THE REPORTER'S
UNLIKELY REUNION

Praise for MaryAnn Clarke's Books

"Loved. Jp and Lucy's journey was heartwrenching and beautiful. You really felt for them, as a couple and individually. I really enjoyed this book. I hope to be able to read more from the author!"

Amazon Reviewer Kyrie Masters for Single Dad in Studio 7D

"Want to read a book where the plot [is] crafted in a way that has a grip on your heart, tears in your throat and laughter on your lips? Then this is the book for you. Who doesn't love romance, art history, and family? The plots twists and tension kept me reading well into the night. The Author M A Clarke Scott gives the reader a run for their money."

Amazon Reviewer Tanya for The Art of Enchantment

"Though, at first, the book appears to be a classic take on the enemies-to-lovers trope (my favourite trope by the way); it was so much more. I cannot believe how well the author conveyed all of the characters' emotions and struggles. The writing style was profound and pulled at my heartstrings more than I can describe. This book has so many things going for it: how Alexa's and Bruce's chemistry evolves, their relationship with the children and their emotional and professional growth. The reader (just like the characters) is not the same after reading this story."

Reedsy Reviewer Karla Danklu for Making Room
For You

THE REPORTER'S UNLIKELY REUNION

Most UNLIKELY To Book 1

MARYANN CLARKE

Ebook ISBN: 978-1-988743-37-0
KDP print book ISBN: 978-1-988743-38-7
Ingram Spark print book ISBN: 978-1-988743-39-4

WANT TO CONNECT WITH ME?
www.maryannclarkescott.com
maryann@maryannclarkescott.com

For Romance Readers Everywhere in search of a friendly place to call home, where everyone knows your name, and you are always welcome. I hope you find your next book boyfriend, or girlfriend, between the covers of these books.

Foreword

The Most UNLIKELY To Series of Contemporary Romance novels.

Get to know this close knit group of twenty-something friends while they learn to cope and grow as their expectations are turned on their heads.

The Most UNLIKELY To series books are full-length, character-driven, adult contemporary romance novels. They can each be read as stand-alones, or read in order to experience the story chronologically. More rom than com, with a little steam, they're perfect for fans of Christina Lauren, Mhairi Macfarlane or Helena Hunting's single-titles!

Welcome to Port Camosun

an idyllic historic small town on the West Coast of Canada.

When you've given it all you've got, and are tired of life's hard knocks, it helps to have a place to return where everyone knows your name and is glad to see your face. Sometimes the answer is going back to the one place in the world you can always call home. And sometimes your happily ever after can be found in the most *unlikely* place.

Let's take a peak into the pages of the Port Cam High's senior annual and introduce you to a special group of friends: ten diverse individuals who grew up together, have known each other through all the trials and tribulations of growing up, and have formed an unbreakable bond. See if you recognize any of these folks.

Introduction

Quinn 'Mom' Roarke, Voted Best Shoulder To Cry On, and also Most Likely To Own A Café

I know that I'll look back on these days as being the happiest of my life. If you leave Port Cam, make sure to come back and visit. Come on in, the coffee's HOT!

Deanna 'DeeDee' Dunham, Voted Most Likely To Get A Facial

Goodbye old boyfriends. Hello new boyfriends! Mwah! (Does this photo make me look fat?)

Ruby Zimmer, Homecoming Queen, & Voted Most Likely To win a Pulitzer Prize in Journalism

Roads? Where I'm going, I won't need roads. If you follow your dreams, you are capable of anything.

Rainy Saraladevi, Voted Most Likely To Change the World

Be who you are and say what you feel, because those who mind don't matter and those who matter don't mind.

I'll never forget these great years with all of you! xo

Jeannie van Bellen, Voted Most Likely To Win The Nobel Prize, and also Cutest Couple

The saddest thing in life is wasted talent.

Graduation is the first step of the next chapter of your life.

Aislin Làska, Voted Most Likely To Get Flushed!

I hate people. So much.

Parker Roarke, Voted Most Likely To Be A Justin Bieber Impersonator in Vegas

All our dreams can come true…if we have the courage to pursue them. Just sayin' —See you at Comicon, losers.

Julian Michaels, Voted Most Likely To Be A Dad

Thanks for all of the memories. I had the time of my life.

Miss you all! See you all at the 10 year reunion!

Tate Foreman, Voted Most Likely To Get a Star on Hollywood Blvd

Stage or screen, stage or screen… Both! If movies have taught me anything, now the real fun starts.

Zach Chapman, Voted Most Likely To Be Late For Class, Also MVP, & Cutest Couple

I'm awake! I'm awake! Is that the bell?

Any pizza is a personal pizza if you try hard enough.

Jae Soo 'JJ' Jeong, Voted Most Likely To Make The Cover of Forbes Magazine

Don't assume the answer is no before you ask the question.

If I still look this good in 10 years, I'll be happy. I'm outta here! See you guys later!

Bethune Douglas, Most Likely To Design Her Own House

Futures don't make themselves, you have to create them.

Thanks for all of the memories. I had the time of my life!

Miss you all!

Peter 'Penis' Corbin, Voted Most Likely To End Up In Jail

Meet me behind the gym if you're lookin' for weed.

Chapter 1

Julian

TEN YEARS AGO, my life plan had been simple. I knew exactly who I was, where I was going, and what I wanted.

I was Julian Michaels, an easy-going, third-generation chicken farmer, and I'd be married to my high school sweetheart with two, maybe three kids, I figured. A dog, of course. A simple, pleasant life stretching as far into the future as I could see.

Then everything came crashing down. My life, my future, my dreams, my faith in humanity, and my self-belief.

I learned that nothing is simple; you can't ever really know or trust anyone—including yourself—and life was random. It was best to take things one day at a time. Be adaptable. Take pleasure in simple things.

Even so, I wasn't prepared.

"Julian! Julian!" A chorus of female voices rose to greet me the moment I walked through Millhouse Coffee. Collectively, the voices belonged to two of my oldest and dearest friends: Quinn, the proprietor of the café, and Deanna, my social media mentor. I'd known them since middle school. They were two-fifths of a dynamic group of clever, popular, can-do girlfriends ironically known as the Kickass Chicks. Quinn, Deanna, and Rainy—who was at work—were the only three that stayed in our hometown, and at the moment were the core organizing committee of our tenth high school reunion. I was a mere hanger-on, their mascot if you will. Also, their caterer.

They leapt from their chairs, swarming me as I strode toward the table where their lists and spreadsheets, seating arrangements and menus were spread. I felt my neck and face heat with embarrassment as they batted their eyelashes in slow-mo, made smooching faces, and fake swooned all over me.

"I love you, Julian!"

"You're so sexy, Julian!"

"Julian, will you marry me?"

"Geroff!" I chuckled good-naturedly, peeling their arms from my neck and pushing them away as they giggled. I was a lucky man to have so many warm and true friends, and beautiful women to boot—inside and out.

I could hardly blame them for the teasing. My newest Instagram Live had gone viral, and my following had grown by ten thousand over the week, thanks to the coaching and technical support of Deanna the social media queen. Or influencer, as she was known, with the 748,000 followers of her Dee+Dun Beauty and Wellness profile. I wondered if the explosion of follows for my farm and food page and gaga girl fans qualified me as an influencer now too. All for tromping around my farm with my dog Finnigan and my goats and chickens like the hick that I was. What a weird world we live in.

"Your following, dude!" said Deanna, giving me a side hug.

"Thanks to you. You really are brilliant, Dee. I'm over the moon."

Swooning girl fans who thought I was some kind of rustic sex symbol was not what I'd expected from the new cooking and sustainable food campaign, nor what I signed up for. I felt awkward AF, but if the attention got me the audience I sought for my brand, and the sponsorships and partnerships I needed to advance my cause—and pay for my animals' feed—I could hardly complain. My actual cost of living was very low, since I essentially lived off my land as much as possible.

They sat down and I joined them, sweeping their papers aside and setting down my cloth-covered tin tray in the centre of the table.

"Ooh! What's this?" asked Deanna, pinching the edge of the cloth to peek underneath. Deanna's diet was too health conscious and frou-frou to allow her to enjoy my cooking fully, and Quinn had rather conservative tastes, though she wholeheartedly supported my sustainable, local approach. But I made sure to include all their needs and preferences when planning the menu, as they were a rather spot-on avatar for my target audience. And I aimed to please.

I swatted her hand away. "Hold on a sec. Where's Rainy?"

"Running late."

She was the most adventurous foodie of the group and loved to sample every new thing I came up with. The highly anticipated event was tomorrow night, and it was my food that would grace the buffet and circulate among the crowd. The food had to be superb, brilliant, and eye-catching, as well as on message. I might be attending the reunion mainly to spend time with my closest friends and reconnect with a few old ones, but I had an ulterior motive.

"Have you got the final numbers for us?"

Deanna pulled her hand back, dragged her laptop closer and clicked. "Yes. There were a few last-minute responses." She scanned her screen. "We heard from Alex whatsit. He is coming after all and he's bringing his husband."

"Any more?"

"Mhm. The four from Boston confirmed. Elsa from Montreal is coming. Dean and his wife from up in Prince George are coming down. Oh! I got a call from James Reynold's mom. He died! She just heard about the reunion and finally got back to me."

"Another one to add to the deceased poster," murmured Quinn, rummaging under the stacks of papers and jotting his name on a list.

I vaguely recalled James. "The theatre guy? With the curly hair?"

Quinn added, "Voted Most Likely To End Up on a Soap Opera." She frowned down at her list, scratching her pen through a line.

"Wasn't he friends with Tate?"

"Yeah, that's what I remember, too," Quinn said, her bright features falling. "They were in the theatre club together. I wonder if Tate knows."

Deanna chewed her lip. "She said it was cancer. Throat cancer. How cruel is that?"

"Fuck cancer," grumbled Quinn. "Want a coffee, Julian?"

"Nah, thanks. I've gotta run. My buddy Arnie is delivering an alpaca this afternoon. I have to get back to the farm."

"A what? Alpaca? Is that like a… like a llama?"

I laughed. "Yeah. Sorta."

"Why on earth would you — ?"

I brushed her question aside with a shake of my head. I didn't want the hassle of learning about a new species, but Arnie was adamant.

"And Jeannie? She still coming?" I turned to Quinn, raising my brows in question. Quinn was the only one who Jeannie had stayed in touch with since grad.

Deanna's face lit up. "I am so excited to see her. I can't believe she's not been back once in ten years."

Quinn gave me her sedate trademark smile, and I caught the undertone of sympathy beneath. She knew I'd never ask directly about Ruby, and that Jeannie was a kind of stand-in for my perverse self-indulgent curiousity about the missing fifth member of the clique. "Jeannie was due to arrive from Toronto tonight. But there was some work thing, and she had to reschedule her flight for tomorrow. It's up in the air but she's still hoping to make it in time."

"She'd better goddamwell make it," Deanna grumbled, making a pouty face. "It won't be a reunion at all without her. I'm still mad at her for cutting us all off."

"Not all of us," I said, elbowing Quinn, who shrugged, pulling a face. Being in Jeannie's confidence, she knew things that she hinted at but never shared. Quinn was like a vault.

We fell silent, as though we all were thinking the same thought at the same moment. Which, undoubtedly, we were. It wouldn't be the same without Ruby either, but nobody expected Ruby to come. And they didn't talk about her in front of me, anyway.

Deanna cleared her throat to break the awkward silence. "So. The final numbers are here. A hundred and twenty-six, give or take. Is that close enough for you?"

"Sure. Anyway, I had some ingredient substitutions and re-jigged a few of the appetizers, so I brought some samples for your approval."

"Ooh. Taste test." Quinn rubbed her hands together, licking her lips.

I swept away the covering cloth with a flourish to reveal my latest creations. I pointed to one. "Harissa grilled baby lamb on sumac flatbreads. You should get a little kick and a gorgeous depth of flavour from the roasted spices, but nothing to knock your socks off."

Tentatively, Quinn plucked one stack off of the tray and popped it whole into her mouth. She closed her eyes and savoured it, humming. "Nice."

"Caramelized shallots on slices of gluten-free Hasselback Jerusalem artichokes for you Deanna."

Deanna picked a sample and peered at it for a moment before touching it with the tip of her tongue. She liked the colour and shape of things as much as their taste and so I'd decorated the tops with a dollop of Creme Fraiche and a pretty sprig of chervil. I thought she'd like that, and as she smiled at it and took a dainty bite, I knew she did. She chewed thoughtfully, and I watched her eyes register the lovely silky texture combined with the chewiness of the artichokes. Another winner.

"Next," Quinn said, waiting for the introduction that always preceded my food.

I picked up one of the dessert items. "How about something sweet, Quinny? This one's maple sugar rhubarb mousse in a cardamom crisp, with wild strawberries and a caramel halo." Quinn's eyes lit up and she enthusiastically gave that a go. I sat back, watching them crunch and chew, listening to their moans of delight, knowing I'd knocked it out of the park.

Without warning, Deanna lurched forward with a guttural noise, her big, dark eyes bulging at something over my shoulder.

DEANNA CLUTCHED at my sleeve as Quinn followed her gaze. As I went to turn around, Quinn grabbed a paper napkin and spit the contents of her mouth into her hand.

What the hell?

"What's wrong? Does it taste bad? What is it?" Had I mixed up sugar and salt? Accidentally dropped chili pepper into the mousse? I didn't do stuff like that. I was exacting and careful; some might say, too precise.

She frowned and hissed, "Don't turn around. Don't turn around."

Deanna let out a long plaintive cry like someone had stepped on a cat. Of course I turned, because whatever had caused this uproar in my girls had to be faced.

Of all the things or people I expected to see entering the café when I turned, it was not Ruby.

My head roared with a whooshing, tidal wave of blood; burning, anguished tears shot from my tear ducts as my throat seized up.

"Did she contact you? Did you know?"

"No. No, I never got a reply to the invitation."

"I thought she was in Afghanistan."

"No, it was Azerbaijan."

I heard the halting exchange between the girls through the thunder in my ears.

I squeezed my eyes closed, opened them wide, shut them again. Surely my mind was playing tricks on me. I'd imagined I'd seen my Ruby a million times over the years. Here on the streets downtown, and even in London, Paris, Rome, and New York; there were times when I was convinced that the person I saw in a crowded restaurant on the sidewalk up ahead was Ruby. But it never was. This, my pounding heart jammed into my throat told me, was undoubtedly Ruby.

Suddenly, we were all on our feet. I don't remember rising. Everything happened at once, in a staccato rhythm.

Deanna rushed forward calling her name, then stopped and glanced back at me, uncertain. Quinn stayed by my side, her fingers digging into my bicep, as though she thought I might topple over without her support. And I might have. I still might.

"Ruby? Is that really you?" Deanna stepped forward.

Ruby, for it truly was her, stood blinking at the bunch of us, disoriented too. Did she come in here by accident? Her lips opened to speak, but she stalled. She reached a hand out, and Deanna clasped then released it.

"Hey… wow… guys. I…" Her gaze skipped across each of us, but kept bouncing back to me, locking on me. As our gazes met, her pupils huge and black, I felt as though I'd fallen into deep space; she seemed as disoriented as I felt.

Deanna stepped back while Quinn released my arm at last, shoving me forward. I stumbled. I didn't know what she wanted me to do. What was I supposed to do?

"Jules?" Ruby's voice reached me, scratchy and faint, like a bad recording. "I didn't expect to see you here. Mom told me about Quinn's new place and I…"

No words came when I tried to find them. Something cottony closed my throat. My eyes burned and my skin was hot and tingling. Confused, I turned to look at Quinn and Deanna. They'd retreated, huddled together like nervous puppies.

"Jules?" Ruby stepped closer and closer. Ten inches away, then eight. I could smell her. Feel her breath on my face. She lifted a hand as if to touch me, but stopped mid air and let it drop. She knew better than to try, this woman who destroyed me. She was part stranger, part lover, part ruination, and it was hella confusing; a storm of emotions swirled inside me.

But then she did touch me. First her palms landed featherlight on my chest, as if gauging my temperature, like a hot stove. Then her arms slid up and around my neck, grabbing fistfuls of my shirt and pulling me closer, tipping her face to the crook of my neck, grazing it with a feather touch. The familiar scent of her, dark chocolate and the cinnamon spice of carnations that I'd loved so much, swamped my senses.

In a flash, my body remembered what I'd fought ten years to forget. The silky feel of her thick hair and smooth skin against mine. My fingers tingled, and my arms ached to grab her and pull her into me, hold her tight. I feathered my fingertips on her back, and felt her ribs and vertebrae jutting, strange in their gaunt hardness. But I could go no further, enveloped by her trembling breath and crushed by the sound of my own heartbeat in my ears.

Suddenly we were at the centre of a frenzied group hug, the other girls rushing us and twining their arms around both of us. Pressed closer to Ruby, our chests, bellies, hips, and thighs connected, a fever of familiar desire washed over me; my body temperature shot up as my skin screamed and nerve endings lit up. Blood surged to my groin in a tidal wave of sexual reverberations. I tried to pull back but was locked into the embrace, painfully conscious of my swelling groin.

They must have all realized they were crowding us at the same moment, because the group broke apart and everyone teetered back a step. My head was on fire.

I drew a breath. Some shards of sense cut through the fog. Finally, I found my voice, a choked, stiff, drowning voice. "Are you here for the reunion?"

She winced and swayed on her feet. Her head tilted to the left. "No. No, I didn't know. My mom and dad just told me about it." Her shoulder hitched up. "That's why I came looking for Quinn."

I said nothing. Did I honestly expect she'd look me up first? Or at all?

She looked great. Fantastic. Strong, lean, and tanned, her brown hair streaked with gold. Of course, I'd seen her on TV. We all had. So it's not like the changes wrought by ten years in her field should shock me. But they did all the same. In the flesh she looked tired, weathered. Not the incandescent, nubile Ruby of our youth. Tiny lines flared out from the corners of her hazel eyes, and cut into the sides of her full mouth. It was a hard life she'd chosen. I knew that. Still, she was as beautiful to me as ever.

I reached up to rub the back of my head, staring down at my rubber work boots, now painfully aware that I'd come in directly from the farm. I was in my rattiest t-shirt and scarf, my baggiest work pants. I never fussed about clothes anymore, but my skin crawled now with self-consciousness. A deep, crippling sense of my inadequacy swamped me.

"Are all of you going to the reunion?" Ruby finally asked, scanning the group.

"Of course we are. We organized it. And now so are you!" squeaked Deanna, leaping closer. I just kept staring at her, as blood roared in my ears to the sound of her name. Ruby, Ruby, Ruby.

"You're going?" Ruby's big green-bronze eyes circled my features, as if she too were taking the measure of time since we'd last been together.

"Ah… nooo, actually. Nope." Tugging on my scarf, I shoved my hands in my pockets and stepped back to give myself a bit of space. I registered the sharp intake of breath behind me. "Have an alpaca to unpack. Got to get it… settled." This couldn't be happening. I took a step to the side, clenching my hands into fists, and angled my shoulder towards her — like a bull intent on plowing through a fence. Anything to stop me from wrapping her in a crushing embrace, burying my face in her hair, drawing the scent of her skin into my lungs like a life-giving elixir.

"You are too going, Julian." Quinn's quiet voice came right behind me. "You have to go. Everyone expects you."

I twisted to glare at her. "No. Can't make it. Sorry." I turned back to Ruby. "You should though. Since you're back. Everyone will be so excited to see you." My God, I have to get out of here. I stepped around her, forcing myself to put one foot in front of the other until I found myself on the sidewalk out in front of the café. The warm summer air washed over me like a silken veil, waking me up from a dream. A volcano of emotion erupted from somewhere deep inside me; I felt like I was on fire. I had to get away, and fast.

Though anguish and horrible humiliation, and latent rage swirled together in my gut, all my nerve endings stubbornly insisted on standing up together and singing a high clear note like a choir.

Ruby was back.

Chapter 2

Ruby

I'M GUTTED.

I know I deserve this feeling of rejection, but it fills me with fear, as if my last thread is about to snap.

My pulse hammered, my breath shallow. It felt a lot like being caught out in the field by an IED explosion or machine gun strafing, catching me unawares and catapulting my body directly into flight or fight mode, all systems on high alert. I'm used to keeping my mind vigilant and objective in those situations, but this one left me with my thoughts skittering incoherently.

I barely knew where to look after Julian stormed out, and still couldn't think of what to say as Deanna and Quinn rushed toward me and smothered me in more welcoming hugs and kisses, patting and squeezing as if they didn't believe I was really here. I could hardly believe it myself. It felt like I was watching a newsreel, floating somewhere over my shoulder, detached.

When I came to find Quinn's new café, after Dad told me

about it and the reunion that I'd inadvertently stumbled upon, I didn't expect to find two of my closest friends together. Nor had I expected to smash right into Julian. My Julian. Never mind under the curious, critical stare of two of my oldest friends.

He couldn't escape fast enough, his eyes pained and panicked.

I twisted to glance longingly out the front window of the café just in time to see Julian pause, rake his hands through his messy hair, shake his head, and stumble out of view. My heart pounded from the shock, the joy and anguish of seeing him again, like that. It was over before I knew what was happening.

I didn't plan to meet him this way. It wasn't fair to him. But I wasn't prepared either. Seeing him again after all this time affected me so much more than I expected. My hands were shaking now that the adrenaline was ebbing.

As my heart rate slowed, I looked around me at Quinn's newly opened café, Millhouse Coffee. It occupied a fabulous heritage brick warehouse space, with tall industrial windows and a high, metal ceiling. The floor was rough and rustic, with an eclectic mix of up-cycled furniture scattered around. The atmosphere was wonderful, a mix of new, old and funky, a perfect reflection of my friend's earthy, bohemian tastes.

Clearly, I hadn't given this enough thought. I should have taken shelter at my parent's place awhile and got the lay of the land first. Sent up a flare to warn people. Julian specifically.

"Ruby, I can't believe you're here!" Quinn said, her palms framing my face.

"We were just going over the attendance list five minutes ago, and I was wondering if you even got the invitation," Deanna added, wrapping her arm around me and pulling.

I shook my head. "I didn't. I'm sorry. I was in Toronto, and before that, South America for months. I just got to town."

"Sit down. I'll make a coffee for you," Quinn said, ducking behind the counter as Deanna sat down at a long table that was strewn with papers, phones and a laptop. In its centre was a tray with all kinds of little food things that looked like something out of a gourmet magazine. Wedding food.

I sat down, putting aside my swirling emotions about Julian to deal with later. "I'm starving, actually. Can I eat some of this?"

There was an awkward beat of silence, and then Deanna replied, "Of course. Help yourself. They're samples of the appies for tomorrow night." Her gaze darted to Quinn's for a second as I picked up some kind of stacked nibbly thing and popped it whole into my mouth. Incredible flavour exploded along with silky textures that melted on my tongue. I'd eaten both fantastic food on my travels and terrible rations, and had even gone without. But I don't think I'd ever tasted anything like this.

"Oh my God! This is incredible."

"Um. Yeah. We have a great… caterer," Quinn said, setting a coffee beside me.

I picked up my cup for a sip and noticed she'd scrawled something on the side with a Sharpie: Most Likely to Win a Pulitzer! I laughed, tilting the cup at Quinn, meeting her gaze. That was one prize I hadn't actually won. Yet.

"This place looks amazing, Quinn," I said, lifting the cup to my lips. "You did it! Your dream come true." While most of the rest of us had planned to go to university, all Quinn ever talked about was her café for as long as I could remember.

She sniffed and sat beside me, wiping her hands on a bar towel. "Yup. It's a start, anyway. Opened about nine months back. But I'm not solvent yet. It takes awhile to establish regular clientele." She sighed, her eyes darting around the space. "One step at a time."

I could see the uncertainty in her eyes and inferred that she was stressed about it. The place was empty except for us three at the moment, but it was late afternoon on a Friday. Most people were probably still at work, or gone to a pub.

"The location is great, though. With that view over the

water. Tables outside on the terrace. I'd come here every day if I lived or worked in the area."

Just then the bell over the door tinkled as it swung open. We all turned to look as a very tall, very thin woman strode in, black hair escaping a messy top knot. Taking in her extra long brown arms and legs, I realized this was our missing friend, Rainy.

"Sorry. Sorry I'm late! Got held up with a chatty client." She stopped, just shy of the table and stared. "Ooh, food. My favourite. Where's—"

"The caterer dropped off new samples," Quinn practically shouted at her.

"The cate—?"

"Ruby's here!" Deanna cut her off, gesturing at me.

Rainy turned to me, brow puckering, mouth falling open. "Ruby?"

"Hey, Rainy." I stood up and we hugged before she pushed me away to peer intently at me.

"I cannot believe you're here."

I shrugged. "Just in time for the reunion, apparently. But I don't think I'll make it. I have to see the family."

"You didn't plan it? Of course you have to come. Where are you headed next?" Rainy picked up another appetizer and bit into it.

"I'm between assignments," I deflected, chagrinned that she assumed I'd be flying off again. "Decided it was time to visit."

That was only marginally true, but what I was really doing in town was best kept secret until I made a decision. That was the million-dollar question. I really didn't know whether I was staying or moving on again. I guess I was hoping my friends could help me decide. Catching up with everyone at this reunion would help, actually. And Jules... well, he was part of the equation. "So... Julian. Does he come in here a lot?"

Quinn cleared her throat, her gaze flicking between the

other girls and me. "Whenever he's in the city. A few times a week."

"Looks like not much has changed with him then. Still on the farm?"

Deanna perked up. "A lot has changed with him, actually." After a quelling glare from Quinn, she babbled on but in a more subdued way and I wondered what she'd edited out. "His dad died about a year-and-a-half back, and he's taken over. His mom and Molly live nearby in the village now, so the property's all his. He's doing things a lot differently. It's not a chicken farm anymore, though he still has some chickens I guess."

I let these details soak in, thinking about the past ten years. How many places I'd been; what I'd seen and experienced. And Julian, apparently just where I'd left him, the same. I couldn't even imagine. "Did he… I mean did he… is there anyone…"

Rainy picked up on my meaning and said, "No. Still on his own." She pulled out a water bottle and took a long drink while I watched her swan-like neck swallow.

My pulse kicked up. I was torn between feeling ecstatic and desolate at the news. Not surprising, my friends also seemed to be at a loss for words as I studied their familiar faces as three pairs of eyes bored holes into my face.

Deanna leaned in. "You're not serious, Ruby. Say you'll come to the reunion. We've spent months planning it. I can't even imagine going knowing you're in town but not there with us."

"Please come!" Rainy clung to my arm, begging me with her eyes, and for a moment I felt like I was back in high school, surrounded by my besties.

I sighed. "I don't think it would be fair to Jules to just crash like this. I didn't even expect to see…" I looked to Quinn, and she kept her gaze cast down. In that, I saw the truth. Of all of us, she'd been closer friends with Julian, and I imagined that after I left, she was someone Julian had leaned on, confided in. "Was he telling the truth? He's not going?"

Deanna and Quinn shrugged uncertainly while Rainy scowled, a question hovering in her eyes. I knew I was making things awkward.

"I don't know. I guess," said Quinn.

"Tell me who else is going," I said, to change the subject. "Will Jeannie be there? And Bethune?"

"Beth, yes. She's back from finishing her architectural internship in Ottawa and job hunting here. Jeannie's coming back too, actually. She's flying in tomorrow; fingers crossed she's in time for the party."

"So, I'm not the only one who's been AWOL for the past decade."

I was having an almost out-of-body experience, watching my friends' faces, listening to them talk over each other, feeling surrounded by love and acceptance. Suddenly, my throat burned and convulsed, the heat rising through my sinuses. My eyes filled with tears, and my chin wobbled. My hot breath wavered with a spasm. "I missed you all so much," I blurted.

Then we were all crying and hugging and laughing.

Once we all settled down, they showed me their detailed plans for the reunion event, and we polished off the rest of the yummy snacks from the tray.

"Promise me you won't get wasted, and stay well away from Zach tomorrow night," said Quinn, giving Deanna a pleading look.

Dee's eyes went wide as blue lakes. "He's my friend. But I hear you. I can hardly—"

"If he was just your friend, and not your friend-with-benefits, we wouldn't worry," added Rainy.

"We don't..." whined Deanna. "Not much." She tucked her neck into her shoulders. "Not. Often. It's only—"

"When you both get drunk and feel sentimental. Gee... I wonder why we're worried about tomorrow night, Dee."

I reeled to think that the two of them were still hooking up after all these years. They were never a couple, and never would be. I'm sure everyone still remembers grad night. It was such a shitshow. I'm sure that's why Jeannie stayed away. If it were me, and I'd caught Julian with someone at the after-grad house party, I don't think I'd have ever recovered. Not that I thought Jeannie and Zach were destined to be together forever, but that year they were pretty sweet. Everyone thought so—the star athlete and the star mathlete. They were in the running against Jules and me for prom king and queen.

"All right. I promise." She raised her right hand. "I vow I will not sleep with Zach Chapman, tomorrow night."

"Or ever again," murmured Quinn.

"Let's not push our luck," Rainy said. "Okay, for my part, I vow I will not give in to my mother's wishes and spend the entire evening on the arm of either Aman Banerjee or Neil Kumar."

"Seriously. Pick something you're not actually motivated to do, so it's at least a little bit hard," Deanna said.

"It'll be hard enough," Rainy sighed, wilting, and we all understood. Mrs. Saraladevi was not to be messed with. And I saw that Rainy still struggled to assert her own wishes over her domineering and demanding mother's.

"What about you, Quinn?" I asked. "Is there someone you'll be avoiding at the reunion?"

Quinn shrugged and shook her head, as if she couldn't think of anyone.

"I'll tell you what," said Rainy. "Since our mutual good friend Jae Soo is back from Seoul, how about not monopolizing him so we can all get our share?"

Quinn's mouth dropped open. "I wouldn't!"

The other two made a chorus of skeptical noises.

"Anyway, everyone will have to beat down your twin brother to get a few minutes with JJ."

After a few more minutes of chitchat, it was time to go. I

excused myself but not before another round of hugs and yet more urging that I attend the fateful event.

"I'll see. I can't promise. My parents want to spend time with me too, you know." As I walked away from the café, I made a vow that I wouldn't go anywhere near that reunion if Julian was going to be there.

Chapter 3

Julian

QUINN: *Hey*

Me: ...

Quinn: *Seriously. I'm worried about u.*

Me: *I'm fine. Farm keeping me busy. Arnie just arriving.*

Quinn: *Won't keep you. Just want to make sure you're coming* tomorrow.

*/*dancing woman/* /*dancing man/**

Me: *Don't know. Having second thoughts obvs.*

Quinn: *Julian!*

Me: *La la la. Can't talk now.*

Quinn: *She said she won't go anyway. :`(*

I didn't even have arguments pro versus con fighting in my head. Instead, it was a fog, while tension held my entire body in a rigour-mortis-like lockdown. Earlier, I barely got to my truck before I fell apart. It was like having my legs cut out from under me by a sickle mower.

My gut was still in knots, and gound my teeth as I strode to the front gravel field, Finnegan bounding at my heels, to watch

Arnie's rusted blue truck crunch toward me with his livestock trailer bumping behind.

"Sit." Finn settled at my side, tail wagging, as we waited for the new addition.

Arnie pulled up and shut off the truck, leaping out with the agility and ease of a farmer who spent all day on the move. I'd been back on the farm just over a year, but I already knew the feel of that sinewy strength, and the vitality that came from spending most of every day outdoors hauling shit around. Literally. My gig might have been food, but farming was farming. And animals, as I had learned, demanded a lot of time and attention. I strode around his truck to meet him at the rear of the trailer where he yanked on the door latch.

The alpaca, which was due yesterday, was a welcome distraction today. The delay was no big deal. Arnie and I understood each other. The animals always came first, so people had to be accommodating and patient. It was too much to hope he'd changed his mind about giving this animal to me. I could only demur so many times.

I led Arnie and the small-headed, long-necked tan creature he had on a lead to the paddock I'd prepared. Most of its coat was short from its last shearing, except for the unruly mop on its head that looked like a mad aunt overdue for the hairdresser. I made a face at it. You'd think living with goats, pigs, and chickens I'd be tolerant, but there was something weirdly alien about alpacas and their wide-set dark eyes. As if some stuffed animal from your childhood bedroom had come to life.

"He looks like you," Arnie teased as I held open the gate, and self-consciously raked a hand through my messy, overlong hair.

I was fully occupied for the next hour as Arnie and I maneuvered the skittish alpaca into the small paddock and gave it some feed. He was convinced the goats would love it, but I wanted to take it slow. Introduce them gradually. I didn't need eight agitated goats. The creature didn't like Finnegan and didn't seem to want to live here with me any more than I welcomed it. God. I knew nothing about alpacas.

"Last chance to take it away."

Arnie laughed. "Not a chance, Julian. You'll figure it out like you always do. You didn't know about goats either, nor pigs. Now look at you!"

I groaned. It was true, but they had motivated me. They were actual food, after all. But this thing… Arnie read my expression.

"It's a he, by the way. Time to give him a name. Aside from the superb fibre, it's very enviro friendly. They eat way less than cows."

"If I'd wanted to diversify my stock, I'd have gotten sheep."

"Alpacas are the same but better. More sustainable."

"Mm." I remained unconvinced. Was I supposed to take up knitting?

"And if you want, you can get him a girlfriend. Then you could milk her. I figured you might like to experiment with cheese-making."

"Uhh… No more alpacas," I pleaded, still hoping I could give this one back after a decent interval.

My phone rang this time, with a distinctive tone that meant my sister Molly was calling. I left Arnie walking and talking to the alpaca, trying to calm it down, and stepped away to take her call.

"Molls!"

"Little brother."

Hm. She only called me that when I was about to get a scolding.

"I heard a rumour."

"Did you?"

A long silence followed my glib reply, and I sobered.

"Julian."

"Molly."

"Are you okay, sweetie?"

Tension clutched my jaw, my eyes swimming with tears instantly. I turned and quickly strode away from Arnie. I swallowed and swallowed again, clearing my throat, working to get a grip on myself.

"It came as a shock." My gravelly voice betrayed me.

"How... how did she look to you? Are you afraid..." her voice trailed off.

"Afraid of what, Molly?" I flinched at my tone. I didn't mean to snap her head off.

She inhaled and sighed, long and slow, giving me the moment I needed. "Afraid you'll fall in love with her all over again."

Her words hit me like a punch to the gut. Again! I'd never stopped loving the damned girl. But Molly didn't need to know that. No one did. "Huh. I'm too fucking angry to fall in love," I chose to say instead. That was true too. Too angry to give into the feelings. Too gutted to take a proper breath.

"Julian —"

Arnie's shout came from a distance. "Julian! Get back here."

I raised an arm to wave at him. He had places to go.

"I've got to go Molly. Arnie just brought the fucking alpaca over."

She snort-laughed. "That's exactly what you need right now."

I grunted in agreement. The necessity of dealing with the thing was keeping me from wallowing. Or it would have if my family and friends would stop hounding me.

"I'll come over in a while to help with more food prep, 'kay?"

I signed off and made my way back to the alpaca pen, leaning my arms on the top rail and watching it shuffle sideways as Arnie held it in a gentle headlock to remove the red harness from its tiny head. It was pretty placid considering the stress of the ride over and the strange environment. They were bizarre looking creatures with their thick necks and small fluffy heads.

Finnegan ducked under the bottom rail and circled around, curious, and the thing started humming loudly. Arnie said, "Call Finn away, Julian. You'll have to get them used to each other gradually. These guys don't care too much for dogs."

I scoffed. "You might have mentioned that before. Finnegan! Come!" I patted my thigh, and he jogged over obediently so I could scratch his ear. "Let's give the new guy some space, okay, buddy?"

Arnie gave the alpaca a pat and ducked between the fence rails, joining me in watching it prance around, exploring its new space. He turned to speak and stopped. "What's up with you? You get bad news?"

Shit. I combed a hand through my hair, shaking my head. "Uh, no. It was just Molly."

"You're sure popular today. Last-minute arrangements for your event?"

I filled my lungs, held the breath then let it go with a huff, staring at the soft dirt underfoot, indented with boot and hoof prints. Only eight years older, Arnie was a good friend. Not a father, but like an older brother to me. With his property only a few kilometres from mine, I saw him as much as my friends in town, and he knew my business.

"Something… happened earlier today. I'm not sure I'm going to the reunion now."

"What! You have to go!"

"I know. I know." I raised a hand, palm out, but Arnie was already fired up.

Arms wide, he faced me with an incredulous expression. He was part of the Farm-to-Table Faire planning group, and was as invested in the event as I was. They were all expecting me to drum up some significant sponsorship through the reunion. My food was only one part of the campaign, but with my experience and public following, I was its de facto spokesperson. After all our planning, it would be stupid and irresponsible not to go.

"We can always adjust the scope if we don't get another big sponsor or two," I hedged.

"Or we could just take Ethan up on his offer."

"Not a chance!"

We critically needed about a hundred grand more to fund the Faire. The only big sponsor that had come forward was the owner of Ragged Mountain Resort and Spa. And their pockets were too deep for comfort. Though others on the committee didn't share my reservations, I wasn't prepared to compromise our mandate for someone like that.

When we were still in school, the old owner, Thomas, had been widely disliked for his sleaze and his greed. There'd been one major dust up that I recalled, when he'd clear-cut a vast swath of his mountaintop land without proper permits or geotechnical engineering so he could expand, causing some severe erosion that affected neighbouring properties and wildlife habitats.

Even my easy-going father had had major run-ins with him, losing money. Worse than that, my gut told me the current CEO, Ethan Garwood, who was between me and Arnie in age, was savvy and ambitious enough to want to leverage my new online notoriety for his own nefarious commercial aims. I didn't feel like lending my name to line his pockets with gold and compromise my own agenda.

"Why, dude?"

I owed him an answer. "My… old girlfriend arrived in town unexpectedly this morning."

"Your old…?" Arnie's brow pinched together. "Uh… what's her name. From high school? That one?"

"None other." In fact, there never had been another. For all the women I'd taken to bed to drown my sorrows, there were no other ex-girlfriends. "Ruby."

Arnie narrowed his eyes and stared at me until I squirmed and cringed. "What?"

He clicked his tongue. "So you're going to scurry back to the farm and hide like a rabbit? That doesn't sound like you, Julian."

I shot him a dirty look. "Just because I told you the story, doesn't mean you know what I'm thinking right now. She's been away for ten years. People want to catch up with her. I thought I'd give her space, that's all." I was now regretting that fishing trip and bottle of whiskey around the campfire.

"Uh-huh. So I guess all these texts and phone calls aren't your army of friends fretting over your bruised ego?"

"Fuck you, Arnie," I grumbled.

He laughed and smacked the back of my head. "You can wallow about the girl if you want to." He turned and strode towards his truck. With his hand on the door, he turned. "Or you can put on your fancy city-boy duds and show that girl you're more interested in investing in your future than cryin' about your past."

"Fuck you, Arnie," I mumbled once more, but under my breath, because what he said was true.

After he pulled away, I kicked at the gravel, sighing; picking up on my mood, Finnegan trailed me. It wasn't my ego that was bruised by Ruby's betrayal ten years ago. It was my heart that had been pulverized. I didn't think it could handle the exposure. But Arnie's comment made me feel like a chump for thinking about bailing on our project.

The girls had said there'd be about a hundred and forty-five people. Maybe we could give each other space in a crowd that big. Or maybe, like Quinn said, she really wouldn't show up. Guilt pinched at my gut. So much planning had gone into this event. I knew everyone was expecting me. I sighed and pulled out my phone.

Me: Maybe I'll just set up the food, say a quick hello and then slip out.

Quinn: Your food! Your plan! Our friends! You have to stay! :'

Me: She's really not going? Don't shit me.

My phone rang.

"That's what she said. Honest."

"Quinn."

"Look. We all urged her to come after you left, but she seemed pretty sure she wouldn't. She said her parents wanted her around."

"Understandable. How much have they seen of her?"

"I don't know. My dad would flip if I went away for years and years. Like your folks did when you left."

"I wasn't gone that long," I argued.

"Six years, Julian. That's almost as bad."

I hummed, half a concession. More like seven since I worked in the city for over a year before I really left town. It felt like a lifetime. I wondered what it felt like for Ruby to be back after a full decade.

"Don't let the idea of her do this to you, Julian."

I grunted, squatting onto my haunches to give Finnegan a rub and closed my eyes while he licked my chin. I just wanted to lie down on the ground and go to sleep and stop thinking, but a decision had to be made.

"Julian. You can do it. You have to. If she shows up, just... ignore her!"

I barked with sudden laughter. "Yeah, okay. Easy. Right.

"So that's a yes?"

I let out a huge breath. "Yes. Ok. I'll... try."

I hung up on her cheering. I needed to face my fear. I could do this for my friends, for my cause. It didn't have to be about Ruby. I headed for the shower. There was a ton of food to prep. That much I knew I could do.

Ruby

"Good morning sweetheart." Dad's warm, familiar voice was like a balm for my weary soul as I joined them in the kitchen the next morning.

"Coffee?" Mom turned toward me, and I smiled at her. She was as put together as ever in a silky blouse and dressy trousers, makeup and jewelry, her hair perfect, and had probably been working for two hours even though it was Saturday morning.

"Yes, please," I said, sliding into the chair beside my dad. He was still in his sleep pants and robe, his hair smashed to one side, his reading glasses halfway down his nose, his phone in his hand—probably reading the news headlines. Mom set a steaming mug of coffee in front of me along with a buttered slice of toast smeared with peanut butter. I could get used to this.

"Have you decided about tonight?" Dad set down his phone and leaned forward on his forearms, peering at me over the frames of his glasses. No beating around the bush in this family.

I twisted my mouth and looked at him, because of course he knows I'm agonizing over it. "I just got here. I want to spend time with you two. And Isaac. He's coming over isn't he?"

"Eventually," Dad said. "He's busy."

"Your friends will want to see you too, sweetheart," Mom set her hand on my shoulder as she walked by. "We'll be here when you get back. Let me know if you need something to wear. I have papers to grade." She left the room, her heels clicking on the tiles and I wondered, not for the first time, why she had to get dressed to grade students' work.

Dad cleared his throat. "I can see why you're reluctant, but the thing is, whatever the real reason for coming home, you have to face your demons Ruby. You've got choices to make, and catching up with all of your old friends could give you some perspective."

I pushed out my lower lip and narrowed my eyes at him. His words were truer than he could possibly know. Naturally he knew exactly how I was feeling, despite how I'd hedged when I explained why I was back and what I was doing. That was Dad. He could read me like a newspaper.

"But I want to spend time with you." My voice came out small, childlike. Was I that desperate to avoid a confrontation with Julian?

"You know I'm very proud of you Ruby," Dad said. "As is Mom."

I looked up from poking at the peanut butter on my toast. His eyes were suddenly, suspiciously glassy.

He continued, "And I would never presume to tell you how to live your life. But if my only daughter should choose to live closer to home, that would make me very happy."

"Dad. Don't get maudlin. I've only just arrived. I haven't made any decisions yet. And you have a son, and a daughter-in-law, not to mention your first grandchild on the way."

He hummed his agreement, chuckling. "Nevertheless. They're not my Ruby. We've missed an enormous part of your life, and it's clear it has been hard for you to be so rootless. It's time for you to think about what the rest of your life is going to look like."

"I'll figure it out."

Mom would say, *Pull up your socks, Ruby. You know what you want, so quit waffling and go after it.* But I didn't know. Not anymore. This next choice felt momentous. I was ready for a change, but also terrified of what I'd be giving up. My hard-earned reputation. The predictable unpredictability of my life. How did I know if this new opportunity would be right for me? Especially if I wrote the book of my heart.

Picking up his phone he stood and turned to put his mug in the kitchen sink. With his back to me he added, "Is it Julian? Is that what's holding you back?"

I let go of the breath I'd been unconsciously holding,

absently fingering my empty ring finger, tension pinching my ribs. "Of course. Partly. How could it not?"

Dad turned to face me, leaning back against the sink. "Are you afraid to see him again?"

I hadn't mentioned to them that I had already seen him yesterday, unexpectedly, and couldn't erase the image or the feel of him from my mind or from my skin; my heart rate racing at the very thought of seeing him again. It would've caused quite the uproar. Their curiousity and concern would get the best of them.

"The girls said he's not going to the reunion now. If that's true, I think it's because of me, and I don't think that's fair."

"That's his decision, isn't it? Even if he decides to go, it's not something you can avoid. Especially if you do stay. You at least owe the man a conversation Ruby."

I made a sound in my throat, in part because he spoke the naked truth, but also because he'd referred to Julian as the man, and that threw me for a loop. Somehow, still, I thought of Julian as the boy. My boy.

"I trust you're staying a while. We'll have our chance to visit. Eat your toast, drink your coffee, and think about it. There's time yet."

I did think. For close to two hours. I didn't have as much time as he seemed to believe. The offer from Maclean's magazine was on the table, but it would expire if I couldn't make up my mind. And if too much time lapsed, I'd be expected to ship out again. The proverbial rock and hard place loomed.

How could I explain to my dad—or to anyone—why this decision was so hard for me? Aside from the infamy that could come if I wrote the book of my heart, I wasn't sure I could do it without support. And at this point in my career—and life—Dad's reliable "follow your heart" and mom's predictable "pull up your socks" weren't all that helpful. I needed a soft place to land. And the only place I could think of was with Julian.

Did I honestly think I could waltz back into town after ten

years away, after abandoning him and cutting him off cold, and expect to be welcomed? No, I did not. I wasn't that naive. And the truth of it was, I knew I didn't deserve it. I didn't deserve him.

Yet I still felt the need to sort things out with him before I could make the right decision.

I went to my room and looked at the pile of dirty work clothes spilling out of my duffel bag and backpack in the middle of the floor. I sighed. A hundred percent rugged, utilitarian, and well-worn. I had long ago given up any pretense of a normal life.

There was not one single item of clothing that I had worn in the past ten years suitable for a reunion. My old jersey knit LBD and beat up ballet flats that I'd kept rolled up in the bottom of my pack for the occasional diplomatic or celebratory event overseas had been tossed into the bin before my last flight home. I'd have to replace them if I went back out in the field.

Kicking the pile of rags aside, I turned to my open closet with a hefty dose of skepticism; anything left in there was from when I was eighteen, and not age, or reunion, appropriate. Even if I did want to go to this event, I didn't have a single thing to wear.

I sat at my dressing table and pushed my shaggy waves back from my face. When was the last time I got a haircut? The past decade had emphatically not been about me, my relationships, or my identity. Of all the things that I worried about, my appearance seldom made the list. Now I looked at myself trying to imagine what my classmates would see. What had Julian seen? I squinted, taking the measure of the lines on my face and the deep sadness in my eyes. I was only twenty-eight, but I felt like a centenarian.

Why did I care now? Was it the way seeing my old friends took me back in time? Was I having an identity crisis? Or was it all about Julian, with whom I'd discovered and shared everything. Everything I knew about my body, every detail of my self concept, my very experience of pleasure, had blossomed under his loving gaze. His touch. It was his love that had given me confidence.

When I saw him yesterday, I noted the difference in his eyes; while yes he was older too, but on the surface he was much the same. Still carelessly dressed like a farmer, smelling of hay, chickenfeed, and fresh country air, his wavy brown hair a wild mess. And under that careless exterior, he was still the most beautiful boy I'd ever set eyes on. I used to swoon over his smooth tanned skin and rosy cheeks and lips, his agile hands and lean, muscular arms and legs. Not bulky, but toned. I trusted that body with my very being.

And for just a split second, before the reality of my return had hit home and put a stunned frown on his face, I'd seen his sweet smile flash and my heart took flight.

I grabbed my phone and dialed Rainy. When she picked up I said, "When you saw me yesterday, did you think I looked older?"

Her tinkling laughter filled my ear. "We are older Ruby."

"I mean ooooold. I mean weathered, worn-out, haggard."

In the thirty seconds or so that it took her to answer, I remembered that Rainy was a practical woman who had spent her life juggling the expectations of her traditional Indian mother to be a proper lady and catch a suitable husband with her own deeply held values about women's rights and emancipation of women from their traditional roles. On the subject of feminine beauty and fashion she pulled no punches, despite being able to transform herself into a Devi goddess in a flash, whenever required.

"You are the most amazing woman I know, Ruby Zimmer. Whatever you're thinking, stop it right now."

"What I am thinking, Rainy Saraladevi, is that even if I did want to go to this stupid reunion… sorry, I don't mean stupid, I'm sure you all worked incredibly hard organizing it and it's going to be really wonderful and lovely…" I was rambling, "but it's really hard for me and I don't know what to… but what I'm thinking is that even if I did want to go I haven't got a single thing to wear." I drew a breath. "I don't even own any makeup, or jewelry, and my idea of doing my hair is scraping it back into a ponytail." My desperation was so apparent in my voice even I felt sorry for me. Was I really whining that I couldn't make myself attractive enough for my old friends? Or for Julian?

"Aha. I see the problem now. I'll call you back in five." And she hung up on me. Just like that. I gave the disheveled, weathered woman in the mirror a gimlet gaze and rolled my eyes. She was right. But it didn't stop me from wondering if Julian still found me pretty, or if everyone at the reunion would think I'd got dragged behind an army tank.

I got up from the dresser and flopped onto my bed, staring at the smooth white ceiling, waiting and wondering. Lying there, my mind began playing tricks on me, and I could swear I heard the thrum of a distant helicopter bending the air. So often I'd had nothing to do for hours but wait for transport, it had worn a groove in my brain. My phone rang but when I answered it, it wasn't Rainy.

Deanna's voice said, "I'm texting you my address. It's a townhouse on the Point. Which, FYI, is trendy now. Be here ASAP." Then she hung up too.

Huh. I guess it was time to put my trust in the hands of my closest friends.

Chapter 4

Julian

I WOKE at five-thirty the next morning to Finnegan bouncing, scratching and barking excitedly at the front door to the farmhouse.

"Finnegan!" Molly crooned in greeting, letting herself in.

She'd arrived early to set to work in the kitchen with the last of the food preparations. Last night we'd chopped and assembled everything that could be done ahead of time. We washed and minced while we bopped around the kitchen and I made sauces and reductions, pre-roasted and marinated as many things as we could. Cooking with Molly was easy and fun. We'd been doing it together all our lives, even though I was Chef now.

Today would be even busier. My extra fridge was crammed full of the ingredients that I'd purchased ahead of time, and I'd gathered and foraged every bit of late summer bounty my land had to offer for the occasion.

I put on some Rihanna tunes, turned up the volume and we got to work. As we assembled the food and piled it in containers for transport, I made notes for the serving staff.

My phone buzzed in my pocket with another text. I sighed. I didn't want to have to deal with Quinn's sympathy all day. I was so torn already, feeling shredded emotionally.

Unlike Quinn, Molly wouldn't nag me about going to the reunion. She knew I wanted to go, had been looking forward to it eagerly, and she knew why. She was as invested as I was in the success of the Farm-to-Table Faire. But she also knew, perhaps better than anyone, how devastated I was when Ruby left, how incredibly difficult it was for me to face her now. It was Molly after all who held me and coddled me and listened and talked and nursed me back to some semblance of functioning after I realized Ruby really was gone, and wasn't coming back.

But it wasn't Quinn.

Parker: *Dude! What you wearing tonight? /*dancing man/**

Shit. Just like Parker not to think about this until the last minute. Nah. Quinn must have put him onto me. She knew me too well. I swallowed. She was probably standing right next to him, telling him what to say.

Me: *Have to cancel. You want to borrow my Tom Ford suit?*

Parker: *(ಠ_ಠ)*

Me: *Ask your sister. She's standing right next to you.*

Parker: *Busted*

ME: *tell your stupid brother to wear his grey suit/pale blue shirt/navy knit tie.*

Quinn: *What are you wearing? :p*

Me: *Lay off, Quinn.*

Quinn: *Please Julian. Everyone's expecting you.*

Me: *What did she say? Is she going?*

Quinn: *Haven't heard anything.*

. . .

I'D BARELY GOT BACK to work when again my phone buzzed in my hand. Damn these guys.

Tate: *Who's the sexiest man in Pt Cam?*

I chuckled.

Me: *Me of course loser.*

Tate: *Wrong! So wrong. It's me!*

Me: *You horn dog.*

Tate: *It's gonna be a great night. All the old squad together again.*

Me: *Yeah, yeah. It'll be amazing to see everyone.*

Tate: *We're doing this right?*

Me: …

I took a deep breath and braced myself.

Me: *You heard Ruby's back?*

Tate: *Fuck me dude* ☉ _ ☉

That exactly summed up how I felt.

Tate: *You want company?*

Me: *No. Busy prepping food.*

Tate: *U do know April will be there too. /*eggplant/**

Me: *Ugh.*

Tate: *Got your back my friend.*

I sighed. With the shock of seeing Ruby, I had completely forgotten about April. I closed my eyes for a beat. What an asshole I was. Another reason to give this fiasco a miss.

At the sound of my groan, Molly asked, "Have you made up your mind about going?"

I grunted. "Forty-seven times."

"You were really excited about this."

I nodded. "I'm actually really psyched about seeing every-one. It's going to be a great night." Regardless of what I decided to do, I still had to drive all the food to the venue.

When we had done everything, and were side-by-side at the sink washing up the equipment, and wiping down the counter-tops, Molly stopped suddenly, drying her hands on the tea towel tucked into her apron and turned to me. She looked up at me, her big brown eyes limpid and sympathetic, and reached up to tuck my unruly curls behind my ear.

"You're overdue for a haircut little brother. Do you want me to give you a trim while I'm here?" She kept her eyes on my face, waiting patiently for me to acknowledge that I was still considering going. And in her subtle way also recognized that I would want to look my best. Despite the fact women seem to love my scruffy farmer look, and my hair when it got long and messy, and my jaw when it was shadowed with a day or two of beard, somehow we both knew that I needed to take it up a notch tonight. If I were going.

Of course I had to show up at least to coordinate with the catering crew and make sure the food was set up and laid out properly for the whole night. The question was, would I get dressed and would I stay.

About the haircut at least, I conceded and went to the bathroom for my barber kit. I settled into a kitchen chair with a towel around my shoulders while Molly spritzed and snipped and trimmed. Only half watching in the hand mirror, trusting that she knew what I liked, I steeled my resolve. Despite the coddling I was getting at Molly's hands, I knew Arnie was right. I couldn't let a decade old slight dictate my future. But that didn't mean that I wouldn't make sure I could hold my head high.

Ruby

Deanna's apartment was an amazing spread of gleaming white surfaces, tan modern furniture, and pink accents. Her family always had money, but I'd never seen her in a place of her very own. It shouted her personality. I didn't know another soul who could get away with pink as a decorator colour. My style was more khaki, rust and dust. You could say I felt a little out of place. It occurred to me that Deanna and I had little in common besides high school. Despite being part of our clique, it was Rainy, Jeannie, and Bethune I was always closer to. But Rainy was buddies with Deanna. And Jeannie was besties with Quinn. So, as a group, we worked. And I guess every clique of girls needs their fashionista. Since I'd been out of the picture, it felt like just yesterday she'd caused a scene at grad by sleeping with Zach and breaking up Zach and Jeannie. But I guess everyone had got over that ages ago.

"Give me your jacket and come this way."

Deanna scooped me up by the arm and dragged me down the hall, bursting through a double doorway into her equally white, and even more shades of pink, bedroom. Colourful clothing was strewn over the backs of chairs, hanging on the doors, and laying across the bed. Kesha sang softly in the background.

Also on the bed, looking even more grumpy and tomboyish than I remembered her, was Aislin. Aislin who was always there in Deanna's shadow even though she was never really part of our gang. She wasn't part of anyone's gang.

"Aislin! Oh my goodness," I rushed towards her to give her a hug. She stiffened in my embrace, leaning slightly away, and I released her. Not everything had changed since high school. She seemed just as reserved and socially awkward as ever. In that respect she had not changed at all. "It's so good to see you again. How are you?"

Her eyebrows pinched together, and I noticed that she had a new piercing through the right one with a small stainless-steel barbell. Her ever-reluctant smile tilted up to one side as though she were half-amused, half skeptical of me. Of anyone really. Of other humans, I guess.

"Hello Ruby."

I stepped back and looked at her. She had evolved; I guess you could say. Instead of just awkward, and plain, she now had a kind of edgy geek look to her with more ink than before. Her pretty heart-shaped face had become more contoured, under a mop of dark hair. She wore a black tank, shredded camo leggings, and colourful socks with what looked like rows of code on them. Like a dusky moth on a lily petal, she sat crossed-legged in the centre of Deanna's wide silky pink bed. It was the most incongruous thing I'd seen in a very long time.

At least we weren't alone. "Can I assume that you too are about to be subjected to a Deanna makeover?" I asked as I sat on the edge of the bed.

Aislin rolled her eyes and let out an exasperated huff. "Apparently because this reunion requires us to revisit our painful childhoods, we have to dress completely out of character so people we don't know or care about will get entirely the wrong idea about us."

"Oh, A. We talked about this," Deanna teased. "It'll give you some closure, and maybe you'll even find a real man to hook up with tonight."

Aislin groaned, twisting her face in disgust. "Highly improbable."

Pouring, Deanna handed me a glass of Prosecco. "Make yourself comfortable Ruby, we're going to start with some internet research. Then, I am going to treat you both to the very best that my closet has to offer." She waved an arm towards said closet like Vanna White, revealing your choice of doors. "You're both a little shorter than I am, but we're all a similar size and I'm sure I can pull looks together for both of you. It's going to be fun!"

I wanted to believe her, but my gut recoiled in discomfort. I hadn't shopped or worried about fashionable clothes in... well, ever, basically. I hoped she wouldn't turn me into some kind of fashion runway monster. I didn't want to hurt her feelings. From the look on Aislin's face, we were on the same page.

Deanna turned to her laptop that sat on her dresser and woke it up. Grabbing it, she edged her way between us on the bed and started clicking through a series of images of women on her Pinterest account. Every imaginable look flashed before our eyes. "See anything you like? Just stop me."

"Hold on a sec. What's the dress code for this thing?" I asked.

"Semi-formal, I guess. Cocktail dress? If that's what you're comfortable with. But some people of course, will take every opportunity to dress to the nines."

"Yourself included D," deadpanned Aislin, scooting back to lean against the pillows and crossing her feet. "I think the whole reason for this reunion is so that you can dress up and impress everyone with your glamour and fashion, and win over even more followers for your Insta account."

"Not true. Don't be mean A." She swatted Aislin's shin with her long fingers.

"I don't know if you're aware, Ruby, since you've been away so much, but Deanna is an 'Internet Influencer.'" Aislin accompanied this statement with elaborate air quotes. "Her Insta account has 748,042 followers, and her beauty and wellness blog has over a million. I don't understand it. A million people tuning in every week to look at yoga pants and face creams." Aislin grunted.

"I didn't really know the extent of it," I replied, "but my family has kept me in the loop and I had some vague idea that you had quite the online presence, Deanna. Let me see some of those pictures." I took the laptop from her and scanned quickly past dozens of images of women in flowy dresses with makeup and hair that just would not work for me. Since I'd spent most of the last ten years in khakis and T-shirts, bulletproof vests, anoraks, and boots, I felt I had more in common with Aislin and her geek girl look then with anything that Deanna's closet might contain.

Then I stopped at a picture that reminded me a bit of a journalist that I admired. She was giving a Ted Talk, and I thought she looked powerful, serious, sophisticated, and very feminine. I could imagine myself like that and smiled.

"How about something like this?"

Deanna leaned over and squinted at the screen. "Aha. Yes, I see what you're getting at. Classic glamcaster. Barbara Walters for the twenty-first century."

"Like Janine di Giovanni," I said.

"I think I have something that will work. Let me find it and you can try it on."

She leapt from the bed and disappeared through doorway number two to the side of her large bedroom. I thought she'd been swallowed up until I heard hangers clacking against each other and cardboard boxes banging to the floor. After a few minutes, she emerged from what I realized was an enormous walk-in closet with a garment bag and a pair of shoes hanging from her fingers. She tossed the shoes down on the carpet and laid the bag across the bed. Unzipping it she pulled out a drapey off-white dress and held it against herself. She'd nailed it.

"Wow. You're good. Not only did you know exactly what I meant, but you actually have it in your closet. Now let's hope it fits."

"It will. That's why they pay me the big bucks. Go into my bathroom and try it on while I find something for Aislin."

I did as she instructed, dropping my chinos and snap shirt to the floor. I was not wearing the correct undergarments for this amazing dress, my black sports bra showing in the deep neckline, and yet it really fit me beautifully. It had a low princess neckline with silky jersey, stretchy bands across my stomach that wrapped my torso snugly, and a sexy ruffle down one thigh. I zipped it up as far as I could, turning to get a glimpse of myself in the vanity mirror. Frustrated, I stepped back into the bedroom to get some help and a better view in the full-length mirror.

When I came back out, Aislin stood in the middle of the room in a cute purple dress with angled lines.

"Where did Aislin go? Who is this sexy woman?" I laughed, then realized this was exactly the wrong thing to say to Aislin.

"Oh, frock off." Aislin buried her face in her hands. "How do I let you talk me into things like this, D?"

Deanna clucked and wrapped her arms around Aislin, squeezing her. "This is so great. This dress is you, A. You look like a super cool gaming avatar."

"This is the reason you organized the reunion!"

A dark blue and green tattoo wove around Aislin's bare arm and twined over her shoulder and up the side of her neck. She had on one black pump and one fluffy slipper, and another tattoo grabbed her calf like a claw. Deanna stood back assessing the outfit while Aislin's head shook back and forth as she moaned. "No, D. No. I can't. My legs show. It's too girly." She plucked at the cap sleeve. "And I can't even walk in these shoes!" She kicked off the pump, and it flew in my direction. I flinched and jumped out of the way as it thumped against the wall.

"I think it's cute," I offered hopefully. Aislin groaned, shot me a dirty look, and squirmed and spun around.

"Cute? Aargh! Get it off. Get it off me." She dropped to a squat, wrapping her arms around her bent head and knees, rocking forward and back.

Deanna rushed forward to help her unzip it. "Okay, A. It's off now, okay? You're super brave for trying it. It's okay."

Three minutes later, disaster averted, Aislin was back on the bed in her underwear, arms still wrapped around herself. "No dress."

Deanne studied her, hands on hips, her face folded up in a scowl. "Alright. No dress. Just let me think a minute."

"What do you feel comfortable in, Ash?" I asked. "What's your power suit? Your favourite kick-ass outfit?"

"If she had her choice, it'd be baggy pants and a tank top."

"And boots," Aislin nodded.

"Well, what've you got that meets those criteria. Can you just take her every day and make it more… dressy?"

Deanna pushed out her lips thoughtfully, tapped the side of her nose, and disappeared back into her closet. Deanna's mumbled self-talk drifted out to us. Aislin met my gaze warily, so I pulled a stupid oh fuck face and she rolled her eyes, almost cracking a smile. Win!

While Deanna searched, I asked a few probing questions, which was what I did so well. "What did you end up doing for work, Aislin? I remember you being really good with math, and also liking art."

"You have an excellent memory, Ruby. I'm a programmer. I work for a gaming start-up."

"That sounds perfect for you. Do you like it?"

"Yes, coding makes me happy. I'm good at it."

Deanna poked her head out of the closet. "You're brilliant at it. Of course. And the best thing is, Ruby, they're all geeks like her, so she fits right in. They love her there." She turned to face Aislin. "It's the best thing that could've ever happened to you. The problem is that tonight we don't want you to stick out like a sore thumb. Some of those mean girls that used to give you a hard time in high school will be there tonight." Back to me she went on. "I've been coaching A on how to put them in their place." Ducking back into the closet, she added, "But you've got to look the part, my little friend, if you want this to work." Clack-clack went the hangers.

Aislin said, "I'm not interested in revenge D. I just want to get through the night without getting upturned into a toilet. In fact, all I want is to be left alone. It's bad enough I have to go to a party with 243 people I can't talk to and don't like. I'd rather die."

"A! Nobody's going to beat you up tonight. We're not teenagers anymore. But you have to stand up to any snark. Defend yourself."

"You don't know them like I do, D."

Deanna didn't respond.

I shook my head. This was getting weird. I felt like I'd travelled back in time to high school.

Aislin and Deanna were the oddest pair. One short, dark, boyish, nerdy, and pathologically antisocial. The other a tall, blonde, gorgeous girly girl and a social butterfly. Also improbably, a liberal-minded social activist who couldn't walk past an underdog. Maybe that's what started it all.

If you didn't know their history, it would be nigh impossible to stretch your brain around their unbreakable bond. Their story was mythic. Deanna, with her ADHD—forever spending extra time in the learning support centre with tutors, catching up on homework, or getting extra time on tests—meeting Aislin, who's on the spectrum and probably didn't have any friends at all until that point, not to mention the bullying. Suddenly A's not only got a protector, but she's forever the sidekick of the coolest kids in school. Aislin was hard to like. Only D seemed to be able to get her to talk. I guess she had grown some, after all.

When I moved to the school at the end of grade nine, I think that was probably when they started hanging around together. I used to wonder what was in it for Deanna, though. I'm sure it started as a reluctant partnership that came from prolonged confinement together. From the stories I'd heard, they didn't get along at first, like oil and water. But between their complementary skill sets, they forged a friendship that persevered through all the challenges and changes that high school wrought. That's how they became A-typical-girl and ADHD-Dee, or A and D for short, though people thought it was just their names. No one walked around calling people by their disabilities these days, but their nicknames had stuck, nonetheless.

Finally, Deanna emerged with a new armful of clothes, mostly black, and dumped them on the bed beside Aislin. "Ok. Let's try this."

Deanna finally noticed me in my off-white jersey wrap

dress. She turned to me, looking me up and down. "Just as I thought, Ruby. You're a knockout. A diamond in the rough. Those sleeves look amazing on your toned shoulders. Same thing though—hair and make up for you, girl. It'll make all the difference. And the proper bra, of course. We'd better get moving."

She rummaged in her dresser drawers for suitable under-wear for Aislin and I to wear under our party clothes. She thrust a handful of silky, lacy things at me and said, "Put those on. Then I'll do your hair and makeup." She turned to Aislin. "You, I'm going to dress myself. I'm sure you do not know what to do with Spanx."

I laughed and returned to the bathroom to change.

When I emerged again, properly underpinned, Aislin stood woodenly in front of the full-length mirror. Her head tilted to the side, her eyes narrowed as she peered at her own reflection as though looking at a stranger. If I hadn't seen her just five minutes ago, I don't think I'd have recognized this woman.

This time, Deanna had dressed her in crepe wide-legged black pants with a high waist, and buttons that went up both sides like old-fashioned sailor pants. The sleeveless top was something stretchy and shimmery with a wide boat neck that bared her long white neck and complemented her ink. She wore some kind of platform heeled boots that peaked out below the hem of the long pants. The extra three inches were transforma-tive, but still sturdy. Deanna stood behind her with the fingers of both hands threaded into the strands of Aislin's choppy brown hair, pulling it up and away from her face, squinting.

"We'll have to do something with this. I can't wait. You're gonna wow everyone, A-typical."

Aislin groaned, and we all burst into laughter. For a moment, I felt like a kid again.

By the time Aislin and I were properly garbed, Deanna had dragged two kitchen chairs into her bedroom and lined them up like a salon. I don't know where she learned to cut and style hair, but she seemed to know how to do anything and everything with fashion and beauty. Two hours later, both Aislin and I had been transformed so that A looked stunning, and I looked something like the glamorous journalist who I admired so much. More grown-up than I felt, despite the lines on my face. Those Deanna had magically minimized with all sorts of potions and creams. And then she'd somehow made my eyes and lips pop and my cheeks glow rosily. All right. I'm ready. Let's do this thing.

Chapter 5

Julian

WHEN I ARRIVED at the reunion venue, I knew the team had made the right decision. It looked amazing, and I could imagine it filled with all my old friends in their finery.

DJ Troy's voice crackled over the PA system, "Test. Test. Okay folks, how's about we get this party started with a few tunes to stimulate your sentimental souls."

A familiar rapid guitar intro began, and I smiled, glancing up at Troy, with a shake of my head. The main opening line of "I Gotta Feeling" by Black Eyed Peas had barely begun as I stepped out from behind the servery having sorted the last of the food. Quinn and Parker rushed me, each grabbing an arm, bopping their heads and laughing.

"Dude, where's your suit? You're dressed like a chef!" Parker was referring to my black-and-whites, which I always wore when handling food.

"I gotta feeling…"

"Please tell me you have your suit in your van." Quinn swiveled to stand directly in front of me so I couldn't avoid her gaze. Quinn looked like herself, but nicer. She, like me, was more interested in comfort than fashion, but she'd cleaned up pretty well for the party. Her voice dropped to a hoarse whisper, "You promised me you'd stay."

"I did no such thing, Quinn Roarke. I said I'd come. That's not the same thing."

"You can't leave now," said Parker, dapper in the grey suit I'd suggested, as he gripped my shoulder. "The other guys will be here any minute. Dude! Seriously."

I let out a heavy sigh, the guilt already swamping me like a tidal wave. I would never get out even if I wanted to.

"You got a haircut," Quinn said slyly, giving me the side-eye. "Don't tell me that was for your goats. Or maybe it's for your new internet girl-fans?" She teased.

"Piss off, Quinny. Yes, I have my suit in the van. I left my options open. I'm still thinking about it." It didn't occur to me that any of my new fans could be part of our grad class. God, I hoped not.

"This place is awesome. Great choice, man," Parker said, his gaze scanning the beautiful space.

Finding a suitable venue for the reunion had been one of the most challenging details for the planning committee. We knew how many had been in our graduating class, but we didn't know how many would make it or bring plus-ones. So we had to stay flexible until we had a closer count.

"Well, it was the best of the lot, since the committee insisted I oversee the catering. All the hotels, both high and low end, insisted on including their own food services, so they were out."

"Plus, we had a budget," said Quinn.

"Not everyone we went to school with is super successful like Tate and Zach, or has piles of family money like Deanna and Jae Soo." Ask me how I know. In my search for Farm-to-Table Faire sponsors, I'd researched everyone, and knew more about how they were all doing financially than I probably should have.

"Still, I would have preferred the winery. My friends would

have made us very welcome and done half the work we had to do ourselves here."

"But literally no one would want to drive all that way," Quinn replied. "My favourite was that rustic community hall."

"But it would have been way too tight with this many people. And the kitchen facilities were completely inadequate."

Quinn pulled her face into a long Python-esque mock-serious expression. "Well, there was the German Cultural Society."

We both burst into laughter.

"What was wrong with that one?" Parker asked.

It had actually been pretty well set up for all sizes and manners of gatherings. "Ask Deanna. She vetoed it based on aesthetic hopelessness."

"I believe she called it pedestrian and uninteresting, and no one dared disagree with her."

"Well, I love what we ended up with."

The Port Cam Public Market could accommodate a group of our size in the large heritage open space. Even better, my foodie friend Matt was one of the vendors and willing to share catering responsibilities with me. Being able to use his kitchen and servery made my job easier. The retrofitted space had a funky, modern vibe and flexibility that worked for our event. We'd made the right call.

"So much better once Deanna and Rainy did the decorating."

"I helped," Quinn said.

"Well then, thank you. It's really perfect."

When I'd walked in to help the catering crew set up, it astonished me how the space had been transformed. They'd slayed it. The long, tall, narrow space with its brick arcade was strewn with strings of patio lights; there were white flowers everywhere, and trees with twinkling mini lights. Since the food was all finger-food and self-serve buffet, we had clusters of bar top, small, and long tables tucked into different side rooms and alcoves, leaving part of the large central area open for mingling and dancing. The DJ, a guy named Troy from school who was not part of our graduating class, had set up on an upper level overlooking a balcony into our party space. It was absolutely perfect. But then this organizing committee was a group of women whom I would trust with any undertaking. They were capable, energetic, hard-working, and creative.

"And your food buffet is to die for, Julian. It looks like a spread out of Gourmet Magazine," said Quinn, squeezing my arm.

I smiled, as proud of the food as I could be. I'd pulled out everything I knew and pushed all the boundaries. My goal was for people to take notice and rave. I wanted the attention tonight so I would have talking points for my sponsorship campaign. Delicious aromas were already wafting out from the kitchen as various foods warmed, and serving staff poised to circulate with amuse-bouche as soon as we had enough people.

"So. You're staying, right?"

"Is she coming?"

She huffed, her hands on her hipbones, evading my question. "I have to find the other girls." She pointed one finger directly at Parker's nose in that bossy big-sister way of hers, even though she was only about forty-five minutes older. "Parker, you're in charge of making sure he doesn't sneak away."

"Yeah, yeah. Don't worry. He's not going anywhere."

She turned away and exclaimed, "Oh, they're here! Later, gator." And she scooted away, her hips rolling with her limp, completely unselfconscious. That was Quinn.

Parker and I spun to watch her go, and in the distance we could see a group of women arriving together. They looked like a flock of tropical birds.

"Shee-it," hissed Parker. "Are we at the Oscars?"

Deanna, with her pinked tipped, pale blonde hair, glowed like a beacon in a black swirly cut-out gown that made it seem as if she were half naked. Peering with lifted brows, I presumed the tan bits in between were fabric and not actually bare skin. Beside her, a petite brunette I didn't know. Just behind them was Rainy, all glammed with makeup, which I only ever saw on her when she had a video call from her mother, or going to some cultural event, except no sari tonight. Instead, her dress was shimmery and electric blue. Shorter, curvier, but no less gorgeous, was Bethune, with her severely cut bright red hair and unique sense of style.

No sign of Jeannie, yet. Quinn hadn't said if she'd made it to town in time. As the women fanned out into the central space as if taking flight, looking around, they parted like curtains to reveal one more bright bird, and my breath left me in a whoosh, my head swimming.

Ah, Quinn. You lied to me.

Ruby, with her golden-brown hair in long, twisting, shiny ropes laying across her shoulders, red lipstick and a creamy white dress that made it seem as if she glowed from the inside out. A goddess.

The excruciating sense of loss slammed into me and my chest collapsed, like I'd been tackled. All these years, I'd been missing a ghost, a shadow of a sweet eighteen-year-old girl. Even as I had grown up, become a man, changed, Ruby had stayed the same in my memory. I couldn't play that game anymore. She stood before me in all her beauty and brains, grace and gravitas. The same breathtaking woman I had ever loved, but more refined.

You'd think I'd be a pro at stomping down and ignoring my feelings for Ruby, but then, I hadn't laid eyes on her for ten years. I found I didn't have quite the same self-control when she was in the room.

Parker's voice barely reached me. "Julian! Holy fuck. Is that Ruby? Julian?"

But I was already racing through the kitchen door out into the back lane.

Ruby

Deanna led the way, with Aislin and Rainy following. I hung back to get my bearings, feeling oddly shy. After checking in, we entered from the foyer and I surreptitiously scanned the room, still not convinced I should be here. My stomach buzzed with a low-grade mixture of excitement and anxiety about what the evening would hold.

Years ago, I'd been to the public market, browsing the vendor stalls and buying lunch. I'd never thought of it as an interesting place you could book for a party. The girls did a fab job of decorating the tall brick space. It was like a fairy forest, full of twinkling lights and shadowed foliage. You'd expect Peter Pan to fly down from above.

Instead, I gazed around for a more down-to-earth figure, half terrified that I'd actually see him. But I didn't. My racing pulse and trembling hands belied any excuses I'd told myself about not caring. I really was hoping to see Julian tonight. Not because I foolishly hoped to rekindle any romance between us, but because I felt I owed him a civil conversation. A proper apology.

It's only that I hadn't yet summoned enough courage.

Not many people had arrived yet. My industrious friends wanted to see that all was going according to plan before the masses arrived.

Across the central space, Quinn charged towards us, smiling broadly. "You all look amazing!" She hugged everyone, taking a moment to compliment every single member of the group on their dress, hair, or makeup.

"You look so lovely, Quinn," I said, when it was my turn. "I love your hair down like that. You look like a boho model." She never would wear a short skirt, because of the huge scar across her knee, but tonight she wore a long batik tunic over leggings with tall boots. She still looked like a tree-hugging earth mother, but it suited her; she was naturally beautiful, with her golden freckles and green eyes, so she didn't need high fashion to be attractive. She was someone as comfortable in their skin as could be.

She waved off my compliment, humble as ever. "Let's give you the tour before anyone realizes who you are." She led me through the space, showing me the bar, the buffet, the DJ up on a mezzanine, and all the little tables tucked into alcoves and side rooms.

"It's a perfect space for the reunion," I said.

Rainy jumped in. "Julian found it for us. The only place we would fit, within our budget, was this boring cultural centre that Deanna nixed. But Jules knows the guy that owns the meat roasters here — some rancher — and made a deal with their event coordinator. So we get beautiful food, and Julian gets to work the crowd to drum up sponsorships for his Farm-to-Table Faire on Labour Day weekend."

What was that?

Quinn reappeared at my side.

"Is Julian here, then?" I asked, my voice low, nonchalant. From the looks on their faces I could see I wasn't fooling anyone.

"Yeah, of course," Quinn said, spinning around, scanning the space. "He was right there." She waved at Parker, who stood next to the bar, raising her voice, "Parker, where'd Julian go?" He didn't react, attending to someone else.

My heart shot into my throat. He came after all. I pulled on her arm, shushing her. "Stop it, Quinn. I don't want to talk to him."

She turned back, squinting up at me. "Sure you don't."

I twisted my face. "Well, not in public. Have pity on me. I need time."

"I'll go find out. He was talking to Parker and I a moment

ago." She pointed at the buffet and before I could stop her she limped off in that direction.

Deanna, a champagne flute in one hand, waved the other elegant bare arm overhead as she clutched her phone, indicating the decorations. "Isn't it beautiful?" She snapped pictures of the space and angled herself into the photos with various other people. She really was, with her mauve-tipped blonde hair, purple lipstick, and black and rose velvet burnout dress with its sheer deep vee neckline. She had such a natural flair and sense of design. The look I'd chosen for myself, that she'd executed so flawlessly, felt stodgy by comparison. I don't even know why I worried about dressing up. I felt so fake.

I obliged when she pressed her cheek to mine and angled her phone camera above us, spinning us until she liked the lighting and the background, pasting on a professional smile, and then waiting while she posted it.

I half-listened to her explanations about this and that while we spun around, while a part of my mind tried to piece together what I'd learned about Julian's life. It sounded like Julian was really invested in his role as a local food producer, and I wondered how he was managing alone on the farm. I was happy for him, I think. He always seemed to know what he wanted. Though a part of me still felt a kind of sadness at his curtailed life.

Even if Julian was here, I wouldn't have been able to strike up an awkward conversation with him. A large group of people arrived and since we were standing in the middle of the tall open central space, we were immediately swamped with old classmates who recognized me, while I had to pretend I remembered most of them. Even if they didn't know me or hadn't paid me much attention in school, pretty much everyone had seen me on the news channels. You'd have to have been living under a rock to have not.

Not that I was comfortable in a crowd of fans, all excited to be in the presence of someone they perceived to be a celebrity.

As I forced a smile, accepted congratulations, and fielded curious questions from my former classmates, I squirmed and darted glances left and right, desperate to find a crack through which I could escape. But anytime I saw an opportunity to slip away, another few people would arrive, notice me and come over.

Aislin seemed to share my discomfort, her neck tucked into her shoulders like a turtle wanting to disappear into her shell. I gave her a sympathetic look and she mumbled, "I hate people."

I let out a gust of laughter. "You're not alone there. Reunions are strange. And I'm not comfortable in crowds either."

"Even with all your awards?"

I shrugged. "Mostly I hear about those through the wire. I think I've personally received awards about three times in ten years. So... not much practice." I laughed.

What people didn't understand was that, while they saw me on their television sets and smart phone screens, they had this sense that I was used to crowds and attention. But a field reporter in fact lives a largely solitary life in remote, faraway locations and communicates with co-workers and editors only by email and sat phone. The reporting that I do, that I mostly did, was into a mic and the only person I saw or spoke to on a daily basis was my cameraman.

Often, there was a handful of foreign correspondents from other countries that shared our divey hotels and seedy bars, or traveled together on buses and trucks. Sometimes they even became our friends. Occasionally, in lonely moments, our lovers. But the idea that I was someone noteworthy. A star. A celebrity. That was an uncomfortable notion to me.

Sure, I'd won awards, but that was... something else. Professional recognition. Something that happened in parallel with the life I lived. Talk about imposter syndrome.

When I felt about ready to burst and run screaming, Quinn returned and rescued me.

"Couldn't find him," she murmured. She probably could see the whites of my eyes, like some kind of rabid cornered dog, and realized I needed a break.

"Oh, look! It's the celebrity douchebags," Rainy barked over the rising hum of voices, and the increasingly loud music pumping from the speakers.

"Excuse us," Quinn said to the few hangers-on, pulling me towards the approaching Tate and Zach. Despite Rainy's disdain, they were obviously still close friends.

Deanna and Rainy ran interference, and we escaped, forming our own little circle.

"Look at us! All these successful, famous people in our graduating class," Deanna crooned, blowing air kisses at the guys, who grinned and ate it up. Though with their looks and reputations, I think they took it for granted. "Group selfie!" She turned her back to the group, trying to get a shot of everyone together.

Quinn made a wry face, popping up in the front row. "Some of us."

I admired her and thought she was brave. You wouldn't catch me starting a new business from scratch. And she'd worked hard to get where she was, working shitty jobs, doing research, apprenticing. But I could see how she felt like the underdog. If only I could make her understand how uncomfortable fame was, and how phony it made you feel.

Someone behind us snickered and snarked, "If you call making fish faces and flashing cleavage on Insta an accomplishment." I turned and glanced over my shoulder to see who was making catty comments about our Deanna, who'd worked so hard to plan this event. Two women had their heads together, a blonde woman who was vaguely familiar, though I couldn't quite place her, and another with jet black hair cut into a sharp bob. Something made me think that maybe they'd been on student council. They slipped away before I figured it out.

Quinn pulled a face at me, and we shared a giggle. I looped

my arm through hers. "Fame's not all it's cracked up to be. Is Jeannie going to make it?"

She sighed. "It's not looking good. And Jae Soo isn't here yet either, though he promised."

Quinn, Parker, and Jae Soo had been inseparable since grade school. It had been a very long time since I'd been with friends that I could count on to be there for me, no matter what.

"He'll be here. He wouldn't let you and Parker down."

Chapter 6

Julian

I STOOD IN THE SHADOWS, safely flanked by Quinn and Parker, trying to keep a low profile, which was exactly the opposite of what I'd planned for tonight. But if I stayed vigilant, I could have a couple of drinks, work the crowd, say hi to a few friends, and still give Ruby a wide berth if I saw her. That was doable, right?

For the moment, her fans surrounded her, fully occupying her and she wouldn't notice me. I allowed myself a minute to watch her in the limelight, unobserved, thinking that she'd found her rightful place. She'd earned that fame. She deserved that adulation. It's what she needed and wanted.

Coward that I am, I'd spent the last ten minutes sitting in my van in the back lane with my stomach in knots, my will frozen. Eventually, I drummed up sufficient self-loathing, resentment and rage to change into my suit, comb my hair, and come back in. I was met by the twins, loyal and steadfast friends that they are.

Quinn wrapped her arms around me in a hug of sympathy. "You've got this, Julian. I'm glad to see Ruby back, but I can't bear the thought of you missing out on this night. It's too important to you."

Parker slapped me on the back in silent support and I grunted my thanks.

"Yeah. Just have to get up the nerve to move around. I'm not feeling very gregarious or persuasive."

Parker shoved a cold beer into my hand, as if that would fix everything. I held it to my forehead and neck in turn. Well, it might help. I took a long swig.

"You can't let Ruby take this from you, Julian. She has no right. And anyway, she wouldn't want to." Quinn dipped her chin and peered steadily at my face. "Please go out there and be your usual passionate self; do what you came here to do." She gave me a little shove.

I filled my lungs, bolstering courage. She was right. I took a few minutes to take my own photos of the venue, some people and, of course, my food; getting the shots just right to upload later where I'd use them to talk about sustainable food practices and pump up the Faire.

Deanna approached, her phone held high, asking me questions as she recorded, which was good. I was glad she still had the presence of mind to think about our respective businesses before the evening got too wild.

She sidled up to me and took a few selfies of the two of us with the food buffet behind us, and I happily hammed it up.

While I checked that Ruby was still busy, and scanned the room for people I wanted to talk to, Quinn bent her head over her phone, flicking a finger over its surface with a scowl on her face. I could guess what it was about.

"What's up with Jeannie? Is she going to make it?" I asked.

Quinn swore softly. "She sent a text that her flight's delayed. I haven't heard anything for hours, so I just don't know."

"I hope she makes it."

"Me too." Her shoulders sagged. "I was counting on it."

I put my arm around her and squeezed. It had been hardest

on her when Jeannie went off to university and never returned. Of all the girls, they'd been the closest friends, and Quinn had missed her, even though they had stayed in touch.

Parker shifted from foot to foot and smoothed back his slick blond hair. "Never mind Jeannie. What about Jae? Anyone seen him? He's coming, right, Quinny? He said he was."

"Yes, Parker. He's coming for sure," she answered with exasperation, as though he'd been asking every two minutes. Which, undoubtedly he had. Speaking of best friends. Jae Soo Jeong was practically an honorary Roarke twin, or triplet, I guess. He'd moved to town and met the twins when they were about nine. And since then, they'd been inseparable. Except when Jae Soo was required to go back to Korea most summers, and — since grad — for longer and longer periods. He was being groomed to take over the family businesses.

"He flew into Vancouver from Seoul two days ago and is on his way. Relax Parker." She lifted her head and met her twin's gaze with a dip of her chin and a nod. Some magical twin woo-woo passed between them because Parker took a deep breath, let it out on a long sigh and seemed to settle. "Go talk to some other friends."

Deanna buzzed by again in a whirl of bright hair, perfume, and waving arms, snapping pictures as she went. Parker took the hint and followed her into the crowd like a mouse after Pied Piper. As I watched him, I realized that Rainy and Ruby were part of Deanna's entourage.

Ruby was laughing and animated, and it threw my mind back to a time when watching Ruby across a room was my religion, my daily devotional. I could never get enough of her dynamism, energy, and intelligence. When we'd bumped into each other at the café yesterday, she was so stiff and serious. I'd thought maybe she'd changed. Lost her spark. But there it was. I'd missed it. I'd missed her so much my heart ached like a lost limb.

Aislin suddenly appeared in Parker's place, swapping out

one glum face for another, effectively distracting me from gawking.

"Hey Ash. How're you holding up?" Quinn asked her.

Expression wooden, she grumbled, "She exhausts me. And I hate crowds. Have I mentioned that?"

"You look really nice tonight, A," I offered, realizing she'd been the unrecognizable brunette I saw when they'd all entered. This was an extraordinarily fresh look for her.

She squirmed, dropping her gaze. "Thanks, I guess. I feel weird. Not like myself." She glanced up and stiffened, her eyes narrowing.

Suddenly, April appeared out of nowhere and leaned into me, gripping my arm, and my stomach clenched with dread.

"Hi, Julian," she purred. "I had to find you before your internet fans steal you away from me." She giggled, and I felt my face heat, shifting my weight and catching Aislin's eye. She raised her brows, blasé about my suffering.

I hadn't precisely been avoiding April… okay, well maybe I had. Our arrangement wasn't a public thing, and I wasn't comfortable with her claiming me as her property. I gently slid my arm out of her grip, turning slightly to make it seem natural, while deflecting with a compliment.

"Hey April." I offered a neutral, friendly smile. "You look great."

"Thanks, Julian. So do you. You clean up really well."

Her gaze travelled up, down, and up again. She peered up at me with her blue eyes wide, and I could easily read the question written there. We're an item, right? Is this the night we tell people? She hooked her hand around my neck and pulled down, hard. I resisted, but I ended up giving in to a peck, keeping it as brief as I could without having an obvious tug of war with her.

My teeth ground together in frustration. I did not want to hurt April, but we were definitely not a couple. We never had been. Surely she understood that. She's the one who first suggested we keep our episodic booty calls quiet. While not my preferred type of relationship, it had served us both well enough. Tonight is when she decides to change the rules?

Surely she couldn't have missed the fact that Ruby was back. She was attracting so much attention. And no one who knew me would fail to understand what Ruby meant to me, both the good and the bad, and maybe give me some space to deal with it. It was almost as if April felt threatened by her and decided to make an issue of it. I swallowed, my chest tight. I'd have to say something. Later.

"You look quite different, too, Aislin," April said in a high nasal voice, tilting her head, her eyes sharp as skewers. "That's not your usual… style, is it?" Her mouth pinched up like she'd sucked on a lemon. "My, you have a lot of tattoos, don't you?" If she was trying to scare Aislin away with that passive-aggressive move, I wouldn't allow it.

Feeling Aislin stiffen and shrink beside me, her glare burning holes in April's chest, I stepped closer to Aislin, bumping her elbow and smiling to show my allegiance. "She looks great, hey? I think the girls had a little makeover party at Deanna's. Didn't you, A?"

Aislin, no slouch, sent me an assessing side-eye, darting her gaze to April and back again. "Yes. We had Prosecco. Deanna insisted."

April made a valiant attempt to keep her smile afloat, but it sank a little anyway. "Oh, that explains it. Well, aren't you a good sport?" April sneered, dragging out the words. "I didn't think you were likely to do that on your own."

April was sidling up to me again, a determined gleam in her eye, and I worried she'd insist on a private tête-à-tête. It was good fortune that just then Tate blasted up like a summer storm.

"Hey, Julian, Aislin. How's it going?"

"There you are, dude," I said, the tension draining away

with an exhale. He said he'd have my back and he always came through.

"Oh, he-ey April," Tate said with a flashy smile, pulling out all the stops, "I was looking for you, girl."

Predictably, April fell into his sticky web of charm, good looks, and fame like an unsuspecting fly. "Hi, Tate!"

"Yeah, uh, you used to be on student council, right?"

"Mhm." She smiled up at him, basking in his glow of fame and general handsomeness.

"You know I always admired you for being so responsible… and involved."

"Yeah?"

"Oh, yeah. And hey, there are supposed to be some announcements and stuff, and they were looking for you. Why don't I walk over there with you?" He caught my gaze over her head and gave me a sly smile, then winked at Aislin, scooped April's arm under his and swept her away, unresisting while he sang along to Rihanna's "I Love The Way You Lie." Because who could resist Tate, our resident movie star?

I sighed, sagging. "Oh, thank God."

With flattened lips, Aislin eyed me critically. "If you don't like her, Julian, you shouldn't be having sex with her."

I groaned. "Yeah, thanks for that. It's complicated, Aislin. Especially now."

"S'pose. It looks to me like it was going to become a problem for you anyway."

I nodded, reaching behind me for a couple of amuse-bouches. I so often forgot to eat when I catered. With all the food in my field of vision, and all the tasting that I did along the way, my brain failed to get the message that I was hungry until my stomach growled, which it was doing now. Redirecting the conversation, I half-jokingly said, "She's got no business throwing shade at you, girl."

Aislin let out a bark of laughter, then sobered. "You know

she was one of the bitches who bullied me in high school, right? She was horrible."

I nearly choked on my own food. "What?"

She cast her gaze up at me as though I were the dullest knife in the drawer.

"No. I'm sorry, Aislin. I did not know that." I may have been self-absorbed in high school. Or Ruby absorbed. But I had heard something about some of her adolescent hardships. That was half the reason Deanna had taken her under her wing, I recalled.

She shrugged.

"It's not okay. And now she's a schoolteacher." I fumed, thinking of the implications, rapidly replaying all our interactions, searching for evidence to support this new image of her. April was a single mother, too. You'd think that would give her some perspective. I frowned. "People's essential character doesn't really change, you know."

"And you wonder why I don't like them."

Laughing, I shook my head. "It ends tonight. I'm done with her."

"How convenient."

"Ash!"

Then Aislin's face did that little side smirk, and her dark eyes twinkled.

"Catch you later." I realized I needed to deal with this. Right now.

Ruby

Weaving to the rhythm of John Mayer's "Heartbreak Warfare", Quinn, Rainy, Beth and I nudged our way through the growing crowd toward the bar table near the entrance to refresh our drinks. Curious well-wishers and celebrity rubbernecks had surrounded me for so long I'd wondered if I'd get any time to mingle, relax, and catch up with actual friends. It had not been my intention to steal the limelight from everyone else, and I was already having regrets.

The Public Market concourse had filled up with classmates and their escorts in the past hour, making it hard to see anyone who wasn't standing right in front of us. Still, I peered through the gaps in the crowd. I may not have been looking forward to actually talking to Julian, but I needed to see him like I needed oxygen. I needed to know where he was, what he was doing. It was a compulsion.

Drinks in hand, Bethune caught my eye, lifted a brow in query.

I scowled. "Have you seen him?"

"Who could you possibly mean?" she replied dryly.

Conceding with a half smile, I huffed. "I didn't expect to be at a reunion party with all my friends and classmates a day after arriving, you know," I explained. "I wasn't prepared for any of this. I wasn't ready to see Julian at all."

"I understand. But you can't blame us for gawking at the show."

I hummed. I supposed not. I kind of got the feeling that everyone was gearing up for some kind of showdown.

Beth sobered. "Are you going to tell him?"

I'd thought about this, but I gazed at the floor for a moment to gather my thoughts. "I suppose I won't have a choice. I can't avoid him all night. We'll have to talk. He'll ask, won't he?"

Beth's gaze locked on mine and she nodded in sympathy and reached to take my hand, squeezing it, and I swallowed. I would tell him. I wanted to. I would explain and apologize at the first opportunity.

A glossy couple stepped into our space. A guy named Adam and... was it Carina? "Hey, Ruby Zimmer!" he said. They both wore wide, amazed smiles. "We didn't expect to see you here."

Dread settled in my gut. Just a few minutes of peace would have been nice. "Hi guys. Yeah, well I—oh, excuse us."

A sudden kerfuffle at the registration table drew our attention. Any excuse to get away would do. I scanned the crowd for Julian as we made our way to the foyer.

The teenaged volunteer manning the desk said, "I'm sorry. This is a private event reserved for PCH grads and their escorts," his voice plaintive.

"Yes, I understand. But as I told you, I am a grad," came the gruff reply.

"I know, sir. But you can't possibly be Peter Corbin. Peter Corbin is, ahem, deceased."

"Look!" We turned to stare as the other volunteer, an older woman—possibly a teacher from after our time—showed the display panel Rainy had made with pictures, names, and dates of all our classmates who had died. When we'd arrived and stopped to pick up our name tags, I'd paused for a few minutes to look it over carefully.

Sixteen classmates, out of approximately a hundred and fifty grads, had not made it ten years into adulthood, and I wanted to know them, count them, remember them. It could so easily have been me. So many close calls. What would all my friends be saying tonight if my face were on that board?

I scanned the newcomer from head to toe. How could he be Peter?

Even though he was marginally part of our group, I never knew Peter Corbin well. I remembered a tough, skinny kid with longish dark hair who skipped a lot of school and hung around with potheads and small gang thugs. I'd assumed he was one too, but Jeannie always defended him, saying he was a good guy, and smart too, but had personal problems. And the guys, Tate and Zach in particular, were friendly with him, if I recalled. I think they would get their weed from him. After he'd died in the fire, I think everyone felt terrible that they had voted him "Most Likely to End Up in Jail."

I had to agree; the tall, clean cut, superior specimen of masculinity claiming to be Peter Corbin bore no resemblance to the kid I remembered. That Peter Corbin had, sadly, ended his young life in a wild trailer fire the night of our grad party. The same night Deanna hooked up with Zach and broke Jeannie's heart. Christ! The drama. I would not wish to be eighteen again.

Quinn stepped forward to intervene. "Hi, there. Can I help you?"

The hunky guy faced her, a small, crooked smile creasing the corner of his chiseled cheek, his grey-blue eyes twinkling. He was built of solid muscle that was straining his dress shirt like fucking Clark Kent. "Quinn Roarke," he said. "You haven't changed one bit."

Quinn stopped in her tracks and reared, studying his face, frowning. She seemed to clock his features one by one, checking them off on some mental list. Then she gasped. Her voice was a choked whisper when she stuttered, "You're... alive? How can it be?"

His wry smile fell and he nodded. "I'm sorry to shock you. I... I'm afraid it was by choice. I was happy enough that everyone thought I'd died in the fire." He had the grace to look sheepish. "I am also sorry for any hurt it may have caused. Since then I've been away, deployed overseas mostly."

The two volunteers behind the registration desk gawped at the unfolding scene, their grins advertising the fact that this was the most exciting thing to happen to them all night.

"Peter Corbin." Rainy stepped closer to him, reaching out to take his hand. "If I passed you on the street, I would never have recognized you. The last ten years have been good to you, haven't they?"

He looked down, chuckling. "Hey Rainy. I grew up is all. And I... well, I joined the Navy."

I'll say. Aside from having grown to well over six feet, his shoulders were broad, his arms and chest powerful, tapering to lean hips and strong, tree-like thighs. I didn't even really know him, and my ovaries were doing little flips.

"I'm sorry about your father," she added. "I guess it's a little late to offer condolences."

"Thanks, though. Appreciate it."

If his father actually did die in that horrible fire, and he ran off as a frightened, grieving teenager to join the Navy, I can imagine coming home now is difficult for him. I joined the little circle, glad to feel like one of the crowd instead of the curious newcomer, for a change. "Hello. Welcome back to Port Cam."

He turned to me, his eyes narrowing. "First time for both of us, isn't it Ruby?"

My brow came down, puzzled. "How would you know that?"

He winked. "I've been overseas quite a lot. I… might have followed your career… path. Bravo Zulu." His grin flashed.

My mouth opened, incredulous. "Well, I'll be damned, Peter."

"Oh, and, uh…" he winced. "I go by Phoenix now."

"What?"

I blinked twice, shaking my head. "Not… really."

At our collective disbelief, he chuckled, "I know it's… FUBAR. The guys in my first unit gave me the moniker when they learned my story, and it stuck." He shrugged those massive shoulders and I laughed. "I don't know if I'd answer to Peter, after all this time."

"Phoenix it is then," Rainy conceded.

Quinn grinned too. "Well, Phoenix Corbin, come on in and get a drink. There are some people here that are going to be stoked to see you."

I followed them to the bar, intrigued to hear more of his story.

"… I saw my mom and my baby sister, Bess, before I left for boot camp. But I made them promise not to tell anyone."

"But why?" Rainy persisted.

He paused thoughtfully and took a draw on the bottle of beer he'd just picked up. "Needed a fresh start I guess."

Quinn nodded, then frowned down at her phone.

"What are you worrying about, Quinn?" I whispered.

She turned to face me, dropping her voice. "Jeannie. I really expected her to make it, but it looks like she won't now." Our gazes met, and she pulled a sad face.

"Jeannie? Jeannie van Bellen?" Phoenix said, frowning.

Quinn, with her back to him, stiffened, her nostrils flaring. "Yeah. She's moving back to town. But it looks like she won't make it tonight." She turned to face him with a broad, tight smile.

"Hmph," Phoenix nodded, apparently having lost interest.

"So what are your plans, Phoenix? Are you back to stay?" Quinn asked, and I wondered why she was suddenly so on edge.

He tongued his cheek, pushing out his lips thoughtfully. "Haven't decided yet. I'm at a crossroads in my career, and I've got a little time off to think about next steps." That sounded all too familiar.

"Oh, here come the douchebags," mumbled Rainy. And there went my chance to ask Phoenix what he meant about following my career.

I turned and watched as across the room four handsome guys in suits broke into motion and strode towards us like the Rat Pack, having heard the exciting news.

"Who? Tate and Zach?" I asked to clarify. Parker was behind them, and nobody would call him a douchebag. He was a goofy sweetheart. I'd hoped those other two would have outgrown their macho tendencies, but even from here, it seemed fame and fortune had done nothing to temper them.

"Mm. Yeah." Rainy said, tugging on Quinn's flared sleeve. "Do you know where Deanna is?"

Quinn shrugged, continuing to ask Phoenix questions about his military career.

Tilting my head towards Rainy, I whispered, "Who's that hot guy in the suit standing next to Parker?" thinking there were more good-looking men in my grad class than I remembered. Or maybe I'd just been away too long.

Rainy dipped her chin toward me, her brow and mouth all scrunched up, disbelieving. "Seriously Ruby? How did you make it as a reporter, girlfriend?" Rainy laughed. What? "I'm gonna go find Deanna. Make sure she's not drinking too much and getting stupid."

Puzzled, I looked again at the guys as they approached and greeted Phoenix, all charming smiles, handshakes, and back-slapping. As they got closer, the handsome, sexy guy in the expensive navy suit turned toward me. Between the heads of his friends, I found he was peering intently at me too, with a dark and dangerous expression, and caught my enquiring gaze. I gasped, my heart hammering in my chest, nearly falling off Deanna's designer heels from the shock. The mystery guy was Julian!

Chapter 7

Ruby

HEART THUNDERING BEHIND MY RIBS, I scooted away from the throng, following in Rainy's wake. Julian? That's Julian? I darted a furtive, curious glance over my shoulder even as I retreated. He turned to the side and glanced in my direction, his eyes narrowing. Our gazes glanced off of each other like opposite pole magnets, sparking and kicking my pulse into a higher gear, and I watched as his Adam's apple slid up and down his toned neck. He was drop dead gorgeous! I mean, he was always gorgeous, but not like this, sleek and sophisticated. What happened to him? Since when did he dress that way? I'd never, ever seen him so beautifully groomed. His hair was shorter, glossy and smooth, his jaw shaved, and his navy suit looked like it had been custom tailored for him. Suddenly, all the other handsome men in the room faded into wallpaper.

Rainy and I caught up with Deanna, who was flitting around the party like a hummingbird on speed, taking pictures with her phone of all the beautiful people, including herself in most of them—her eyes fluttering, her lips puckered, the lighting perfect.

"We're trending!" Dee announced, giddy.

"Hey, sweetie," Rainy said, pulling her away from a group of grinning grads. "How 'bout a time out?"

"Hiiii!" Deanna draped her swan-like arm around Rainy's neck and air kissed the side of her face. "You having fu-un? Is this a great party or whaaat?" The volume of her voice was a titch too high even given the loud dance music that had driven the excited hum of conversation louder as the room filled with people. I could see why Rainy was watching out for her. Deanna had always been a wild party girl.

"Let's get something to eat," I suggested as I glanced over my shoulder at Julian. I was fascinated, drawn like a moth to fire, and yet wanting to put more distance between us, understanding the danger he posed. We all needed a little space. Despite my determination to talk to him, I found I was still short on courage. "I'm starving and I want more of those yummy things I tasted yesterday before they're all gone."

They followed me as I plowed through the crowd toward the buffet.

"No need to worry, Ruby," Deanna crooned. "Julian would never short us. He knew exactly how many people were coming and he made sure there would be loads of food."

"Julian? Did he help with the planning?" It seemed I couldn't avoid thinking about him if I wanted to. We stopped at the table where a gap between shoulders revealed platters and stacked tiers of delicious things to eat.

Deanna said, "Julian? He made aaaaalll the food. He catered for us." Then she picked up a tiny plate and carefully chose some green and white things. "He said these are dairy and gluten-free," she murmured, taking a nibble.

"What?" What was she saying? I cursed Troy the DJ for cranking up the music to the point it was getting impossible to hear. Lady Gaga was chanting "Bad Romance" at top volume now. I filled a small paper plate with several amazing tidbits and popped one into my mouth. Again, the flavours exploded into an ecstatic medley of highs and lows. The textures, both smooth and rough, were a delight. Quickly swallowing, I exclaimed, "I love this stuff. I've never tasted such great food. And it's so beautifully arranged, too. What did Julian do?"

"He's the chef, Ruby. You didn't know?" Rainy smirked.

"What do you mean... the chef? Why didn't you tell me?" Why was I so clueless? Everyone knew things about Julian that I had no idea about. Nothing added up. "Can we..." I grabbed several more items and piled them onto my plate. Mystery or not, I wasn't passing up on these treats. I hadn't had food of this quality for years. "Can we please find a quiet table so you can tell me what I'm missing?"

The three of us wove through the crowd, Deanna definitely tottering a little on her heels, and found a vacant high-top table tucked around a corner in an alcove where some other people, at least, were managing quiet conversations. We set our plates and glasses down on the black tablecloth and I grabbed the edge of the table as I leaned towards them.

"Did I hear you say Julian is a... a chef? Since when?"

"He went to culinary school, a couple years after grad. When you left, he didn't stay on the farm for more than a couple of months."

My chest muscles pressed in on my heart and lungs, making it hard to breathe. I sensed it, and yet I didn't want to hear the details. I'd been running from them all this time. "He left the farm? But he's there now... didn't he say?" I shook my head, befuddled. Yesterday, he'd looked as much the farmer as ever, and didn't he say he was getting an alpaca?

"He left and came back, Ruby! Just like you." Deanna reached for her wineglass and Rainy intercepted her, handing her a glass of water instead. "He worked at a pub, and then a restaurant in the city for... how long, Rainy?"

"Over a year. And then he skipped town. We didn't really know where to for a while. We all worried about him, actually.

Then he finally contacted us to tell us he was at culinary school in London."

My head shot back in surprise. "London! England?" To their nods of agreement, I repeated, incredulous, "He went to culinary school in fucking London, England while I was studying journalism in Wisconsin?" How is this possible? All these years I figured he was raising chickens with his dad on the farm, the way I thought he'd always be, and he was... "Then what?" I demanded, looking at the food I'd been shovelling into my gullet with fresh eyes, and this time, amazement.

Deanna waved at a passing friend. "Heeey, Armand!"

Rainy kept a loose hold on Deanna's wrist and went on. "He graduated with honours, and apprenticed, I guess. You'd have to ask him for details, but I know he worked his way around Europe, at resorts, hotels, restaurants. He was doing really well, and I think he was working on his first Michelin star somewhere in Italy maybe, when he suddenly quit."

"His dad died!" hollered Deanna above the music, distracted.

I made a face. I couldn't react fast enough to all the new information. A Michelin star, for God's sake? And poor Mr. Michaels died? "When?"

Rainy picked up the tale. "About a year and a half ago. Julian came back for the funeral and never left. He took over the farm and changed everything. About the farm. About his life. I told you yesterday, didn't I?"

My mind reeled. I monitored the crowd, sifting through the faces for another glimpse of Julian, more curious than ever. How was this possible? "You mean he's been back just over a year? And he left a couple years after grad? So, he was gone..." I shook my head. I could hardly comprehend what I was hearing.

"Yup. Almost as long as you were," nodded Rainy, smirking with a naughty glint in her eye.

This, I suppose, explained the transformation from rustic

farmer to smooth metrosexual in a designer suit. I guess it also explained the amazing food we'd been eating.

"I guess he wasn't what you thought he was."

I couldn't stop myself from glaring at her. "I didn't leave Julian because I thought he wasn't good enough. He always..."

Speaking of Julian, my roving gaze snagged in the middle of the room. He strode confidently up to Tate and the same blonde woman and snatched her away, possessively taking her arm and leading her to a quiet corner opposite. My stomach hardened with an ugly feeling of outrage, though I didn't want to name it. He turned away, sheltering her, and bent his head as her hands came up to embrace him. And then they kissed! My heart lurched at the sight. It never occurred to me that Julian was with someone. "Is he..."

I nudged Rainy's arm and gestured with my chin toward the cozy scene opposite. "Who's that?"

Rainy followed my cue, glanced over and shrugged, but my stomach remained unsettled at the sight. "He's got a lot of fans, Ruby. He's a very sexy, attractive single guy. And right now, a media darling." She shot another glance over her shoulder. "Can you blame her?" She relented, sighing. "I know, hon. I'm completely on your side, about leaving and all. But the way you did it... you hurt him. A lot. And he didn't deserve to be treated that way."

As if I needed her help to feel guilty; I knew she was right. Even Rainy, one of my closest friends, saw me as a transgressor. I sighed, drooping, feeling sick. "But what now? Is he working in a restaurant here? Is he involved with someone?"

"I've been helping Jules with Insta live." Deanna waved an arm at someone behind us.

Bethune, with Aislin in tow, slid up to our table and parked.

Deanna explained, "He's worked hard on his new sustainable venture, and he's so invested in the local food scene. I help him with PR and monetization through social media sponsorships."

An impressive mouthful of jargon for Deanna, especially in her condition.

"With Dee's help, his social media following has mushroomed. He started his whole sustainable farm and food site, and works to educate and inspire people to look at where their food comes from. He's committed to self-sufficiency. And now he's organizing a Farm-to-Table Faire," Rainy explained enthusiastically.

I was thirsty to learn about all Julian had done these past ten years. "I need to know more."

But tonight was not the right time or place to get details.

Rainy shook her head, preoccupied by Deanna's increasingly erratic behaviour. "He's on a mission. You'll have to ask—"

The sudden appearance of a grinning Zach, who flung a heavily muscled arm around Deanna and bent to kiss her on the cheek, interrupted her. "Hello, my beautiful. You did a great job, Dee. This is dank AF!"

"Thanks, sweetie," Deanna sang, spreading her fingers over his chiseled pecs. I bugged my eyes at Rainy, who pulled her mouth into a tight smile and turned to Zach. She levelled him a narrow-eyed glare. "Hello, Douchebag."

"Hi, Raincloud," he chuckled, his eyes hard.

"Deanna, drink your water, hon," Rainy urged, picking up the glass and pushing it towards her; Deanna obligingly took a small sip and set it down.

Rainy gave Aislin a meaningful look. "Hey, you want to take a shift keeping this one out of trouble?"

Aislin sidled up between her friend and Zach. "I've got her."

Zach pulled Deanna closer, crowding out Aislin. "You are still the hottest chick in our entire grad class, Dee."

"Zach, you're sweet," Deanna crooned, as Aislin elbowed him out of the way.

Rainy said, "He's not. What did you do? Did you go around the room checking every single woman out?"

"Course." He grinned, tilting his head, oblivious.

"Did you check their teeth?"

"I did actually," Zach said, smirking. "You know the tall skinny chick, Louise, she had her teeth straightened, doesn't look half bad now that she's filled out a bit. Still a little anorexic for my taste. You're far more luscious, Dee Dee, darling."

"Women are not cattle, Zach Chapman," Rainy growled, rolling her eyes.

He chuckled, as if she were teasing instead of ready to scratch his eyes out. Assessing Aislin, he cooed, "Awww. Look. I see you dressed up your pet for the party, Dee."

Aislin glowered at him.

Deanna gave him a scolding look, pouting. "Zach-y, be nice."

"I'm always nice."

"You're always a big dick," said Rainy.

"Why, thank you. Thank you very much."

"Why are you here?" Aislin added.

"Why're you here, weird one?" he retorted.

"Stop it, you two," Deanna said. "I love you both."

Rainy said, "I swear Dee, if you have sex with this asshole tonight I will never speak to you again."

"Don't be silly, Rainy, Zach and I are just friends."

"That's what you said last time." Aislin frowned at Rainy, her gaze darting to me and back to Rainy. "We all have to do our part. Watch them like a hawk." Glaring menacingly, Aislin said, "Go away, Zach. Come with me to the ladies, Dee. My Spanx are slipping." She hauled on Deanna's arm until they were both veering off into the crowd, Aislin propping up the wobbling Deanna.

Bethune sidled up to the high top, set down her drink and propped her elbows on the table. She leaned closer to me and tilted her head to the side, resting it on my shoulder with a happy hum. I put my arm around her and gave her a squeeze, kissing the top of her red head. God, I missed these people. My people.

My smile fell, remembering the distance I'd put between these special friends and myself for so long. Why had I done that? For all the excitement of each new assignment, the adventure of travelling to unknown places, and the momentary intimacy that danger and intrigue lent to the relationships with various colleagues, it wasn't the same. Those moments were like flashes of light through a sliding door. Transitory, unreal, unreliable.

These friends were different. They were solid. I had history with all of them, even though they didn't know me anymore. Somehow, it didn't matter. They knew what I was made from.

Zach didn't seem to mind the intervention and laughed good-naturedly. I was gathering all sorts of interesting intel about my old friends, and it all swirled in my head. I would have a lot to puzzle about over the next few days.

"So, Ruby, Ruby. You finally came back." He toasted me with his beer bottle. "I see you and Julian are giving each other a wide berth."

Whoa. I pulled back. Nervy much? "Not at all, Zach. We just haven't caught up yet. There are a lot of people here."

He pulled his mouth into a sly side smile, nodding. "Uh-huh. I understand. I do. Challenging turf there. Playing some width in defence, heh? I don't blame you. Julian's a great guy, but really, what did he expect? You guys were just kids. And he should have gotten over it long ago, don't you think?"

He should have? But he didn't? I chewed my lip, unable to formulate a snappy reply to his soccer babble.

He continued, unphased. "These are not the days to be settling down with the first person you meet. We're young! Am I right?" He raised his beer into the air in a general salute to the crowd and received a few drunken shouts in response. "These are the years to be sowing our wild oats. Playing the field.

Exploring our options. Finding ourselves. Y'know what I mean?"

Stony silence at the table met his ridiculous speech. Zach pished, and glanced around, searching for a more receptive audience.

"Anyway, that's what people have been doing. When I look around this crowd, I realize how many have been away. Faces I haven't seen in years," Rainy said.

"Tell me about what's been happening with everyone. Fill me in," I said.

"Beth left, right after you," Rainy said. "Broke Tate's heart."

"I did not," Bethune said.

"Did him a favour," Zach mumbled.

"We had an understanding. I knew I had eight years of school ahead of me, and travel, co-ops, internships. I had to be free to move around. Just like you, Ruby."

I let that slide. "I can't believe you've been in school most of the past ten years, Beth," I said. It seemed strange that she was only just starting her career as an architect and I felt like I'd been working forever.

"It's been over a year since I graduated," Bethune added.

"What've you been doing since then?"

"I got a position in Toronto, helping one of my profs with a special project after grad. But now I'm thinking about where I really want to build my career."

"Well, congratulations. That's a big deal." I raised my glass to her.

Other than the few I'd heard about who'd studied medicine, or law, she'd had the longest academic road of any of us. "Who else has been away, then?"

"I've been stuck here." Rainy said sulkily.

"You could have done the same, if you'd wanted to," Beth said, her eyes narrowed.

"I couldn't." Rainy said. "If I didn't stay here with my brothers, Mom would have hauled me back to Jaipur and married me off to the first eligible bachelor with a job."

"You might have stood up for yourself, Raincloud," Zach tossed out, his gaze still scanning the crowd, drawing a long, dark look from Rainy.

"Did your mom pay for your university?" I cut in, trying to ease the tension. "Or your brothers?"

"Yes," she said. "And I wouldn't have my career at all if I hadn't been willing to compromise."

"I don't know, Rainy. You're brilliant at what you do," I said "I remember your mom. I am sure she would support your career if you were honest with her and stood up to her."

"No travelling, at all?" It made me sad to think Rainy was stuck here because she wasn't free.

"It's different for you, Ruby. It was easy for you. Your family expected you to get educated and have a career. They didn't just indulge you while waiting for you to get married and start a family."

Taken aback, I fingered the empty ring finger on my left hand, spinning my ghost ring, a reminder of the fact that I had almost got married, regardless of my family's wishes.

Zach seemed to jolt awake with a grunt. "Still too young to settle down. Seriously, people."

"That's true," I said, ignoring him and answering Rainy. "Mom would have disowned me if I hadn't pursued a career and a life of my own. She encouraged me to…" I stopped myself before I said it aloud. It was Mom as much as anyone who'd convinced me I had to cut ties with Julian and strike out on my own; that we were too young and couldn't know that we were meant to stay together. But I told no one that. I'd barely thought about it myself for a long time now.

At first, away from home at university, I missed Julian so much I thought I'd die. But the years ticked on, and I had so much to do. The pain dulled. But I never felt that way about anyone else. My life became all about the work, the calling, my need to excel.

Zach drew a breath, seemed to wilt, then pulled his shoulders back, lifted his beer and said, "You all are bringing my party mood down."

"You're lucky you got recruited by the local Pacific North team, Zach," Rainy said. "Professional athletes rarely get too much to say about where they work, do they?"

"Sure they do. Some. They let me stay because of Mom." Zach turned to the side, resting his elbow on our table, glancing away into the crowd, and I got the sense he might have enjoyed playing for different teams, but was too macho to admit he had a soft heart, and was loyal to his family. His huge bicep flexed as he brought his beer to his lips. All these tall guys with their big muscles and full beards. It's true what they say about guys continuing to grow well after twenty. My girlfriends looked much as they did ten years ago, plus or minus a few curves, but the guys all looked very different.

"See, we all make compromises for the people we love," Rainy replied. "And I love my job. It's important to me."

"Someone had to hold down the fort," blurted Zach. "If it weren't for Deanna, Raincloud, Quinn, Parker and me, there'd be no us to come home to."

We all nodded, and I felt truly grateful. "Who else went away?" I asked.

"Besides you, Bethune and Jeannie, from our circle, well… Pete… I mean Phoenix, obviously."

"What a mind fuck!" Zach blurted, facing us again. "Did anyone know? I mean, shit." He shook his head. "How could Penis let us think he was dead?"

"Don't call him that. That's mean. I don't think he wanted anyone to know," Rainy said of Peter-slash-Phoenix's mysterious resurrection. "I don't think his life was too great, during school. He probably wanted to put it behind him."

More crazy shit to think about for another day. I'd forgotten that guys used to call him Penis. Because he really was a dick, too. That's why it surprised me that Jeannie liked him. It didn't fit with most people's experience. But maybe he had his reasons.

"I think it's fuckin' weird he didn't stay in touch with his old friends," Zach grumbled.

I felt my stomach tightening, my gaze darting past my friends, unconsciously seeking an escape. I may not have been able to come back, but I had stayed in touch with Rainy and Quinn as much as I could. Some, anyway.

Although that was partly a lie. I was too cowardly to come back and face Julian. I peered hard into my glass. "I don't know, Zach. I think… getting through school, starting your career, can be very absorbing. It's easy to… for the years to slip away while you're just figuring shit out, you know? Getting established in a career. Adulting."

Arms came around me, one from each side. "Never mind Zach, Ruby. Don't feel bad," Rainy said.

Beth added, "We always knew where you were. And we knew why you were doing it. It's not like you could do your job without travelling. It's not the same thing at all."

"Well, maybe that's true for Phoenix as well," I said, suspecting it was.

Veering away from the subject of delinquent friends, Rainy lifted the fingers on one hand and counted off as she continued. "Anyway, Aislin was at university in Vancouver for four years but came back right after. Jeannie left for uni and stayed away until now. And even though Jae Soo goes away for long periods, he comes back all the time, so it never really feels like he left. And then…" she hesitated, her voice dropping. "Well, Julian was away quite a long time."

I swallowed, letting that roll past, still stunned. "It's funny that everyone is drifting back now. Isn't it?"

Beth sipped her drink, glancing at the crowd. "I don't know. This city is one of the best places to live in the country. It's on the ocean, has a mild climate, it's not too big or too small, it's artsy and clean, with recreation and a lively pub and food scene. I'm tempted to move back."

Rainy and I nodded in agreement. "I wonder if our age has anything to do with it, too. Ten years seems just enough time to explore, have some adventures and then come back down to earth with a sense of your own mortality," I added. "I know I for one don't feel like the girl I was ten years ago."

More general agreement around the table.

"Ugh, stop. This conversation's getting way too heavy, girls. I'm outta here." Zach spun on his heel and slid into the crowd.

Bemused, I ventured, "He hasn't changed much," and we all laughed.

Changed or not, I felt a sense of belonging and togetherness with my friends, in my hometown, like someone had dropped a warm blanket over my shoulders.

"Uh, shit," Rainy said, perking up, eyes fixed over our shoulders.

"What is it?"

"Speaking of dodging suitors, it's fucking Doogie Kumar, MD, six o'clock. Help me, Beth."

Beth glanced over her shoulder. "Oh, Lord. He's heading right for us."

I looked too, and recognized the short, chinless mouth-breather Neil Kumar from our grade twelve biology class. "Did he actually become a doctor like he planned?"

"Oh, yes," Rainy moaned. "A most eligible doctor. And my mother is still friends with his mother. I'm afraid he's been instructed to hunt me down tonight. Beth, you promised!"

"Yup. Cloaking activated."

"Go, go, quickly!" I urged. I loved catching up with my best friends, but I wanted to mingle. I knew I'd see more of them tomorrow. And I had questions for the elusive Phoenix. Something he said earlier raised my investigative antennae, and I was looking for answers.

Julian

Cutting across the dance floor area, I jogged to catch up to Tate and April. "Hey!" I grabbed his arm, needing a moment before he dropped her off with her women friends on whatever false pretence he'd dreamed up.

They stopped and turned to face me; April's face lighting up in a smile, while Tate's was wearing a puzzled grimace. "Dude?" Wasn't he supposed to be bailing me out from one-on-one time with April tonight? I closed my eyes and nodded at him. Yeah, yeah. I sighed.

"Can I have a word, please, April? Alone?" I squinted at Tate, letting him know he should skedaddle.

Tate's brows shot up, and he gave an exaggerated rapid blink, pulling in his chin, lifting his hands up. "Ri-ight. Got it. Smell you later, man." He melted into the crowd, only too pleased to be relieved of duty.

I cupped April's elbow and led her to a quiet corner against the front windows, away from anyone I knew, angling us so my body shielded her from the people around us. One of Deanna's trees, covered with twinkling white lights, stood right beside a tall brick pillar. It could have been a romantic spot for a tryst, but I hadn't given it much forethought. Misunderstanding my intent, she slid her hands up my chest, gripped my neck, tilting her face up for a kiss. Giving her another cool peck on the corner of her lips, I took her wrists and pulled them down, off of my body, and held them together between us, creating a little space.

"Look April. I owe you an apology."

Predictably, she stiffened, tilting her head to one side.

I nodded. "What we have… had…" I stumbled, glancing over my shoulder, uncomfortable doing this here, in public, when I really ought to have ended it long ago. "Has been great.

You're really sweet…" I wasn't sure I believed that anymore after the way she treated Aislin, but a little honey might help the medicine go down. "But this," I released her hands to gesture between us, "this was never meant to be anything more than… momentary comfort. Okay? I was never going to be available for anything more than that."

Her chin hitched, and I watched her process this news, adjusting her expectations, pulling on a defensive posture. "Of course, Julian. I knew that," she snapped. "I'm the one that told you we had to keep it quiet, because of school, and Lisa." Her daughter.

I nodded. Great. She was going to make it easy. "Right? I know —"

She cut me off, throwing a coy look up at me. "My interest might have grown a little lately, that's all."

"Uh-huh." I frowned. "Nothing to do with my sudden celebrity status?"

Her mouth fell open. "No! I knew you were a sexy thing before the rest of the world discovered it." She bit her lip, and I squirmed at her obvious flirtatious advances.

Ugh. "It's just, you know, I think it's time we let it go."

Her smile looked stiff and pasted on.

I smiled back with as much genuine warmth as I could muster. "We're good? You're okay?"

"Of course." She shuffled to the side, seeming eager to get away from me now.

"I'll see you around."

As I walked away from her, sober and sharp-eyed, I knew I'd got out of that entanglement in the nick of time. Thankfully, with minimal consequences.

Chapter 8

Julian

AFTER I SPOKE WITH APRIL, and before my inevitable showdown with Ruby, I had work to do. And I hoped to make quick work of it so I could focus on what was really on my mind.

I looked around for the faces I'd hoped to connect with tonight. From my mental short list, the first I spotted was Noah Saddler, the owner-operator of a local heli-tour company. I figured we could both win with his sponsorship of the fair. All I had to do was talk him into it.

I caught up with Noah at the buffet, talking to another couple of guys from our class who also ran local businesses. Perfect timing. I could give my pitch to all three of them at once. You never know.

"Hey Noah. Hi, guys."

"Julian! Hi, there. So you're the man responsible for all this, are you?" He swept an arm over the buffet, while smiling and nodding, I took a measure of how well the catering crew were doing keeping it stocked and tidy. It looked good.

"Well, the committee pulled the event together, but if you're referring to the food, yeah that's me. What do you think of the spread?"

"Amazing, Julian. I wish I could have eaten at one of your restaurants."

I shrugged, only a little heartbroken at the mention of my former glamorous life abroad. The choice had been mine, and I'd made it. "Life goals, eh? I might just do that again someday, right here in Port Cam." I pointed at one platter with a wink. "Try those."

While I had Noah and the guys cornered at the buffet, sampling all the food I'd so carefully planned and prepared, I gave them the Farm-to-Table Faire spiel.

"And so… with enough of us small producers and hospitality, tourism and food service businesses supporting the Faire, we can avoid the necessity of charging too much, or depending on large corporate sponsors."

Noah turned to face me, washing a mouthful down with a sip of his drink. "You can count on me for a share. It fits nicely with my late summer marketing goals. Have you talked to Ethan? I think he'd be —"

"Uh, no. That's exactly what I'm trying to avoid. Big companies like his are not a good fit for this event."

"I don't agree, Julian," said Noah. "Whenever I see him at Chamber of Commerce events, he is going on about their new company mission statement. He's all about natural living and protecting the environment. It sounds like a perfect marriage, if you ask me."

"That's what I keep tryin' to tell him," rumbled Matt, the chef who had provided some of the roast meats for tonight's spread, coming out from his kitchen behind the servery. "But he won't hear it."

"I'm afraid I can't agree with you there, guys. I've been familiar with the Garwood family and the way they have run the Ragged Mountain Resort since I was a kid. My fa—"

At a slyly raised brow from Matt, and a sudden head jerk

from Noah, I spun my head to see what had caught their eye. Or whom? It was Ruby, sashaying through the crowd in that white dress, tall, tan, and sexy with her long legs and confident stride. She glanced our way, and our gazes snagged, and again my breath rushed out of my lungs as my pulse thundered at the sight of her. She hesitated, paused briefly and turned toward me, her mouth opening, as if she'd thought of something she wanted to say.

"Whoa. You know her?"

"Julian. Hey!"

I jerked back to the conversation, scowling. "What? Sorry."

"She's a beauty. You know her, man?"

Glancing back her way, I nodded absently, answering under my breath, "Yeah. Yeah, I do." Our eyes danced with each other for a moment longer, and I saw the instant she frowned and pulled back, deflated, and disappeared into the crowd. I swallowed, my throat dry as flour, as I shook my head to clear it of the chorus Ruby, Ruby, Ruby that echoed in my mind. I turned back to the guys, giving them my full attention. "And I know the Garwood family, too. It would be a mistake—"

"There's Ethan now. Why don't we just talk to him? Hear what he's got to say," Matt said.

I whipped my head around. "He's here? Who invited him? He's not in our grad class."

"His girlfriend is, maybe?" Noah replied. "I think she—"

"I'll talk to him," Matt cut in, waving Garwood over.

"No. Matt. Don't." I frowned at him, but it was too late. Garwood headed our way, chin up, grinning.

"Julian. I know this Faire was your idea, dude. But we're all partners. And we need the sponsorship or there won't be a Faire."

I scowled at Matt. I was just a spokesperson, a champion, a farmer. We'd had this conversation at planning meetings, and so far I'd prevailed. It didn't make me happy, but I couldn't dictate. "That's what I'm afraid of. He knows we need the money and he'll use it to manipulate the program." I turned to Matt, clenching my teeth. "Go ahead. Speak to him, but be wary. I don't trust him." I turned to leave, determined to catch up with Ruby. I could barely keep my mind on the Faire tonight.

"Aren't you staying?"

"No." I shook my head and strode away.

<hr>

Ruby

Still rattled after catching Julian's eye by the buffet, I drifted through the crowd, restless. He'd been preoccupied talking with a group of other men, but when they all turned to gawk at me, I couldn't bring myself to approach. Somehow, we needed to be alone to talk. I didn't have the willpower to stride up and pretend like we were just old friends. I couldn't erase the ghost image of that blonde hanging off his neck, kissing him.

I mentally slapped myself. Did I think a man like Julian, who was smart, handsome, sexy, and kind, hadn't touched another woman in the past ten years? I was a fool.

I crossed paths with Quinn on the way to the foyer; she was en route to see if Jae-Soo had arrived yet. It looked increasingly like her two closest friends were both going to disappoint her tonight. Heading toward the check-in table to ask if he'd arrived, we found Phoenix and Tate standing together.

"Hi guys."

Tate beamed his sexy, charming smile as we approached. "Ladies."

I was a little wary, since he and Julian had always been really close. I expected he was not a big fan of mine. "Hello, Tate. How've you been?"

"Ruby Zimmer. Welcome back to Port Cam." If he felt any

animosity towards me, he hid it well. But then, he's a professional actor, and that's his job.

"Thanks."

"Be right back," Quinn said, "I'll just check the list." And she stepped over to speak to the volunteers manning the desk.

"So, you're kind of a big deal this year, I hear," I ventured. I looked Tate up and down. He was always one of the best-looking guys in school, buff, charming, and confident. Though I remember him being quiet and bookish until middle school, when puberty hit and coincidentally when he'd discovered drama club. But now, he really was handsome, with a beard-shadowed, chiseled jaw, symmetrical features, and a smooth, suave manner.

Phoenix hung back, tonguing his cheek with suppressed humour, and hid a wry smile by taking a swig from his bottle of beer. Maybe he thought it was funny, watching women swoon over Tate. Even me, the one that was supposed to be hardened and serious. Though Tate was never my type, anyway. But beauty was beauty. I also suppose Phoenix had been getting filled in on everything he missed since grad, just like I had. Including my personal business.

"Have you kept up with your writing, Tate?" I asked. He and I had been close once, since we shared top honours in English and both wrote for the school paper, and he used to write plays, I remembered. He came from a literary and academic family, just like me, and had real talent. It surprised me, frankly, that he'd redirected his creative efforts to the screen instead of the page. I wondered what his family thought of that, and of his newfound success.

"Ah, well. I dabble, you know." He waved a hand dismissively, swinging it up to smooth back his wavy brown hair. "But the new show keeps me pretty busy. We've just started shooting the third season, so I don't have much time for that these days."

I nodded in understanding, but there was an odd tension in the way he answered, and an assessing gleam in his brown eyes. It was like the old, shy Tate was in there somewhere, behind his new polished veneer. I'd have to ask the girls about him. Rainy casually tossed out the tag "douchebag" to refer to him and Zach together, but there was always much more to Tate, in my opinion. He was, or had been, a smart, thoughtful guy.

Quinn returned, sighing. "No sign of Jae yet."

"He's probably planning to make an entrance," Tate said, chuckling.

"Oh, I thought that was your thing," Quinn teased, and was rewarded with a flashing grin that belonged in a glossy magazine.

The unwanted Dr. Neil Kumar appeared beside us suddenly. "Good evening, ladies," he said. "I wonder if you've seen your friend Rainy?"

Quinn caught my eye, pulling a face behind his back. I was glad Rainy had made herself scarce, and I could honestly answer, "No, Neil. Not for a while. How have you been?"

He lingered to answer politely, but his gaze was already wandering, searching the crowd for the object of his interest. "Very well, uh… thank you. But I must find Rainy. I have a message for her from my mother. Excuse me."

Thankfully, he wandered away, and I hoped wherever Rainy was, she had an exit route planned.

I wanted to talk to Phoenix, but I'd have to wait until I could get him alone. For the moment, I stood by while he answered the questions Quinn and Tate were asking about his career.

"Ruby Zimmer!" A woman's face pressed close to mine, and though she was whispering, she was also sort of shouting. I pulled back a few inches to get a better look at her.

I recognized her. "Hi," I said, stalling while I fished around in my memory for her name. Tiffany? Tianna? Tamara! That was it. I remembered her and her friend, the really tall one, always overdressing for school, as if they were heading straight to a club when the bell rang at three, and humble-bragging about their college-aged boyfriends.

She swayed on her feet and leaned closer again, grabbing my arm. "I'll tell you a shecret," she hissed, and I smelled alcohol on her breath. A lot. Lifting my brows, not sure I wanted to hear any more, I waited. "I used to be jealoush of you. I admired you sho much."

This came as a surprise. My remembrance was that she thought rather highly of herself, and had nothing but disdain for anyone else, myself included. I glanced side to side, hoping for an opportunity to escape.

Undaunted, she went on, draping a hand over my shoulder. "You're very lucky, Ruby. I have not been sho happy, y'know. Life doesn't turn out the way you want. My husband, is such a jerk." She stumbled into me, her face smashing into my hair, and I helped her right herself. "But thash okay." She leaned back and flicked a hand into the air dismissively, dropped her voice to a hiss. "I have a lover now. An' you'll never guess who?"

Wow. I was pretty sure I didn't want to know.

"Ish Misser Dixon."

I blinked, confused. Who called their lover mister?

"Y'know. Our chemishry teacher? Remember him? He's a cutie." She grinned conspiratorially. "We have chemishry." She giggled.

Our teacher? Mr. Dixon? The bossy little middle-aged South African guy with a handlebar moustache? That guy?

"Oh. All right. Well... um. Hey, nice to catch up with you, Tia... Tamara. You take care now." I slid away from her as she stumbled off into the crowd. Life does indeed not turn out the way you expect.

I sighed, shaking my head, and rejoined my group just as Jae Soo burst in the door like a K-pop star in a creamy white suit and pastel green shirt, doing some kind of weird dance moves like he was making an entrance on the Tonight Show with Jimmy Fallon. Everyone turned to watch, and I burst into laughter.

"I guess you were right, Tate. An entrance has indeed been made."

"It's about time you showed up, you jerk," Quinn announced, striding over to him, punching his arm and wrapping her arms around his middle, just as Tate, Rainy, and a couple of others piled on for a group hug. "Parker's been driving me nuts asking about you."

I didn't know what to expect. We were never very close. Jae Soo had, in the past, been in turns shy, arrogant, silly, reckless, rude, and sweetly responsible. I guess it was all a part of growing up and figuring out who he was. Certainly, the warm welcome he received spoke to his popularity, so he seemed to have turned out alright in the end. At least in the eyes of the friends whose judgement I trusted.

After a flurry of hellos and explanations for his tardiness, he shook hands with Phoenix, expressing his astonishment, as everyone else had before him. Then Quinn dragged him by the arm to stand in front of me.

"Ruby?"

I grinned. "*Annyeong*, Jeong Jae Soo. Nice to see you."

"Wow, wow, wow," he said, flashing his beautiful smile and taking my hands in his. "Look at you, flesh and blood Ruby!" He gave me a quick hug, then pulled away. "Does that mean the old squad is all here, together again?" He turned to Quinn, his boyishly handsome face alight and expectant.

Her smile drooped. "No. Sadly not. Don't get me wrong, I'm thrilled that Ruby is here." She tucked her arm around my waist. "But I'm sad that Jeannie didn't make it in time." Her voice quavered and tapered off. Quinn, usually so even-tempered, seemed to have hit her limit for the night. Maybe she was just so happy to be finally looking at Jae Soo, or maybe it was the sum of all the emotions we'd all felt this night, but her face trembled and collapsed, and she drew her lips between her teeth as her eyes filled with tears. I felt my throat burn and eyes flood in sympathy.

Jae pulled back his shoulders and dipped his chin, a sympathetic smile popping a dimple in his cheek. "Ah, Tsundere. I know you're happy to see me. I'm glad to see you too," he said, taking her head between his palms like a basketball and bending to plant a big smooch on her hair, accompanied by a melodramatic sing-song, "Mmmmm," to which everyone added a chorus of "Awwww."

Quinn's head snapped up; throwing Jae Soo a playful side-eye, she planted a hand in the middle of his pretty face and pushed him away. "I'm not crying stupid. My eyes are just watering from looking at your obnoxious designer suit, pretty boy."

Jae-Soo tossed his head back, laughing, bending over with his hands on his knees. Righting himself, he grabbed her in a headlock and gave her a noogie. He stepped back, shaking his head and stroking a palm down one lapel of his jacket. "Hey, this is a KimSeoRyong. You're just jealous because I wear twenty-first century fashion, hippy-girl. And don't mess the hair. I just had it done."

"What colour is it this time, anyway? It looks…" She squinted at him with an exaggerated sneer. "Kinda purple?" She turned her palm up and scowled down at it. "And are you wearing lip gloss?"

Jae licked his lips, shook his head again, and rolled his eyes. "Where's your stupid brother? I have news to share with you both."

"Come on. Let's find him," she said. "He's been asking about you every five minutes." They grinned stupidly at each other and strode away, he with his arm slung over her shoulders, her elbowing and tickling him like twelve-year-olds. He gave us a wave over his shoulder.

I drew a deep breath and smiled, watching them go. "Okay, then. What the heck was that?"

"Oh, you know those two. Always at each other." Tate stepped closer. "I'm going to trail along and see what the news is. Every time he comes back from Seoul he's got some crazy scheme or his family's jerking him around again." Then he was gone too, dodging through some dancers to catch up.

I turned to Phoenix. Finally, a chance to ask him what I wanted to know.

He smiled down at me. Sort of. His firm mouth twitched and tucked a little. I guess that's what counted as smiling for him.

"Hey, Phoenix."

"Hey there, Ruby. How are you enjoying the party?"

"More than I thought I would. How about you? How does it feel to be back?"

He lifted his gaze over the top of my head and scanned the room slowly, and I got the impression of a highly trained, tightly contained tactical expert. I'd seen military guys like him in the field. Like mountains. They were prepared to move through unfamiliar and threatening environments at a moment's notice; continuously assessing danger, reading people for threats, strategically mapping out their path, their next action. Like chess players projecting forward in time, anticipating every possible move, every probable consequence.

"I haven't decided yet. I'm still gathering intel. Doesn't feel too bad." He sounded like he was waiting for something bad to happen.

"What are your plans?"

"Haven't decided that either. I'm at a fork in the road and have to choose what my next steps will be." He glanced down at me, making steady eye contact, and I wondered how I ever could have thought ill of him. He seemed solid, steadfast... trustworthy.

"That's always good."

"What about you? Are you heading back overseas?"

"No. Not right now." I hesitated.

"Are you and Julian… still a thing?" he asked, twitching his head to the side and peering at me.

"Aah. No. I guess you really have been out of the loop. Julian and I… split up right after graduation. We never, I mean, we haven't been in touch."

"Huh." He seemed to think about that for a while, studying me. "I guess I thought you and he would…" He shrugged. "Somehow I imagined you were juggling your career and still…" He gave his head a shake, a question in his eyes.

"No." My gaze skipped away from his and hopped from face to face in the crowd, unable to settle. I swallowed and pasted on a smile, looking back. "No time for that these past few years."

"Sorry. Not my business. I get it."

After a beat of silence, I asked, "How about you? Anyone special?"

He gave a quiet chuckle, sliding his hands into his pockets. "I haven't even had a permanent address for ten years."

"Are you staying in town?"

"Up for a PCS. I have a few choices. I've got a month off to think about where I want to land."

I mentally translated his acronym. Permanent Change of Station. Just like me. Maybe. "Yeah, me too. Maclean's magazine has recently offered me a new job as a foreign correspondent. Thinking it over." I hadn't really told anyone what I was doing here, but I felt a kindred spirit in Phoenix. Someone who could understand. "They have offered me a contract to write a memoir about my years in the field, and it could take me a while. I just have to decide whether I want to do it here, or somewhere else. Or not at all."

Phoenix nodded. I sensed we were kind of in the same place.

"It feels," I paused, catching my breath as I surveyed the room again, "Surprisingly good," I confided, "to be with my friends and family again. I wonder if this is what I needed."

Again, he nodded. "I hear you. It's very welcoming. The question is, do we fit in, or have we changed too much?"

I hummed. That was it, exactly. It was clearly a rhetorical question, but one I wondered about, too. I sipped my drink to signal a change of subject. "So. Something you said earlier raised questions in my mind."

He smiled slightly, his eyes sharpening on my face. "I'll bet it did."

I flashed a grin. "You implied you'd followed my career path. And I wondered, or rather I thought you meant more than watching the news on television. I got the sense that you knew where I was."

Phoenix nodded. "I did. When we were deployed overseas, which was often, we generally got rumint about where Western journalists were embedded, and monitored them. So, I knew where you were, most of the time. And I knew, better than most, when there was the potential for problems. Getting blown up, political upheaval, or hostage takings. I was ready to jump in if needed, but you always managed to be okay."

My eyes widened in astonishment. It's not that I didn't know that the military were there to protect us. Often I was provided a military escort when venturing into the field to interview locals. Although, just as often, we'd use locals as drivers, guides and interpreters, because we didn't want to be constrained by the presence of Western military when we were talking to local people.

He was quietly watchful, smiling pleasantly, but very contained, like a coiled spring, full of potential energy. It also got me wondering about his role in the military actually. I knew there were highly trained special operatives who moved around like ghosts, "meat eaters" they were called, and I wondered how much skill he had, and how much autonomy. I knew, from my time overseas, that there were certain military personnel who were known as secret squirrels. Guys who's work was so classified that nobody knew what they did. They never talked about work, and certainly never bragged about it. But they seemed to know everything, had eyes everywhere. I knew nothing about Phoenix's training or time in the navy, but I had this funny feeling about him. How else would he know things about where I was?

It was surprising to think that there was someone I knew, not very far away, watching over me. And even though he said he never had to get involved, I was sure he wasn't telling me everything. I peered at him, listing some of the places I'd been assigned. "Afghanistan? Syria? Crimea?"

He shrugged noncommittally.

"Venezuela?"

He chuckled again, non-committal. "I had my own assignments. But my reasons weren't entirely selfless," Phoenix went on.

I glanced up, puzzled. "Oh?"

"You know how it feels to be adrift. You meet people, on the job, here and there. It's always temporary."

I nod to encourage him.

"So, somehow you need to feel a connection with who you used to be. A reminder of your humanity, when you were all alone out there, dealing with shit. And because you were nearby, you were a kind of... a kind of beacon for me. I want to thank you for that. And I guess I wanted to return the favour, if I could."

I found myself suddenly tearing up, a most unexpected reaction. I bit my bottom lip to stop the quiver, sucking back the rush of salt tears that flooded my mouth.

He lifted a hand, lightly touching my arm. "How you doing, really?" Phoenix asked. "Do you get... counselling for PTSD, due to the stress and fatigue of embeds?"

My breath left me in a huff of surprise. Somehow I didn't expect this big reserved alpha sailor dude to be asking me about my mental health.

Not waiting for a reply, he continued. "Don't know if you

knew much about my family," he went on in a slow, steady way, talking through my reaction as though it was nothing, giving me time. "My dad was Navy too, and a really amazing, upbeat, super guy. Totally committed to the job. Until he got fucked up. And then he wasn't. So…"

I got the impression there was a lot more he could tell me about his dad and his life at home, but wouldn't. At least not tonight.

Phoenix shifted his weight, widening his stance to bring his eyes closer to my level, and locked his hands together behind his back. "Point being, I know a thing or two about PTSD, about living with ghosts. About re-entry. I joined the Forces with my eyes wide open, Ruby. Knew exactly what I was getting into. What horrors were possible. And I've been in a good number of FUBAR situations myself. Thing is, I'm also pretty attuned to the mental health side of conflict. I vowed, when I joined up, that I would be kind to myself. And others."

I met his steady, dark bottle green gaze that seemed to see and know all, and nodded.

Then, out of the blue, he said, "Just because you did a thing doesn't mean you have to continue doing it. There's no shame in changing direction." He paused. "Your time in the field has already exceeded a standard military tour of duty by a magnitude of five. Think about that before you ask any more of yourself. Sometimes… you need to stop and rest so you can keep moving toward your ultimate goal."

He stopped there, and I realized he'd said all he was going to. The rest was up to me. He was inviting me to talk, if that's what I needed. Or get help, if that's what I needed. Or just maybe, to be kind to myself. And in that moment, I realized it wasn't weak or cowardly to acknowledge my suffering, or even to let go and move on to a different life if I needed a change.

Phoenix shifted slightly, turning away from me, and we both stood in silence for a second or two, just watching the crowd.

After a moment, Phoenix nodded at me. "I'll send you my number, if you want to talk."

I realized now that I had come back to Port Cam because this was what I really needed. I wanted to be home. At least for the foreseeable future. There were decisions to be made about the book I might write. I had doubts, questions and concerns about how I would handle it. It was one thing to whisper this change to myself, and quite another to announce it to the world.

But before I could do that, there was someone I needed to talk to. It was childish and wrong to avoid Julian. I owed him a conversation. And I was burning to hear about his life these past ten years. If he would talk to me.

Chapter 9

Ruby

A SQUAWK from the PA system cut short my contemplation of the interweaving paths of Phoenix and myself in the far-flung corners of the earth. Troy the DJ cut in to say, "Yeah, so, the grad committee, uh… have something they want to say to you all."

With another squawk, the sound switched from Troy's sound system to a microphone at the front of the room where three women stood on a slightly elevated platform covered in blue carpet, a spotlight now trained on them.

"Good evening, Port Cam alumni and friends! If you can't see me from the back, I'm April Neilsen, president of your grad committee. I'm here with Suze Campbell and Bonnie Retten. You might recall we were on the executive of grad committee ten years ago."

Stiffening, I recognized them as the women who'd thrown shade at Deanna earlier.

Responses from the crowd ranged from cheers to grumbling complaints at the interruption.

"We wanted to welcome you all back together again. Isn't this a great evening?"

April paused to give the crowd a moment to applaud politely, and a couple of good sports in the back gave a loud cheer.

"It's so nice to see everyone again. First of all, I want to thank the reunion planning committee for putting this event together for us tonight. Deanna Dunham, Rainy Saraladevi and Quinn Roarke. Let's have a round of applause for everyone involved in the planning of our ten year Port Cam High reunion!"

The crowd broke into genuine applause and cheers, and I felt a moment of gratification for my lovely friends who had worked so hard to make this happen. It made me wonder why one of them was not making this welcome speech, until I found Rainy and Quinn in the crowd, and by their scowling faces inferred that this was an unscheduled and unwelcome announcement. The applause was cut short by April's droning yet nasal voice yet again.

"And a big thank you to volunteers from the school who are helping out at the sign-in table, and to Troy for agreeing to be our DJ tonight." She continued speaking over the smattering of applause. "We have a special surprise for you tonight. Before you resume your drinking..." More hoots and hollers from the crowd. "Ha, ha, ha, dancing and catching up with all your old friends from high school, and of course eating that fabulous food prepared by our very own celebrity chef Julian Michaels..." The crowd again broke into applause and hollers of appreciation.

"How about that Julian Michaels everyone?" Her voice rose, clearly trying to rouse a reaction from the crowd, yet there was a biting aggression to her tone. "We really do have more than our fair share of celebrity talent in this graduating class. As you know, we have a professional soccer player, star midfielder for the Pacific North FC and Canadian National team player

…" More applause. "Zach Chapman. And we have a rather famous actor from the new hit fantasy series, Skycastle. Hey, Tate, can I have your autograph?"

Laughter from the crowd, on cue.

"And of course many more very successful grads, both those that have stayed here in Port Cam and those that have ventured far afield and returned to see us all today." April cleared her throat, and there was an awkward pause before she resumed with a squawk of the speakers. "And of course we're all especially blessed today to have back amongst us the world-renowned, award-winning investigative journalist Ruby Zimmer." The crowd broke into even louder and wilder applause at the mention of my name, and my shoulders hitched up towards my ears.

Phoenix and I exchanged a jaundiced glance and I gather he understood, perhaps better than most, how uncomfortable this sort of adulation made me feel. Though I noted April failed to welcome him back from the grave. But my discomfort at that moment was the mere tip of an iceberg of awkwardness, because it was clear April was just getting warmed up.

She looked up at the mezzanine and raised her arm to wave up at Troy, sending some kind of signal. Then a song played that created an instant ache in my chest. Our song. "Only Girl in The World" by Rihanna, and my stomach filled with dread. What was going on?

Over the music, April spoke to the crowd. "Now you all remember one very special part of our grad night ten years ago. And that was the announcement of our prom king and queen!"

At her words, adrenaline swamped my body. The panic and dread at what I knew was coming next nearly had the contents of my stomach heaving while I broke out in a cold sweat. "Oh God. Oh God, no. Please don't."

But she did.

"Aren't we fortunate that our very own prom king and queen are both in attendance tonight? Please join me in welcoming to the podium, our very own royalty, Julian Michaels and Ruby Zimmer. Come on up here, you two. We have something for you."

Having the tall, muscular and imposing Phoenix Corbin at my side, self-appointed guardian of my safety, was no protection from what happened next. Those that stood nearby, excited at the prospect of having their prom king and queen remembered and acknowledged, rushed me, surrounded me, their smiles and laughter menacing in my ears, and they swept me forward through the crowd to the small carpeted platform and podium, where April and her committee stood.

When I got close enough, I recognized her as the woman who Julian had kissed earlier. The same woman who had dissed Deanna. What was going on here?

As I reluctantly stepped onto the dais beside her, I knew, naturally, the same fate had befallen Julian. Of course it had. He, too, had been propelled through the crowd from the back of the room to the front. The next thing I knew, we were both being jostled together to stand side-by-side at the podium, all eyes turned toward us.

Julian

Suddenly shoved through the crowd by what felt like dozens of hands pressing against my back and arms, I narrowed and focused my vision on the bodies parting in front of me.

"What's happening?" As I approached the podium, I saw April standing there, speaking into a mic, but I couldn't make out what she said in the din of the crowd. "What the hell is this?"

I stomped up onto the podium next to a wide-eyed and nauseated looking Ruby, already standing there under the lights like a shell-shocked prisoner. As I neared I saw how vulnerable and frail and broken Ruby looked in the glare of the spotlight. My gut curdled in a mix of anger, guilt and pity. Seeing Ruby like this filled me with an overwhelming urge to protect her. To shield her from danger.

As one of April's accomplices jammed plastic crowns onto our heads, I realized what was going on and was filled with fury over April's spiteful cruelty.

Suddenly, there we were standing side-by-side, like we were ten years ago. Somewhere from the balcony above, I suspected Troy the DJ, angled a spotlight down onto our faces, and I blinked and squinted in the sudden glare, raising a hand to my face.

Still clutching the portable mic in her fist, April met my furious gaze coyly, fluttering her eyelids. She smiled broadly and I felt the knife twist in my back, knowing I was wholly to blame for this spectacular moment of humiliation. The last time Ruby and I stood in the spotlight together, our hands were intertwined, our hearts as one, and as far as I knew a shared future, a blissful one, stretched out before us.

While April droned on about our distinct characters, and how we'd each carved out our own way in the world, loved by our fans for being, in my case sweet, charming, caring and creative, and in Ruby's case, smart, tough, courageous, and independent. She couldn't have made us out to be more unlike and incompatible than she did, while ensuring that our characters branded us as victim and villain. Lest anyone in the room had forgotten our ill-fated relationship.

It was unavoidable. Shoved together against our will, our shoulders and elbows brushing, my heart aching, our eyes lifted and met. I winced, swallowed and mouthed, "I'm sorry." Ruby, of course, could not know what a petty act of vengeance and jealousy this was, and shrugged, grimacing at our joint discomfort.

Jostled together by April and her friends crowded onto the dais, my arm bumped into Ruby again and again. The backs of our hands brushed, sending jolts of awareness through me, burning like fire. I felt us circling each other like fighters in a ring, like a toreador and bull, in this electrifying dance of attraction and repulsion. Sooner or later, we were going to crash together, and the suspense was killing me, building up like a volcano ready to rupture.

For all I fought it, I wanted it too—like a moth intent on its own destruction. Even though we had so much unresolved business between us, so much hurt, I felt closer to Ruby than any other person on earth. There had to be some way for us to connect without destroying each other. My gaze slid up her body, so gloriously feminine in that ruffled creamy dress. My eyes snagged on the vee of exposed tanned skin of her breastbone, and again I wondered at how thin she'd become. She was beautiful but frail. I needed to feed her, heal her, nurture her back to a robust and glowing health. I wanted to make her mine again.

Of its own accord, my gaze danced over her jaw, her ears, her high cheekbones, the elegant arc of her brow, and landed on her wise green-brown eyes. They shimmered with a profound sadness, and what felt like an echo of our familiar intimacy, and maybe even a remnant of the intense love we once felt for each other. That I, reluctantly, still felt, despite what she had done to me.

It was so horrible, it was comical. And trapped there together, we couldn't help but feel sympathy for each other's discomfort. As Ruby's expression gentled from pained, to pitying, to kind, to affectionate, I felt my chest compress with a familiar ache of longing.

Against my wishes, almost against my will, my hand moved, sliding between her arm and her side, hooked around hers, sliding down, and opening, pressing her fingers apart, softly, gently tucking my fingers between hers. The slide of my skin against hers, finger tips to palm, shimmered with sensation. A tsunami of want mounted inside me, blood rushing from my head to my groin, and made me faint with desire, my vision narrowing, darkening. Ruby, my brave and big-hearted Ruby, opened her hand, laced her fingers in mine, and squeezed. My heart lurched.

Then she let go.

Chapter 10

Ruby

I'D REGISTERED Julian's anger and recoiled, believing, deservedly, that it was directed at me. It made me feel even more hateful, awkward and humiliated to be forced to stand in the spotlight, as though everyone were taunting me, drawing attention to how much I'd hurt and betrayed him, how selfish I was, how I'd broken his heart.

My chest was a jungle of snarled vines. Panic filled me. How could I stand this? How could he? When I lifted my gaze to brave the wrath in his, I was shocked to find that his eyes shone with sympathy, and with the kindness that I always saw in Julian's eyes. I saw sadness and regret, and I knew he hated this, too. How humiliating for him, and for this woman, April, who, of course, must resent my presence so deeply.

Why had he touched my hand? Was it for show?

Yet as our hands interlocked, suddenly the whole vicious world faded away and the two of us were left alone in our bubble. More visceral, powerful attraction than I've ever felt for another person. My knees went weak, and my heart stuttered.

Flung back in time, my body was achingly aware of how

much the two of us had been one. How our trust and intimacy had been complete. Nothing and no one had ever made me feel the way Julian did.

I'd missed him. I'd missed him more than I'd realized. I wanted to be alone with him. We had so much to say. I had so much to explain and to answer for.

Somehow, we had to get through this dreadful moment and move past it. I would take this bullet for him.

I tore my gaze from Julian's face and scanned the crowd. I could do this. I was a professional, accustomed to delivering the goods on demand under pressure when the camera started rolling. All I had to do was to imagine that little red light, imagine the voice in my ear saying, "Over to you, Ruby."

I plastered a wide smile on my face and turned to wrest the mic from April's grip. My crown slipped to the side, and my hand instinctively jerked up to catch it and right it, pressing it firmly onto my head while a barrage of 'fix your crown queen' memes flashed on parade through my head. I glanced once at Julian.

Gritting my teeth, I pulled back my shoulders and jutted my chin, facing the podium, intent on taking the fire and minimizing Julian's discomfort. Putting an end to this charade. "Thank you, April. Thank you so much everyone for your kindness and warm welcome. I didn't know that coming here tonight would garner so much attention. I am simply grateful to see you all and to connect with all my old friends again. I appreciate so much that you have followed my career and taken such an interest in my work. I'm humbled. Thank you again."

I paused, my smile slipping, and gazed at the floor under my shoes for a long moment. My heart pounded in my chest like a war drum as I watched the movie of our life together, our love, so much the envy of our friends, when we had been crowned king and queen of grad as if the very fact of us made us worthy of the titles, played out in my mind.

"I also understand that the stunning menu we have enjoyed

this evening was the creation of our very own Julian Michaels who's on a mission to save the planet." My voice trembled. I paused momentarily at a loss for words, my eyes darting, wishing I could be anywhere but here. Then I drew myself up. "We should be very proud of our own.

"I am astonished at the talent that this class has produced, and am humbled to be a part of this special community. Thank you…" My gaze lifted to Julian, and I saw him swallow. I felt the heat rise in his body, so close to mine, and a matching fever rose on my skin. My face flushed as tears rose to my eyes "Thank you… Julian."

And suddenly I was gut-punched by the magnitude of my betrayal. Of him, yes, but of us both. How much we had both lost because of my actions.

A quaking began in my gut and worked its way up my body, through my stomach, shaking my ribs, my heart, pounding, quivering, as though a muscle that had been long petrified were dissolving. I feared I would humiliate myself further by breaking down in ugly tears right here in front of everyone, under the spotlight. The tears surfaced. My bottom lip began to quiver, and then my jaw. Desperately, I thrust the mic at Julian and catapulted myself off the stage and into the crowd, needing to find shelter.

***

Julian

Catching the mic and clutching it to my chest, I was convinced it amplified the loud thud, thud, thud of my heart crashing against my ribcage and everyone would know the magnitude of my anguish and humiliation. I looked out at the upturned faces of my classmates, frozen between expectation and disappointment, and couldn't think of a single thing to say.

I muttered, "Excuse me," and handed the mic to April. "I'm

sorry," I apologized, for more than anyone could know, and leapt from the stage, desperate to find Ruby.

Before I could break out of the dense crowd, my squad closed in around me, hustling me off to the foyer.

Everyone was clearly embarrassed for us both.

"That was horrible. I'm so sorry, Julian," said Rainy.

Quinn added, "We didn't know she planned to do that. She just—"

"That was a shitty thing for April to do," Tate snapped, meaningfully, pulling me to one side. Zach elbowed in on my other side, throwing a heavy arm over my shoulders, shutting out the rest of the crowd.

Agh. My chest tightened like a clamp, strangling my breath in frustration at the delay and I bent my head into my hands. I needed to escape. I needed to find Ruby. But these were my friends and they cared.

"I asked for it," I murmured to Tate, knowing no one else would understand what I meant. Except for Aislin, who met my gaze across the group with a tiny shake of her head. "It was bound to be awkward."

"April has designs on you, though, bro. She's scary as fuck."

"I shouldn't have let it go this far. It wasn't fair to her."

Zach jumped in, surprising me by adding up the clues. "Look at me, dude. Look at Foreman. You don't see us nursing every fan girl we hook up with, do you?"

"It's not the same. April was a friend."

"Yeet. You gotta swerve. She's so basic." He thumped me in the chest with his finger. "You are dank. A limelight dude living your best life. Girls are thirsty for that. Don't apologize. You got to chill for once, Jules."

It made me wonder if Zach had to deal with clingy fans. But this was different. April and I, well we didn't have a relationship, but we had an understanding. I thought.

"Man, April really laid it on thick. Ruby was tight," said Tate, shaking his head at Zach's extra emoting.

"Yeah," I sighed. "Did you see where she went?"

"She's a big girl. Don't worry about her." Zach argued, his voice slurring.

I pulled a face at him, narrowing my eyes. "What?"

"Aw, I know you're getting all kinds of pressure to hook up, like you're the OTP," he said, waving a hand. "Don't worry 'bout it. Let it go. It's history."

I had to figure out what he was really saying. "You used to be sympathetic, Zach. What do you mean?"

He shrugged his wide shoulders, his gaze sliding away. "Well, maybe she did you a favour, dude. You should be glad you didn't get married at fuckin' eighteen years old. Where'd you be now? A chicken farmer with a whack of kids to support?"

Tate pulled the corners of his mouth down thoughtfully. "Same. You both got to do your own thing. We all did."

"Like you?" I threw back. "Mr. Celebrity Series guy with a new fangirl on your arm every week."

"That's not real and you know it. It's my job to keep up the man whore act. What about Zach with all his ball-bunnies?" Tate teased Zach, and he shrugged it off, unapologetic. "And I wasn't talking about women, anyway. I meant space for goals. If I met the right girl, I'd settle down in a flash."

"Yeah, you would," Zach scoffed.

"I would," argued Tate. "I'm tired as fuck of the dating scene. Hey, I'll tell you guys a secret I never told anyone."

I wanted to find Ruby, but I couldn't resist the allure of Tate telling a story, true or false, so I forced myself to take a breath, to slow it down.

Tate chuckled. "I actually proposed to Bethune the summer after grad. But she told me to go to hell."

"Nah!" Zach and I both jeered. That couldn't be true. Tate had a knack for stringing people along with made up shit. He loved an audience.

Zach guffawed. "Bet she's sorry now that you're a hot property."

Tate shook his head, sobering, and I suddenly believed him. "No, it's ok, though. It was an adolescent crush. She did me a favour by turning me down. And she was really committed to her career. I got that. I had ambitions too." He raised both hands and shrugged. He looked at me, more than a subtle hint in his eyes.

Yeah, yeah. I tongued my cheek thoughtfully. But it was different for Ruby and me. So different.

Zach had obviously been drinking a lot, and seemed low in spirits. His party vibe had worn off.

"You all right?" I asked him.

Tate shoved him and grumbled, "Drank too much again. How the hell you get up and train I don't know, bro."

Zach swore under his breath. "Maybe I'm not gonna tomorrow. Maybe I'm gonna quit. I'm nearly washed up, anyway."

"Bullshit. Why are you saying that, asshole?"

Zach swung his head, and I feared he was more drunk than we realized, and was aiming to pass out.

"You're just a miserable drunk, Chapman. Maybe we'll head out soon, huh? Split a taxi, bud?"

Zach grunted.

I was feeling the same way. April's little stunt worked like a cold shower on my mood. Not that I'd been able to relax and enjoy this night the way I'd hoped.

Just then, Deanna split off from the girls, chatting a few yards away, and spun over towards us. "Hi, guys." Speaking of drinking too much, she was wasted.

She hooked her arm over my shoulders, and I stumbled under her loose-limbed weight, even though she was light as a runway model.

Zach and Tate kept on with their mumbled argument, Zach droning on about his injuries, his chronic aches and pains, and his fears about getting traded to a lesser team, or being forced to go overseas in search of work.

"S'matter, baby?" Deanna crooned, shifting herself over to Zach, looping her arms around his neck. "You saaad?"

Tate caught my gaze, rolling his eyes. "Here we go again." This is how it started. Drinking, depression and then, well, whatd'ya know? These two old friends went home together. Again.

I didn't have the patience or the attention span to babysit Deanna and Zach tonight. We had plenty of friends who could intervene, maybe, if they were motivated. I had problems of my own.

I shook my head and excused myself, resuming my search for Ruby. I had to talk to her. I couldn't wait another minute.

Julian

I finally caught sight of Ruby's white dress disappearing into the service corridor that led to the washrooms and back entrances of the market shops that ran the perimeter of the building. My pulse pounded with a primal excitement, knowing we were done with the dance of evasion. Like a soldier marching onto the field of battle, I would finally face her, excavate the truth, get some resolution, some closure.

Even if I never came back.

"Enough! Stop running."

Her head whipped around at the sharp sound of my command, her eyes glassy with tears, wide and apprehensive. She turned away and carried on. It took only two determined strides to catch her before she slipped through the entrance to the ladies' washroom, as if that would have stopped me.

Grabbing her by the wrist, I pulled her back, and she coiled toward me, unresisting. She spun against the wall, tossing her head back against the painted cinder block, closing her eyes.

I loosened my grip on her wrist, letting my hand slide down across it until my palm pressed against hers against the wall to her side, letting my gaze dance over her. Finally. She stopped resisting, opened her eyes and stared back.

Widening my stance, I faced her with my feet flanking hers in case she thought to evade yet again, my knees touching hers lightly. Uneasy, my stomach in knots, I scanned her face, her lean shoulders, her anxiously twisting hands. Her chest rose and fell rapidly as she gulped air, drawing my attention to the soft mounds of her breasts under the smooth white fabric, a hint of tanned cleavage taunting me in the deep vee of her neckline, and, to the rapid flutter of her pulse in the elegant hollow above her collarbones. The semi I'd sported all night, just knowing she was here, roared to life with her so close to me.

"Ruby." My voice choked on ancient words, unable to prevent them from slipping off my tongue. "Sweetheart." Unable to call them back, my gaze devoured her white neck like a starving man. Finding myself standing alone with her at last knocked the air out of my lungs, making me dizzy and weak.

"God, it's good to look at you."

My trembling hand reached for the long coil of gold-streaked nut-brown hair that draped over her shoulder. I slowly, gently wrapped it around my fingers like a lifeline, closing my fist in the silken rope. I pulled ever so slightly, and her chin came up, her gaze meeting mine, heavy lidded. Her tongue darted out and dragged along her lower lip, wetting it, and my cock jerked in my pants. The green flecks in her brown irises drew me in like talismans, hypnotic, and I slowly, so slowly, angled our heads and slanted my open mouth over hers in a slow motion ballet. Close enough that our breaths mingled, and I could taste the wine she'd drunk tonight on the vapour, along with the flavours of my food on her palette. But not touching. Not quite. The choreography was so familiar, our bodies, our mouths, knew their place as though it were written in some ancient text, etched on the wall of a prehistoric cave, inevitable.

That was me and Ruby.

Instead, I slipped my hands around her lower back, pulling her close, stroking down the ends of her long hair, just breathing her in. She fell against me willingly, her embrace swift and tight, our bodies flaring alive again as though it had not been a decade since we'd touched each other, as if we'd just woken from a trance.

But it wasn't enough. I felt the pull of our cells, crying out for each other. Tilting my head back just enough to meet her dark, hooded gaze, I succumbed to the force of attraction that had always been bigger than either of us, than our will.

Her lips were soft and cool, her cheek hot against mine. I was a man parched in the desert, come upon an oasis of life. The first touch, tongue to tongue, nearly made me black out with the sheer pleasure of it. How many times had I imagined just this one sensation, rolled it over in my mind, bringing it back to life, as I pounded out that ancient ache?

Chapter 11

Julian

MY GAZE RETURNED to Ruby's face. Tears glistened in her shadowed orchard eyes while the ones that had escaped streaked down her cheeks. The compulsion to kiss her again almost swamped me, my knees as weak as saplings.

With a throbbing head and my pulse pounding with desire, the urgency to claim and possess this woman that had always been mine and was here, in my arms again, clouded my mind.

I was panting, the skin under my dress shirt and jacket damp with sweat, tingling. My nostrils flared as the warm scent of her rose to my nose. Chocolate, the cinnamon spice of her perfume and the unique musky scent of her skin, triggering a flood of memories, both emotional and deeply erotic.

There was nothing in the world I wanted so much as this woman, to take her and make her mine again, and she stood before me, so close it was torture, and yet she wasn't mine.

What was happening to me? I mentally shook myself, reigning in my emotions. That scene had upset me, of course. How must it have made Ruby feel? Her eyes swam with unshed tears and my mind was in my pants like a savage teenager.

I exhaled, trying to let go of my pent-up tension. "Are you all right?"

She gazed up at me with a rawness that shredded me. Everything I felt was reflected there. It was too much. I waited for my heart to slow down, trying to calm my breathing, but it was like I was standing at the precipice of a cliff, leaning out, knowing I would go over willingly, unable to stop myself from hurtling to my death.

"Oh, Julian," she whispered, closing her eyes, squeezing two fat tears from the corners.

A heavy weight pressed on my chest, and my throat felt tight. I lifted a hand and dragged a knuckle gently across her cheek, swiping away a tear. "I'm sorry about that whole scene with April. It's my fault she did that. She is angry with me, and she's hurt."

Ruby's throat worked through a swallow. "Is she your…"

I shook my head. "She isn't my anything. She's… confused."

Ruby studied my face. Testing the truth of my answer, or just reacquainting herself with my features, I didn't know. She let her gaze roam over me and I could see the admiration in her eyes. "Why aren't you with her now?"

"There is no her. There's only us." My breath caught, but the words kept coming from some deep dark place, unbidden. "There never has been any other woman for me."

Ruby shrunk away from me, tucking her chin and frowning up at me. "You're together." It wasn't a question. "I saw you. Don't deny it."

Jutting my jaw, I shook my head. "It's nothing. Truly, it's nothing. I ended it." Guilt roiled in my stomach, belying my words. I was an asshole. It had been nothing to me, but April didn't deserve this. I may not have loved her or even admired her, but she didn't deserve to be hurt and humiliated this way. I sighed. "She's a friend. I'll speak with her again, to explain." I shook my head, my gaze skipping away from Ruby's knowing gaze.

Her shoulders slumped as she exhaled. "I didn't come back to disrupt whatever life you have built for yourself here. I didn't know you'd left. I hardly know anything about you."

"Why did you come back?"

Instead of answering me, she whispered, "You look so good." Her lips quirked in a half smile. "So amazing." Her face lit up with a smile that stopped my heart and started it again, like a jolt of life. "You've grown up."

I felt my cheeks heat, pleased that she still liked the look of me.

"You're really not…"

I shook my head. "No." I frowned. "Are you?" It had never even occurred to me that she had someone, somewhere.

"No."

I grunted, flattening my lips and squinting at the irony. Why were we strangers to each other? This was never meant to be. "You look good, too." Words could not express how beautiful she was to me. I let my gaze slide down her body and sighed, shaking my head. Good enough to lose myself in.

Ruby lifted a hand and set it lightly on my chest, lifting her eyes back to mine. She could hardly have failed to notice the proud ridge in my dress pants.

I swallowed, praying my uncontrollable arousal didn't anger her, or turn her off. "What are we doing? Why are you back?" I didn't know why I asked, nor why I asked in quite that way. As if I had a right to demand answers. I didn't. She'd left me, and made that clear choice ten years ago.

Yet she answered me as though I were entitled, soft and yielding. "I'm… at a crossroads. I might be changing jobs and I need to decide what to do next."

My stomach turned over, sinking. She wasn't staying, then. "So… nothing to do with me? With us?"

"I didn't say that."

Was I supposed to feel better? "When I was abroad," I said, pulling a hand across my jaw — already scratchy with late-night growth—and blinking to clear my head, "It was easier—sometimes—to forget you. To imagine you'd never existed at all." Her face registered hurt at my words. If she only knew how much I'd hurt, thinking she'd discarded me, forgotten me.

I backed away a step, hooking my hands on my hips. "I was busy, thankfully. My life was a whirlwind of work and travel. I was surrounded by exciting, glamorous friends, clients, and colleagues." I shook my head. "But since coming home, it hasn't been that easy. I've thought about you so much more. Wherever I go, every time I'm with our friends, memories of you, of us, are lurking. Haunting me." I inhaled deeply and sighed. "Yesterday, I thought…" I paused, swallowing, remembering the intense shock I felt at seeing her for the first time. "I thought I'd conjured you. All the reunion planning, the talk of classmates, how could you not be on my mind?"

"I didn't know I'd see you at the café. I hadn't planned—"

"To see me? At all?" I cut her off, blurting the words in response to the intense stab of pain that idea caused. A rush of anger came out of nowhere. "Really?"

"No! Of course not. I just hadn't prepared… I wasn't ready."

"Well, I really don't know what to think, Ruby." I grit my teeth, pushing down the bitter resentment that had overtaken all the other emotions I'd juggled today. My voice came out choked, watery. "You're the one who left me. You're the one who broke my heart, broke our vows, betrayed me…" I stopped, realizing that my mouth swam with salty tears, and if I kept going, I'd be crying too, and have not one shred of dignity left.

The pain of that confession tore my heart out of my chest. My hands tightened into fists at the remembered sense of betrayal, the confusion and hurt.

Ruby's hand came to her mouth, holding back a sob as her eyes pooled with fresh tears that spilled onto her cheeks.

The muffled sound of her grief pierced me. I dropped my

forehead to hers, hot skin to hot skin, our moist breath mingling while we each scrambled back from that dark place.

"I'll leave you alone. You have your own life now, and I'm not part of it." I stepped back, out of the sphere of her heat, breaking the hold her body had over mine, trying to hold onto sanity. Steeling my nerves, narrowing my eyes at her, there was just one unanswered question. "Tell me just one thing. Why did you do it?"

Chapter 12

Ruby

DO WHAT? What was he asking?

Why I left? Why I left the way I did? Or why I abandoned our love, our family and our future?

I wanted to tell him everything, to explain and ask forgiveness, but I couldn't stop crying. I was a heaving wreck. Despite wanting to talk to Julian, the reality was more than I could bear. I couldn't stand there another second with all those eyes on us, feeling like a fraud, knowing we were both feeling raw and exposed.

I needed a moment alone to calm myself after that spectacle, never imagining he was right behind me in the corridor.

Voices in conversation reached us, and I whipped my head up, aware that someone was about to discover us. Panicking, I clutched Julian's solid arms, my mouth falling open, dismayed at the prospect of getting caught in this state.

Julian darted a glance to his left, realized what was happening, and turned back to me, his face a mask of determination. Cupping my tear-streaked face between his strong hands, his mouth came down onto mine, firm and possessive, leaving me stunned. Pulling away, he grabbed my hand and dashed down the corridor, hauling me behind him, stumbling on unfamiliar high heels.

We reached the bend at the end of the hall just as a group of people came into it at the party end, talking loudly and laughing. Around the corner, the oppressive sound of loud voices and music faded slightly, but so did the light. I came up short, panting in the dark, disoriented by the sudden changes. Images flashed in my mind, bringing with them visceral responses. My heart pounded in my throat and a cold sweat flushed on my skin, my muscles tightening.

"Come on," Julian urged, tugging on my hand. But my feet refused to move. He turned back, stepping close, lifting my chin and looking closely at my face, his voice soothing. "Hey. I know a quiet place where we can talk. What's wrong?" He gripped my upper arms and my shaking fingers found his forearms, holding on. "Ruby?"

"I-it's dark." I mewled, suddenly rigid with fear. "Don't leave me." He couldn't know how desperately I meant that.

"I'm here. It's all right."

He pulled his phone from his pocket, flicking on the flashlight, then gripped my hand and carried on down the ever darkening path. White metal doors in white frames, each of them identical, lined both sides of the white painted concrete blocks of the narrow corridor, flashing in the dancing beam of his light. The image brought to mind military hospitals and institutions I'd seen. He pulled me past several doors before slowing and shining his light on individual ones, searching the simple letter-number addresses. We passed one, two, three more before he finally came to a stop in front of 25J.

Standing close, creating a halo of light for us to stand in, he fished in his pants pocket, coming out with keys on a ring, and lifted them to show me. I caught a flash of his sweet smile in the light of his phone before he turned away, shining it on the door.

Fitting a key smoothly into the lock, he shouldered the door open and dragged me through into another pitch black space as the heavy metal door clicked shut like a tomb. I stood immobile, trembling, struggling for breath.

Disoriented, this place reminded me of assignments overseas, sneaking into strange bombed-out buildings to meet contacts and interview locals, always at the mercy of interpreters and guides to show me the way, never knowing what I would encounter. A shooter, a bomb, or a body as likely as a pot of tea and a biscuit.

"Hold on."

I heard him in the dark, scrambling, crashing into something and cursing under his breath, slapping at the walls until he finally located a switch and a light blinked on overhead, blinding us. I flinched again, covering my eyes with my hands, letting out a squeak.

Julian's hands cupped around my forearms, rubbing with his thumbs, holding me steady, and I sucked in a breath.

"Where a-are we?" My voice shook as I shivered. Pulling my hands down, he held them in his warm, steady grip, his thumbs continuing to rub the backs of my hands in circles. I extracted them, suddenly embarrassed that they were bare, worrying that he'd ask about my ring. I wouldn't have the heart to tell him I'd lost it.

"Hey, hey. It's just a storeroom." He wrapped his arms around me lightly, rubbing my back until I lifted my head, blinking at the harsh brightness.

"I'm okay. I'm okay." Come on, Ruby. Pull up your socks.

"Seriously. What's up? You're so jumpy."

"It's just… jetlag. I'm tired."

"Yeah. Right." But he dropped it.

After a moment, when our eyes adjusted, I saw that we were in a sterile utility space, lined with stainless steel shelving, stacked with cardboard boxes and white plastic tubs, a commercial refrigerator at one end. Piles of cardboard boxes cluttered the linoleum floor.

"It's my friend's place. The back entrance to the Roastery, where our food was laid out. I came through this way earlier, when we set up." Pointing, he stepped to an inner door with a small wire-mesh window, pressing close, and peered through, his face briefly tinted by lights from the dance floor beyond. The thump, thump, of the music's base notes penetrated louder again. "It's okay. Most of the catering team have left already. Just the bartender and a couple left to clean up afterwards." He turned to me. "People will be leaving soon. We have a few minutes before anyone comes back here."

Julian took my hands again and led me to a stack of boxes, pushing me gently down to sit on it, and I sagged, getting my bearings. Shrugging off his jacket, he pulled a hanky from his pocket and handed it to me before I remembered my face was streaked with tears, and likely smeared with mascara. He tossed the jacket to the side, then he stood back and let go his breath, as if he'd been holding it. A muscle ticked in his jaw as he ground his teeth, a tic I remembered well that told me when worry got the better of him.

After our mad dash, my heart rate pounded again. I took a moment to tidy my face, needing to think. I hadn't had a chance to process the kiss before we were on the run. He'd kissed me! Did he even realize he'd done it? My lips still tingled at the memory of it. It felt so natural, so familiar, as if we two were back in our old life, always together, moving as one being, as familiar with each other's bodies as with our own. I stared at him. Part of me just wanted to fall into his lap, curling into his embrace like a kitten, forgetting everything.

Now, though, he was calmer. Dipping his chin, he considered me without words, blinking, watching. The ball, so to speak, was clearly in my court. He unbuttoned his cuffs and rolled up his shirtsleeves, waited for my answer.

I lost myself for a long moment, my eyes caressing his sexy, sinewy forearms.

When I remained silent a beat too long, he plunged his

hands into his pockets, angled his head, looking around the storeroom, his mouth twisted in a wry expression.

"This could be anywhere. Any commercial kitchen in the world." He snuffled, laughing to himself, his eyes, crinkling at the corners, cast down in that bashful way that made me fall for him the very first time. "Behind the glamour and style and crisp white linen, kitchens are all the same. Stainless steel, white plastic, iron, flames, slop buckets and steam." He shook his head. "Wow, this takes me back."

He was giving me space to calm down. Or maybe he was weirded out by my panic attack and didn't know what to do about it.

His raised brow reminded me of what an expressive face he had. So charming and boyish, under his usual tumble of brown waves, which had lost some of their slick styling through the evening—likely as much from his restless hands as our dash to find privacy. His heavy brows, this incongruous slash of masculinity, arched over laughing eyes such a dark blue I'd always said they were navy. New laugh lines fanned out from their corners. He still had that sweetness, especially when he smiled. His lips were rosy, but his jaw angled sharply, and shadowed with the heavy beard of a man. A study in contrasts.

His hands intrigued me, too. Strong, well-shaped, and calloused from working on the farm. But now they bore unfamiliar scars on the knuckles and backs from adventures and mishaps I knew nothing about. Sharp knives and hot flames, I presumed.

"I can hardly picture you in that world. My concept of you just doesn't accommodate…" I shook my head, baffled. "Tell me everything. Tell me how you got there. I want to know about your life as a chef."

He reeled back, lifting those brows and blew out through those lips with a familiar expression that had not changed, though the wariness in his eyes was new and brought me pain. "I wouldn't know where to start."

I smiled softly. "At the beginning?"

He scrubbed a hand over the back of his head, mussing his hair further, then stepped to the door with the window, peeked through, then slipped out, leaving me alone. I sat up, alert. What the hell? But before I could form a thought, he was back, clutching a bottle and two glasses and wearing a smug expression.

"I know where the bar staff hid the extras." Then he squinted at the over bright fluorescent lights above us, spun away and yanked on a chrome handle and opened the large commercial refrigerator, triggering the interior light.

He hummed and pulled something out, then closed the door loosely, so it didn't latch, letting out a narrow stream of yellow light. Then he flicked off the overheads, leaving us in semi-darkness.

I let out a shaky breath I didn't realize I'd been holding.

He sat on his own stack of boxes, our knees a mere few inches apart, and poured us each a glass of red wine. As he handed me one I pondered his resourcefulness. He'd always been that way. His mind sharp. Quick to find a solution to any problem, he was agile, coordinated, ingenious with found objects, and skilled with his hands. It took my breath away, and I had to push aside the images and sensations that threatened to overpower me. He could always make the best of a less-than-ideal situation. I'd admired that about him.

"You'd be a good chef."

He swallowed a sip of wine, his eyes twinkling in the dim light. "I am a good chef. I'm an excellent chef."

I knew that from the few samples I'd eaten tonight and yesterday. But his casual confidence about his skill, that was new.

He picked up a package he'd got from the fridge and set it on a box beside us, winking. "We can have a private party." He lifted the cloth wrap to reveal some of his h'ors d'oeuvres and I smiled as he picked up an item and held it toward me.

Not sure if I was more wowed by his effortless charm or the prospect of being fed, I opened my mouth and closed my eyes, the ultimate act of trust, knowing that it would delight my palate, but also wanting to show him my trust. The brush of his knuckles against the skin of my jaw sent a shiver of anticipation through me. I wasn't disappointed, and a moan of pleasure escaped as I processed the wonderful salty flavours and textures. When I opened my eyes, his intense expression focussed on my face, his eyes hooded, his lips parted, revealing clenched teeth.

"I'd love to cook for you. Cook a proper meal. Come to the farm. Meet my dog Finnegan. My goats. They're really fun." He quirked that brow again, smiling.

I swallowed, my gaze dropping as I felt my face heat. His invitation brought with it a whole host of suggestions, memories, sensations, and desires. "Um. Rainy, or maybe Deanna, said you went to culinary school in London?"

He nodded, a hint of a smile pulling at the corners of those lovely lips. "Eventually. I worked my way up from busboy to… mmm, I'd have to say competent kitchen help, and discovered my love of food."

"More. Tell me the whole story."

He tilted his head to the left and smiled at me, meeting my gaze steadily. "What are we doing, Ruby?"

Chapter 13

Ruby

"I'M INTERVIEWING YOU." I grinned. Feeling my cheeks heat, I dropped my gaze, feeling an overwhelming shyness. What are you doing, Ruby? Aside from flirting shamelessly, I knew I was deflecting, stalling. The longer I could keep Julian talking about himself, the longer I could avoid the words I needed to say. "It's what I do."

"Oh, I see," he dipped his chin and quirked a smile, shaking his head. Then he turned and grabbed a big wooden cylinder from the metal shelf beside him. He gripped it in his fist and held the bulbous end under my chin.

My pulse kicked, and I felt a spasm of carnal need shoot through my core. "What… is that?" I pushed it away.

He held it away and peered at it. "A pestle," he said, matter-of-factly. "A… mic?"

"Oy," I squeaked. "I thought… it looks like a…" I snapped my mouth closed, meeting his gaze as my face flushed with heat. I was pretty irreverent, usually. That was normal in my business. But somehow I couldn't bring myself to joke about 'dildos' out loud to Julian. "Schlong." My lips parted, and my tongue darted out to wet my lower lip. Realizing I'd done this, I bit my lip, feeling heat flood my body.

"Oh." His eyes widened and fixed on mine. The blue deepened when he realized what I meant, his wrist going limp, his wooden pestle drooping. Then he cleared his throat and chuckled, dropping his gaze shyly as his ears went bright pink. There was no doubt in my mind that he, like me, was seeing mental images of us at sixteen, seventeen, eighteen, fucking like bunnies every chance we got.

We both burst into self-conscious laughter, and I closed my eyes for a moment and tried to pull myself together.

I sniffed. "Fine." I took the 'microphone' from him and my hand overlapped his. A thousand sparks flew when our hands touched, and my breath drew shallow as my pulse raced ahead.

He let go, and I held it close to his chin, my voice a mere whisper as I said, "You were telling me about the summer after grad."

Lifting a dark brow quizzically, he blew out a breath and squinted into the darkness. His gaze dropped and our playful mood fell away.

"I don't want to talk about me." He lifted his dark gaze to mine, insistent. "I want to know what the hell happened to you. To us."

I dropped the flirtatious prop to my lap, staring at it, my heart heavy. I was in the habit of pushing those memories away. "I reacted."

"To what? What happened? We had plans!"

I swallowed, my throat a tangle of knots like one of my knitting projects in the bottom of my pack. My gaze flicked up to his, reticent, and I shook my head. "Not yet," I whispered. "Please. Keep going."

He frowned as my request hung in the air between us like a vow. "Well. At first, nothing. I didn't believe you were gone. My mind wouldn't accept it. I frantically looked for you, and I sought explanations. The gang knew nothing. Except Beth, and your parents, who were evasive and tight-lipped; after a while I realized they were covering for you." He raked his hand through his hair, his eyes dark as midnight. "Finally, they admitted you'd gone off to Wisconsin to start your program, as planned."

The raw expression of remembrance caused pain to grip the back of my throat as tears fought their way to the surface again. How I wished I could go back and change the way things had unfolded. I never meant to cause Julian so much anguish. Never again. I reached for his hand and he allowed me to hold it limply between mine. I noticed a nasty scar on the knuckle of his left hand as though he'd tried to slice it clean off. Hazards of being a chef, I guessed, and touched it lightly with my fingertip, wishing I could bring it to my lips.

"I never meant…"

"What?" His voice snapped, demanding, and I recoiled.

Anger simmered under the surface of his charm. It would be harder than I thought to get him to listen. To summon the courage to tell him everything.

We froze like that, breathing in sync, pain throbbing on the surface; our gazes locked on each other's faces when the door burst open. My heart catapulted to my throat with a scream as I jerked back, lifting my arms to my head.

"Oh!" One of the serving staff stood there in his all-black uniform, propping the door open with his foot, holding a tray in each hand, his eyes wide. "Sorry. I didn't expect to find anyone back here." He began backing out, turning his face away.

My heart rate settled back to normal again. Come on Ruby. Pull up your socks.

"Aaron, it's okay," Julian said, shooting to his feet. He lunged for the door, opening it wide. Taking the trays from Aaron, he said, "I'll put these in the fridge for now."

"Okay. Uh, it's just that, we have to put the food away."

"Right. It's okay. We'll…" Julian turned to regard me pensively. "We're just heading out. Give us a few more minutes, ok?"

"Sure." Aaron hesitated. "Matt was looking for you. Should I mention you're here, or…" He shook his head. "Not."

Julian nodded, closing his eyes with a quiet groan. "Yeah, yeah. I'll talk to him in a few minutes, okay?" His voice was tight, a muscle in his jaw twitching with tension.

"I'm keeping you from…" I wasn't a hundred per cent clear on the what, but Julian obviously had some business he was trying to conduct tonight.

As Aaron let the door swing shut behind him, Julian said, "It's okay. This is Matt's kitchen. We're… I'm supposed to be soliciting sponsors for the event we're planning for end of summer. That's all."

"I'm sorry. I'm in the way."

"It's okay." He sat down, slid an arm around me and pulled, and kept pulling until I slid into his lap, my happy place. His arms came around me, tightening as his cheek pressed against my back. "Hey. You're so jumpy. What happened to you, sweetheart?"

I sighed, not wanting to sift through my disordered thoughts for words to explain something I wasn't sure I completely understood myself. Letting my body relax into his, I gave my head a tiny shake. "Go on. What did you do that summer? I need to connect the dots."

He hummed against my back, the vibration sending shivers through me, and I let my head fall back against his shoulder as he rocked us back and forth. His thighs were solid muscle, but it didn't mean I couldn't feel his cock rise up to meet my ass between them. I clenched my muscles as a shiver wracked me, and heat pooled between my legs.

Tightening his grip on me, he went on. "I wallowed. I

couldn't bear to be on the farm. I didn't want to be there, anyway. I don't know if you knew that Dad and I had been arguing for a while about it. I wanted to live my own life, have my own experiences, and he expected me to take over our family legacy." He scoffed.

I nodded, remembering Mr. Michaels, stoic and hard working. "To your dad, it would have made sense."

Julian's grandparents travelled from England after the war and built a strong business, became an important part of the community. They were justifiably proud. I had assumed Julian felt the same way. Evidently, I'd missed the signs of his discontent. I realized now that I had been rather self-absorbed, thinking my own career ambitions were the only ones that mattered. To me, being with Julian meant being tied to that farm.

Julian hummed in agreement. "Dad didn't understand why I would want anything else." He sniffed and I felt his forehead lean to touch the back of my neck. "Anyway, your leaving tipped the scales for me and I don't know... I guess I took it out on Dad. We fought, and I left." He shrugged as if it didn't matter, but it saddened me that a rift had formed in a family that I had always seen as idyllic, loving, and supportive.

I turned to the side so I could look at him, lifting my legs across his knees and wrapped an arm around him. He hooked a hand over my thigh and pulled me tight against his torso. The scent of his body surrounded me like a spell, warm skin, cotton, cologne and man, and I dipped my head closer to breathe him in.

"I am so sorry to hear about your dad."

He nodded, swallowing.

The lull in our conversation carried the dance beat of the party music like a heartbeat. I felt it thump in my chest, my womb, my head and my pulse raced to keep time.

"It's ironic, isn't it? That you're back now?"

"Yes. But you're jumping ahead." He chuckled. "Then, I had no sense of direction, just had to get away. I got a series of shitty jobs and ended up in the back end of a bunch of restaurants, bussing, scrubbing pots, and then helping out with food prep. One thing led to another and somehow feeding people, nurturing and creating, healed me or it healed a part of me and gave me a reason to go on."

I tried to picture him at eighteen, peeling potatoes or something. "You always enjoyed cooking with your grandma," I reflected. "And she loved feeding people so much."

He nodded. "I thought about her a lot. I drew inspiration from Gran and all the things she had taught me and I thought — I can do this, I would actually enjoy this. My chef at the time liked me, thought I had potential. He told me about this scholarship program to the Cordon Bleu Institute in London, where he had connections. I applied. He wrote a reference letter and set me up. I ended up getting accepted." He drew his bottom lip between his teeth and shrugged, lifting his eyes.

I raised my empty wineglass, and he picked up the bottle and refilled it and his own and set it down. I silently toasted his success, our gazes meeting with a warm familiarity. He touched his glass to mine and we sipped. We'd shared so much, I didn't think, for all our differences, that Julian and I could ever be cold strangers.

"Keep going," I whispered. I loved his mouth, his lips and the way they moved when he talked. Such a kissable mouth, it took me back to when we'd first met; fifteen years old and I'd never wanted to kiss a boy before Julian. Then suddenly it was all I could think about.

Slipping my arm back across his broad shoulders, I touched his face, stroking his ear and cheek with my thumb, dipping my fingers into his hair. His eyes darted to the side, acknowledging my touch, and then he sighed. I felt his fingers tighten slightly against my ribs, just grazing the side of my breast, and knew he was as agitated as I was by our proximity.

I could listen to him forever and I'd been deprived of this addictive delight for so long, I didn't want him to stop. "What was it like, working in European restaurants?"

His throat moved as he swallowed. "At first, I determined to work with the best, and it was all about finding the right jobs, knowing the right people. So I could learn. I didn't have much free time, but I learned about the cultures and local cuisines through chefs, restaurant owners, suppliers. I moved around a fair bit, and that took me from London to Paris, to Italy, to Switzerland and back to the south of France."

His hand slid down my side until it rested over my hip, sending electric tingles through my nerve endings. I squirmed again, feeling his hardness beneath me, feeling desire overtake my brain functions.

"That's amazing. I'm so jealous."

Julian drew back his chin, scoffing. "Jealous of me? You've done nothing but travel."

I sighed. "Sure. London was my base. But many of my assignments took me to some miserable places. I mean, the countries themselves were interesting, if they'd not been in crisis. Bombed-out buildings and hungry, homeless people tend to detract from the tourist attractions."

"I'm sorry." He shook his head, as if to rid it of the images my words evoked. Then he ran his left hand up my thigh, gripping it hard, digging his fingers into my flesh, effectively ending any pretence of conversation.

"I missed your body, Ruby. I know we're not…" He stopped, grimacing as if in pain. "… not a thing anymore. But my body remembers yours and wants you as much as ever."

I lifted my free hand to caress the side of his stubbled jaw, looking into his mysterious eyes, nodding. When he lifted his face, I bent my head, dropping my lips slowly onto his like I'd been wanting to all night. Even more so since he'd kissed me in a frenzy in the corridor.

Our mouths came together like two halves of a whole, fitting like puzzle pieces into a familiar hot pattern. There was no awkwardness in the kiss, no hesitation. He was bold and certain, taking possession. We hadn't forgotten the feel of each other. Not at all. Opening my mouth, gliding my lips over his, I let my tongue reach for his, and he took the cue, lifting his hand to cup the back of my head and deepening the kiss. Oh, what a kiss. Our tongues danced, slowly, languorously, relishing this sensation that we'd been deprived of for ten long years.

A low moan rose from his chest as he pulled us closer together, pressing my breasts against his hard chest.

Heat suffused my body, my skin coming alive with goose-flesh, my core clenching with a stab of need as his hands slid hot and hungry over my body, as if he wanted to feel every bit of me at once. While his right hand slid to the cleft of my ass, his strong fingers slipped beneath me, curling. His left hand grasped the hem of my dress and pushed it up, his thumb dragging up the inside of my thigh, seeking my centre.

It was my turn to moan into his mouth. Everything inside of me pulled me towards him, crying to open wide and invite him inside. I shifted my weight, and he shoved my skirt up to my hips so I could straddle him, pressing my hot centre against his urgent need with a gasp. I rocked my hips, feeling his hard shaft rub against my aching mound. Our mouths fused in a desperate hunger, our teeth clashing as our bodies took over, compelling us to connect in every way possible.

Julian's hands dug into my hips as his fingers curled around my ass and explored the crease between, reaching to stroke the tiny crotch of my silky thong. Thank you Deanna!

"Fuck, you're so wet." He groaned, plundering my mouth with his tongue, diving in time with his rubbing fingers, tracing the edges of my scant covering, snaking underneath, seeking my slippery skin.

I was practically climbing him in my need. "Just hearing your name makes me wet." I spoke against his lips, unwilling to part from him, my voice hoarse. "Julian."

"God." His other hand slid up, dragging his palm across the top of my breast, sending shock waves through my hard nipples; I arched my chest towards him, hungry for more pressure. My response brought his hand fully around the curve of my breast, squeezing; the tips of his fingers curling at the neckline of my dress as if he meant to yank it down.

I brought my hand over his, gasping. "Deanna's dress. Don't hurt it."

With a groan, he backed off, pulling his hands from me, his breath shuddering. His voice was deep and gravelly when he said, "We have to get the hell out of here before I explode." He pressed his mouth to the low open vee of my dress, dragging his tongue along my sternum between my breasts, one hand on either side of my ribs, his thumbs stroking the sides of both breasts at once. I nearly buckled as my head dropped back, sensation rippling through my entire body, screaming for him.

My hands shook with need as I stroked his chest from neck to abs, my gaze locked on the prominent bulge in his pants as I slid from his lap, standing on wobbly legs, panting. I wanted his hard cock in me, now. All other thoughts had flown from my mind.

He stood up, grimacing as he adjusted himself, a few inches of super-heated air between us. Then he dropped his damp forehead against mine, peering up into my eyes. I was stunned by the unguarded and overwhelming want in his dark gaze.

"I'm sorry." He forced a breath out. "This is wrong. I'm sorry."

"No. No, I want to… I need you Julian." I reached forward, setting one trembling hand on his chest. "But not here."

"Where—"

Before he could finish his question, the door opened again. We both jerked in shock, Julian turning his back to the door, pressing hard on his erection.

I darted further along the shelving, seeking privacy,

yanking my dress down, checking for exposed body parts as my heart thundered behind my ribcage.

"Julian! There you are. Damn it. We need you."

"Matt."

I glanced over. Matt saw me and froze, his face registering what was going on. He cleared his throat, hesitating.

I stepped forward, smoothing my dress self-consciously, turning my face away as Julian stepped in front of me, toward his friend. "I'm sorry, I—"

"I'm sorry to barge in, Man. But why aren't you working the room like we planned? We're almost out of time here."

"I know. All right. I'll come."

"Listen, I really want you to hear out Ethan Garwood. He really impressed me with what he had to say. And he's game to be a major sponsor. It would make our operating budget and take the pressure off."

"I'll be right there," Julian growled as Matt stomped out.

We faced each other. He was rumpled, flushed, his eyes dark with desire. I reached to smooth his hair with my fingers and his jaw ticked. Dropping his head to my shoulder, he took it gently between his teeth and bit down softly into me with a groan. Then he straightened his shoulders, obviously trying to shift his thoughts, giving his head a small shake. He smoothed down his shirt, tucked it in, shoving his hand in his pants to straighten himself, and sighed.

He stepped away, then stepped back, reaching for my arm. "I'll be back. Don't take off. We're not done." Then he took my face between his hands and kissed me, slow, deep, and passionate, ruining me. It was the only kiss in the world. Nothing compared. Pulling away, he peered into my face, then turned to leave.

I twisted to look at him over my shoulder, nodding as he slipped out, the door closing behind him. Alone in the storeroom, the remains of our private party scattered around me, I felt bereft, my chest heavy.

Rejoining the party was the last thing I wanted right now, but standing and waiting for Julian made me feel ridiculous; all my nerve endings were firing at once, turning me into a jittery mess. I smoothed my hair and headed out, intending to check my face in the bathroom mirror and prepare for whatever came next.

Chapter 14

Julian

MY BODY SCREAMED with frustration at the abrupt end to our make-out session, every cell in my body crying out to touch Ruby, reliving each sensation.

But a part of my mind reeled at what had just happened. What the fuck was I doing? How could I let that happen? As if I had any choice, any self-control with Ruby.

Even so, a saner part of me was thankful for the interruption. We needed to cool our jets. I couldn't let my raging libido and memories of our perfect love confuse me.

As our mutual desire had escalated, a dawning awareness grew of the reality that, however much I wanted her, she was not mine. She had left me, betrayed me, and broken me. The person who had loved her ten years ago… well, a part of him had died.

Yet she was acting as though no time had passed. When I'd pulled back, waiting a moment to let my saner self gain control of my primal urges, she'd seemed… unhesitating, unrepentant. As if she'd wanted nothing more than to go down that slippery slope.

I did too, but I couldn't let go. I still had got no explanation from Ruby, let alone an apology for leaving me ten years ago. Never mind my need for self-preservation, my pride alone wouldn't let me go there.

We'd have more time together tonight. I'd make sure of that, even if I had to drive to her parents' house and break down the door. And I'd get the answers I sought once and for all before I touched her again and let her weave her magic around my heart. Or my throbbing cock.

If there was one thing I knew, no matter what happened, my heart would never withstand another betrayal and abandonment by Ruby Zimmer. So I had to guard against it with every ounce of self-control I possessed.

I wanted answers, yes. But I didn't trust her. How could I?

Standing to the side of the bar, I saw Matt, Noah, another of our smaller sponsors, and of course, Ethan Garwood at the other end. I knew tonight was critical. The opportunity to show off my food and give my pitch to a captive audience was unprecedented. There wouldn't be another opportunity like this before the end of summer. And if our Faire was to go ahead as planned on the Labour Day weekend, this funding had to be secured. We all knew it, me most of all. Too much was at stake.

Noah noticed me, and I raised a finger. I just needed one minute to pull myself together.

Why was I being such a prima donna about whose sponsorship I accepted? Because of something old Thomas Garwood had done decades ago? Was I being unfair? I wasn't my father, and I wasn't running a farm like he did, so why couldn't I give Ethan a chance? At least a chance to say his piece. Convince me.

I faced the bartender.

"Whiskey, please." Once I had the glass of ice and golden liquid in hand, I tossed back a good gulp, and then another. My nerves were frazzled, and I needed to be both calm and sharp-witted for this encounter.

Then I stepped forward to do my best.

Noah greeted me first, having seen me coming. Then Matt turned, slapped my back. "Here's the man, at last."

I smiled tightly. "Sorry to keep you waiting. Has everyone given the food a try?" It would be great if everyone looked away while I gave my face another brisk rub.

To a backdrop of exclamations and grunts of approval, I slipped in my short spiel about the source of the various ingredients I'd used for tonight's menu. I sold them on the idea that my brand, my social media strategy, emphasized food that I could grow, forage, or husband on my own acreage, twelve months of the year. I didn't share the fact that Deanna had devised the plan to turn me into a minor celebrity. She thought my cooking, my cozy country lifestyle, and my looks would do more for the cause than all the speeches I could make in a year. So far, she'd been right, but that was private.

"This time of year, the bounty is endless and varied, so the menu for the Farm-to-Table Faire over Labour Day weekend will be impressive indeed. There are few places on earth as clean and plentiful as our valley." I let my gaze move from man to man as I spoke, subtly reading Ethan's expression as I did, gauging his attitude.

"Are you overseeing all the food production for the Faire, Julian?" he asked.

"Overseeing, yes. But there are many suppliers, producers, and individual cooks involved; everyone will bring their personal brand and style to the table, so to speak. It will benefit everyone."

"Not least of all the consumers."

I nodded. "And the planet. Part of the educational component is helping consumers understand they can't eat strawberries twelve months of the year without paying the price. No matter how close we live here to the Californian growers, we have to learn not to depend on their irrigated desert, or produce shipped from Mexico and Chile in the winter to indulge our spoilt palettes. It's not as much about the economy as the sustainability of those practices for the earth."

"I'm very impressed with what your group has organized so far," Ethan continued. "And if you'll have me, I'd very much like to play a part. I've been reorganizing and rebranding my resort for almost two years now, and I won't lie. Aligning myself with your cause will make my re-launch much easier. But the reason I want to support you is simply that, I agree with everything you're doing, and I want to help."

I didn't say anything, still assessing the sincerity of his words. He clearly saw how I felt on my face.

"I look forward to the opportunity to work together, Julian," Ethan said, reaching out a hand for me to shake.

I ignored it, mumbling, "That makes one of us."

Matt scowled at my rudeness, but I ignored him. "He's a tough customer, our Julian."

Ethan, undaunted, persisted. "It would mean a lot to me if you'd meet me. Come up the mountain and see what I've been doing." He set a hand on my shoulder. "It's not the same resort my father ran when we were kids, Julian. Please give me a chance to prove it to you. We can hash out the details at the same time."

I could hardly refuse an appeal like that. He certainly gave the impression of meaning what he said. I offered him my hand.

He shook it firmly with a smile. He was a smooth operator, no question, but I had to give him credit for trying. "When can you come?"

"In a couple of days. I have some personal business I have to take care of before my time opens up." At my words, Matt's expression told me what he thought I meant, and I sent him a steely glare. "Set it up, okay?"

Ruby

. . .

THE PARTY CROWD had thinned considerably, but a few people were still scattered across the dance floor or sat in clusters around the edges of the open market hall. I caught a glimpse of Julian standing with a group of men by the bar looking very serious and businesslike. I managed to sneak across the room without encountering any close friends, and ducked through the doorway to the washrooms, having made a full circle.

I almost laughed aloud. Nothing felt the same now as it did an hour ago, when I'd first dashed off of the dais in search of privacy.

Slipping into the women's washroom, I quickly relieved myself and washed up, dismayed at what I saw in the mirror. Dabbing at my messed-up face with a dampened paper towel there seemed little doubt about what I'd been up to. I may not have looked thoroughly fucked, but halfway there had a similar look. In addition to smudged mascara around my eyes, my lipstick was smeared half off. And my lovely shiny ropes of hair were tangled and frizzed. Deanna would be disappointed if she saw me now, having destroyed her handiwork.

"Ah, Ruby. What the hell are you doing?" I murmured to my reflection.

"Ruby? Is that you?"

I jumped, spinning to look at the toilet stalls. I'd assumed I was alone in here. "Who's that?"

A sniffle, followed by a nose blowing honk and a flush followed. Then a door opened and Quinn emerged. She looked like she'd had a rough night too, and had been crying.

"Quinn! Are you all right?"

She sniffed again and shrugged, turning to a sink. I met her eye in the mirror as she washed her hands and dried them. "I just got some bad news."

My pulse kicked up. "Is everyone okay? Did something happen? Your dad?"

"Oh! Oh, no." Quinn's eyes went wide. "Nothing like that. Sorry to scare you. No." She closed her eyes and dropped her head, leaning on the vanity. "It's only that, Jae Soo told us tonight that he's..." she looked up. "He's engaged to be married."

"Oh? Is that a terrible thing?" My mind whirled with reasons why this would make Quinn cry her eyes out. I knew they were close friends, but...

She swallowed. "Well. Not for him, I guess. Of course we knew it would happen eventually. But it feels too soon. Parker is devastated." She shook her head as if Jae'd been sent to the gallows.

"Is he happy about it? He must be."

She shrugged. "Resigned, I guess. His family has been setting him up with all the right society girls forever. He'll be thirty next year, so they turned up the heat. I guess he decided to pick someone tolerable before he got stuck with someone worse."

"Huh. So, it wasn't really a surprise, then?" I was still searching for an explanation.

"No. But now..." Her face buckled and she pinched it all up trying to hold back fresh tears. "Now we won't see him anymore. Instead of coming and going he'll be stuck in Korea with the business, and his new family."

"Ah." I nodded, finally understanding. "So you'll miss him, is that it?"

She stiffened. "Of course. He's my friend too. But Parker..." A single tear escaped and trickled down her cheek. "Parker is so broken up. They're best friends. He lives for the months that Jae is here. And now we'll never see him." Her chin quivered again.

"I'm sure he'll still visit. Don't you think?" What else could I say to cheer her up?

"I'm sure you're right," she said, but the words were muffled as she buried her face in her hands and bent over again. "I'm sure you're right." Scrubbing her face roughly, she stood up, straightened her shoulders, and lifted her face. "We can always go visit him and his wife in Seoul."

"There's an idea. Now you're thinking." I smiled. "Is he leaving right away, then?"

"No. He's staying for Julian's Faire. He's got about a month actually, before he has to go back. Oh! I just remembered."

She yanked on her small shoulder bag and rummaged, pulling out a key ring. "Here. Deanna said you left some stuff at her place? She's gone home with Zach, sadly. She said to let yourself in, get your things. Crash even, if you want to. It's closer than your folks' place."

I took the keys from her and tucked them into my evening bag. "Thanks."

It was Quinn's turn to check herself in the mirror and rub her face, but since she hardly wore any makeup, if any, all she needed was a splash and a little smoothing of her auburn hair and she was good to go.

"Uh… so… Deanna and Zach. Are they an item? How long has that been going on?" I'd been gone a long time, but somehow that was one change that surprised me. They seemed very ill suited.

Quinn paused, her hand on the door pull. "No, they are not an item, exactly. No one knows precisely what they are. Fuck buddies, I guess? But 'it' has been going on for ten years. Ever since grad, when they hooked up and broke up Zach and Jeannie."

"Oh, right." I vaguely recalled that was the reason Jeannie split from Zach. But I hadn't stayed in touch with her, or rather, she hadn't stayed in touch with me or anyone else, except Quinn. "That is puzzling, I'll admit."

Quinn pulled the door open. "We agree on that. I'm heading home now, but come to the café tomorrow, okay? We can hang out. A few people should be there. Bring Julian."

My head went suddenly fizzy at her words. Julian. She was

almost gone by the time I eked out the words, "Will do. Good night, Quinn."

I emerged from the washrooms, feeling on edge. Julian had said not to leave, but maybe he'd had second thoughts. He'd seemed torn about the way things got out of control in the storeroom. What did we think we were doing, anyway?

A couple of the guys Julian had been speaking with turned to look at me, despite my efforts to slink invisibly into the shadows. One of them was Matt, who'd walked in on us, so I guess he knew who I was.

After a few more words were exchanged, they all shook hands and the group broke up. Julian turned to face me. It took him no more than a second to find me in the shadows by a column, his face tightening with determination.

A sudden weight pressed down on my chest, making my next breath difficult, and the back of my throat ache. His focus on me carried a dangerous intensity and my pulse thrummed at what might happen next.

He approached, slowing as he came within a couple of feet, slipping his hands into his pants pockets and rocking back on his heels, as if he wanted to maintain space between us. "You sure made an impression on those guys. Their tongues were lolling out like Finnegan after a run."

"Finnegan?"

"My dog?" His mouth quirked up on one side, and he stepped closer, into my personal space. He leaned toward me and inhaled deeply. "I missed you."

I shivered and breathed in his scent too; it was citrusy, musky and sophisticated in a way that was unfamiliar and yet pulled at my libido like a drug. It wouldn't matter what cologne Julian chose, he would always smell like home to me, and that smell stirred a wild hunger in my blood.

In the dim light, he raised his hooded midnight eyes and peered into mine. "You ready to leave?"

My mouth twitched, relieved that he hadn't decided to cut and run. "Where will we go?"

"We can go make out in my catering van," he murmured, lifting a hand to run a finger down my arm. "Who needs a bed when you have cold bare steel to lie on." He growled. "Sexy."

I dropped my head, laughing quietly. "When did you get to be so funny?"

"I've always been funny. Did you forget?"

I glanced up at him through my lashes, my face warm, and my skin tingling. "No. I remember."

He took a deep breath and stepped back, inclined his head toward the nearest door. "We have to get out of here. You're staying with Mom and Dad?"

His casual reversion to calling my parents Mom and Dad, the way he did in high school, made my throat spasm with sudden sweet tenderness and crippling grief. A swelling warmth suffused my chest. How had I managed without him for ten long years? He was my person. He'd always been my person. I felt tears prick at my eyes. Again. I was a sentimental mess tonight.

"I am. Though I'm sure they'd love to see you, maybe not… like this." I smiled.

He made a disgruntled sound in his throat. "It's almost half an hour drive to the farm." The muscle in his jaw ticked with frustration. "We can get a hotel room. I suppose." He pulled a face at the implicit tackiness of that, and shrugged.

I nodded, holding back the smile that pulled at my face. "Or." I opened my bag and pulled out Deanna's keys; holding them up threaded over my pointer finger, I teased, touching my tongue to the corner of my mouth. "We could go to Deanna's, where she is not sleeping tonight because she's gone home with Zach, apparently."

His expression froze as he processed my news. "Fuck me. You just made my night."

I grinned.

His face lit up, eyes glinting, sending a shiver of anticipation through me. "Problem solved." His heated gaze met mine, and suddenly I felt as if I were going home with a stranger. A far more worldly, experienced, and bold man than I knew, and my pulse quivered at what that might mean.

He held up a finger and mouthed, Don't go anywhere. I'll be right back.

I swallowed and watched him duck behind the servery once again, and a few minutes later, re-emerge with a carry bag.

"Got us some beverages and snacks." His brows quirked up. "For later."

Chapter 15

Julian

"WE LEFT THE PLACE IN A MESS." Ruby opened the door and led the way inside. "I'm sure Deanna would be mortified if she knew you'd be seeing it like this."

I flipped the light switch on, since I doubted she knew where it was. "Not likely." I'd spent plenty of time at Deanna's during planning sessions for my branding and social media campaign. Dee was a pro, and she'd grilled me for hours, then sweated over a plan, and put a presentation together that left me amazed. Without her, I wouldn't be doing what I was now.

Ruby tossed her light shawl and bag on the sectional and switched on a low light on the end table. She stood and turned toward me, flapping her arms, pressing her palms to her cheeks. "Turn off those bright lights, okay?" Her cheeks and chest were rosy with a blush.

It had been a tense drive. We found ourselves suddenly alone, no one to put on a show for or hide from, no one lurking around the corner watching us critically or silently cheering us on. I felt suddenly naked and raw. I'm sure Ruby felt more than a little self-conscious too.

By the time we got to Deanna's condo, I'd gone from desperately, unrepentantly turned on to wracked with guilt at what we were unwisely heading here to do. My mind raced through different options, different outcomes, dragging my emotions along for the ride until I was catatonic with indecision.

My original goal had not been to hook up with Ruby, nor even to get back together with her; I'd let go of that hope a long time ago. I'd finally reached a kind of equilibrium. Everything was finally coming together. But here she was. Here we were. And I had questions I wanted answered. Issues that I could finally resolve and put to bed.

I'd waited for years for this moment, wondering, thinking, planning. And what had happened? Despite the shock and fresh pain at seeing Ruby again, what had overwhelmed me, maybe both of us, was the instantaneous attraction and the effortless connection; understanding each other was the unmatched bond that had always held us together. Even while we'd been thousands of miles apart all these years, living separate lives. The pull to be closer to her, to draw her inside of me, was irresistible. My body screamed for hers, to the exclusion of anything my mind, or my heart, might need.

Almost.

What exactly was I doing here with Ruby now? What did I want, or need, from her? And how long could I keep lying to myself?

I looked up from staring at a spot on the floor, gnawing on my cheek, deep in thought. "She won't care." I cracked my neck and sighed, toeing off my shoes and stepping further into the room.

"Just wait here a minute, okay? I have to…" She darted down the hall and disappeared into Deanna's bedroom. I thought she had to use the bathroom, but I heard her scuffling around in there, muttering and swearing, doors thumping and banging. She was tidying, for fuck's sake.

"It's okay, Ruby. Leave it." My voice came out an impatient bark, and I ground my teeth in irritation at my lack of composure.

She returned, more flushed than before, shaking her head. "Really, there were clothes and shoes all over the place. On the floor, on the bed…" She darted a glance my way, self-conscious.

I dragged a hand across my mouth and chin, my beard already long enough to rasp against my palm. I let out a non-committal grunt. She was worried about the bed. God. I grimaced.

She froze mid-motion, her voice emerging short and uneasy. "What's wrong?"

I raked a hand through my hair, stepping to the kitchen. "How about we have some tea? I'm thirsty and…" With Deanna's kettle in my hand, I looked up, "…tired. I think if we do anything, we need to talk."

Ruby's face fell, and her throat moved as she swallowed, setting aside any delusions that we could barrel past the necessary, painful conversation and straight into bed. She nodded, nibbling on her thumbnail, looking me up and down. "I'm going to change." She disappeared back into Dee's bedroom and quietly closed the door.

Ruby

I froze in the middle of Deanna's bedroom, uncertain. I knew I was stalling. I was overwhelmed. Had I really believed, just because Julian and I had fallen so effortlessly into each other's arms, into our old patterns, that we could skip the hard parts?

I'd nervously tidied the bedroom in a crass assumption that we were here to have sex. Which was, I guess, not off the table. But Julian would not make this easy on either of us. But what did I truly expect? What was I here for, anyway, if not to do an accounting? To confess and explain and beg forgiveness.

That didn't make it easy.

I strode to the chair where I'd draped my own clothing after tidying up the rejected garments Deanna, Aislin, and I had considered earlier. I had to get out of this dress. Though Deanna's styling had made me feel beautiful and given me the courage I needed to face that roomful of classmates — strangers and old friends who I'd basically neglected this past decade — it wasn't me. Suddenly, I felt fake and uncomfortable in my skin.

I stripped off the white dress, realizing that I'd have to get it cleaned, or at least pay for dry cleaning as I hung it on a hanger.

Shit. I hadn't told my family I would be staying out all night. Accounting for my whereabouts was not something I was used to. At least, not this way. I dug out my phone, which I'd left here, to send a quick text to dad. He was likely already asleep, but if he were worried, I wanted him to know I was safe.

I flicked it on and started thumb-typing.

Thanks for convincing me to go to the party. It was a lovely evening. I'm crashing at De —

And my phone died. Fuck. I let out a frustrated sigh and turned to my discarded clothes. Cold wrinkly cargo pants and a thin t-shirt didn't feel even remotely comfortable, or sexy. Chagrinned, I turned to Deanna's drawers. This woman had enough clothing to supply an entire army. I rummaged until I found something soft and stretchy, and not too new looking, and tugged them on over Deanna's fancy lingerie. That I would hang on to for a while longer, because… who knew?

In the bathroom, I flicked on the light and cringed at my mangled reflection. All of Deanna's beauty woo-woo had pretty much worn off. My gorgeously curled and coifed hair hung limply in ratty tails more closely resembling my everyday mess, which was why I usually scraped it back into a no-nonsense pony. Sighing, I dragged a brush over the worst of it but left it down, tucking it behind my ears. My face, though. Ugh. After my crying bouts and make-out session with Julian, my mascara was irreparably smudged, and what lipstick I still had on wasn't quite in the right place anymore. How had I got out of the reunion venue without people staring at me like some kind of sad hooker?

Using some cleanser in a pump bottle, I scrubbed my face clean, then stood back to see the result. Twisting my mouth to the side, I mentally told the girl in the mirror: This is who you are, Ruby Zimmer. Older, wiser, weathered from a challenging but fulfilling life on the road. If he doesn't like it, well, them's the breaks. If Julian was naïve enough to want my eighteen-year-old self, then he'd better get over it pretty quick. I wasn't that girl anymore. I had scars. Inside and out.

Just like him, I realized, my heart softening.

I flicked off the light and ventured back to the living room to face my inevitable fate.

Julian

I carried two mugs of chamomile citrus tea to the living room just as Ruby slid onto the sofa, tucking one bare foot under her thigh. She avoided my gaze, nibbling her freshly scrubbed lips and plucking at the sweatpants she'd put on, along with a pink tank top with some sparkly shit on the front. It was so Deanna and so not Ruby.

I laughed. "Are those Dee's?"

She nodded. "I didn't feel like putting my day clothes on this late. She won't mind, will she?"

"Nah. Course not." I sighed and sank down beside her on the sofa, leaving a couple of feet between us.

"You didn't laugh earlier when I was wearing Deanna's

borrowed frilly white dress and high heels." She quirked a rusty brown eyebrow at me with a wry smile.

I sobered. "That's because you were fucking hot as Hades in them, and you know it." Our gazes met in a sudden intense tangle, and I cleared the cotton from my dry throat.

I could not let my libido decide how this was going to go. I leaned forward to retrieve a mug and hand it to Ruby, then took my own and leaned back, trying to pull my shit back together.

"Oh," she said, "Can I use your phone to send a text? Mine died."

"Mm-hm." I handed it to her.

She opened the text app and then paused, her finger hovering. "Um. Do you know my dad's number?" She knew better than to ask if I communicated with her mother, which was unlikely. It's not that Mrs. Zimmer disliked me, she'd just always seen me as an obstacle in her daughter's career trajectory.

I smiled. "It's in there." I couldn't believe she didn't know at least one of her parents' numbers by heart and told her so with a look.

"They got rid of the old land line." Smiling wryly, she entered her dad's name, and seemed genuinely surprised when his profile popped up. "Have you... spoken to him recently?"

"A few times since I've been back. He came to Dad's funeral."

Her mouth formed an 'o' of surprise. "He never said anything."

I shrugged. "I guess he figured you'd catch up with me sooner or later once you got back to town." I waited a beat, taking a cautious sip of my hot tea. "Did you tell them you were coming back?"

She hummed while thumbing a quick message to her dad, handing back the phone. "Not long before landing. I tend to... not make plans far in advance, because I get yanked around a lot. Something comes up and they want me overseas on pretty short notice. I don't like to get Mom and Dad's hopes up and dash them."

"Have you truly never been back home in ten years?"

She pulled a face. "I did sneak in for a quick visit once about..." Her eyes studied a spot on the ceiling. "About four years ago? Very hush-hush and quick. Even the girls don't know. Mostly we met up overseas. Once in New York. And even then, not very often."

"You've been busy. It's hard to connect with someone who's hanging out in..." I lifted a finger at a time. "Afghanistan, Syria, Crimea, Myanmar, North Africa..." I shrugged. I couldn't begin to list all the places she'd reported from, though I'd watched many of them. I had become a bit of a news junky, when my life allowed it. Working in restaurants tends to eat up one's free time.

"Chile, Peru, Bolivia, Venezuela..." she whispered, her voice tapering off as her eyes drew inward.

"Your dad has always been—" I began.

"You seem very comfortable here." She cut me off. All right then. She turned her cup in her hands, trying to find just the right grip on the hot mug, her eyes evasive, darting. "Are you... have you and Dee ever..." She tapered off, her gaze landing on Deanna's photo booth and worktable in the corner, strewn with electronics and heaped with product samples and clothing still in its packaging.

She didn't really think that. I scoffed, smiling and shaking my head. "Deanna works from home. This is where we laid out my... my business and marketing strategy, I guess you'd say."

"I see." She took a sip of tea, her fingertips tapping the side of the mug. "Are you... making money with this?"

I tilted my head from side to side. "Nothing significant yet. But she's convinced I can make a living at it with sponsorships and endorsements. The new viral videos will attract them like flies to honey, she says. And I don't need much, anyway. It doesn't really cost much to live, since I really do try to walk my talk."

Her brow pinched together. "Meaning?"

"Subsistence farming. I basically live on what I can raise, grow, trade, or find."

"Seriously. You can do that?"

"Mhm. I can't grow coffee or sugar, and I don't have room for wheat, obviously. But I do as much as I can, and buy as locally as possible anything that I can't. And the point is to change your habits. Don't eat the stuff that has to be shipped twelve thousand kilometres, like pineapples, mangos, and avocados.

"Impressive. You're on quite a mission."

Enough evasion. Time to be an adult. I stared at her, letting my gaze roam over her face, her hair, her body, so familiar and yet not. My throat tightened and my eyes stung. I swallowed back the salt that rose on my palate. I filled my lungs, bracing myself.

"When I..." I paused, frowning. "Once I'd become so involved in my work, even though my goals shifted, I remained passionate about what I was doing. My skill, my purpose. It helped me."

"Helped you what?"

"Helped me understand you... your passion." I met her gaze straight on and held it. I wanted her to understand this part of what I was saying. "You always knew what you wanted to do, and I admired that."

Ruby clutched her mug close, blew over the surface and drew a sip of tea, her eyes wary and watchful. "I'm glad you figured it out."

"I came to understand why you chose your ambition, your education. Your career. I really did. Do. That's who you are, and I loved you for that. But I really couldn't understand..." I pressed a fist to my sternum, my ribs closing in on my lungs, making steady breath difficult. "I won't say it didn't hurt me,

Ruby, that you couldn't see a place for me at your side. It hurt. God, it hurt so much when you were gone. Like my heart had been torn from my chest. I didn't think I could go on without you."

Her face went tight, her beautiful full mouth pressing into a tight line.

"Ten years ago, your dreams were my dreams. I would have done anything for you. I expected to." I shrugged, a bitter laugh gusting from my throat. "Once we were married, I'd have gone wherever you needed to be. Stayed by your side. Helped you. I knew as long as we were together, everything else would work out."

Tears welled in her eyes, her chin quivering. "That would have been lovely," her voice was a hoarse whisper. "I believed that once too."

I pulled my lips between my teeth, barely hanging on, and shook my head. I had to keep going, so she understood where I was. Who I was, now. "But I understand, And I don't resent you for that. In fact, I have to thank you. Maybe I wouldn't have become a chef, and discovered my own passion if you never left. But..."

She shrank back into the sofa cushions, as if she could avoid talking about this, as if she could disappear.

"The one thing I need to know. The one thing that I could never reconcile, is what the hell you did with our child."

"What do you think?"

"What was I supposed to think, Ruby? You left me completely in the dark. I certainly didn't see any evidence in the press, nor a hint from our friends, to suggest you have a nine-year-old child in your life. Or maybe everyone I know is really good at lying to me!"

A mewling cry came out of her, and her tea wobbled and slopped onto her lap. She jerked, flapping her hand and I lunged forward to grab it before she burnt herself, setting it and my own on the low coffee table. Her hands came to her bowed face, her shoulders curling, and her cry grew more plaintive.

"I know if you'd kept it, I'd have heard. So I assumed…" My head kept shaking, my disbelief and resentment rising fresh and hot in my chest like a bitter wind. "I assumed you'd terminated the pregnancy, or gave our child up for adoption? That's why your parents whisked you away so fast. You'd have given birth around Christmastime." I shrugged, still baffled. I'd gone through all this in my mind so many times, coming up with nothing. "You were starting to show. Is that why you left so suddenly? To hide it?"

"No," she cried, rocking forward and back, her face a mess of tears now, sobbing and shuddering.

"How could you take my child from me and give it away to strangers?" How dare she? I felt cracks forming on the surface of my composure. Of my control. Maybe I didn't want the answers I'd waited for so long.

"No-o-o."

I grabbed the hair at the back of my head and yanked on it. "Then what? What the hell happened? Help me understand!"

"I never had the baby, Julian."

Blood pounded in my ears. My vision flooded with rage, frustration, resentment, grief. "It was too late for that!" I shouted. "We talked it through. That window had passed. It wasn't what we wanted, anyway. What we'd decided." I gripped her upper arms, peering into her streaming eyes. Could she have been so desperate she'd have done that and kept it from me? "Was it? Did you change your mind?"

Her face folded in anguish, her head shaking from side to side rapidly. Her shoulders shook, and she cried so hard she couldn't speak, but her head continued to shake back and forth, back and forth.

My body went taut, my hands fisting. A fresh sense of betrayal swamped me at the thought of her making these decisions about my child—our child—without me.

"Is that how little you think of me?"

"What else could it be? You realized being with me, and having a baby, would weigh you down. It wasn't the life that you had planned for yourself. We would be an anchor strapped to your leg, and you needed to be free. I know what you wanted, Ruby. We had no secrets. I would've slowed you down. A child would have stopped you in your tracks. Our lives would be completely different."

Her head swung back, her face flushed pink, tears streaming. "No." Her reply was a barely audible squeak. "That's not it."

I glowered at her, my nostrils flaring, waiting. Waiting for some kind of answer that made sense of it all. What could she tell me? There was nothing she could say to me now that would…

Another thought popped suddenly into my mind like a flash of light, shoving aside all my accusations and fears. The cracks opened further. Something I hadn't thought of before. Horrified, I waited for it.

Ruby tilted her tear-streaked face up at me, her mouth contorting as she tried to speak through her sobs. Then she whispered, "I lost her."

Chapter 16

Julian

MY BREATH RUSHED OUT of my lungs, leaving me taut, spiky with shooting pain throughout my body. It was my turn to grimace in pain as my throat tightened, choking me. Confused, disbelieving, I croaked, "Lost her. Our baby."

With a sniffle, she nodded. "Beth and I were a-a-at the spa that day. Everything was…" She lifted her shoulders jerkily. "Everything was b-b-beautiful. And then… suddenly," Ruby couldn't speak then anymore, and gestured vaguely at her legs. "Cramps." Her sobs were silent gasps now. "And bleeding."

At first I didn't hear her words. They didn't penetrate my brain in any meaningful way. A sound like a storm approaching rushed through my ears, filled my head with red and black, acid and bitter.

"I couldn't accept what was happening. I was distraught. Beth drove us to the hospital."

My head heated, my eyes stung with tears, unable to stop myself from crying now. I found myself closing the gap between us, pulling her crumpled form into my embrace, pressing my face against her hair, kissing her, and holding onto her so tightly, my arms shook.

Stroking her back and hair, I asked, "How could that happen? I thought we were safe. Was there an acc... did you fall?"

She moaned into my chest, murmuring, "They said it was a chromosomal abnormality. After. In the midst of it, I knew nothing but panic. Pain and panic. I didn't understand that she was gone."

"Oh, God, Ruby. Why did no one call me?" I rasped. "Beth was with you?"

Her forehead pressed to my shirt, she nodded. "I hardly know anything. They said I was hysterical, in shock. I guess she freaked out and called my parents." A shuddering sob wracked her. After another moment, she settled and leaned back, wiping her face with her palms, dragging her arm across her running nose.

"I wouldn't let them call you. I also think my parents were angry with you, disappointed, thinking we'd been careless. I screamed whenever they suggested it. I guess I was in shock, and a bit mental."

"Ah, fuck, Ruby." Everything inside me broke at once, like glass hitting the floor. My world cracked apart and exploded in shards around me. Nothing fit together, nothing made sense, least of all my emotions, that I'd learned to keep in orderly boxes, lids nailed tight.

"I was... completely irrational. I lost a lot of blood. They said I blacked out. The only part I remember was lying there in the emergency ward, staring at the ceiling, waiting for an ultrasound, I guess, bleeding out. I was alone. It felt like a thousand hours. I felt my heart pumping, felt blood flow out of me with each beat of my heart, feeling life ebbing away like the tide, emptying me. I was as good as dead. And after a while, I started to believe that it was meant to be. That I was meant to be alone. That it was a sign. A sign that... that I couldn't have everything.

That I was a fool to think I could have everything. I was being punished for my arrogance and greed. The choice had been made for me."

"Choice? About us?"

She nodded, then lifted her shoulders helplessly. "I was so clear about my goals, and… it felt like too much. Like I would have been terrible at everything. Mediocre and miserable and compromised and nothing. I wasn't worthy. And then I slid from shock into depression. Numb."

I let out a long, shuddering sigh. I felt so helpless. That she had suffered such a trauma, and I knew nothing. Somehow, I should have known. I should have sensed that she was in trouble, that she needed me. I should have fought harder to see her. I bent my head, hooking my chin over her shoulder, and pulled her into my lap. She curled into a tight ball and I held her, covering her body with as much of mine as I could, wrapping her up safely, and we sat like that, silent, for a few minutes.

"And then."

"All I remember was feeling so ashamed. As if I'd done something terrible."

I jerked back. "What? That's crazy! It wasn't your fault."

"All I could think was how heartbroken you'd be, and if you didn't know, then you wouldn't be sad. I could keep you safe. I don't know. It doesn't make sense. I was in the hospital for a day, day and a half. I don't know how long, but Mom and Dad took me home and nursed me."

I felt her shoulders hitch. "In that yawning void that followed, in that numbness, I realized that all the joy and excitement that I'd felt about us being together forever, about us being a family, it really would've stolen my dream."

My own breath stuck in my chest, and I tensed, waiting for the rest of her words.

"Later… Dad asked me again… if I wanted to see you, or if he should call you. And I…" Ruby lifted her red and swollen eyes to my face, her lips twisting, shuddering. "I told him, no. I made him promise not to call you. I insisted I didn't want you to know."

"Not know what? We'd made a child together. We'd made promises." I tried to keep my breathing steady, but the same old bitter mix of wrenching loss and fury shook me, so that my breath stuttered. "Mom told me you'd gone away for a couple of days for a girls' retreat before the end of summer. I never questioned that. But then it was one excuse after another. You were sleeping. You were hung over. You were packing. And then you were gone. It didn't make any sense. I was bewildered, trying to make sense of events. How could you just vanish? Why weren't you calling me? I went mad with it, imagining all kinds of reasons."

"Somehow in the fog that followed, while my body healed, my mind hardened, and I knew I had to make a clean break. I could never have said goodbye to you, Julian. I could never have left you."

My throat spasmed as fresh pain shot from my heart to my neck to my burning eyes. "But you did leave. What the hell happened to us?"

"Maybe you felt it. The baby."

I grunted, skeptical. "All I knew was I didn't have my Ruby." I stroked her hair, damp from tears and sweat, back from her face. "And then they took you to Wisconsin?"

She nodded. "I didn't plan it that way. When I was well enough. Mom and Dad threw everything I owned into the car and drove me south. I had a residence already booked. They moved me in, set me up while I sat there like a straw man. Mom helped with completing registration and getting organized, then when classes started, Dad left."

I laid back, pulling Ruby down on top of me, holding her tight, stroking my hands up and down her back. My arms tightened around her and pulled her closer. She lay her head on my shoulder, her voice soft and muffled as she went on, pressing her body along mine. Her familiar scent, warm and wet, grounded me.

"Mom stayed with me for over a month. I remember nothing about the first semester. I was on meds. I must have been like a zombie. I have no memories."

I continued to stroke her hair and her back until she calmed, her breathing evening out, the tears on her face drying. "I am sorry I kept the truth from you, Julian. I've never regretted anything more."

"If I'd known, I would have grieved the loss of our daughter with you." I kissed her temple, her cheek, and she burrowed closer, tucking her face against my neck, breathing against my skin, sending tension through my body, awakening it, dredging desire out of the depths of our shared grief. I lifted her hand to my face and kissed her palm and felt a soft mewling moan against my neck.

"I felt enough loss and grief for both of us, Julian."

My mind spun through my memories, visceral and real, of the weeks and months that followed Ruby's disappearance from my life. I'd grieved, gone numb and hardened, too. I took it out on my friends, and on my father. Pleading with her parents for some information, which they stoically denied.

"I went to your house a hundred times, thinking you'd be back and there'd be a perfectly logical explanation. I remember your parents were away for a while. Then one time, Dad answered the door, and he cried when he saw me. He hugged me, said he was sorry, and then just closed the door in my face."

Her arms tightened around me, her tears tracking down my neck, her voice muffled against my shirt. "I just went through the motions for a while until the learning grabbed hold of me. I could shift my focus to my dream again and shut that door behind me, between us."

She shrugged, giving her head a shake, and I understood, as if the events of our own lives came as a surprise. As if they'd happened to someone else. Where had ten years gone?

"I went on year after year, lost myself in study, in the writing. Graduated."

"How did you end up in Europe?"

"In my last year, I did an exchange year at the University of Amsterdam. I made connections overseas. Went on a trip, wrote a piece, got it published. I got my first job in London through an acquaintance. Did some contract work, got some essays published, and that led to assignments. The rest is history."

Indeed. It was only when I'd finally accepted that she was gone and never coming back that I embraced my own new reality and took steps forward to have a life of my own.

I shifted to the side, sliding her off of me, wedged against the back of the sofa, and took her face between my hands, stroking her brows with my thumbs. Her face and breath were hot and wet from her tears. The next thing I knew, our lips were locked together in a hungry, needy kiss, biting, sucking, fighting as though our lives depended on the connection between us.

Her body molded more closely to mine, her leg sliding over my thigh, pulling me closer, pressing my stiffening groin to her fiery core. I responded by jerking closer, blood rushing to my cock in delirious welcome. My leg slid between hers of its own accord, finding its place, and we rocked against each other. My tongue swept into her mouth, feeling the inside of her, once as familiar to me as my own body.

Her arms slid behind my neck and applied pressure to the back of my head, touching our foreheads together as we paused to share a heated breath, our gazes locked. My hand caressed her thigh, her hip, tracing up her ribcage—too thin—my fingertips counting her ribs as they slid over the ridges. I pulled my mouth away, staying close, sharing breath as my hand covered her full breast, resting there, feeling her tightening nipple against my palm with satisfaction.

I tore my mouth away from hers, gasping. "Ruby, Ruby." I trailed kisses over her jaw, pressing her chin up as I sucked on her neck, one hand grabbing hungrily at her breast. We were almost at the point of no return, our gazes meeting, burning with love, pain and desire. Being swept up in burning lust felt like a healing balm over the fresh wound of our lost child. Searing, it came almost like a hot iron to cauterize our wounds, allowing us to move forward together.

"My body never forgot you, Ruby," I whispered. "I'm mad as hell, torn apart with sadness, but I can't stop my body from wanting you. I'm possessed. Since I saw you yesterday, I've been in a fever. I've been hard non-stop just knowing you're here in the same city. It's driving me crazy."

"It's the same for me, Jules. There has never been anyone to replace you. I might as well have been in a monastery these past ten years."

***

Ruby

At my words, he pulled away, his face hard, his eyes dark with desire, and a frightening intensity I had never seen in them before.

"You're not saying you haven't had sex in ten years. I might wish it were so, but that's—"

I scoffed. "No." I quirked a brow at him, smiling, then sobering at the look in his eyes. My voice dropped to a whisper. "But I haven't made love in ten years."

He swallowed, his midnight blue eyes shining with the sheen of tears. Shifting to stand, he lifted me in his arms. The sensation was strange, being lifted and held like a child. Julian was bigger than I remembered, stronger than he looked, I supposed, from his farm work, and I felt small and safe as his long legs ate up the distance to Deanna's bedroom. He set me down by the bed, frowning at the broad expanse of pink, and fisted her duvet, yanking on it, tossing it to the floor in a shimmering heap of satiny fabric.

Then he faced me, jutting his jaw with a quirk of a smile that was almost predatory, stepping closer, setting his fingertips on my bare shoulders. His chest rose and fell as his touch slowly traced my neck, my arms, the sides of my breasts, my ribs, sending shivers of desire racing over my skin. When his hands reached my hips, he gripped me and lifted, tossing me bodily onto the bed like a bale of hay. Before my gasp of surprise left my lips, he flung himself on top of me, both of us bouncing on the bed like kids on a trampoline. I exploded in laughter as he growled, wrapping his arms tightly around me and burrowed against my neck, his beard scruff scratching and tickling.

It was just the thing to break the tension and dispel some of the melancholy that hung over us. I couldn't recall the last time I'd laughed unreservedly. Or felt so at ease in someone's company. That was Julian. He was my person.

Where had that girl gone? How had I forgotten what it felt like to completely let go?

Frenzied, he grabbed me like a fire flaring on dry tinder, swamping us both in desire, a hunger so intense it would never burn out. Both our hands roamed, groped in a life-and-death quest for familiar textures, handholds, comforting shapes, signalling both need and ownership.

Julian had never been a rough lover with me. Sex was always hot and energetic, not surprising, since we'd been teenagers, but still sweet, caring, tender. He was always the most attentive, nurturing lover. That was half the attraction. Julian's gentle, knowing hands, so sensitive, so capable, so empowered to awaken in me a primal desire. Knowing he was burning with desire for me, but holding back, always giving me what I needed first, always taking care of me—was so hot.

Now, though, he was a force of nature. A storm. And I sensed a new darkness in him, the weight of his maturity, and the scars of his pain. If it were possible for him to be even sexier, even more virile, hot-blooded, ardent, more essentially man—then I didn't know how. I became a molten pool of desire under his midnight gaze, under his wise and possessive hands.

Our shirts disappeared, our hands roaming hungrily over each other's hot skin as our mouths fused again in a deep kiss that went on and on, desperate, seeking. I stroked my fingers over the intriguing ink that marked my Julian's skin. Ink I had never seen before. My eyes raked the patterns, searching for clues about his life, his journey, the people, maybe, who had helped to shape the man he was now.

Then I saw it, my hand freezing in place.

In amongst some weaving vines and flowers and maps that adorned his chest continuing around his left arm, was a smallish black and grey anatomical heart with a fancy dagger plunged clean through it from top to bottom. Nothing overly morbid, very artful black blood dripped from the wound, and on the hilt of the dagger was a heart-shaped gemstone, blood red, the only spot of colour in the design. It was easy to miss it in its bed of thorns and roses. It didn't take much imagination to figure out the symbolism. As I stared at it, he lifted his hand to cover mine while meeting and holding my gaze, pressing my hand flat over the design, and sliding it down.

I felt tears searing my eyes. The compulsion to get closer to him released me from my usual reserve, and I explored his mouth, his tongue, his teeth, unreservedly. Hungry for more of him. He tasted subtly of wine and citrus, his scent masculine and earthy, his skin as I licked him, tangy with salt.

He raised himself onto his elbows, looking down at my breasts, his fingers stroking lightly over the edges of the fancy bra Deanna had lent me. Shaking his head, he murmured, "I'll have to send Dee a thank-you note." Chuckling, he lowered his face to the valley between my breasts, breathing in, dragging his tongue across my skin, moaning. Sliding his hands beneath me, the clasp of the bra opened like magic, and he slipped the straps off of my shoulders, lifting the cups away, baring my breasts.

"You taste so good. I'm in heaven."

His breath came out long, slow and pained as his gaze caressed my naked curves before he brought his hands near. Again his fingertips touched me first, featherlight, worshipful. Dropping his mouth to my skin, he sprinkled delicate kisses over the curving flesh of my breasts, under and along the sides, his fingers drawing their edges. My nipples puckered and pebbled, screaming for his attention while he teased, touching them only with his hungry gaze.

At last he kissed first one erect nipple, then the other before his hot mouth finally connected. He licked from below, scooping my left nipple into his mouth and pulling long and hard, while his fingers grasped both breasts, firmly and softly at once. The fingers of his left hand brushed over the other nipple before pinching, pulling and gently twisting it into a peak of ecstasy. In an instant, I was incoherent with desire, his attentions sending jolts of pleasure through my core, setting my pussy afire, molten with need. I clenched my muscles, writhing, suddenly wet and in desperate need of him.

A whimpering moan emerged from my throat as I squirmed under his hands and seeking mouth. He switched sides, intensifying the impact of his touch, and I gasped, my voice hoarse and needy. "Jules. Jules. I need you."

"I know, sweetheart." He backed away, pulling a moan of longing from my throat at the loss of his touch. His hands didn't lift from my skin, though, only slid down, hooking into the soft waistband of the sweats and achingly slowly pulling them down, down, over my hips and lower, until they disappeared onto the floor. His own pants dropped seconds later, my gaze drawn to his tented boxers like an eagle to its prey. I reached for him.

He shoved my hand away. "There's no way I'm rushing this, Ruby. I've dreamt of you for years. Literally dreamt, waking hard and sweaty and throbbing at the memory of your body.

Missing the feel and smell of you like air. I–" His words choked in his throat as he grimaced. "Oh, my Ruby."

A primal growl emerged from his chest as he sat over me on his haunches, his gaze and his fingers exploring newly revealed parts. His strong hands roamed, his calloused fingertips driving me mad with sensation, his hard palms caressing my ribs, my belly, my mound, sending heat radiating through me. One hand slid back up to hold a breast while his mouth came down to meet the gooseflesh of my stomach, laving and nibbling and planting soft kisses as he travelled its terrain. His other hand slid beneath me, cupping my ass, his fingers curling hungrily between my legs, his long fingers caressing my pussy from behind. He'd always said that was his favourite place, that crack beneath my heart-shaped ass, where he could slide a finger and feel my heat, like a promise.

"Fuck, you're wet for me. You want me." His voice cracked, hoarse, as if he were in pain.

"I am. I'm aching for you, Jules." I spread my legs, inviting him closer, needing him next to me, inside me. He was like a drug that held me captive in its grip, and my body remembered the feel of him under my hands, the feel of his hands on me, so strong, so safe, so perfect. Made for me.

He shifted his weight, moving between my knees, pressing my thighs apart. He dragged his chin slower, scratching over the silky fabric of my panties, dropping between my legs, his hot breath penetrating the thin fabric to envelop me in a cloud of heat. My hips bucked, pressing closer to his mouth. "Jules! Julian. I need you."

His hands gripped my thighs, thumbs possessively dipping into the valleys to either side of my aching pussy, spreading me further as he sucked me through the wet silk, his tongue confidently tracing my creases, his teeth grazing my throbbing clit through the fabric. There was no hesitation in his movements. He knew my body, knew his way around, and knew what set me on fire.

Moaning, I pressed against his hands as they held me against the bed. Then he hooked one thumb across the crotch of the panties, yanking them aside, drawing a groan from both of us. Then his lips were on me, and I was home again, for the first time in ten long years, trembling at the very idea that this was Julian between my legs. My Julian.

"God. My Ruby." His gravelly voice vibrated against my sensitive skin, just as his tongue laved my folds, dipping into my wet heat, drawing another moan from my throat.

Quivering uncontrollably, I raked my fingers through his hair, tugging on it, pulling on his shoulders. "Jules!" My pulse throbbed in my clit as he took it between his lips, flicking, nipping and sucking, while his thumb dipped into my wet core, driving a spike of exquisite agony through my spine, drawing my muscles into a full body spasm, pulling a keening scream from me as I trembled, suspended in a state of bliss.

Julian kept his mouth pressed to me through it all, like an embrace, taking in my release. When I drifted back down from the ceiling, my limbs limp as a popped balloon, he crawled back up my body and wrapped his arms around me, tucking me against his body like an envelope around a love letter.

Even though I knew he still burned with need, he waited patiently, revelling in my release, in my pleasure, as I swam in it. His words came back to me, as if he'd spoken them just yesterday. *I feel your bliss like my own, my love. I'm there with you through it all, Ruby. When you're satisfied, I'm content.*

I knew what he meant. I felt it too. A love so selfless, a union so complete, that we shared in each other's happiness, sadness, pain and bliss, as one body. The very memory sent warmth coursing through my veins, and his need fuelled my own second wind. This was only the beginning. My Julian waited for me, and I wanted him.

I reached down between our bodies, taking his hard, throbbing shaft in my hands, embracing him. "Tell me you have a condom."

He grunted, closing his eyes. "Wouldn't come near you without one." He scooted off the bed, digging into his pants, and was back in a blink. I angled up to watch him sheath his gorgeous cock for me, caressing his thighs, reaching for his sac and gently caressing it as I waited. The moment he was ready, I lay back, lifting my knees and spreading them, opening myself to him.

"Fuck, Ruby, I'm going to pass out. My head is exploding. I can't believe this is you. This is us." He dove at me, one hand on either side of my shoulders, holding his body over mine, just an inch of heated electrically charged air between us.

He angled his mouth over mine, kissing me gently, lovingly, his tongue pressing into my mouth, betraying his desperation, mine answering by entwining with his, fucking first with our hearts.

I stroked his tensed arms, the bulges of his biceps, his pulsing veins. "You've grown up, boy," I murmured, caressing his contoured chest and rippled abs in awe. "I couldn't have imagined you being more beautiful than you were. But I didn't know what a man felt like." His arms trembled as I reached down and nestled him against my opening, sliding it back and forth. I looked up, capturing his gaze. "Now."

In reply, he looked into my eyes, as if he could see right through me. Without breaking eye contact, he pressed forward, into me, slow but steady, unhesitating, filling me up, until he was fully buried, our pelvic and hip bones pressed tightly together. He held there, and we just looked at each other, connected.

"My God, Ruby, I love… love the way you feel. Nobody feels like you."

He held me in his gaze, lovingly, and I believed him, as I had always believed him. He made me feel precious and true, and I knew I had never stopped loving him. I couldn't blame him, but he did not say those words to me, and I didn't have the courage to say them to him. To open myself up completely. Not now. Not yet.

What was also true? I saw it clearly now. What I'd become in order to survive. Hard, defended, bottled up. I hadn't let go for ten years. I'd held on so tight, I'd forgotten what it felt like - to fall, to float, to trust.

His face buckled in pain as his eyes filled with tears and he slowly began to move, pulling out and slipping back into me. Achingly slowly, out, out to the edge, and back in, all the way in deep and hard, pressing his weight against my clit with just the right pressure, just the right amount of friction. Fire built and shot through my core. I burned for him, my head tilting back to give him access as he kissed, licked and sucked my neck. We plundered each other's bodies, connecting up parts that belonged together.

My desire was so complete, and I felt his was too, that our movement, our slowness, was more about limiting sensation that stimulating it. Holding back, riding the edge, prolonging that incredible, unique feeling that we had been gifted. I knew that now. I'd had other lovers, and no one brought me to such heights of quivering want, of ecstasy, the way Julian did. Always had. But we'd been so young, and inexperienced, we couldn't have known then that ours was a one-in-a-million connection.

By unspoken consent, we stretched it out as long as we could, teasing and edging, but there was only so much a body could take. I felt us floating up together rung by rung, coming apart stroke by stroke, cell by cell until, our gazes still locked in awe and wonder, we crested the deluge of sensation together.

After that, no words were necessary. Our connection was complete. Nothing had changed, and yet nothing would ever be the same.

Chapter 17

Julian

THE FUNNY THING about sleep is that even an hour or two wipes your short-term memory clean, so that you begin anew upon awakening, at least for a minute or two while you make sense of your world. Mine had irrevocably changed in one night. Again.

After making love for the first time in a decade, Ruby and I had fallen asleep like an old married couple, completely at ease with each other. Utterly unselfconscious in our intimacy, as if the years fell away like scales, leaving something smooth and young exposed, unmarked.

I awoke at my usual hour, more rested and relaxed than I remembered being in ages. It had been only a couple of hours since we'd slipped into exhausted slumber after another exquisite round of lovemaking, the sort of which I had never experienced. Not even with the beautiful, nubile version of the woman beside me. There was something sublimely deep and poignant about the experience. I don't know if it was that our mood was tinged with melancholy or that we brought the gravitas of our experience to it.

I sat on the edge of the bed, watching Ruby sleep like the dead. She curled like a kitten around her pillow, one foot cast off the side of the mattress, as she had always slept. I'd always admired how tough she was on the outside when she was, in fact, soft and sweet inside. I imagined that sleeping so soundly had helped her survive in her tumultuous life of travel and work in what can only have been a host of less than comfortable circumstances. After watching her twitch and jump at every light and sound during the reunion, I had worried that perhaps she did not sleep well. Something, I couldn't imagine what, clearly tortured her mind.

I didn't have the heart to wake her now, though I had to leave. My animals would not wait for my indulgence and I hadn't arranged for anyone to come to the farm and care for them. Poor planning, but I truly had not imagined, in my wildest dreams, spending the night with Ruby.

Finding my clothes in the dim dawn light, I quickly dressed, slipping silently from the room. I searched for paper and pen on Deanna's work table, bending to scrawl a message for Ruby when she woke.

I left the note on the coffee table where we'd sat, hoping she found it there. On the quiet dawn drive out of the city, back to the farm, I thought about our reunion, what it meant. What did I want it to mean?

As I pulled into the gravel drive, Finnegan bolted from his doggy door, leaping and dancing with joy at my return, and I felt my chest warm, and my face stretch into a broad smile. No matter what life dished out, my dog always made it better. That was one thing about having a home base and staying put, something I couldn't have for all my years moving from job to job overseas.

"Hey, boy," I greeted him as I hopped out of the van.

"Arf," he replied, and continued talking to me as we entered the farmhouse, filling me in on his time alone.

"Good job, buddy. I knew the place would be safe in your paws."

After quickly changing into rough clothing, I fed Finnegan while waiting for a pot of coffee to brew.

Before leaving the house, I grabbed the overfilled compost buckets from all the party prep. Then, with a tin mug in hand, we made our way to the pig pen first, tossing it in and causing a stir as the two older pigs snuffled over. "Morning, Clover. Hey there, Mack." With little spotty Acorn nosing around, I rinsed out the buckets and set them out to drain and pick up later.

"Come on, Finn."

Then we headed to the goat barn. I'd been a little worried about the young alpaca, leaving it alone overnight in a strange environment, but he seemed quiet enough as I passed his pen.

The goats bounded out, tumbling over each other when I opened the barn door, pulling a laugh from my throat like they always did. The alpaca I had led inside to a separate pen yesterday afternoon, with some difficulty. Fortunately, Arnie had left the halter and lead on him to give me a chance to get used to him. Or him to me. But first the goats.

They all dispersed quickly, kicking and bucking out into the pasture area with Finnegan on their heels. He circled around, telling them what for, and returned to me a few minutes later. I always added a fresh hay bale to their feeder, and between the six of them they ate most of it every day on top of foraging. Then I drained and filled their water trough and added a splash of apple cider vinegar.

As we approached the alpaca's pen to open it up, it hung back against the far wall, humming. "Come on, you. Might as well get to know your roomies." Arnie assured me he'd be fine with the goats, who would keep him company until I added more alpaca to my herd. Hah. As if.

Swinging the gate wide, I encouraged it to come toward me. "Come on. Out you go." I stepped back and waited. It took a few tentative steps towards me, dipping its neck nervously, its huge brown eyes following Finnegan's movements. "Okay, Finn. Go on outside for a bit." I shooed him out to hang with the goats and reached in for the lead to help guide the newcomer.

Once I tugged, he followed tentatively, but just as we emerged into daylight, I felt a tug on the lead. I grabbed it quickly before it took off, pulling back and unclipping it from the harness so it couldn't drag it around in the mud, or tangle and trip itself. "There you go. Hyah!"

It stepped away, circling around, taking in the other animals and then turned back to me. Its ears were twitching, and mostly flattened back, and I had the sense that it was uneasy. Finnegan made his way back towards us and I lifted my palm to hold him off a moment longer. He stopped in his tracks, but the alpaca noticed him, of course. Then suddenly, it raised its fluffy head high, lifting its toothy hairy chin to the sky, making a weird throaty mwa-mwah noise that wasn't the typical humming I'd been told to expect. I watched it warily for a moment, then suddenly jerked back as a stream of green spit flew in my direction, hitting me square in the chest with a splat.

"Ugh! Fuck." I lurched back, giving the demon more space. "Bugger off, you!" Eyeing the foamy green goop dripping down my shirt, I was grateful I didn't get it in the face. I thought they only spit when they were fighting. Or, I guess, super stressed. "Get on. Go play with your goat friends and leave me alone." I picked up a handful of hay to wipe the goo from my shirt. "Come on Finn. Let's leave these ruminants to their business."

As I was in the habit of doing, I took a stroll to check the veggie garden and then meandered through the apple orchard, monitoring for projects that needed my attention later. There were always projects on a farm. A bit of fence that needed mending, some pruning, weeding or messes to clean up. Being out of doors, in nature, soothed me like nothing else, and calmed my thoughts. Or, while not calm exactly, they at least began to fall into some kind of order and perspective.

Everything had been in a turmoil for two days, since I'd seen Ruby again, and had just wound me tighter and tighter. Last night was amazing, but not easy. Despite the shattering sex we'd shared, my gut was still twisted in knots, my neck and jaw tense with worry. I could hardly breathe for the tightness in my chest.

What did it all mean? What was going to happen?

Being together confirmed the feeling I'd always had, that Ruby and I were made for each other - two halves of a whole - but it changed nothing. I still had more questions than answers. Somehow, I thought once my suspicions and fears about the baby had been confirmed, or denied, as it turned out, that I'd feel more settled. Instead, I was wrought by doubt and, strangely, simmering with resentment even more than before. Given all she'd suffered, shouldn't I be feeling more sympathetic? More understanding?

I got that she was in shock, but it still hurt that she'd pushed me away. Why shut me out when she needed me most? Why did she exclude me from such a traumatic loss, one I shared, and head off into the wide world without a backward glance? The answers didn't make me feel better.

And worse, even if I never entirely understood why she left, I had even greater doubts about why she'd come back. After all this time. She never got to that. What did it mean? Surely she could not be planning to stay. Nothing about Ruby—her work, her character, or her circumstances—would lead me to that conclusion.

Leaving me wondering, what just happened? Was last night just for old times' sake? Was it just a sentimental pity fuck in the end? It sure hadn't felt that way in the moment.

It occurred to me then to wonder where my grandmother's ring had ended up. She didn't wear it, obviously. She hadn't mentioned it either. She certainly had never returned it, though it was a treasured family heirloom. Maybe she lost it. It felt like an ominous sign.

We strolled to the chicken coop last; I put out feed and then gathered up the eggs into my shirt while the hens were distracted. "Seven! Enough for a quiche for lunch, maybe? That'd be nice for Ruby, wouldn't it boy?" If she showed up. I glanced at my watch.

Ruby belonged out there, engaged with the outside world, in pursuit of her next grand adventure or her heart-wrenching humanitarian story.

And me? I belonged here on the farm, with my animals, in my hometown, with my own worthy causes. Our lives didn't mesh any better now than they ever had. Ironically, I'd come full circle, returning to my roots just in time to cross paths again with my one true love.

Unless…

Maybe she wanted a change? Maybe she needed a home base? Maybe if I showed her my home, my life now, my mission, she'd… she'd what? I didn't know what to expect, but the turning nausea in my gut warned me not to expect much. Contrary to my tortured, desperate, hopeful thoughts, my body was already preparing itself for rejection and abandonment.

But I could deal with that. I had before, and I could do it again. And my life would go on as before, without Ruby.

***

Ruby

Jarred awake suddenly by a loud bang, a scream left my throat before I had a chance to process my surroundings— pink, white, disconcertingly feminine, and definitely not mine —and remembered why I was here. Deanna crashed noisily into her bedroom and found me standing naked on the far side of the bed with the duvet pulled up to my chin, disoriented.

I'd slept! My head felt clear in a way it hadn't in so long.

My nights of late had been cut short by insomnia and night-mares, my cumulative fatigue pressing down on my mood.

As memories of our night together shot back to the front of my mind, and my nerve endings caught up with memories of their own, I only knew that I'd been utterly sated from the intensity of our reunion, and felt relaxed and safe in his arms.

Safe enough to sleep deeply for the first time in ages.

Only then did it occur to me to wonder where Julian had disappeared to.

"What time is it?" I croaked.

"Ruby?" Deanna stood blinking. She wore an oversized sports jersey over her gauzy dress from the night before and was kicking off her high heels. "Jeez, girl, you scared the crap out of me. I didn't realize you were staying over."

"Quinn gave me the keys so I could change and…" I grimaced. "Sorry to impose. She said you'd gone home with Zach, and I really needed to crash." Should I mention Julian stayed with me? I tugged the sheet from the bed and wrapped it around my naked body, dropping the quilt and inching closer to the door as Deanna dropped her bag and stripped off her clothes, tossing them here and there as she stepped toward the bathroom with her long slender legs. "God, I need a shower. You all right for a bit?"

"Mm-hmm." I shot a glance toward the open bathroom door, praying that a naked Julian wasn't in there either. A second later, Deanna disappeared into the room without inci-dent, and I heard the water start. Then I realized I had to pee something awful, so I followed her in. "Hey, can I use the toilet before you start? I don't think I can wait."

She was already sitting on it, her messy blonde head in her hands. She grumbled, "Sure, sure. Sec."

A minute later, we'd swapped places, and with a sigh, I relaxed and let my clenched muscles go. I blew out through my puffed cheeks. Where did Julian go? Why didn't he wake me?

By the time I'd done with the toilet and washed my hands,

Deanna had stripped off her underwear and stepped into the shower, steam billowing out over the glass wall. It looked fantastic, but I'd have to wait my turn. Besides, Dee looked like she needed it more than me. "Feeling rough?"

She groaned, turning her face into the stream of hot water, her hands to her head. "I can't believe I did that again."

"I gather it's happened before?"

"Too many times." Her words were garbled as she lifted her face to the stream, raking her hands through her wet hair, eyes closed.

"I'll see about making coffee. I think we both need some." I left her to her cleansing ritual and dragged the sheet to the kitchen, glancing around for evidence of our tryst. Used tea bags on a saucer. My gaze jumped to the coffee table where we sat and snagged on a piece of notepaper tucked under our dirty mugs. Aha!

I wondered if he'd gone out for coffee or food and was coming back while I searched through Deanna's cupboards for coffee. Unsuccessful, I abandoned the effort and went to pick up what I presumed to be Julian's note.

His familiar handwriting hit me in the stomach like a fist. So many details about Julian were such a deep part of my growing up, I could hardly separate him from myself. Our lives and memories were braided together like strands of wool, all the colours blending into one glowing rainbow, one integral whole.

RUBY,

Good morning, my beautiful goddess.

I couldn't bear to wake you. My animals need me, so I'm heading home to do farmer stuff. Come out as soon as you get yourself together. I assumed you'd want a shower and change of clothes. Finnegan and I will wait for you. You remember where we are.

Julian

• • •

HE'D SCRAWLED a heart in front of his name, like he always used to, and I couldn't help but wonder if it still meant the same thing. Did he love me still? How could he? After last night, I could confidently say I was as much in love with him as I had ever been. I hardly knew him, had learned just the slightest sliver about his last ten years, and yet he was as much the beautiful boy I'd fallen for when I was fifteen. He was everything that I admired and craved, and had missed. I realized how much time I'd spent thinking about him over the long years, and how I'd held him in a kind of preserved bubble, just the way I'd left him.

And yet, he was harder, wiser, stronger, and more reserved. He held himself back. Under his grieving and longing and lust, I felt his anger and his hurt. I'd done that to him.

A burning corkscrew of sorrow shot up from my chest, tightening my throat, and shocking my eyes with hot tears.

I couldn't read him anymore. He no longer wore his heart on his sleeve.

Had I ruined any chance at happiness in a careless moment of shock, grief, and confusion all those years ago?

But he wanted to spend more time with me. He wanted me to come to the farm. Maybe it wasn't too late for us. Maybe healing was possible, and a new beginning.

I was beginning to understand what I needed and was searching for. But was it fair to impose on him this way? Did he want this tired, broken version of me? I didn't know, but I needed to find out. I needed to know if he would take me back, because if he wouldn't... then I didn't know what I'd do.

Deanna emerged, wrapped in a fluffy white towel, her hair up in another, looking like a model for some high-end shampoo or spa. Then her face cracked open in a gigantic yawn, ruining the picture.

"You look better." I smiled.

"Getting there. You want to shower?"

"I do, if that's okay. I struck out with coffee."

"Yeah. I usually get it from Quinn's café. I'm there so often. We'll head over there after, if you like."

"Sure. I've got to… I'll…" I didn't know what to try and explain first, but tucked Julian's note behind my back as I stepped toward the bedroom.

Deanna noticed though, her eyes narrowing. Then she lifted her chin and looked around, taking in details she'd missed in her fog earlier. The two mugs on the coffee table, the wildly messed bed, with its bedding mostly pushed onto the floor. "Ooohhhh…" She nodded. "Huh. Now I understand." She flashed a smile at me, her gaze boring into my eyes, trying to get a reading.

I felt my face flush with heat, and swallowed. "I'm, ah, heading to the farm. Later."

She laughed, a high light tinkling sound that lifted my spirits and warmed my chest. Following me into the bedroom, she disappeared into her huge walk-in closet with only, "Hurry, I'm starving. Do you need something to wear?"

"No." I laughed and went to shower. I was happy with yesterday's clothes for now. I'd be back at my folks soon enough, and be able to change.

NO ONE WAS around when I got in, so I went to my room, plugged in my phone; and changed my clothes; I chose my usual leggings, tunic, vest, and Blundstone's that made me feel safe and at home in my body and in the world. It was nice to dress up like a girl and get all pretty last night, but it wasn't me. Being androgynous could be a lifesaver in my work. And some-times familiar clothing was the only comfort to be found in an alien environment, so I had my attachments.

I grabbed my laptop and headed for the kitchen, interested in finding something to eat while I caught up on email. I may also have checked out Julian's Insta profile, smiling at the charming gentleman farmer photos of him with his hair all windswept, his face stubbled; I sighed a little as shivery warmth slid up and down my spine, and swirled around my pussy. I squirmed in my chair, sipping my coffee, remembering his touch and feel.

Then I fell down a rabbit hole of videos of Julian feeding his baby goats, them climbing all over him like a jungle gym, videos of Julian cooking, just listening to his sexy voice saying things like lovely juices, delicious silky emulsion, and creamy unctuous texture. I nearly fell off my chair. He made food so sexy; it was a revelation. I wondered if he learned to talk about food that way in culinary school, in European kitchens, or whether it was all part of Deanna's brilliant marketing plan to get millions of swooning fans for Julian's movement. Whatever it was, I could see why he'd gone viral. It was addictive to watch.

Mom wandered in after an hour, filled her coffee cup and stood eyeing the scene in front of her; me with my laptop and papers spread out, my plate, crumbs, and crumpled napkin.

"Hi," I said, smirking at her, daring her to ask if I was planning to clean up after myself. I wasn't a teenager anymore, but I doubted she had changed much in the last ten years. "Busy day?"

"The usual." she set her mug down and swept my debris away, stacking it in the sink, and I chuckled to myself. She couldn't help herself, I guess.

"You guys got my text?"

"From Julian's phone. Yes."

I huffed out a laugh. "Oh, you noticed that, did you?"

With her face pinched up like she'd sucked a battery, she replied, "How could we miss it?"

I smiled, waiting for it.

"Did you enjoy the evening?"

I nodded, "It was... interesting. Great to see everyone. Not the best place to catch up with my closest friends, but a good warm up."

"You spent the night with Julian?"

"We needed a private place to talk. Deanna was out, so we went to her place."

She hummed, picked up her mug and sipped, her gaze studying me, thoughts and opinions swimming behind her sharp eyes. I knew she still carried some of the guilt for the way they handled things, but I also would have hoped she'd believe I could deal with it, after all I'd seen and done.

"Where's Julian now?"

"Home. I'm going to head out to the farm in a while to… see it. See his set up."

Her eyes narrowed. "What do you think you're doing, Ruby?"

I scoffed and sat back. She wasn't asking about this minute, sitting at my laptop, or even about my plans for the afternoon. Not in that tone. I leaned my head into my hand and peered up at her. "Hell if I know, Mom. I'm trying to figure it out, remember?"

She pursed her lips, her tongue stroking over her teeth thoughtfully. "Well, I'm worried, Ruby."

What else was new? "About?"

"You seem… off. You've never hesitated before. I wonder what you're doing with your career suddenly. You're at the top of your game now. This is no time to ease off the gas."

I sighed, stroking and tapping my keyboard, listening to the gentle clack-clack of the keys, a self-soothing habit of mine. She was right. She was always right, a voice in my head grumbled. That voice bore an uncanny resemblance to my mother's.

But was she? What did Mom really know about what I'd been through, and what my work life was like? She only saw the polished, finished product, like everyone else in the world. Few people knew what happened behind the broadcasted reports. Or what I went through to get those stories. Phoenix probably had an inkling. Aside from that, Mom still believed my motivation for my career choice was the high-profile status associated with it, because that's what mattered to her, when all I'd ever cared about was giving a voice to those dispossessed by war and strife. And an opportunity to see the world. Perhaps it was psychological, or maybe biological, but I wondered if I'd experienced enough novelty for one lifetime.

Was that why I felt so numb?

We stared at each other for another minute, not speaking, both of us waiting for answers. Without warning, her face pinched up again and, blinking rapidly, she strode out and back to her home office. I bent my head to my laptop, scanning through more of the emails that had piled up.

Oh, shit. Oh, no.

My assignment editor with the Times. I clicked it open, scanning quickly.

Zimmer

Report from Middle East Bureau Chief just in. Shit hitting the fan all over the region. They need an extra pair of boots on the ground. I'm sure you'll find a good story or two. You up for it?

Richard

MY BREATH STUCK in my chest while I absorbed the words. Richard typically had to make personnel calls within a matter of days, if not hours. This message had arrived at one AM. He'd be champing at the bit already, no doubt, not having heard back from me yet. I quickly scanned, and sure enough, there were two more messages that came in afterwards.

But I'd negotiated a month off after everything in South America went down. I wasn't ready, and I was only halfway through it. Not that Richard cared two pins for my private life, or my need for R and R.

Was I ready? Had I got the rest I needed? I felt the familiar thrill of adrenaline at the prospect of a fresh challenge and sat with it for a moment. A healthy fear was always part of the anticipation, but maybe this was different.

I quickly typed out a reply, asking when he needed a decision, and when I'd need to fly out if I accepted the assignment. At least the time it took to exchange a couple of emails would buy me some time to think. A few hours, at least. Not that I expected clarity about my future to materialize suddenly this afternoon.

The problem was twofold. I really didn't know if what I was feeling was going to wear off, with time, or... I don't know. Was this terror that gripped my stomach my new normal? Was this damage permanent?

Did Phoenix have answers for me? Should I call him? Would it help?

These days all I could think about were the correspondents who didn't come home. Pile, Capa, Silva's colleagues, Pearl, Colvin, Foley, spinning in a continuous loop in my mind. I had no wish to be remembered on the wall of the Newseum, or to return home blown to shreds by a mine. I cared and was committed, but was I willing to risk everything? Was this job all I wanted? My success, the fact that my face and name were well known, increased the risk for me with each successive assignment. Everybody knew that. It had been no accident that they had taken me in Venezuela. I'd been targeted.

My other option, accepting the book contract from Maclean's, was no less terrifying. I felt trapped between what I believed they wanted from me and my truth. Which story would I tell? What would I have the courage to do in the end? And would I be able to live with it?

Maybe Phoenix was wrong, and it was too late for change. Maybe I ought to keep doing what I've been doing. I'd achieved a rare success. Why throw that away now?

Who was right? Mom or Phoenix?

Why ask for trouble? Wouldn't it be easier to keep going? I knew how to do this. But... it was different now. I couldn't seem to remember what it felt like to burn with curiosity and compassion; alive to the point of recklessness with courage and conviction, ready to cross any bridge to get my story. Now, I felt only fear.

Visceral memories of my capture in the Venezuelan jungle came to me at random times. It had been perhaps just a few hours, but it could have been minutes or days. Either way, I was convinced my life was over. When I thought I was about to have my throat slit and be tossed off the truck, only one thought had filled my mind. Only one regret. Julian.

And here I was, alive. Home again. What was I going to do about Julian? I had to be honest with him, and he was waiting for me.

I'd just grabbed my bag and jacket, ready to head out when I heard the shouts.

Chapter 18

Julian

As the afternoon wore on, my doubts and insecurities started to get the better of me. How had I convinced myself that this would be easy? Finding a handful of mushrooms under the oldest apple trees, I'd gathered the eggs, cleaned up, and made a quiche for our lunch. Was she even coming?

"Face it. She's not coming, Finn." From his spot on the rug under the dining table, he lifted his head slightly at my words, his eyebrows twitching.

I frowned at the quiche cooling on the counter. "I guess we're having mushroom quiche for dinner."

Finnegan stood up, slunk over to me and leaned against my leg in sympathy, his tongue lolling.

"I know. I promised you could meet her. I'm sad about that too. You're a great guy. She'd like you. And I know you'd like her too."

He sat on my foot with a heavy sigh, mirroring my own sentiment.

"Well, we can't sit around all day. Let's get some chores done, huh?"

By the time I had my feet shoved into rubber boots, Finn was standing by the door, tail wagging, and we stomped out together. There was always something to do around the farm, and no better way to distract myself than physical labour.

"Last night was good, though, Finn. I'm not gonna lie. It was tough, at times, but… you know. That was to be expected, right? But Ruby and I are so good together. We really fit. I'd forgotten how well." I shook my head as we strode past the vegetable garden towards the animal pens, thinking about what Ruby confessed to me last night.

I'd spent ten years imagining reasons, yet somehow it had never occurred to me she'd experienced grief like that. The loss of our baby hit me hard, as though it had just happened, and I was still processing it. All these years I'd been seeking an explanation, and I'd always blamed Ruby. That was my pain speaking. I realized now though that, in her moment of heartbreak, she had abandoned me, but I had also abandoned her. I had given up too easily. I had not tried harder to find her, protect her, and keep her safe. That was my job. My duty. My promise.

"To be honest, I don't even know if it's what I want. But how will I know if we don't spend more time together?"

Finnegan glanced up, listening intently.

I shook my head. "What does it mean if she doesn't even show up…"

At the sound of our approach, the alpaca, who quietly grazed at the hay hopper, lifted its head, ears twitching. Then it took off at a gallop to the other end of the paddock, like a bolt.

"Man, that little creature can move, hey? Silly thing."

Finnegan darted forward, then stopped to look back at me.

"No. You still can't chase that one. Sorry, dude. He's not your problem."

He was mine, however. Arnie was already pissed off at me about my lack of attention to securing sponsorships, so bailing on the alpaca was the least of my worries. But I knew he really wanted me to give it a shot. Now I wondered whether he wanted to offload it because it had an attitude problem. Or was that me?

Finnegan stayed at my heels while I put out more feed for the animals, shovelled manure, and hauled some hay. Then I grabbed my tool belt and hiked to the edge of the paddock to fix a bit of fence that I remembered was loose.

Finnegan's ears perked up before I heard it, but moments later, the crunch of tires on gravel had my heart racing and thundering in my chest.

I looked at Finnegan, who looked at me.

"Let's go see."

Leaving the task of twisting wire half done, we stalked back around the barn to the driveway. But it wasn't Ruby.

I recognized April's station wagon, and my heart tumbled downhill.

She stepped out, watching and waiting as we drew closer. I was so not in the mood for a showdown with April this afternoon.

"Hi, Julian."

"Hey."

I stood a few feet away, my hands in my pockets, and Finnegan sat beside me, a low, almost imperceptible growl emitting from the back of his throat. I showed him my palm. I guess I owed it to her to hear what she had to say.

"So. About last night. I am so sorry for embarrassing you. I behaved badly."

I pulled a rueful face. "I guess the occasion pulled us all back into high school, huh?"

"Hmm. I don't know about that. I... I had been wanting to talk to you. And I was so thrown when Ruby showed up that I just..." She pulled her lips between her teeth and shook her head. "I don't know. I felt jealous and irrational."

"Nothing to feel jealous about, April. We had a mutual understanding."

She glanced down. "Yes. About that. Um... I've really

enjoyed our time together, Julian. And I've grown fond of you. I thought maybe we could…" Her gaze flicked up to my face and then down again, suddenly shy. "My interest in you has been growing gradually, and I've reconsidered the things I said. Before."

Finnegan made another attempt to growl. "No," I commanded, and he lay down, setting his chin on his paws, looking very unhappy as he pretended to ignore us.

From the beginning, April had made it clear that she was only interested in letting off steam. That she wasn't interested in a relationship, or even in being seen together. She'd made kind of a big deal about being discreet, not wanting parents at the school to get any ideas about her being involved with anyone. With me, I'd inferred. Now she was singing a different tune.

"Right, well. I'm afraid nothing has changed for me. And I meant what I said last night. I really think… I think we're kind of done here."

"It's truly nothing to do with your Insta account and all that. I'm sorry if you think so. I'm not that shallow."

I grimaced. My suggestion obviously offended her, though I still believed there was something to it. "Again. I'm sorry. I didn't mean to be an asshole."

She pulled a tight smile. "All's forgiven. I hope we can still spend time together, sometime."

"I actually don't think that's a good idea, April." Wasn't it long past the time she should say goodbye and drive away? "I have been very distracted since Ruby showed up in town."

"About Ruby…"

I tilted my head, waiting. I certainly would not help her with this, whatever this was. And besides, it was none of her business.

Suddenly April's tone changed, taking on something of the righteous teacher's voice I'd heard her use at civic meetings. "Everyone knows what she did to you after grad, Julian. You can't honestly think she's staying. That you can have a life together. Look at what she does. How does your life fit in with hers? I'm afraid you'll be hurt again."

Stunned, I couldn't get a word out of my open mouth. Unbelievably, she kept going.

"You and I are much better suited. We're homebodies. We're both invested in our local community, and we belong here. She never will."

"Yeah, well, that wouldn't concern you. But thanks for your opinion." I nodded towards her car, taking a step back. "See you around."

After she finally drove away, I stood in the drive for a long time, staring off across the paddocks and fields, just thinking. I didn't want to give nasty April's words credence, but they'd echoed my own fearful thoughts.

I couldn't resist Ruby. Every fibre of my body still wanted her, needed her like air, like food. But my poor bruised heart may not know what was good for it. And indulging it in a hopeless fantasy may very well conflict with my true mission, and her intentions for her own life, whatever they may be.

The afternoon had worn on and long summer shadows stretched across the yard, adding to my forlorn feeling.

"Let's settle the animals for the evening and head inside." Who was I kidding? She wasn't coming. I hung my tool belt back in the shed and grabbed a woven willow basket. "Come on, Finn, we might as well gather some salad while we round up the goats."

Later, after struggling yet again to get the stupid alpaca back into the barn, the quiche tasted like mud and cardboard in my mouth, my disappointment was so profound. I barely registered the creamy eggs, or the morels and shallots I'd so eagerly added to it in anticipation of pleasing Ruby with my skill. Now I went through the motions robotically, putting away the leftovers and washing up the dishes before bed.

Melancholy though I was, I knew I was a fool for dreaming of a different outcome, even for a day.

Chapter 19

Ruby

"RUBY? Someone told me my sister is in town! Ru-by!"

Hearing my brother's voice, I dropped my things and raced downstairs. I hadn't seen Isaac since his wedding to Yasmin three years ago, when I'd got a few days off to meet them in St. Barts. Since then, they'd both finished their teaching degrees, gotten good jobs in town, and were close to having a baby.

"*Shalom*," Isaac said as he wrapped me in his brawny arms, so reminiscent of Dad, he even smelled the same.

"Hey, you," I murmured, burying my nose in his chest and inhaling his scent of spice and coffee. We each took a step back and looked at each other, half assessing the changes in each other, half just soaking in the comforting sight.

"Hi, Ruby," said Yasmin in her high, sweet voice. Picture the quintessential elementary school teacher, that's Yasmin. It made me want to start school all over again. I wrapped my arms around her curvy shape.

"Oh, my, look at you!"

"I know," she groaned. "I feel ready to pop and I've still got two months to go."

"*Mazel tov*. Are you excited? Are you ready?"

"Thank you. We're as ready as can be, but I'm a bundle of nerves. Isaac is like a rock. You'd think he'd done this before."

I nodded, smiling. "He's like that." Just like Dad. Nothing rattled him.

"Do you think you'll still be in town in September?" Yasmin's dark eyes were as wide as a doe's. "It would be so awesome to have you here."

My face went slack, jaw dropping. Not only did I not have a ready answer, but I was touched and taken aback that she'd even think of me. Babies were not my forte, obviously, though I'd jiggled a few while interviewing women all over the world, pitching in to buy a few minutes of their precious time. Before I could think of a reply, she jumped in again.

"Oh, I'm sorry. Of course you can't. I understand." She gave me another quick squeeze. "But wouldn't it be nice?"

We moved into the living room *en masse*, where Yasmin lowered her off-balance form onto a stiff armchair.

Isaac glanced over, "Okay, Sweets?"

"Yup. Just have to get off my feet."

Stealing a quick glance at my wrist, I ventured, "So what brings you over?"

Isaac's face pulled tight in a mock grimace, his dark brows climbing. "Just got off work. Mom invited us for a family dinner. You... knew? Right?"

I nodded in a slow and exaggerated way. "Ah. Of course. Yup. Sure."

We both laughed, our gazes locking in mutual understanding. My suspicions were raised the moment they crashed in, and they were confirmed. Mom the machinator, doing her thing as only she could. If I wanted to know what she really thought about my spending the night with Julian and rushing out to the farm to see him again, I had my answer.

Right on cue, the familiar click-clack-click of Mom's heels

on the tiles approached from her home office, and I smiled ruefully. She was a tank, my mom, but I loved her.

"Well! Great. I've been so looking forward to seeing you both," I said.

"Hello, my darlings!" Mom gushed as she breezed into the front room. "I'm so glad you could make it, Izzy. Ruby's been asking to see you since the moment she got back." She swooped in and took his head between her hands, kissing both cheeks. Then she moved on to bend over Yasmin with hugs and pats and murmured questions about her health.

"You didn't have plans for tonight?" Isaac gave me a side-eye and a wink.

Tilting my chin up, I answered truthfully, "Nothing that couldn't wait." That was the truth. Julian and I hadn't seen each other in ten years. Another day now could hardly make a difference. I hoped he'd understand. If I had his number, I'd send him a quick text. Thinking I might get his number out of Dad's desktop, I stood up.

"Ruby, honey. Help me lay the table," Mom said, leading the way to the kitchen. "Dad will be here soon with the food."

Again, Isaac and I smiled knowingly and exchanged glances. It was okay. I really was so glad to see him again. My chest swelled and fizzed with the pleasure of it. Isaac was only three years younger than me, and we'd always been close, even though I hadn't been around much since high school. But we exchanged emails regularly, and I had been there—virtually—during his university years, his girlfriends, meeting and falling in love with Yasmin, the jobs, the wedding, everything. And he got as honest an account of my life as a journalist as I could give him. As much as anyone got.

Isaac served drinks for us while Mom made a pot of fruity tea for Yasmin and I brought a bowl of pretzels in; we sat and caught up for a half hour or so before Dad stumbled in with a cardboard box. Clearly, the two had conspired in this little idea of theirs.

"Food's here!" He bellowed cheerfully. "I got us roast chickens and potato salad."

We laughed. What else? This was Dad's favourite meal, his go-to if given any latitude. I swear he'd eat the same thing every day if allowed.

Then it was chaos as we all moved to the kitchen, then the dining room, putting out the food to share.

"To Ruby's return!" said Dad, raising his glass with a wide smile, and everyone followed suit. "It's wonderful having the entire family together again."

"To Yasmin and Isaac's impending family addition!" I added.

"*L'Chaim*," Isaac said.

We were a noisy bunch while we ate, several conversations criss-crossing the table at once, and the hours slipped by before Isaac rose and claimed he had to get his pregnant wife home.

That night, mellow and tipsy from too many glasses of wine, I collapsed into my bed in a dead sleep, only to awaken abruptly as I hit the floor. I'd been dreaming of Venezuela, my heart racing as I struggled in the dark against my bonds, and flailed and kicked myself right out of bed. I got up to drink a tall glass of water and rehydrate; my mind swirled with all the things I'd left behind, the things I'd returned to, and the uncertainty about what my future held. To some extent, it was up to me, and yet it filled me with nothing but doubts, fears, and insecurities.

Returning to bed, I slept poorly for the rest of the night, tossing and turning, reliving the kidnapping in neurotic detail, and wishing I had Julian's arms around me so I could find peace in slumber.

Julian

The next day, resigned to life as usual, without the faint hope of Ruby, I fed the animals and did my usual series of chores. Though I loved the farm and this delightful slow routine that I'd developed in the last year, I felt a keen sense of loss. All I needed was to reframe my expectations and all would be well again, but for the moment I was grieving some half-formed dream.

Finnegan suddenly let out a short, sharp bark and I spun to see another car pulling in, this one unfamiliar.

"Who has come to scold me this time, Finn?"

The strange sedan coasted into the drive and stopped. Ruby got out, squinting towards the house.

I almost couldn't breathe, never mind call out. Finnegan, though, knew exactly what to do. He barked again and dashed toward her, coming up short as she turned to him.

"Hey, there, doggy." She glanced up, raising a hand to shield her eyes from the sun, and saw me walking toward her. "Hi, you."

Joy and relief warred in my chest, my throat tightening. How could I be so happy to see her? I raised a hand in greeting, still unsure of my voice.

"I'm so sorry, Julian. I fully intended to follow you out here yesterday."

Ruby waved her hands around jerkily, scratching Finn's ears, her gaze jumping, avoiding meeting mine while she spoke.

"Deanna came home, and it took a little while before I found your note. Then when I got home, I kind of got stuck dealing with a bunch of work emails."

I nodded. Work. Of course. "It doesn't matter. You're here now."

"I'm sorry I didn't call. I don't have your number."

"Your dad has it." Did I sound peevish? I didn't mean to.

"I... I thought he might, but then Isaac came." She looked

truly remorseful, her frantic movements stalling. She looked full at me for the first time, her features softening and her eyes roaming my face, taking in my rough clothing.

She was back in her cargo pants and vest, like she was on that first day. But despite how stunning she looked all done up for the party, she was still the most beautiful woman I've ever seen. My pulse, already racing when I realized she had come, thundered ahead in anticipation. I didn't know what it all meant, but I knew I wanted her.

Without a word I stepped up close, pinning her against her car—in the wedge of space between her seat and the open door—and took her face between my hands. I bent my mouth to cover hers, pausing to breathe in the thrilling scent of her, desperate to taste her again, to show her how happy I was to see her again, hungry for her.

Fire ignited between us instantly. I was having the most amazing flashbacks to our night together. My whole body turned on and my cock leapt in anticipation, semi-hard in seconds, straining against my pants for more.

With a little whimper in the back of her throat, she melted into me, her knees softening, surrendering to my possessive touch, and mentally I pumped my fist in the air. Mine. She's still my girl.

Finnegan continued to thrash around us, tail wagging, nudging between us. I laughed weakly against her mouth, reluctantly backing away. "He wants a proper introduction. I told him all about you."

Ruby laughed too, bending to look him in the eye. "How do you do?" She glanced up at me, and I supplied, "Finnegan."

"Finnegan," she said, putting out a hand, and he obliged by setting his speckled white paw on her palm. They shook. "Nice to meet you, too." The smile on her face made my entire body heat, and if the smile on Finn's face was any measure, he liked her just fine. An expert judge of character, my dog. If I had a tail, it'd be wagging harder than Finn's with his ass end swaying back and forth.

"Let's walk. Finnegan and I were just heading out to bring the goats in for the evening." I handed her the basket. "We need to gather some greens for supper."

"You're cooking? After all that food you made for the party?"

I nodded. "I had quiche for our lunch yesterday. With morels, and some other wild mushrooms."

"I hope I didn't ruin your plans."

I shrugged. "There's always work to do here. And I'm always cooking. Nothing ruined. This is the way I live." I glanced down to see what she had on her feet. Sturdy boots. Good.

"Come this way," I said to both Ruby and Finnegan, and we set out past the paddocks.

Falling in at my side, our elbows and arms knocking gently, she tilted her head and peered at me sideways with a questioning look and a wry smile. "Are you happy here?"

"Yes. I am. I grow my own food, eat seasonally, and spend my days with animals. I feel very connected to the land that I live on. What's not to love?" I looked over to see what she thought of my statement and caught her smiling as she looked off into the distance. I bent to scratch Finnegan's ears, embarrassed by my rambling.

"I can appreciate what I have here so much more, having lived abroad. My grandparents chose well when they settled here seventy years ago. Our property sits in the warm, dry rain shadow of the mountains, and creates a very special climate that's not unlike Provence."

As I spoke, I felt my passion stirring. It was easy to be distracted by Ruby's return, but my homecoming was fuelled by a deep need to connect with my roots and sense of purpose. This was who I was now. This was what mattered to me.

Ruby… well, Ruby could accept that or not. It wouldn't change anything.

I just wished…

"I can grow almost anything. Besides the old apple orchard, I have plums, quince, and any vegetable and herb I need. The only challenge is the deer, which make themselves at home, and the occasional goat that escapes the paddock. But it's a challenge and a thrill for me, to cook with what's on hand, and in season."

We walked the pastures, scrubby knolls and dales, and trudged along the shady tree-line, picking wild greens. The way the golden rays danced over Ruby's hair, loose and wavy, and glanced off her tanned cheeks and chin mesmerized me. I tried to let the landscape calm me, and just enjoy the late summer evening air and soft light, and ignore the insistent question hammering at my thoughts like a fist on a door, demanding entrance. Will she stay? Will she stay? My rational mind fought back, far more interested in self-preservation, scolding. Of course, she won't. You don't expect her to. Just enjoy this moment for what it is.

While Finnegan crashed through the woods in pursuit of birds and squirrels, I talked to her about the various plants we found as I picked them and laid them in her basket. I found some garlic mustard greens which I could steam. For a salad, bits of wood sorrel, purslane, peppergrass and pennycress that grew at the edges of a muddy trench that filled with water after it rained. We lucked out and found a small patch of wild violets, and I picked both leaves and flowers, which would make the salad prettier and more appealing, lest she think I was feeding her weeds. Which, technically, I was as I surreptitiously added a few young dandelions to the basket.

She walked with a stride long and sure no matter how uneven the ground, and I could tell she was lean and strong from her life of roaming. I had the feeling she hadn't spent much time lounging around these past ten years.

"Are you tired?"

"A little. Restless last night. But I slept well Saturday night."

"I noticed. You were out cold when I slipped away." I smiled at her. "But we were up rather late."

She nodded, her gaze focussing somewhere far off in the distance. "I haven't been sleeping well for a couple of months. It surprised me to be so..." Her glance flicked toward me, her cheeks flushing pink, and desire stirred in my blood. "So comfortable. So relaxed. I missed you last night."

I laughed. "You earned it." But my chest warmed and puffed out, flattered that perhaps I'd worn her out, or that being with me felt just that right to her. As being with her felt to me.

"It's more than that," she said, sobering. "You make me feel..."

I twitched a brow in question.

She sighed. "Safe."

Ruby

After failing to show up yesterday afternoon, I was almost embarrassed to come; unsure if I'd still be welcome, or if Julian had changed his mind. The drive out to the farm took a good twenty-five minutes or more since there was traffic out of town on a Monday, even though I'd waited until midday. The late afternoon and evening had swooshed by in a blur of conversation and celebration, while under the surface I'd continued to worry about Richard's insistent emails. There was no way I could have met my work and family obligations and still indulged in a visit to the farm yesterday, but now guilt consumed me for not trying to contact Julian. I should have tried harder to call him.

Relaying a message through a friend felt too public for this tentative exploration that was unfolding between Julian and me. Now, though, I was glad I came.

I had to stop myself from running to him, throwing my arms around him and covering his beautiful face with kisses. As he strode toward me, he looked almost stunned that I'd actually come, and I could only hope that bright shining hope in his eyes was a sign that I was welcome. It matched the giddy joy that fizzed in my chest and belly at the sight of him; he was strong and tanned and ruggedly handsome in his work clothes, his brown hair a wild wavy mess with bits of straw stuck in it. How many times over the years had I dreamed of Julian's smiling, welcoming face and had to make do with my faded memories?

But that kiss? Wow. I did not expect that. Was he always so hot, so assured in his movements, able to melt my panties with one look, one touch? I let out a shaky breath, pressing down the bubble of hope that rose in my chest too early.

I sorely wished I had someone to talk through my dilemma with. But there was no one. Mom and Dad knew I was at a career crossroads, and that's why I had taken a few weeks off. It was the first time in years that I'd done so, and I think they felt some kind of momentous turning point lay ahead. But confiding in them would undoubtedly trigger an argument—Dad was only too happy to have me nearby, while Mom would question my desire to quit when I'd achieved so much recognition and success. They wouldn't understand that neither option felt right.

My deepest wish was to talk it through with Julian. But dare I? I couldn't rid myself of the deep desire to curl up in his embrace and sleep for a hundred years. But it wasn't fair to burden him. He had his own life, his own problems to deal with. He wasn't responsible for me and didn't need to be thinking about my issues.

Taking the basket from his hand and silently following him out toward the pastures and woods, Finnegan loping at our heels, was the best thing I could have done. We fell into stride, side by side, like no time had passed, and my chest hurt at the synchronicity. The sense of belonging I felt at Julian's side was profound. Did he feel it too?

He talked as we walked, about the land, the climate, his crops, and the wild things he'd gathered and set in my basket. I listened, and in between, when he fell silent, the silence was comfortable and easy. I let my gaze follow his confident movements, admire the sinewy muscles that rippled on his arms, and beneath his shirt as he bent and reached, feeling warmth tingle inside me.

I could see the old apple orchard out beyond the vegetable garden, with its gnarled, moss-covered branches.

"Are you still making cider?"

"Yes, starting to. A little. That was always a sideline, but there's a new market for it. The old trees still produce, but they need some work. And everything is organic now. Not certified yet, of course. That takes time. It's been a lot of work." He kicked a fir cone out of our path, sending it sailing into the distance. "It's all part of my sustainable food mission."

"That's amazing. So ambitious. And if the food you made for the reunion is an example of what's possible, it will inspire others."

"I hope so. That's the plan. To lead by example, to inspire and teach. That's why we're doing the Farm-to-Table Faire. Hopefully, the first of many."

"I'd like to write about you and your mission. About the fair."

"We don't need help. The committee has PR under control."

"That's not why I want to do it. I'm interested. I believe in what you're doing. Tell me more about this fair of yours. What brought it on?"

"I needed a soapbox to stand on because I was so angry. I needed to show the world."

"Is that why you came back? What started it? Tell me about changes you've made."

I knew this farm well, had spent time here growing up, but

it was different now. Julian had kept the old farmhouse his grandparents built, and several of the original outbuildings. I recognized the big barn, the hay shed, the creamery. But the huge industrial aluminum-clad poultry house, with its giant vents, skylights and feed silo, was just gone. Without a trace. If I didn't know the sort of operation his father ran while we were in school, I wouldn't be able to tell. Julian had reclaimed the area with rustic paddocks and a couple of new-looking storage sheds, and expanded the vegetable garden, ringed by a new fence. We circled the fence, pausing as he pointed out the crops he grew there.

"As my skill as a chef grew, I became increasingly discerning about the ingredients and their origins, who had handled them and how bringing them to market had affected the farmers, ranchers, animals, the land itself. I began to take an interest in the little traditional farmers and the local suppliers. They were the ones who brought the best ingredients. I could see, smell, and taste the difference. And they were the ones closest to the land. I was envious of them, but also worried."

He opened a gate, indicating the direction, and we tromped out through the grassy paddock, the land rising gently under our boots. I could see small goats grazing way off in the distance, their heads popping up when they noticed us before dancing off over the rise.

I loved the feeling of the farm. The relaxed yet purposeful arrangement of utility and pastoral emptiness was so soothing. I blew out my breath, trying to re-centre myself. "This farm reminds me of the traditional farms I stayed at in Peru and Bolivia earlier this year. Even there, the impact of big business is felt."

"I heard you were in South America." Julian's knowledgeable gaze stayed on the horizon ahead, ever watchful for something we could eat. It amazed me, the things he bent and harvested, showing me and telling me their old-fashioned, romantic names. Pennycress and cleavers, huckleberries and Queen Anne's lace.

I nodded. My memories of that time were mixed. Some of the most beautiful and comforting places I'd ever been were tangled up with some of my most frightening experiences. I wasn't sure I could talk about one without triggering the other, so I stayed silent.

"So you came home," I redirected.

I think he felt my discomfort, so he didn't push. He nodded. "I got word that Dad died… and even though I'd been back to visit, our relationship was strained. We never fully mended the rift that formed when I refused to carry the torch, so to speak, the family legacy."

"I'm so sorry. That's sad. I hadn't heard that he died. I'm surprised Dad didn't tell me."

He pulled a sympathetic face.

I had been out of touch a lot these past couple of years. Maybe the opportunity never came up. Despite Julian and I living in each other's pockets throughout high school, our parents were never close. Too different, from such different worlds, they'd have had nothing to talk about except us kids. I was touched that Dad had gone to his father's funeral in my stead.

I laced my fingers through his, squeezing, and his gaze darted briefly to my face, then back toward the sky.

"At his funeral, I said to myself, I'll do one better, Dad. I'll fix everything that was broken and take our family's love of the land—the animals, food production, cooking, nurturing people—to a whole new level. I'll heal and create and educate and inspire; then maybe when it's my turn to die, I could do it with pride, having spent my life doing something that I believed in. It was important to me to create my own legacy."

Again, I squeezed his hand. My chest swelled with pride in everything he'd done, both before and now, on the farm. He'd grown into exactly the kind of thoughtful, capable, principled man I'd always known he'd be.

"Anyway, that's how I started doing what I'm doing now. There was so much to take care of. After Dad died, Mom didn't want to be on the farm anymore, so we got her an apartment near Molly."

"Molly! How is she?" I remembered his older sister. She'd married already by the time we were in senior high.

"She's good. Happy with Jake. Molly and Jake had already moved away and were raising their kids in the village. They stopped at two kids. Charlie and Sunny. They're nine and seven now. I love being close to them."

"Your mom must enjoy her grandkids."

He nodded, but his brow twisted, his eyes darkening with a memory that skewered me. I was running out of time.

"And then it was just the farm and me. I had some capital. I dismantled the commercial chicken operation and started from scratch."

As we crested a sweeping rise in the land, the vista opened up over a long valley in the shadow of the higher hills to the West. The sun hung low in the sky, and the green meadow was chequered with light and shadow, shimmering with golds, greens, and blues.

"Oh," I exclaimed. "It's breathtaking." So peaceful, I felt the weight of my worries lift off my chest.

Julian led the way over to a rocky outcrop and gestured. We sat down and just took in the view for several minutes. Finnegan caught up with us and circled around, laying on the grass to rest, his eyebrows twitching as his gaze flicked from Julian to me and back again, watchful. We stayed there a long while, just listening to the birds, letting the sun warm our faces and limbs. Julian seemed to sense that I needed time, and silence; the space between us lay quiet and comfortable.

"I'm so proud of what you've done here. And all alone."

He moved his fingers lazily in my hair, and I closed my

eyes, revelling in his touch. "I have friends I can call if I need a hand for bigger jobs. Arnie." He chuckled. "But the everyday tasks I handle. Slowly, sometimes. It makes a difference that I'm only subsistence farming. I don't have clients, quotas, or deadlines that Mother Nature doesn't impose herself."

"Still. It's a lot of work."

"It is. But I love it. And I do spend a fair bit of time cooking, and taking photos and videos." He pinched his lips into a thin line and rocked his head from side to side. "Still getting used to that."

"That must be tricky. If you're in them."

"Deanna taught me a few tricks so I could be self-sufficient. You can do a lot with a small tripod. But Molly comes over and helps sometimes."

We fell silent. After a moment, I glanced over at Julian. His gaze lay heavy on my face, and I knew he was thinking, as I was, about our own baby. Thinking of how she'd be nine years old too, like Molly's eldest.

"Our daughter would have grown up with her cousins," I said.

A tiny, choked noise emerged from his throat in acknowledgment. "Did you give her a name?"

"Nuh-uh. I just think of her as… baby… not even that. Just a little spirit person. Too ephemeral to picture."

After another minute of silence, while we continued to watch the sun play across the landscape, Julian spoke.

"I'm sorry."

My head shot up. "You're sorry?"

He nodded. "I've been thinking. About my own actions, or lack of, and it shames me. I realize I… didn't act like a husband, or a father. I let your parents decide for both of us, and though I didn't like it, I didn't question their authority. That was wrong. I'm disappointed in myself. I didn't protect you like I should have."

My chest squeezed at his words, my eyes suddenly burning. "Jules! No. You were eighteen. We were kids."

He shrugged, his mouth pulling down in a grimace. "Still. We were old enough to make a child together. We'd made promises to each other." He glanced at me, and his gaze fell to the ground at our feet. "I guess we both broke them."

I thought for a while about that. While technically he was right, I would never—could never—hold him responsible for any part of what happened that summer. Certainly not for our estrangement. I may have been in shock, but I had facts. I had left Julian with nothing but questions. No choice. The weight of my betrayal and abandonment added to his burden.

I reached out a hand to him palm up, and he ran his calloused fingertips along it, sending shivers up my arm, before slipping his hand into mine and lacing our fingers together. He tugged, and I went to him, settling onto his lap, relishing the feel of his powerful arms as they wrapped around me, pulling tight. I hooked my chin on his shoulder, setting our heads side by side, sighing through the intense feelings of grief that pulsed through me. My throat thickened, convulsing, and my eyes burned with tears. I felt his chest heave and his arms tighten.

After a moment, he sniffed and pulled away. He kissed me tenderly, and said, "We'd better get those animals and head back."

We stood up and strode off through the meadow toward a few little goats that grazed a couple hundred yards away. Finnegan loped off towards them, circling around, doing what he'd been bred to do. Julian called out, a high-pitched staccato laughing sound, and in an instant, their heads shot up and they bounded towards us, their long ears flapping. Laughing, I joined in the call, imitating his sounds. They answered his call with their own bleats, and before another minute had passed, other goats were coming at us from different directions, all of them bleating in a chorus.

As they drew near, Julian greeted them with enthusiasm,

and his love for them was obvious, as was theirs for him. There were little black ones, hairy white ones, and a few spotted ones. He was so adorable, together with his little goats, I pulled out my phone and snapped a few pictures, then took bits of video I thought maybe he could use. Or if not, at least I'd have them to remember this afternoon.

"Hey, you!" He hugged them and scratched their ears and necks as they crowded around, jumping, nudging him, butting him with their heads and their baby horns. He pulled some biscuits from his pocket and gave them treats. "Hi, Oreo, hey, Milkshake. Time to go to bed. Come on." Laughing, he continued to greet them all by name. Taco, Milo, Otis, Pan and Puck. With each name he called out, I laughed harder.

Once the big welcome was done, we walked back towards the farmhouse and they trailed and danced around us in a swarm.

"That was easy. They love you."

"Well, I raised most of them from babies. It's mutual."

As we marched through the meadow en masse, a shaggy, long-necked creature appeared and galloped towards us, then shied and turned on its heel to dance away, then came back again. Each of its movements tentative and unsure. Finnegan let out a single sharp woof.

"Stay," Julian barked.

"That's not a goat!"

Julian groaned. "No, it isn't."

"You have alpaca, too?"

He sucked his teeth. "Just that one. He arrived two days ago."

I remembered then that he'd said something about an alpaca delivery when we'd first encountered each other at the café on Friday. I'd been so shocked to see him, it had flown out of my head.

I stepped forward, calling out the sound they used on the Bolivian farm where I'd stayed. A kind of high moaning moo.

The little animal halted its retreat, its ears twitching towards us, and I called it again. "Mmmm. Mmmm."

Julian looked at me. "What is that?"

"You know goats. I know alpacas." I laughed and called again as the alpaca inched a little closer, curious. "Come on, sweetie, come here."

"Be careful. I don't think he's all that sweet. He gave me a pretty hard shove on the ass yesterday."

I laughed. But sure enough, the shy alpaca circled around, giving Julian and his goats a wide berth and sidling up to my other side. I turned to scratch its ears and neck in welcome. "Hi, there, darling." It seemed to welcome my attention and gave me a gentle body check. "He seems perfectly gentle to me. What's his name?"

Julian grunted. "No name. I haven't even decided whether I'll keep it."

"Aww. Why not? They're lovely creatures. Let's see." I looked at his shaggy brown head, pulling back his long coat to gaze into his big, soulful eyes. "How about Chewpaca?"

It was Julian's turn to hoot with laughter. "That's good."

"Or maybe, in keeping with your food theme, Nutmeg. His coat is that colour, kind of dark taupe."

"I like that." Julian eyed us skeptically. "How come he likes you and not me?"

"How come you like your goats and not him?"

He pulled a face, making me laugh even harder. Bashful, he pulled me closer, and we bumped into each other, flirting. My hands laced behind his neck, and he dipped his forehead to touch mine briefly before lowering his mouth to mine for a kiss.

In my relaxed state, the mere touch of his lips set off fireworks in my blood, my body remembering every intimate thing we'd done Saturday night. The playful, tender kiss deepened in an instant, Julian's tongue teasing then seeking more as he explored my mouth, his arms tightening at my back. Fisting his hands, he slid them down, pulling me against his hardening groin with a moan.

We pulled apart, breath shaking, his gaze searching mine for confirmation that we were going to do this again. That last time wasn't just a liquor-inspired lapse down memory lane. I hoped my expression conveyed how badly I wanted more of him. How intensely my body craved connection with his.

He inhaled deeply as he let go of me, stepping back a little. "How do you know alpacas anyway?"

I took a moment to ground myself and push the desire down to a slow burn. "I got to know them in Bolivia, on a farm. They're sweet animals. And they like to be in packs too. So he needs to be accepted by you and your goat buddies. Unless you're planning to get him some alpaca friends?" I glanced up, raising my brows, teasing.

"Uh. Err. Well, no. I hadn't planned on it."

"Maybe you'll change your mind once you get to know him." I raked my fingers through his short coat. "Their wool is amazing to work with."

In response to Julian's questioning frown, I lifted a shoulder and said, "I knit."

"Knit?" His delighted grin was crooked, curled up at one side, triggering his dimple there, and I wanted to lick it.

His incredulity was expected. Knitting is not something anyone would associate with me. I'm neither crafty nor domestic. "It's something to do while I'm in transit, and waiting around for things to happen." Though I'd done it for years now, I'd recently picked up some fascinating techniques and patterns in Bolivia, and learned to card and spin alpaca wool as well, from the women who hosted me.

We sauntered the rest of the way back, hand in hand, and I felt a deep sense of satisfaction being surrounded by the peace of the late summer evening. The chorus of birds sang down the sun, and our four legged companions trotted along beside us. They were like a balm on my bruised heart. When we got to the barn the goats, followed obligingly by Nutmeg the alpaca, went into their barn for the night. They were no less encouraged by Julian shaking a pail of oats and dishing it out into their feeding troughs. We latched the door and walked toward the farmhouse as the light finally started to fade.

"Are you hungry?"

"For anything you cooked? Of course."

"Since you waited an extra day, you get to watch me cook. I have nothing prepared."

"Sounds absolutely perfect. How can I help?" The thought of a live demonstration of his sexy cooking techniques made my knees feel weak.

He halted outside the farmhouse, turning towards me. Taking the basket from my hand, he set it on the ground and took my other hand; holding them both loosely, he jiggled them a little, his eyes cast down, and his long dark lashes lay against flushed cheeks as his ears turned red. The old self-effacing Julian had returned. How easy was it for me to steal his confidence away, if I could be so presumptuous? My stomach pinched with guilt. I was doing a poor job of persuading him to trust me again.

"Everything okay?" I asked.

His chin jerked up a little in a tiny nod, and I saw his throat move as he swallowed. His mouth quirked to one side, flashing a dimple, and I smiled. Our gazes met, mine questioning and patient. He seemed to want to say something, but was hesitant.

Finally, he cleared his throat. "I'm really, really happy you came. I so wanted to show you around." He turned his head away, squinting towards the barn and garden. "I wanted you to understand what I'm doing here. What I'm about."

My heart thudded a little harder at his sweet admission. "I'm glad too." I waited for him to say more, but he dropped my hands and led the way into the house.

Chapter 20

Julian

OUTWARDLY, I remained calm and cool. On the inside I was twisting and turning, jumping up and down and bleating like my goats. She came! I couldn't even talk to Finnegan about how hard my heart pounded in my chest. I had to keep it all to myself, though I ruffled his ears and I'm sure he sensed my excitement. She was right here, on the farm, in my home, about to spend the evening and, dare I think, another night with me.

I didn't mean to kiss her. Repeatedly. It just kept happening. I couldn't keep my hands off of her, or my mouth.

I didn't realize how self-conscious and unsure I was about my choice to return here until the reality was reflected in Ruby's eyes. I'd built myself a prestigious career and a glamourous life abroad. This was its polar opposite. All those years I had, on some level, been trying to impress her from afar. Trying to be the desirable something that would have kept her with me, if only in my dreams. Now that she was here, I still didn't know why or for how long, and I was trying to impress her by being the same old country farm hick she'd abandoned the first time around.

It was enough to send a farm boy running for the hills with his tail between his legs.

Inside the farmhouse, warm from the day's sun beating in through the windows and onto the old tin roof, it was cozy but stuffy; the scents of this morning's freshly baked bread and last night's dinner lingered on the air.

"Mm. It smells so nice in here."

"Leave the door open for a while. Need some fresh air," I said as I shucked my flannel work overshirt and hung it on a hook by the door. Finnegan circled around, lapped up some water, and flopped down on his mat with a tired huff and a sigh. I turned to Ruby. "You thirsty?"

Her gaze jumped to my face, and I realized she'd been checking me out in my thin old t-shirt. The way she blinked, flashed a shy smile, and swallowed before nodding made me quirk a smile. I may even have flexed a tad, enjoying her admiration. Even without her nearby, my nerves were doing somersaults just thinking about her. My Ruby. My hands were shaking, and I felt my body surging with need. Slow down, boy.

"I'm… um… going to grab a quick shower. Wash off the farm. Make yourself at home." I handed her a tall glass of ice water and a glass of Pinot Noir and slipped out to my bedroom for the fastest shower and change in history. Before I was done combing my hair, I heard soft music wafting from the living room.

She'd chosen one of my playlists, and the strains of Kelly Clarkson's "Because of You" drifted quietly from the speakers. I wondered if she remembered all the hours we'd lain together, wrapped in each other's limbs, listening to this song and so many others, talking about life and what we wanted from it.

Letting off steam in the shower did nothing to diminish how rocked I was in her presence. I stepped close to her, running my hands up and down her arms, and she signalled her openness by lifting her chin and arching her back slightly, setting my heart fluttering wildly in my chest. I bent my head to kiss her, lingering to soak in the sweet feel of her lips, the scent of her sun-warmed skin — like buttered toast. I held back the burning need to a civilized level. We needed food.

"Pasta okay?" I asked as I pulled away, turning to my kitchen. My place of comfort and control.

She cleared her throat. "Sure. Of course. Anything you make will be wonderful." She followed me, leaning against the counter, sending my thoughts meandering to the feel of her hip bones in my hands, riding me. "I'll take some pictures for your feed." She held up her phone, snapping a couple of pictures of my incredulous face.

I let out a soft laugh, feeling my cheeks heat. "Okay." Bending to retrieve my big pot, I filled it with water and set it on the stove while she leaned against the counter, sipping her wine, driving me insane. My gaze traced the soft curves of her shoulders and breasts beneath her old t-shirt, remembering the feel of her skin under my palm. On my tongue.

"You like pesto?" I asked, pulling apart our foraged greens from the field and rinsing them. "I make a great super green pesto with local hazelnuts, and a combination of garden herbs and wild things." I sorted the greens and began chopping the ingredients roughly on my old wooden board, my big chef's knife rocking rhythmically, soothing me, then transferring it all into my big stone mortar, drizzling in olive oil, and pounding it into a smooth paste.

"I am loving watching you do this. You're so comfortable and competent in your movements, it's like art. You have very sexy arms."

"Uh-huh." I laughed, reaching for the block of cheese and grater. "I have this luscious nutty Parmigiano-Reggiana — "

"Say that again," she said, her voice deep and throaty, tugging my attention away from my task.

"What?"

"About the cheese."

I blinked. "Parmigiano-Reggiana?"

"Yeah. And the other bits."

"Uh. Luscious and nutty?"

She nodded, her eyes darkening. "Do you have any idea how fucking sexy you are when you talk about food. You are like sex on a stick."

I froze, speechless, feeling my eyes widen. Who me? Did she have any idea how hot it was to hear her talk like this? My cock roared to life, tightening in my pants, and I stared.

"It's no surprise to me that your Insta videos have gone viral, Jules. There must be girls with wet panties all over the world watching them on repeat."

"You… you watched my videos?"

She nodded again, slowly, a smile creeping across her face. "I did. Even though I didn't make it out here yesterday, I might have taken a little detour onto your video stream and exercised a few fantasies of my own."

I swallowed, my tongue suddenly dry. "You don't have to fantasize, Ruby," I croaked. "I'm all yours."

She sidled around the end of the island and stood behind me. "I was hoping you'd say that." She set her warm fingers on my forearm, stroking upward and hooking her fingers sensually into the crook of my elbow. She continued up, stroking my bicep, then sliding back down and covering the back of my hand with hers, lacing her fingers between mine on the cutting board in front of me and pressing her front against my back. "Tell me about your green sauce. Is it creamy?"

Her sexy tone, the suggestive way she turned my words back on me, the tail end of Bruno Mars singing Just the Way You Are in the background, lit me on fire.

"Fuck Rubes. I'm trying to be a gentleman here. You're killing me." I laughed and turned to face her, bending to claim her mouth, stroking my tongue inside, feeling her silky textures.

She lifted her jaw and angled her head, inviting me deeper. Murmuring against my mouth, licking me, she said, "I don't want a gentleman. I want a sexy chef. A laughing goatherd. I want you." And we kissed like that, increasingly hot and slippery, for as long as I could stand it. My hands slid down from her arms and across her ribs to grip her hips the way I had in my imagination, digging my fingers into her firm flesh. Then, on autopilot, I grabbed her, lifted and spun, setting her on the kitchen countertop. My place of comfort and control.

Her legs opened to let me step between them, and I pulled her forward, pressed her tightly against my stomach, my swelling, aching cock feeling the heat she emanated from her centre. We both let out moans of pleasure at the same time. The easy way Ruby and I were together, talking, walking, touching, was blowing my mind. I expected more…I don't know what. Awkwardness? Distance? Shyness? There was none of that. It was like ten years hadn't passed. We were a natural.

As we kissed, my hands stroked her thighs, hips and ass that were spread on my countertop; her hands threading through my hair, feathering against my ears and the back of my neck. She undulated in a wave against my body, pulsing.

"I want you here. Now, " I growled. "A dirty girl in my dirty kitchen."

"That's what I want too." She breathed out, the words carried on a whisper.

I dipped my fingers under the edge of her shirt and peeled it slowly off, and as her arms came back down, she gripped my ratty old t-shirt and ripped it off over my head. Groaning, I leaned in, pressing my face between her breasts, inhaling her spicy scent, dragging my tongue along her warm skin, up to her collarbones, sucking and nipping at her neck.

She arched her back, pressing her breasts closer, and I covered them with my hands, squeezing and pinching gently through the smooth fabric of her bra. Which suddenly had to go. I slid a hand behind her to release the clasp, tossing it away as it slipped from her body, hoping it didn't land in the pasta water humming on the stovetop.

Grunting, I stepped back, quickly turned off the stove and returned to her. I hauled her off the counter, flicked open her fly and stripped her pants off, lifting her back onto the counter in three seconds flat. Now she was naked, and I just stood and ate her up with my eyes. My Ruby, lean and warm and willing, sat with my hands resting on her ribs. My fingers flared over her gorgeous hips. "You're so fucking beautiful." I shook my head, as if this were a dream. "I dreamt of you so often, remembering you, the way you felt against me, but you're even better now. I absolutely love the way you've grown up, girl."

I bent my head to lick her breasts, one and then the other, as she leaned back on her hands, giving me full access, pushing the soft globes closer to my face. I dragged my tongue over her hardened nipples, sucking and nibbling at their tender peaks as she shuddered under my touch.

"Mmm. Julian. The feeling is so, so mutual. I'm really wanting your pants off already, babe. I'm so wet for you. I'm throbbing."

"Mm-hmm. I hear you. I'm throbbing for you, too." I slipped a hand between her legs, feeling the slippery wetness she described. I closed my eyes at the silken texture of her folds against my calloused fingertips as I stroked her erect nub with my thumb and slipped two fingers into her slowly, enjoying the way she trembled and lifted her hips toward me, opening further. Pushing my fingers all the way inside, curling them and stroking her inside, feeling her textures, her pulsing muscles trying to draw me in was driving me crazy with need.

"You're so hot. So beautiful." I pressed my other hand into the small of her back, making sure we stayed glued together as I slid my mouth along her damp skin across her ribs and stomach. I dropped lower, my nose filling with the sweet scent of her.

She let out a groan of pleasure and I pressed harder into her back to let her know I had her as she laid back fully onto the wide island, opening to me.

Finnegan whined, confused by the strange behaviour in my kitchen tonight, and I chuckled and soothed him. "It's all right, Finn. I'm just cooking up a gourmet meal." Skeptic that he was, he turned on his mat and faced away, pretending to sleep.

Withdrawing my fingers, I pressed her knees further apart and replaced them with my mouth, sucking briefly on her swollen nub before diving into her with my tongue. Then I went to town with my tongue, my teeth scraping gently against her, sucking at her folds until she moaned and spasmed under my mouth, calling out my name, and I drank in the powerful energy of her release.

My cock was exploding with pulsing blood, demanding its turn at Ruby's luscious wet heat. Remembering how she liked the way I described food, I pulled back. "You are luscious and nutty, Ruby. Touching you with my tongue is better than the creamiest sauce ever to come out of the Cordon Bleu, babe. You are three star." While I talked, I stripped off my pants and grabbed a condom from my pocket, slipping it quickly over my throbbing girth. I was so eager my hands shook.

Then I pulled her to the edge of the counter, panting, my chest heaving as I slid inside. "Oh, Ruby. Oh, Ruby." She lifted her knees, wrapping her legs around my torso, holding me tight as I drove home. Home. For the first time I was grateful the old counters my grandfather built were a good two inches lower than modern standards, making this incredibly erotic option not only possible, but comfortable.

Moving slowly at first, waiting for Ruby to catch up with me again, I simply relished the amazing feel of her. I slowly built-up speed and force as I sensed her rising need. She lifted onto her elbows to look at me. Then time became meaningless as I lost myself in Ruby, our gazes locked over her heaving sweaty breasts, my knees threatening to give out as I thrust rhythmically against her to the drumbeats of Adam Lambert's

"Whataya Want from Me." *Ba-dum, ba-dum, ba-dum* until an intense spasm clenched the base of my spine and I felt myself get swept away in the sensation, white lights flashing in my vision, losing myself in her. And then I collapsed over her body, gasping for breath, revelling in the glow of one of the most intense sessions of lovemaking I'd ever had.

Chapter 21

Ruby

AFTER THE MOST mind-blowing kitchen countertop sex of my dreams, Julian and I showered and threw our clothes back on, and he resumed making dinner. But now, everything was symbolic and loaded, redolent of sexual associations.

I continued to snap pictures of his capable hands and his intense, blissed-out expression as he effortlessly mixed flour and eggs into pasta dough, a cloud of airborne flour particles floating in a late summer sunbeam that cut through the kitchen. He teased me by describing what he did in the most suggestive sexual language he could.

As he shaped, massaged, and stroked the ball of pasta dough, it became soft, smooth, and round as a woman's breast. Then he turned to me and explored my mouth with his familiar, searching tongue as he squeezed and pinched my breasts until I moaned—getting flour all over my shirt—and then turned back to his task, laughing.

He shaped it into oversized *orecchiette* that he coined *piccolo labbratto*, which he said was going to produce and sell at the Farm-to-Table Faire in September, because they were the perfect shape for holding the creamy sauce and melting cheese. He dropped them slowly into boiling water, stirring and cooking them until they were al dente like an aroused clitoris, sucking and biting one to show me how it should feel. He followed it up with a deep kiss as he tucked a hand between my legs to hold me in his warm palm, sliding his fingers along my heat and pausing to press a fingertip against my aching nub, like a placeholder.

The chopping and grinding of the green herbs, garlic, nuts and olive oil into a creamy green pesto was a process of slow, repetitive, grinding circular movements, and he made sure I caught every nuance and suggestive movement with timely moans, grunts, and hot glances. We were both hot and squirming by the time the sauce was ready.

Then he decided the homemade pork sausages from a local farmer that he had in the fridge were the perfect accompaniment to our pasta dish. Turning to me, pressing his hard groin against my thigh and grinding a little, he said in a fake Italian accent, "The *prendi salsicce*," quality sausage, "would go very well with the *piccolo labbratto* and pesto, making a most delicious combination that would cause me to *svenire* with delight, like an *orgasmo*."

"Do you actually speak Italian?" I asked. It amazed me what he'd learned in our years apart. I realized other languages were entirely possible. I spoke smatterings of Russian, Spanish, and Mandarin, after all.

"I speak food," he said, chuckling, "… in several languages."

Despite all the fun and games, dinner, when we finally got to eat it, was incredibly delicious; I realized everything Julian touched was blessed with his innate talent, sensibilities, and skill. We lingered at the farmhouse kitchen table, its surface scuffed and scarred from decades of family use, slowly savouring our pasta, sausages, wild salad greens with vinaigrette. We nibbled on the sourdough bread Julian had made himself and sipped the wine that he'd brought home from the reunion. Neither of us wanted it to end.

He held my hand over the table as we talked, as though he was afraid if he let go, I'd disappear. I had a similar desire to keep him close. It was the most erotic meal I'd ever eaten, a culinary dance of innuendo and foreplay. The air between us simmered with anticipation, and an unspoken agreement that, in time, we'd make love again.

"Deanna mentioned you were about to get a Michelin star."

He scoffed. "Easier said than done. But yes. For a while, it seemed within reach, and I was working on it. I had a lot going on and I was on a roll; I was making good money, winning awards, and was very successful." He tilted his head. "I had friends in the business and I had clients with influence. It was fun, challenging, exciting, creative. I went a little crazy on the high of it all."

"I get it now," I said. "You're so hardworking, and sensitive, you'd do well no matter what you did. But food makes so much sense, now that I think about it."

He shrugged, releasing my hand to take a swallow of wine, and I watched his throat move. Every part of him was beautiful and erotic to me.

"An exciting life." I shook my head. It sounded like a dream. Hardly what I'd imagined Julian to have done in the years I'd been gone. "And here I was picturing you quietly raising chickens all this time."

He raised his eyes to meet mine with a wry smile. "If your intent was to insult me, mission accomplished."

"Aww. No!" I bent at the waist, trying to hide my fiery face in my hands, and crashed into his hand and snort-laughed at my awkwardness. I sat up and met his gaze with embarrassed remorse. "Sorry. Sorry. It's my lack of imagination. Please?"

He huffed, flashed a bashful smile, then nodded. "Yeah, sure." Squeezing my hand, drawing his thumb over my knuckles absently, he sobered. "Mostly, I was a mad workaholic. Living too fast, sleeping too little. The stress was brutal." His gaze slid to the side, pensive, and I knew there was more to it than that. More that he didn't want to tell me. He picked himself up and smiled. "Despite that, it all seemed to be going in the right direction. Life was good."

He protested, but he'd clearly had a grand adventure and enjoyed it. "You loved it. And you were successful. But you quit."

He stroked his bottom lip with a finger thoughtfully. "I haven't quit. But I was losing heart. Losing myself. I've just… taken a new direction, for now." He took another big pull on his wineglass, and I swooned a little, watching his tongue dart out to swipe his lips. Every move he made drew me further back in time, and my body betrayed me by heating up as my stomach fluttered.

I tilted my head, waiting. I wasn't an award-winning journalist for nothing. Listening and drawing people's stories out was what I did. I'd never hungered for answers so badly.

"It was good for a while. Making delicious food. Feeding people, taking care of them. It felt good, and I started to feel whole again. It was healing. It was something I could do that I thought had value. At first it was about healing me and then I realized it could be more than that. I could take care of others. Just like you, going out into the world because of your desire to help others, I could too in my own small way."

"What was the fly in the ointment?"

"I loved learning things about food and the hospitality industry, but the more I learned to love and care about food, the more I saw in the world that I hated. That made me angry."

"Such as?"

He bristled. "Things that were just wrong. That I couldn't support any more." Julian's dark brows came down in a cloud of frustration, but he sat upright and his eyes sparked with an angry passion. "The food that was sourced for the fine restaurants where my friends and I cooked was not the same as the rest of the world had access to. I wanted to feed, delight and nurture, but I'd become part of this vast system. "We were hurting people and hurting the planet and I couldn't bear it anymore."

"So now you're trying to heal the earth. With food."

He stood, moving the dishes from table to kitchen countertop, and dropped a sausage into Finnigan's dish on the floor. "That's right. I want to take us back to a more natural balanced relationship. We have to learn to husband the land so that the land can nurture us."

Finnegan sidled up, woofed softly in thanks and ate the sausage, snuffling as he chewed. It took all of two minutes.

Julian's passion was contagious. I could see that while his fans, some of them anyway, might have been going wild for this sexy young chef-farmer, it was so much more than that. When he spoke, his eyes lit up, his cheeks glowed pink, and he became magnetic, seductive, irresistible in his conviction.

I picked up the bottle and filled our glasses again while he talked, fascinated by his journey. The wine was giving me a little buzz. I may also have been a bit euphoric, just sitting with him, drinking wine and listening. I knew I'd never stopped loving Julian, but sitting quietly with him like this? Discovering him anew? I was falling in love with him all over again.

He was indulging me. I didn't know where it would end, but I knew my turn would come. And that filled me with dread.

Resting with full stomachs, satisfied palettes, and intensely enjoying each others company after dinner, he took a sip of his wine and said, "The fitting dessert for this meal would have been fresh figs poached in sweet wine, but it's too early in the summer, and my second crop of fruit from my trees is still green." When I asked him why, he laughed and told me *figa* was a slang term in Italian for *genitali femminili*.

When he added, "We'll have to do this again later in the season," my laughter stalled, and my smile fell as I busied myself with clearing the plates.

"I'll clean up, since you did all the cooking. Why don't you look through my photos to see if there are actually any you can use?"

Agreeably, he dropped the subject, scrolling through my photos. "Are there any that are not X-rated?" He laughed, but I heard the doubt and tension in his voice, the unasked question about our future. One I couldn't yet answer.

Chapter 22

Ruby

CARRYING our glasses and partly empty bottle of wine to the sitting area, we settled onto the sofa and I nestled close to him, our bodies fitting together comfortably like sliding into favourite old jeans.

"I love the way you feel against me," he murmured under his breath, tucking his nose against my neck and inhaling deeply, sending shivers down my spine. "You belong right here, under my arm, like you used to be."

"I missed you, too. My body missed yours." Unable to resist, I lifted one leg over his lap, straddling him, pressing my burning need against his hard heat, a moan escaping my throat as I dropped my face to his shoulder and inhaled the scent of his skin. It was a heady mixture of wine, herbs and garlic, mingled with his shampoo and unique masculine smell.

I drew back, licking his neck, pulling his pierced earlobe into my mouth and sucking gently.

His strong hands gripped my ass possessively, and he pulled me close and kissed me again, the heat building between us now that nothing stood in the way. The way he talked, I could easily believe he meant to tell me he wanted me to stay. That's what this felt like. But that was a leap. Or a dream.

Right now, we were both simply floating in the pure delight of being together again, of the sound of each other's voice, the feel of skin sliding over skin. Maybe it was something innate, something genetic, some pheromones at work, but my God, we were good together. Every cell in my body sang a chorus of joy at his mere touch.

We took our time, but our clothing disappeared, item by item, as we delved closer, hungry for each other, greedy for more, until we lay naked and tangled together on his sofa.

He paused the pulsing movements that drew us closer together just at the moment he entered me, pulling away so he could look deeply into my eyes and mouth the words, I love you. This was something he had always done, as though to acknowledge the significance of the moment, our physical union. He never took it for granted. It was always powerfully intimate and meaningful. How could I not be in love with that? With him? He was perfect.

My Julian.

Though we moved slowly, relishing every sensation, the feelings were intense, expressed through hot black steady gazes, slow motion bites on shoulders, open-mouthed sucking and licking of necks and breasts. Before long we linked both hands, Julian holding them above us as we rose together and broke at the crest of a forceful wave of sensation. Afterwards, lying in each other's arms, he leaned into me and in a barely audible voice, he whispered, "I've always loved you, Ruby. You're my one and only. I never stopped loving you."

Barely awake, breathing deeply, I whispered back against the hot skin of his neck, feeling his pulse thrumming under the surface, "I love you, too, Julian. I always will."

Julian

"You comfy?" I murmured, some minutes later, when our heart rates had slowed to normal, and we could breathe without panting.

She hummed.

We lay in silence for a while longer, caressing each other lazily. Despite the night being the best moment in our history, I couldn't put it off any longer. I needed to know what Ruby had planned. Our words of love were a balm to my healing heart, but I needed to move forward. I wanted to do it with Ruby at my side, but I didn't know where she stood. Had she decided if she was staying or leaving? I took a deep breath and jumped into the dark, ice-cold water.

"You got me to talk about myself all through dinner. Now it's your turn. Catch me up. I want to know about your uni days. The start of your career."

At the sound of our voices, Finnegan stirred from his nap on his mat in the corner, added his two cents with a soft "whuff" and set his head back down, closing his eyes again.

"Oh," she replied. "That feels like a century ago."

"Yet I have not read about it in the history books."

"Hmm." She quirked her mouth to one side. "Three years of journalism in Wisconsin."

"Was it everything you hoped it would be?"

She nodded. "And then some. I threw myself into learning, found some great mentors and loved it."

I was happy for her. "How did you end up in Europe?"

"In my final year, I applied for an exchange with the University of Amsterdam and got it. Got a couple little pieces published. From there, a contract with the London paper."

"So… a dream come true."

"Yes and no. Being a correspondent is not really like having a job. You're just out there in the world travelling, going to strange new places, meeting people, learning things, eating weird food, sleeping in uncomfortable beds…" she paused and sighed deeply, "being lonely. Every assignment, you have to prove yourself again."

"Which you did. I read your pieces whenever I could find them. You have true talent for getting to the heart of a story."

Her shoulders lifted minutely against my chest, in the cage of my arms. "You immerse yourself in the place and time, in the culture of the moment. You look around you and see what everybody else's life looks like. That's the important thing. That's what sustains you. The humanity. Telling their truth, bearing witness. That's what it was always about, for me anyway."

"And you're exceptionally good at it. As everyone knew you would be."

"I learned. I gained experience. I made mistakes. And I gained skill." She looked up, meeting my gaze, and I saw some hint of the price she'd paid. She paused, smiling wistfully. "You've accomplished a great deal, too, and achieved mastery in your field. You know what I'm talking about."

I sighed, acknowledging her words with a sad half smile.

Ruby bent her head and kissed me as she snuggled against me, drowsy. She hummed. "I feel so comfortable here. So, at home," she murmured, wrapping her arms tightly around my torso and snaking her leg between mine.

"Do you mean that?" I couldn't help asking, though my skin suddenly felt raw, and my chest squeezed with fear.

After a pause, she responded. "Yes, I do. Being with you makes me feel safe, and I can relax in a way that I never can when I'm on assignment." She squirmed, and we shimmied until we were reclined against the throw cushions, able to see each other's face.

As I searched her eyes, and gently stroked the hair from her brow and temple, I wondered if I dared ask the question that had been burning my throat since Friday. "Why did you come back? What's really going on with you?"

Her gaze dropped, and I thought she would pull away, evade a straight answer, like she had before. But then she looked at me again and spoke.

"I've been offered a new opportunity. It's a big change, and a lot to think about. I couldn't consider the implications while on assignment. I needed some quiet to mull it over. And I was due for a bit of a break, after the… after South America." Her voice hitched, and I wanted to know more, but I'd come back to it.

I frowned. "A promotion? Like editor or producer or something?"

She shook her head. "More of a sideways move, I think. And I'd have to resign my current position to take it on. Give up my job with the London paper. I can't do both."

"Do you want the change?"

At my confusion she continued, "Maclean's has tentatively offered me a contract as a correspondent. But first a book deal for a memoir of my time as a foreign correspondent." She shrugged. "It means I can move back to Canada. Travel less."

My brows shot up in surprise. "That sounds like a tremendous honour. Isn't it?"

She nodded, grimacing. "It is, but also an huge responsibility. One I'm not sure I'm up to."

"You'd stay here? To write the book?" I wished my heart didn't swell up in my chest like a balloon ready to burst, straining to take flight at the very hint of a suggestion that Ruby might be back to stay. That she might be here within reach, somewhere I could see her and touch her. If she would be mine to touch. If not, having her nearby would be particularly cruel. My ribs squeezed at the possibility.

"I don't know where I'd be. I haven't even decided whether I'm going to write the book, never mind how. I've never written a book before, let alone a memoir. What am I going to say?"

"Surely you can do it."

She sighed, tilting her head. "Maybe. But also, I don't know what they want. What if it's something I don't have, or can't give? I'm afraid they want to hear about the courageous, intrepid female war reporter, surviving gruelling, life-threatening conditions to bring in the news. Adventure and idealism. What if my story is the wrong story?"

"How can it be wrong?"

"Not glamorous enough? Not heroic enough?"

"Unlikely," I murmured, thinking of all the dangerous places she'd reported from.

"I think they want me to write about my altruism. But I'm not a humanitarian. I don't help people. I've only ever written about them. Their experiences. Their struggles, resilience and heroism. That's my signature thing, but it was only ever possible for me to bear witness while I was invested in their lives. How can I write my own truth? No one will want to read about it."

"I doubt that. So, that's not your truth?"

"Not really. Not all of it. The job is, in some ways, even harder than that, because of the way women are treated in the industry."

"Do you think they would have asked you if they didn't want your true story, in your own words? Whatever you have to tell will be fascinating."

"I don't know," she whispered.

"Do you have a commission?"

"No. Just an offer, and a deadline. My London paper doesn't even know."

"How long have you got to decide?"

She shook her head, her brow pulled low. "Not long. I got an email from my London bureau chief yesterday with a new assignment out of Jerusalem, so I have to tell him if I'm taking it, or… quitting. "

"They won't give you time?"

She shook her head. "No. I'm expected to jump when they call. They'd have to replace me immediately."

"What will be the deciding factor?"

She lifted her chin, searching my eyes while I searched hers. I looked for anything that told me if I might have something to do with this. Or nothing.

She inhaled and let out a long, thoughtful sigh. "People always think of me as tough, ambitious, and independent, because of what I do. But I'm not. Not really." She swallowed, her gaze focused on my chest as she ran a fingertip back and forth across my clavicle, down my sternum, and around my heart and dagger tattoo. Then she lifted her chin, as if determined to get it all out, now that she'd started.

"I've had to make significant sacrifices to achieve my professional goals, and to maintain integrity and honesty in my work. Yet, this is my identity. This is who I am. Who am I if I quit?"

"You said being here reminds you of who you are. That never really changes."

"Yet I feel changed. I'm tired of pretending." Her shoulders slumped as if to highlight this feeling of defeat. "I... I don't know if I can do it anymore. That's who I used to be, even with my evolving motivation. I'm tired of fighting. At the moment, I'm anything but tough and brave. I feel frail—damaged and unlovable, most unlike myself. Uncertain and fearful."

She'd become agitated, her voice wavering and her eyes glazed. What was she trying to tell me? "You will never be unlovable. Maybe you're just tired and need a break. That's understandable."

"Being with you, like this, is exactly what I need right now, Julian. When I'm with you, I remember who I am. But I..." she tapered off, as if uncertain whether to speak her next thought aloud.

I gave her a squeeze and dropped a kiss on her forehead to encourage her.

After a moment, she continued. "Being famous is a burden, as I'm sure you're discovering. Knowing that everyone watches me makes me edgy. My colleagues, of course, expect me to get the job done. No sympathy from that quarter. My parents have their own opinions about my success. Even our friends see me a certain way, never mind the public."

I touched her chin with my finger, tilting her face up to meet her gaze straight on. "No one here wants anything but the best for you, Ruby. You must know that."

"Sure. I guess that's one reason I came home. But what is that? I don't think I know anymore. I'm at a crossroads in my life, and I can't see my way through."

Not for me then. I was an afterthought. "You'll figure it out. You've always been able to."

"I don't know, Julian. Somehow I feel as if… I owe you something. As if I can't go forward until I resolve our unfinished business. Coming back, I see the way Quinn, Rainy, Parker, and Tate look at me. Look at you. I broke more than your heart. I broke some part of my world when I left, and I want… I need to fix it."

I filled my lungs, holding myself still for a moment while I processed her words. There's no way those events couldn't ripple outward and affect everyone in our circle. After all, I left town and some of that hurt spilled over into my relationships with family and friends. What did she want from me? What did she need to hear? Not platitudes, surely.

"Well. You can't undo what you did, Ruby. We can't go back in time." I hesitated, steeling my nerve. She sucked in a harsh breath, surprised and silenced by my words, but I pushed on. There were things I'd wanted to say to Ruby for years. This was my chance to get them off my chest.

"I have to be honest with you… I gave you my heart unconditionally, and you truly broke it."

Her eyes locked on mine, and my throat tightened as her eyes flooded with tears. "I'm sorry. I'm so sorry Julian. I was arrogant. I thought I knew what was best for both of us. But I never stopped loving you." She lifted her hand, resting her fingertips lightly on my cheek. "I was persuaded that our dreams didn't align, and that what I knew I had to do with my life, would hurt you."

"Sure. We were young, and naïve. But… you know what we were to each other. My only dream, Ruby, was to be with you. No more and no less."

"After the miscarriage, even though my thoughts were muddled for a long time, I convinced myself that I'd done the right thing, for both of us.

I grunted softly. "You betrayed my trust, and that changed me. Part of me will never recover from that."

Ruby's head fell to my shoulder, and I felt her tremble in my arms; a wave of remorse fluttered through me for speaking my thoughts so fully. She wasn't the big bad, hardened journalist tonight.

"But… despite all that, I have to thank you," I continued.

Her head snapped up, and I saw the confusion in her eyes that my admission aroused.

I lifted my mouth in a half smile of concession. "Because… without that pain, the loss, the wound, I would not have gone out into the world in search of… I don't know, distraction at the least, but more than that, some kind of restitution. Some balm for my broken heart and something to lose myself in so I didn't have to wallow in it."

Ruby took my face between her palms, shaking her head. "Don't," she whispered. "Don't try to ease my guilt."

"I'm not. This is the truth." I swallowed, gazing into her anguished eyes, and went on. "Because of that, I found my passion for food, which led me into the world of haute cuisine and restaurants; it was both my salvation and my purpose. I carried my cynicism and my pain with me, and it gave me a deep well of inspiration, but also a willingness to break rules, upturn expectations, and challenge traditions. And that gave me my signature food style, and also the courage to leave that world and devote myself to challenging its practices and institutions. To forge my own way and set a new, higher bar."

Ruby shook her head. "You'd have got there, anyway. I know you would. Eventually, no matter what."

"I don't know that. I may not be the naïve, trusting boy I was. But I know myself now, and I'm very clear about my purpose in life. And for that I am grateful."

Chapter 23

Ruby

I HEARD what Julian was saying. Despite his admission of past pain, he was, in his most diplomatic way, telling me he'd moved on. He was over it. He had a new life and didn't need me anymore. Certainly, he was unwilling to make sacrifices or compromises for me. I'd discarded that possibility when I'd self-ishly betrayed and abandoned him.

But it was as if my remorse, and my words of apology, meant little to him. He'd come to terms with who I am. Was he also challenging me to embrace it?

I hated to take away his new sense of empathy with my so-called passion for my work. And I couldn't say I didn't have it, still. But what drove me wasn't as idealistic as he thought. Reluctance filled me with tension, roiling in my gut, unsettled. If I argued the point, I was afraid he'd ask questions I was still too cowardly to face.

I was getting a picture of how he lived, what he valued, and what drove him. But I wanted to know more. Could I fit in here? Would he even want me to?

It was one thing to reconnect like this, our minds and bodies as sweetly compatible as ever. It was an entirely different thing to rearrange your whole life to accommodate another person.

I thought maybe I was ready, finally, to do that. How ironic that after the depth of his commitment to me, Julian no longer wanted that.

He couldn't know how much I needed him now. No one could help me heal like Julian could, and find myself again. But would he want anything to do with that? Maybe Julian wouldn't love this side of me that needed to hide and heal. I didn't know if I had the courage to express these feelings to Julian and the world.

When he'd confessed how deeply I'd wounded him, instead of revealing that pain, all the emotion seemed to drain out of his face. He became detached, as if he were talking about someone else. My heart broke seeing how much faith he had lost, not only in me but in the possibility of our love. He was always a person who believed in the essential goodness of humanity and understood his place in the world. He carried with him a comfortable worldly wisdom, that I took completely for granted. While I had to travel the world and see so many things, both horrible and wonderful, to find a kind of equilibrium and perspective, Julian had somehow been born with that gift. And yet he was not immune to the damage my betrayal of him, and our love had caused.

And I couldn't blame him.

⁂

Julian

We'd fallen asleep, lying there, not speaking, just pondering and being together. I awoke shivering, my arm numb and my bladder bursting. Slipping out from under Ruby, I pulled a fleece blanket over her cool limbs and kissed her bare shoulder, neck and cheek, feeling an ache in my chest. She stirred, turning to nuzzle her face into the cushion, murmuring, "Be there in two minutes."

When I returned from the bathroom, I scooped her gently into my arms and headed for the bedroom. We needed a proper, comfortable night's sleep. Before I made it to the threshold, Ruby suddenly went rigid in my arms, kicking and flailing as a sharp scream rent the night air.

"Hey, hey. Sweetheart. Shhh."

I got a pointy elbow in the gut, a palm in my face and a Charley Horse, and nearly dropped her on the floor, before I struggled my way into the bedroom to set her down on the bed.

"Shh. Ruby."

By that time, she'd woken herself up, and lay there blinking and disoriented. Clearly, it had been a night terror of some kind. I pulled the comforter up over her and slipped under it to wrap myself around her as she curled into a ball, stroking and soothing her with soft sounds. The tension finally drained out of her body, and with a whimper and a moan, she quietly cried herself back to sleep.

I may have dozed a little, but I was too shaken to let go completely, my mind spinning with questions. What had happened to her to trigger such a violent nightmare? Had someone tried to hurt her? Or had she just witnessed such upsetting things on assignments that she carried those memories with her?

Another hour or so later, time blurred in the still of the night with only my thoughts for company, she stirred awake and turned to face me, stretching her legs and tucking her feet tentatively between mine. I cradled her in my arms, as if she might snap in half like blown glass.

"Tell me."

She buried her face against my chest, shaking it back and forth, saying nothing, but lacing an arm under mine to wrap around my back.

"You can trust me, Ruby. I love you. Tell me anything. Everything."

She pulled away, sighing, and rolled onto her back. Her eyes stared up at the dark ceiling, the moonlight picking up the silhouette of her profile and the glint of moisture in her eyes.

"A few months ago, when I was in South America, we were investigating the aftermath of the sham election and international sanctions in Venezuela. But we'd gone in under the pretext of doing a feature on changes in coffee exports. We knew it was dangerous. The country is still strongly divided between supporters of Maduro, and those of Guaidó, and it's hard to know who to trust. Foreigners have to tread very carefully. But we'd done our homework, had solid contacts, and prepared well. We had a plan, and more than adequate security with us. We thought."

Her voice, flat and quiet to begin with, quavered as she remembered. I remained silent as I listened, my terror mounting as my imagination filled in the blank spaces with questions.

"We were driving from Caracas towards Mérida to interview a couple of contacts. Me, Raoul the photographer, our guide Estevan, and our paramilitary guards in a second jeep. We'd taken Highway 5 down, and turned up from Barinas, to cut through the Parc Nacional Sierra Nevada."

She paused to swallow, gathering her thoughts, and I held her tighter, rubbing her arms and neck, because she'd begun to tremble all over. My heart hammered in my chest, thinking of the hard reality of Ruby in such precarious danger.

"It's a semi-arid, very mountainous region, and we were on a deserted stretch of rocky road when we got a flat. Before we had time to make the repair, what looked like government officials pulled over and began questioning us. They may have been trailing us, or even compromised our vehicle. I don't know. We were naturally wary. There's been political turmoil continuously since the twenty-eighteen election, and there are supporters of both sides everywhere. You could never know where anyone's political loyalties lay."

I waited in silence for a few minutes while Ruby's breath shook, her hands clenching the sheets in a frantic rhythm. She'd begun to hyperventilate, and I could feel heat coming off of her in waves as she'd begun to sweat.

"They… were aggressive with their questions. Making accusations about whether we were supporters of Guaidó. We knew enough how to answer without implicating ourselves. Staying friendly. But then they got pushier, and the guards tried to step in."

Her voice rose on the last words to a squeak, fading.

"There was a scuffle, and shots. The next thing we knew, the guards were dead, lying in the dirt. We knew we were in trouble then. They bound and gagged us, threw bags over our heads, and tossed us into separate jeeps. I wasn't sure where Raoul and Estevan were, but I thought I was alone in the back of this one jeep. I was on the floor, getting tossed around as we drove over rougher and rougher terrain. I was sure we'd left the main road. All I knew was that it grew cooler, like we'd moved into shade. I smelled water. A heavy boot pressed down on my chest, and I could barely breathe."

She was panting now, remembering, her hand clenching mine in a death grip. She'd stopped talking, but her eyes were still open wide, searching the dark. The image of her, manhandled, hog-tied, tossed into a jeep. Terrified.

I waited.

"I was certain I was dead. Another statistic for the wall. Maybe it was hours. Maybe only minutes. I don't know. I was alone with my last thoughts. And in those moments, Julian, my only wish was that I'd spent my life with you."

I turned her away from me and wrapped my body completely around her, but loosely. Rubbing her, kissing her shoulder and neck softly. I wanted to know what happened.

How she got out. But if that's all she could tell me, it was enough for now.

Her breathing eventually slowed to near normal while she lay as still as death. I didn't know if she'd talked to anyone else about this, a therapist or her boss, or what it meant that she was confiding in me. Reliving the details must be horrific, and I was ill qualified to respond, so I stayed quiet, just trying to comfort her by being with her.

"I'm so tired," came her barely audible whisper a few minutes later, and I felt her breath even out as she drifted back to sleep.

Now I understood what she meant by feeling safe here, and being able to relax. I get that. But at the same time, she was in no condition to be making commitments. With a sinking heart, I realized she's not really choosing me. She's just retreating into a cave like a wounded animal.

Yet I could offer her refuge. Did I owe her that? Would I be taking advantage of her vulnerability? And would it last? Or would she rest, heal, and then leave me again? These were not the right conditions to be deciding about our future. If, indeed, we had one together.

I always thought of myself as a good guy. Caring and responsible. But offering a place for Ruby might come at too high a cost to me. Maybe it was time I learned to put my own needs ahead of others, for once. To ask for what I wanted.

I thought back to the summer after grad, when we found out Ruby was pregnant; how proud and excited I was, but also how terrified. She needed my protection. I'd reassured her I'd take care of her, though I did not know how. I'd take care of all of us—our little family—even if it meant I had to stay and work the farm with Dad. It wasn't what we'd planned, but we'd be okay. We had each other.

Before her announcement, I'd been about to talk to her about my options. Whether I'd move with her to Wisconsin for school. I'd work or study something. I didn't know or care at that point. As long as we were together. I wanted to be with her. I knew I'd figure out my own path in time. It hardly mattered.

But after I found out, I realized I'd need to stay on the farm and work with my dad. I'd swallow my pride and do it. For Ruby. For our child.

I believed our love was forever. That was the hardest part for me when she left. Thinking that she didn't feel the same way. Didn't need me. And maybe questioning everything I thought I knew about her, about myself, about the world. I didn't feel that I knew anymore what love was, or that I could trust it.

Strangely, I'd come full circle. Even though I lived alone and everything had changed, I was content with a simple life. Would Ruby be? Should I ask her to stay? Make a life with me here? Have the family we always wanted?

But I had no right to make demands on her for myself. No. She had to pursue her career. She'd achieved so much success, fame, awards of excellence, even. She couldn't give that up for me. Unless she wanted to?

It was foolish to expect anything beyond this delicious moment, but I still hoped that maybe her desires and ambitions had changed. With everything she had gone through, did she long to find her home here again?

Could I bear to let her go again? How could I live with that? My chest squeezed, pressing in on my sad, hardened heart, my throat closing up in a spasm at the thought of letting myself love her, and then losing her again. How much loss could one man take?

Ten years ago, the most important thing in my life was Ruby and our love. Now, I had a history, skills, a sense of purpose. But I also wanted love, companionship, and intimacy in my life. And I wanted a family. Were there other ways I could follow my own calling and be with Ruby, too?

Could I compromise? I had contacts all over the world. If she was based out of London, I could work there. I could get a job teaching at my old school. Or I could pursue my sustainable food mission in a different way. Maybe work with people in different countries. I could research traditional cuisines and techniques, maybe collaborate with someone on a series for food tv, and get my message out that way.

I didn't think I could do nothing, though. Just follow Ruby around, or hang and wait for her to come home. That wouldn't sit right with me. If there's one thing I'd learned in the past ten years, it was that I mattered too. I almost didn't know Ruby anymore. Obviously, her experiences over the last decade had changed her. But there was no doubt in my mind that they had irrevocably changed me.

Chapter 24

Julian

I JERKED awake at the sound of my phone's text notification. Rolling away from Ruby's limp warm form, I slapped in the general direction of the bedside table, searching. No phone. Where's my phone?

Finnegan's head shot up when I stirred and I pointed down at his mat, and whispered, "Quiet." His eyebrows shot up, curious, and his eyes followed my movements, but he obeyed.

The phone bleeped again, and I rolled out of bed, suppressing a groan as I registered a nasty red-wine hangover and stumbled to the living room, discovering my phone on the coffee table. Our discarded clothes lay all about, evidence of the passion-filled evening we'd shared. Images, sensations, and emotions flashed in quick succession in my mind and body, remembering; I laughed to myself over how worked up Ruby got about my cooking. Who'd have thought?

After a moment, Finnegan silently followed me, sniffing around at the wreckage.

I grabbed the phone just as it beeped yet again—whoever it

was possessed little patience. Aah. Matt. I'd already missed several messages, starting at seven this morning.

Julian. Dude. You're not backing out, are you? You want to go over the presentation points?

What the — ?

Julian? If you blow off this meeting, I'm going to throttle and rotisserie you like a chicken.

My heart kicked me in the ribs like a mad donkey. Fuck! The meeting with Ethan at the spa! It's today! I completely forgot.

I know I'm forcing you to do this, buddy, but you have to trust me. Ethan's not what you think. This is exactly what we need.

Yeah, yeah. We'd see about that. But I gave my word.

Would it help if I offered to go with you this morning?

Typing a quick NO! in reply to stop the onslaught, I jogged back to the bedroom in a panic.

Ruby stirred, mumbling. "What?"

Now, of all times, was not the time to run off on her. After her revelations last night, she felt closer to me than ever. She needed me.

"I completely forgot, babe. Today's my meeting with Ethan at the resort. At the reunion, he insisted I come up for a tour and chat. I promised him and the team." I looked at my bedside clock. Shit! After nine already. "I've barely got time to dress and get there. I'm so sorry. I have to go." And somehow feed the animals beforehand. God! I never slept til nine.

Bleary-eyed, her chestnut waves a wild tangle around her head, she leaned up on one elbow to squint at me. "It's okay. Go. Go."

I chuckled softly. She needed more sleep. "Stay in bed. Sleep. I'll only be a couple of hours, tops. I'll see you when I get back. Wait til you taste my eggs."

She moaned and flopped back onto the pillow, her arm over her eyes.

I quickly showered, because I couldn't go to any meeting smelling of sex, not even with the vile Ethan Garwood. I almost wished I could go smelling of goats, hay, and manure. That would give him a clear picture of who he was dealing with.

On the other hand, I briefly considered dressing up in sharp business attire, so he'd know he wasn't dealing with a country hick, and could put away his mercenary plans to exploit local farmers for his own greed. But no. That wouldn't do either.

In any case, I really did need to toss around some feed and hay quickly before I left, and let the goats out into their paddock. So, I opted for the cleaner, less ragged version of my daily work wear, combed my wet hair but did not shave, threw on a soft fleece jacket, and shrugged at my rugged image in the mirror. I filled Finn's food dish, flicked on the power switch of my espresso maker to pre-heat the pump for Ruby, and headed off. Whether she could figure out how to use it was another matter.

Following the rough dirt and gravel road up the mountain to Ragged Mountain Resort and Spa, my four-wheel drive bumping over the terrain, I had a few minutes to gather my thoughts. Unfortunately, instead of rehearsing the presentation to Ethan about the Farm-to-Table Faire and its purpose, my mind strayed to thoughts of Ruby and our night together.

Ruby and our respective futures.

She was clearly at a point in her career and in her life where she needed to regroup. That was clear from her unsettled and melancholy mood, and her rambling disclosures about the book deal she was considering. And there was more than that. Her life-threatening experience in Venezuela was reason enough to reconsider her career direction. Could I go back and carry on as if nothing had happened if that had happened to me? I thought maybe not. No matter what she decided to do, she obviously needed some downtime to heal from the stress and trauma.

Would I be content if she stayed a while as she did that, and then left me again if she felt the need to return to that life?

Fuck. That would hurt. But not in the same way, I realized, as last time. If she rejected me and left me forever, then yes, that would suck. My chest squeezed, and my mouth filled with the sour taste of bile at the mere thought of it. I'd survive, but I'd be miserable and lonely. Again.

If she wanted me to go with, could I leave to follow her? Leave the farm? My family and friends? My hometown now that I'd returned? I chewed on that for a kilometre or so. I had left, so it was no mystery what I'd experience. I'd travelled the world. I had a thrilling and successful career to go back to, should I choose that. But did I want to? Right now, no. My vision for my own future was more of a continuation of my current mission.

After the Faire, I wouldn't mind having my own restaurant again. As owner and chef this time, not chef for someone else. And this time, it would be here in Port Camosun, and would align with my current philosophy. It would be a showcase for my clean and natural, locavore diet. I could continue both paths at once, on my terms. These thoughts, this vision, filled me with excitement and pride.

The thought of working abroad, hopping from hotel to resort, from city to city, trying to stay within somehow in Ruby's orbit as she jaunted around the globe after stories. Not so much.

I'd discovered my purpose, and was committed to it. I knew who I was now. I loved Ruby with my whole heart, and would never love another woman. But still, I had to live my own life, and let her live hers.

But if she left with an understanding—that we belonged to each other, that she'd be back when she could, that we'd be together again. Could I live with that? The pressure lifted, the bitter fading to a mellow sweetness. Yeah. Maybe I could. Not a conventional marriage, but it could work, with understanding. We could even have kids. I'd raise them on the farm happily. I could do that, if she could.

I'd tell her. Right after the meeting, after talking with Ethan, I'd tell her.

And that's all the time I had to think of Ruby for the next hour, because I pulled into the broad circular forecourt of the resort and spa.

THE OPEN SPACE was ringed by trees, and there were a few discreet wooden signs at the start of paths, presumably leading to other buildings that I couldn't see from here. Ethan waited for me at the main entrance.

"Good morning, Julian." He strode forward, hand extended, a wide smile on his face as I stepped out of my truck.

Hesitantly, I shook his hand. "Ethan."

He huffed out a laugh. "You need a good cup of coffee. Then we'll start the tour, hey?" He led me inside an attractive, very rustic chic West Coast lobby, with slate tiles and wood walls covered with indigenous prints of whales, salmon, and crows. Somehow, I was expecting more faux Santa Fé, with pastels and perfume.

To the left, we entered a lounge area with floor to ceiling windows that overlooked the forested mountaintop. Somehow I'd expected overly groomed land, with panoramic views down the mountain to the ocean. He signalled to a staff member behind a long counter, and I heard the rumble and hiss of a top end espresso maker, my headache already kneeling in submission to the anticipated coffee hit. I strode to the edge of the subdued, casual room to look out at the view.

Confused, I turned to him. "Didn't your dad clear cut a fair bit back in the day?"

He walked towards me, handing me a tall foam topped cappuccino. "You all right with dairy? We have alternates if you prefer."

I took the coffee and saluted him in thanks. "Nope. This is

good, thanks." I sipped and sighed. This ordeal would have been much easier if I'd got up at my usual early hour and had time to prepare my thoughts.

He gestured to follow him and talked as we walked. "He did cut a swath of trees, about ten years ago. I was away at college then. But he got a lot of flack for it, and didn't get as far as he'd planned. Thank God."

Curious, I stayed silent as he walked us through the main spa area, a labyrinth of softly lit corridors and small rooms, equally simple and clean, white with a lot of fresh green accents. The logo, I noticed here and there was a simple leaf inside a mountain peak, in a hand drawn circle.

"I got back here in time to at least begin talking him down from his plan. I think he even had golf course aspirations, which would have devastated the mountaintop. I'd been in business school, so I could show him a different vision."

"I don't recall your father being a man willing to negotiate with anyone." Nor was he an honourable man, in my experience. His dealings with my father and other local producers spoke to that truth. I'd met many like him in my travels—interested in profits and status, and attracting wealthy business clientele, celebrities, and socialites. Completely out of touch with the real world.

Ethan chuckled. "Not that he really got it. My father was ambitious—and ballsy—but not that sophisticated when it came down to it. But thankfully he was getting old and tired, and willing for me to take over so he could step back. That's when I pivoted."

"Pivoted?"

He nodded, leading the way out a door to an exterior pathway through the trees. He stopped talking, and it was suddenly silent and peaceful. Morning sun filtered through the evergreen boughs, birdsong, and the rustle of the soft mountaintop breeze were the only sounds. I felt tension leaking out of my chest, and took a deep breath of incredibly clean, brisk mountain air.

"I'd travelled and toured a lot of resorts and spas around the world. And I realized that, while panoramic views of water and rolling meadows are beautiful, they're common enough to be... almost commonplace. When friends from abroad came here, I'd naively take them to show off our ocean views, and they'd turn their backs on it, and stare at our mountains and forests in awe, watching the eagles circle and swoop in a graceful dance on the currents. That's when it hit me."

I couldn't say my experience was much different from his. I'd seen a few similar environments as I moved from restaurant job to restaurant job. Europe has a lot of beauty, but very little of it, except perhaps in Scandinavia, looks like home. Sometimes you have to go away to appreciate what you left behind. Still, I had no reason to trust him, and plenty of reasons to be skeptical.

"What role is your father playing these days?" Ethan might talk a pretty story, but if his old man was still involved, there was no way—

"Dad's fully retired now. His health isn't great, and he and Mom spend half of every year in Tucson. He needs the heat."

Hmph. I snuck a glance at the man before me as he looked out at the forest, trying to take his measure. Even if our Farm-to-Table Faire would be good PR for him, it didn't mean the association would support our mission. In retrospect, I supposed, my own father had been no more sensitive or sophisticated to the concerns I had. And I had pivoted too, so to speak, using the resources that he'd built, and left to me. Perhaps Ethan and I weren't so different, after all.

"Why should we associate with you and your resort, Ethan?"

His smile was wry, as though he expected to be grilled. "You mean other than my deep pockets, Julian?"

I nodded.

He continued walking. "The areas he cleared have been put to good use, or reforested—at personal expense—and will fill in, eventually. In the meantime, I did what my friends showed me how to do. I turned and looked at the trees. After a few years of building and renovation, we have a very different perspective and feel up here. I want to share that message with the world."

As we walked, we passed a series of wooden cottages nestled into the trees, with gentle, serene landscaping, trickling fountains and sculptures set around them. "We can use these cottages for any number of things, mainly massage therapies, small meditation retreats, workshops and the like. But guests can also book them for more extensive, luxury treatment packages on request. That's very popular with the bridal parties."

"You do weddings up here?"

"Sure. It's a good bread and butter trade. Helps pay for the improvements. Our summer tourist season is expanding, but I'm currently working on connecting more with our own local market so we can make full use of the facilities year round. Our climate is mild enough that locals can still make it up the mountain even in winter, and hopefully in time we can do more stuff around the fall and winter holiday season."

"That's why you want to sponsor the Farm-to-Table Faire."

"Sure. Of course. To let people know what we're doing up here. There are still people..." he paused meaningfully, dipping his chin, "... who have preconceived ideas about what we are, based on what was going on ten or twenty years ago. I want to change that perception, and build a loyal local clientele."

I hummed, acknowledging that I'd judged him based on some very outdated information. His passion about this rivalled my own.

"But it's more than that, Julian. What I want for this place, what I believe in, is completely in alignment with your mission. I want people to come here for an experience that's... almost spiritual in its connection with the natural world. And maybe realign their own values in response. That's what we need now."

His passion for sustainable local food and hospitality seemed to rival my own.

We'd looped through the woods and returned to the main complex from another direction, and I saw there was a separate entrance on this side, covered by a generous, log-beamed portico flanked by huge planters tumbling with attractive flowering plants.

"The pièce de résistance, I hope in time, will be our restaurant." Ethan held the door for me, and we entered the dimly lit, quiet space. It was clearly a restaurant, though obviously unused at present; chairs were stacked on tables, pushed to one side of the large room, and a polisher sat in the centre of the wide plank wood floor, its cord snaking off to the side.

We're getting the space ready for a grand re-opening sometime late this year or early next year, depending."

"Depending on what?"

He flicked on overhead lights as we entered the kitchen space, which was only partially equipped, with various gaps and equipment sitting about. "On whether I can find an executive chef to run it who shares my vision for an elite dining experience based on local and sustainable food practices?" And at that, he stopped talking, and let me look around as the penny dropped.

My pulse raced as my imagination ran away with me. It was a great kitchen with top end equipment, though it was incomplete, almost as though whoever was building it didn't know what to put where. This made sense, since every chef worth his or her salt had preferences and specifications for a kitchen layout. One side of the kitchen opened to the dining space, but this was even less finished, a plastic sheet draped from ceiling to floor, and my mind filled in the blanks with details I'd seen in various places, of my ideal workspace.

When I'd seen my fill, I stopped and turned toward him,

taking in his expectant, patient expression. "It's yours Julian. If you want it."

My heart thumped against my ribcage in a steady hammering beat. My heart was saying, Yes! Yes! Yes! An even bigger stage to showcase both my talents and my beliefs. But my brain was more cautious. I swallowed, my throat dry. "This is a lot to take in. Let me think about it, Ethan." I turned, making another three-sixty degree scan of the space, absorbing details. "I'll have questions. Maybe we can start with the Faire and see how it goes."

His face split into a broad, satisfied grin. He slapped me on the shoulder. "That's all I can ask for."

Blinking and shaking my head to suppress an eye roll, I reluctantly gave him a chagrined smile, and we shook on it. "The planning committee will be in touch. I have to meet with them to discuss your involvement. I know you've already got an ally in Matt, but we'll see how everyone else feels. All right?"

He nodded. "Thanks for your time today, man."

Chapter 25

Ruby

I WOKE ALONE, parched, with a headache as sharp as machine gun fire, slowly realizing that it was as much from crying as from the wine we'd consumed last night. Again, surprisingly, I'd slept deeply after my crying bout. Upon first waking, an hour back, I'd had a moment of disorientation looking up at another unfamiliar ceiling, forgetting where I was. Then I'd remembered last night, and reached out for Julian, needing reassurance after baring my soul to him.

Then I remembered he'd left and felt relieved. I needed some time before I could look at him, as I'd withdrawn deep into myself, as I often did after a bad night. Having revisited those events and shared them with Julian, I felt even more raw and exposed, more uncertain in my skin.

Why had I confided everything? I'd not spoken about the kidnapping to anyone since it happened. Not even the military and staff counsellors that coddled me afterwards, prodding gently at my fresh wounds with questions about my mental state.

Finnegan greeted me as I sat up, shoving his cool nose into my palm.

"Hey, there, boy."

Shuffling into the kitchen in search of a glass of water, I saw that Julian hadn't had time to tidy in his mad dash to get to his meeting. Finnegan, however, seemed to have food in his dish, so I expect Jules had taken care of the essentials. Good thing because I had no clue how to feed goats or chickens. I decided I'd better check anyway, to make certain.

The farm was dead silent, except for birdsong, and was so peaceful. Not another soul around for miles. No shouting voices, no thumping bootfalls, no gunfire echoing in the distance.

I had ample opportunity to think while I showered, dressed, tidied up. It was only ten-thirty. Waiting around for Julian to return felt strange. As much as I loved this place and found it comforting, it wasn't my home. I was just a mere guest.

I strolled outside intending to visit Nutmeg, Finnegan loping agreeably at my heels, my thoughts circling around last night's complicated series of events. I'd been shameless in my admiration of Julian last evening. Seeing him here, in his element, both with nature and in his kitchen, made me weak with longing and desire. My skin tingled and my core heated as I visualized his muscled back reaching to pick herbs, his tanned sinewy forearms flexing as he chopped them and kneaded the pasta dough into soft round shapes. His playful, flirtatious, sexy voice as he teased me, and then his intent, focussed passion as he took me, and gave me boundless pleasure.

Then later, his tenderness, patience, and longing surfaced as he looked into my eyes, cradled me and stroked me through my dilemma, my nightmare, and my memories. He was, quite simply, the perfect man. The best in every way. And I was as smitten with him now as I was when I'd first laid eyes on him the summer before tenth grade. No one would ever compare to Julian in my eyes, or displace him in my heart.

I let my eyes scan the farmyard and the far horizon, filling my lungs with pristine country air. Finnegan snuffled at the gravel around my boots. This was what I needed. More of the peaceful, pastoral healing I'd experienced in Bolivia immediately after the kidnapping. This visit, my time with Julian, however brief, had already done me good.

In fact, given my choices so far, I couldn't imagine a life with any man other than Julian. And I knew he loved me too, despite everything.

Finnegan and I peeked into the barn, just enough to confirm that Julian had let the livestock out into the pasture before he left. We meandered out into the field, Finnegan bounding ahead over tussocks of tall grass toward the other animals.

"Finnegan!" I shouted. "Leave Nutmeg alone!" I jogged ahead in case he was bent on harassing the poor stressed alpaca.

A trio of the smaller goats danced towards me, frolicking and curious, and then bounced off, romping like puppies. I envied them their mindless trusting sense of belonging in a group. Not that I wanted to be a mindless groupie. I valued my independence and individuality too much. It was a part of who I was, but I still needed to find my flock. I still wanted belonging and companionship, so absent from my last few years.

Nutmeg stood amid the goats, and I was happy that they'd seemed to accept each other, but he still seemed lonely somehow. Alpaca were social creatures. I hoped Julian grew to love him and even considered getting him some companions.

I wasn't cut out to be a lone wolf, either. The thought of heading back out on assignment, shifting from place to place, never having a home base to relax in, made my blood run cold and my chest tighten with dread. I gazed sympathetically at Nutmeg again, standing apart.

"Hi there, baby," I crooned, approaching slowly. His ears perked up, rotating towards me like antennae, curious and alert. I waved Finnegan off and he hung back, watching curiously as I sidled up to Nutmeg, reaching for his head. He let me scratch his ears, obviously enjoying the touch. After a few moments, I dug in with both hands and gave his ears and woolly neck a good scrubbing. They loved that.

The first alpaca I'd ever met was on the farm in Bolivia three months ago. After Raoul and I were reunited and debriefed by the authorities, the military and the news agency, an acquaintance in Caracas suggested I visit her friends in Bolivia. One thing led to another, and I found myself on this farm, just existing, for a few weeks. I was still in shock, withdrawn, bewildered. I couldn't sleep or eat. No one made demands on me. All I could do was sit and think, reliving those terrifying moments, asking over and over, "Where's Estevan?" I knew he was never found, but still couldn't believe the same fate had befallen him, my friend, as those guards he'd hired. But it must be so. Either that or he was with our captors and had betrayed us. I didn't know which was worse.

Eventually, the quiet, steady kindness of my hosts penetrated my fog. I hung out with the animals a lot, and then started knitting with Belen and her mother Carolina, learning traditional patterns. That was therapeutic, I guess. It gave me something to do, anyway. I came back to myself; at least I was functional during the days, and could help out with chores on the farm.

Then, amongst all the messages of consolation and concern from various colleagues, the offer from Maclean's had come in out of the blue. Like a gift, or a sign. I didn't know why, or what to make of it.

After a few more weeks, I was ready to come home.

When I came back to Port Cam and take a break, I hadn't had a coherent plan to reconcile with Julian. Reconnecting with him, or with my tight circle of friends from high school, hadn't really been top-of-mind. I hadn't, in truth, thought it possible, never mind so easy. They'd all been far more welcoming and forgiving than I'd expected.

But what I'd said to him last night was true. The damage I'd caused when I ran away weighed on me. It was baggage I carried with me always. In some ways, I'd never stopped running after that summer. As long as I kept moving, kept throwing myself into situations far more disturbing and tragic than my own, kept striving to do justice to other people's stories, I could avoid having to think about my own.

Now, I realized, the offer to write my memoir had thrown me into a panic because... I didn't know what my own story was. It was incomplete.

I had some deep thinking to do, and I also knew that many of my experiences as a journalist and foreign correspondent were not as glamorous or honourable as I feared people thought. Not only would I likely disappoint Maclean's with my grim reality, but I might do damage to the professional reputation and contacts I'd worked so hard to build. And yet, the thought of carrying on as before terrified me.

How could I impose on Julian at a time like this? Yes, of course I wanted to be here, safe and nurtured by him and his lovely, peaceful home.

Why was the thought of telling him so terrifying? Could I overcome my fears and ask him for what I wanted?

I needed to sort myself out first.

And though I knew Julian would say I was welcome, and would love me and accommodate my needs no matter what — because that's who he was — I also knew he'd do so at a personal cost. He would take time away from his projects and his work to care for me. And, he wouldn't complain. That was Julian. He was selfless to a fault. It was one of the many things I loved about him.

God, I was such a shit. Promise to love him forever, then promptly abandon him without a word and never contact him for ten years. Then the moment life gets too hard, I run to him hoping he'll take me back?

He deserved so much better than that.

I marched back to the farmhouse as quickly as my legs

would carry me. Making sure I gathered all my things into my backpack, I found a scrap of paper and scrawled a quick note to Julian. I wouldn't say goodbye. That was too definite. But I couldn't be here waiting when he returned.

Julian

Driving back home to the farm from the Ragged Mountain Resort, I was floating. Still reeling from Ethan's offer, but feeling positive and excited about the future, all I could think about was getting back to Ruby. I wanted to share everything with her. My body was hot for her already, my heart thrilling at the mere idea that I could have her near me always.

I knew I couldn't ask her to stay; she had to make that decision for herself. However, I'd held back, my mistrust and fear preventing me from telling her how I really felt about what I wanted. But I would. She could go away, anywhere, for any length of time, and would always be welcome here. In this city. On my farm. In my bed. That was part of who she was and I could and would make space for it. But I wouldn't tie her down.

There would never be another woman for me. I had my work, and she had hers. We made a good team.

Finnegan met me at the door of the truck as I pulled to a stop and hopped out. "Hey, boy. Had a run around, did you?" I was relieved Ruby had let him outside, as he would be restless with me gone. It meant she'd got up at least.

"Hey sleepyhead," I shouted as I walked through the door. The farmhouse was still and silent. Finnegan slipped past my legs and made a circuit of the living room, sniffing. I scanned the room. The place was tidy, clean dishes sitting in the rack by the sink, my clothes from yesterday folded neatly on the sofa. But Ruby's clothes were gone. My heart thudded in panic before my mind caught up. "Ruby?"

Finnegan sidled up, sitting down on my boot. "Where's Ruby, Finn?" He answered with a whine.

Something bright and colourful lay on the farmhouse table. I stepped closer to look at it. A pointy knit toque, with ear flaps in vivid pink and blue, with a banded yellow, white and green diamond pattern, and braided tassels. As I lifted it, a small note drifted out. In Ruby's bold, blocky handwriting, the words:

DEAR JULIAN,

Last night was lovely. Thank you. But also, I'm sorry for everything. I'm not okay, and I don't want to bring you down when you're at this bright, shiny place in your life. That would be unfair. I have my own stuff to work out, and you don't need that.

I made this with the last of my alpaca wool from Bolivia. I can imagine you feeding the goats in it when winter comes. A taste of what you can do with Nutmeg's lovely wool. He needs you, and being here would be good for him. I hope you give him a chance. And that your meeting went well!

x, Ruby

WHAT THE HELL? Where did she go? What did this mean?

For all my deliberations, the point was moot. Ruby had decided for us how it would be, just as I always feared. She was gone.

Chapter 26

Ruby

DESPERATE FOR A COFFEE, and disinclined to dealing with either of my parents in my current state of mind, I drove straight to Quinn's café in Old Town once I got back to the city.

In some ways, I felt like a coward for running away instead of telling him in person. Especially after last night. But right now, I just couldn't. I needed time to think.

Though it was late morning, some of the gang were lolling about on the big sofa and armchairs, which seemed to be their second home. Quinn was behind the counter with her barista, as usual. I wondered if she ever sat down, but that was in the nature of starting a new business. Deanna and Aislin sat, deep in conversation, Dee's hands drawing circles in the air, while Zach slouched in the corner with his eyes closed, a coffee clutched on his lap. Phoenix sat in one armchair, fiddling with his phone, the only one even remotely available for conversation, and I didn't feel ready for that. It's not that he intimidated me or anything. I was comfortable with military guys. And Phoenix was kind and seemed to want to help, but... maybe a little too much.

I decided to get my coffee and breakfast first, rather than disturb them.

"Morning, Ruby," Quinn greeted me, her steady gaze assessing. "How'd things go at the farm?" Our big group of friends had always been tight, but that didn't mean there weren't BFFs, rivalries, and alliances within its ranks. Because of her twin, and their mutual favourite person, Jae Soo, Quinn had always seemed to me to be closer to the boys than the girls. Except for her best friend Jeannie, who'd been AWOL as long as me. Clearly, I was not yet back in Quinn's good graces.

I swallowed. My answering smile felt tight on my face, but I zhuzhed it up and answered cheerily, "Rather well, actually. Julian and I had a terrific evening. He's done so much work on the place. He cooked a lovely dinner for me."

"Lucky you. How long are you going to be in town?"

I gave my head a minute shake. "No plans yet."

Her brow hitched slightly, and I wondered how a teeny tiny twitch could carry so much threat. "What'll you have?"

"Large *Americano*, please. And one of those pretty orange muffins." I looked around at the crowd. "Pretty busy today."

She shrugged. "Weekdays and Saturdays are my busiest times. Evenings and Sundays are dead, so…" She clicked her tongue. "I've got a way to go before I have the volume I need to stay afloat."

"You'll get there." I picked up my coffee. "Any word from Jeannie?"

Quinn gave me a grateful half smile. "Yeah. She made it back, but she's spending time with her folks first."

I moved aside for the next customer, feeling a twinge of guilt in my chest. Jeannie was a better daughter than me, since I'd spent too little time with my own family on this visit. Other than the dinner with Isaac, I'd kept to myself a lot. It ate at me, another factor in my decision-making.

While I waited for my drink at the other end of the counter,

Rainy came out of the toilets, just as Dee looked up from her conversation with Aislin.

"Hey guys," I said, sidling over to the group with my hot coffee. "Do none of my friends have an actual job you're required to go to?

"Ruby!" Rainy and Dee greeted in sync. "Of course we do. We just love to support our girl."

"Come her and sit down," Deanna said. They slid over, making space for me on the sofa between them and Zach.

"Move Zach." Rainy elbowed him. "Make room."

Aislin stood up. "I've gotta get back to work, anyway." She gave a shy wave and left without another word.

Zack stirred awake, grunting, and pulled himself up. "Oh, hey Ruby."

I slid into the empty slot, sighing, and took a long, grateful draw on my hot coffee. This was nice. Having a place to come and hang out, always finding someone you knew there. Made me laugh a little inside, thinking of that old sitcom Cheers my parents used to watch when I was little.

"Late night?" Dee asked, giving me the side eye.

I laughed, opting not to provide details. It seemed everyone knew where I'd been, anyway. My non-answer drew knowing chuckles from several of them.

"Where's Julian?" Rainy asked.

"He rushed out early to meet with that resort guy. About the Faire, I guess."

"What're you up to today?" Deanna asked.

I shook my head. "Nothing, really." I caught Phoenix staring at me, cool as ice, and he glanced back down at his phone.

Just then, someone bustled in the front door, and we all turned to see who it was.

"Quinn! Somebody, help." After a second look, I realized it was Tate, all in a flap and strangely disguised. He had his collar pulled up to his ears, a baseball cap tugged low over his eyes, dark shades, and carried four shopping bags close to his chin. He looked like a mad street person.

"What's up?" Quinn said, her eyes bugging out at him.

"They're after me. Hide me," he gasped. "Can you hide me?"

"Who's after you?" asked Phoenix, shooting out of his chair, his enormous hands clenched into fists, ever the alpha rescuer. He took two huge strides toward the door, ready to take down whomever was hot on Tate's tail.

I moved to follow him, pushing up, but Deanna put a hand on my knee, laughing. "His fans, silly. I doubt you'll be able to help, Phoenix, though you do look like a scary bodyguard."

He turned, his scowl morphing into confusion.

Zach, Rainy and Dee laughed, as though this was a common occurrence. I simply sat, my head swinging back and forth, trying to keep up with the drama.

Tate's head cranked over his shoulder, checking outside. "Ahh! No. They're coming! They saw me come in here!"

"Run upstairs, quick!" said Quinn, pointing to the door that led to the back, behind the bar. Tate dashed in that direction, his bags swaying and swishing, his hat flying off his head. "Parker and JJ are up there. Just go in."

Parker and Jae Soo were upstairs? Seriously, did nobody work?

Tate disappeared into the back just as three teenaged girls burst in through the door, giggling and squealing. "He's in here. I saw him."

Our entire group turned away, pretending to look at their phones, or take sudden sips of their coffees, myself included, watching the action from the side of my eye. Phoenix was the only one who remained standing, but he turned a shoulder to the girls, running a hand through his hair, making a stern, questioning face and darting glances at the teen fans. Obviously, this was a brand of danger with which he was unfamiliar.

Once inside, the girls tumbled to a halt in the middle of the room with their cell phones in their hands, all three of them looking around—like a mob of meerkats—ready to pounce on their tv idol. When they couldn't spot him, their excited expressions fell, morphing into bewilderment. "Where is he?"

"I don't see him," said one.

"Maybe he went to the bathroom," said another, a tall, thin teenager in shredded jeans and a cropped t-shirt.

The third, a girl with badly dyed green hair and several facial piercings, wearing black mesh stockings under cropped short-shorts, and shockingly high, black platform shoes, stepped up to the counter. "Did you see Tate Foreman come in here?"

Cool as an iced *mochaccino*, Quinn slowly raised her head, donning an oh-so-bored expression. "Who?"

More squeals and expressions of outrage from the girls. "Tate Foreman!"

I smothered a laugh, biting on my lips, at Quinn's hilariously blasé pose. "Never heard of him. What'll you have?"

"Seriously? You don't know who Tate Foreman is? What is wrong with you? Don't you watch Skycastle?"

Collectively, they expressed their disgust at Quinn's lack of sophistication while she stood there, the picture of someone who couldn't care less. "Are you ordering something or not?"

They glanced around to see if everyone in the place was equally ignorant. With huge, melodramatic sighs of disappointment and heartbreak mixed with disgust at Quinn's lack of discernment, the girls ordered sickly sweet caramel macchiatos and mint chocolate chip things with extra whip, finally settling down, comparing photos on their phones while they waited. Resigned that Tate would not appear magically, they took their drinks to go and we all let out a breath and laughed at the outrageous episode.

"Does that happen often?" Phoenix asked, his face creased up like he'd eaten a shit cookie.

"More often lately," Deanna replied. "Almost every week now."

I thought I had celebrity problems.

"And now Julian's got women fawning all over him, too. Pretty soon we won't have any peace," Rainy said.

"Now Ruby's back, she'll fend them off," Zach said as he winked at her.

Oh, no. I hope not. That's part of his brand," argued Deanna. "I carefully curate his content to maximize the sex appeal, and I've got him trained now. We can't afford to scare off fans by attaching a woman to his image."

My stomach spasmed. "Um…"

"Ruby will fend them off. She doesn't want all those fangirls falling all over her man," Zach said, taking a sip of his coffee and smiling at me. My lips pulled into a small, tight smile of thanks.

"Who says Ruby's sticking around?" said Rainy, sitting up, indignant on my behalf. "She's got more important things to do than be an appendage to Julian. Her own fame will enhance his cause. Sex doesn't sell everything, Dee." And there went Rainy, advocating for women's autonomy as she always had, despite her own contradictions.

"Yes, it does," Deanna said. "You'd be surprised how much."

"Er… I don't think —" Luckily my phone trilled right at that moment, foregoing any need to engage on this most uncomfortable topic. "Excuse me."

Glancing down, I saw it was the executive editor at Maclean's who'd offered me the book deal. My heart shot to my throat like machine gun fire, and I stood up, moving away from the group to find a private corner.

"Hello?"

"Ms. Zimmer! It's Stuart Goddard at Maclean's. I'm glad I caught you. Do you have a moment to chat?"

"Yes, Mr. Goddard. Of course."

He chuckled softly. "Stuart, please. Mr. Goddard is my father, and I hope we'll have plenty of reason to be on a first name basis in the future. May I call you Ruby?"

I hesitated, clearing my throat. "Uh, okay. Stuart. That's fine with me. But… it might be premature to—"

"I know, I know. I'm not counting my chicks yet. Only being my natural, optimistic self. Don't fret."

"No, it's only that I'm still deliberating."

"Can you tell me what your sticking points are?"

It was my turn to let out a soft guffaw of cynical laughter. "Oh, there are so many."

"I hope there are no serious flaws in our offer. But I trust you'll tell me if there's something I can do to sweeten the deal for you."

"No. Don't worry about that. It's all on me. This would be just such an enormous change for me, and I have so many variables to consider. It would be nice to have more time to mull them over."

"We're in no mad rush, although it would be nice to know you'd got started this year, for publication planning purposes. I hope we haven't placed undue pressure on you."

"No, no, no." I turned my back on the others, dropping my voice. "It's my current obligations that I have to deal with. It's not so easy to… cut ties."

"If money is an issue, I hope you know your advance will come immediately upon signing."

"No. That's not the issue. Thank you, though."

"Good. Good." He paused a moment, and I waited, unsure where this conversation was supposed to go next. Did he want an answer from me? If so, I really wasn't ready. "Listen, Ruby, I have a request I hope you can accommodate. I know it's very last minute, but…"

Chapter 27

Ruby

"YES?"

"Our senior editor, Marzieh Farahdi, happens to be out West right now," Stuart continued.

Marzieh Farahdi! She was one of my idols, a ground-breaking, glass-ceiling shattering journalist who I'd admired since even before university. I waited, not wanting to assume anything.

"She is the very person who I would like you to work with, if you come on board, of course. She has an interest in your career, and this project, so there's no one else I'd rather take it on."

"I said you didn't need to sweeten the deal, Stuart."

He laughed heartily. "Well, this is something we've had in mind all along, so you'll have to take it or leave it. But seriously, Marzieh is in Vancouver this very moment interviewing a subject for a piece. But she's scheduled to fly out tomorrow morning, and we only just thought of this plan. I was wondering —very much hoping, actually—that you could somehow get yourself over the Strait to have a quick meet up with her. You could even intercept her at the airport if necessary. But today would be even better."

"In Vancouver? Today?" I couldn't stop my normally contralto voice from jumping into the soprano range. My pulse did a repeat sprint up the stairs to my throat, thumping wildly. Meet with Marzieh Farahdi? What would we talk about? What would I say?

When he affirmed, I asked him to hold and strode back to the sitting area. "Hey, guys? Do you know the fastest way to get to Vancouver. Like, right now?"

"Sure," Deanna, fountain of all logistical knowledge, spoke up. "Do you want to go by seaplane or heli-jet?"

Uuhh. I shook my head, lifting one shoulder. "Do I really have options? I just need to get there ASAP. Anything."

"Let me check," Deanna bent her head over her phone, tapping away while I waited. "Oh, okay. There's a flight at 1:30, and then three, four, five and later, but they're all full."

My heart fell. It was impossible. Too good to be true.

"Oh! There's a Heli-jet scheduled also at 1:30. To downtown though. Not the airport. Where do you want to land?"

Checking the time—12:18—I put my phone to my face and asked, "Stuart? If I could get there this afternoon. Where would I meet her? Downtown? Or is she staying at an airport hotel?"

"The Waterfront. Not far from where you'd come in, I believe."

"It looks like if I can catch the 1:30 flight out of here, I can do it."

"Okay. I'll let Marzieh know and text you details for a meeting place. This is great. I'm so glad you can accommodate us."

I signed off and tucked my phone in my pocket. I hoped I could follow through. The rush of adrenaline felt good. This was more normal to me than anyone could know. Always foot-loose, ready to fly off at a moment's notice. I glanced down. Yesterday's less than fresh clothes were smelly and wrinkled, far from stylish or professional. That was normal too, but hardly appropriate to meet with a top editor who might determine my future.

"Deanna? Can you book that flight for me, either one, and…" She looked up. I raised both hands helplessly. "Is there anything you can do to get me ready for a work interview? I haven't got time to go home, and I have got nothing nice to wear, anyway."

She leapt to her feet. "My specialty! Quinn!" She dashed over to the counter. "We need to use your boudoir."

"What? I don't have a boudoir." Quinn looked flummoxed at the suggestion.

"Rainy, take over!"

Rainy obeyed, running behind the counter to cover for Quinn, pushing her gently back in our direction.

The three of us headed for the back door just as Tate, Parker, and Jae Soo burst out of it, falling all over and laughing about Tate's close call with adolescent fandom, presumably.

"Hey, girls!" Tate said, stopping in our path.

"Sup?" Parker asked, confused to be surrounded by us.

Jae Soo blocked Quinn's path, grinning. "Love your new house, Tsundere." She shoved him in the chest, growling.

"Outta the way, guys," Deanna barked, shooing them with a wave of her hand. "Fashion emergency."

"Uh, yeah… wouldn't want to get in the—"

With no further explanation, she ushered us upstairs, where, when we arrived, I could see Quinn, and evidently Parker, lived. It was a funky apartment on the second floor, with big old windows in the brick wall overlooking the harbour and the parking lot to one side. A lot of Parker's shit cluttered the space; there was a heap of kicked off men's sports shoes and gear by the entrance, an obvious gaming setup in front of a large screen tv that I knew was not Quinn's, and empty beer cans here and there.

"This is amazing, Quinn."

"Thanks. Another reason to make the café work. No café, no great inner city water view apartment. Though it would be really nice if both me and my stupid brother could afford separate places. But he's my mortgage helper for now."

"You own the building?"

She scoffed. "The bank does. But someday..." Her gaze scanned the open living space fondly. "So... what do you need?"

I shrugged. "Something clean and professional, but not, you know, stuffy. I'm not a banker."

Deanna hummed, eyeing Quinn. "Ok. Clean underwear?"

Quinn nodded and went through a door into her bedroom. Meanwhile, Deanna shrugged out of her cropped jacket, a cute navy-blue thing with a peplum hem. "You can wear this. We just have to coordinate."

Quinn returned and thrust some small undergarments at me. "Go change into these and we'll figure out the rest." She pointed towards her bedroom. "I also have this?" She held up a floral peasant skirt.

I slipped into Quinn's room, a simple, under-furnished space with a plain bed, old wood dresser, and a crate for a bedside table. A burlap coffee sack, printed with some Mexican or Brazilian company name and logo, hung from the brick wall behind her bed; a bow to her obsession with all things coffee and free trade. It would be charming, but reminded me too much of being in South America. I turned my back, quickly stripped down and put on the clean undies.

We used to do this all the time in high school, the five of us, Deanna, Quinn, Jeannie, Rainy and me. Somehow, even though we were all different heights and shapes, we could always trade clothing and it all more or less fit.

The girls joined me in the bedroom. "I don't know about this skirt, Quinn. It doesn't feel right," Deanna said, holding it up against my bare legs. "I could pull it off with boots and an off the shoulder blouse for a boho look, but..."

"I agree. I'm not one for skirts, anyway."

There was a knock on the door, then Rainy came in. "Hello? Can I help?"

"In here!" shouted Quinn.

As Rainy walked in, we all turned to her at the same moment and exclaimed. "Take off your pants and shoes!"

Rainy pulled back. "What? I have to go back to work."

"You can wear this skirt."

Shaking her head, Beth unlaced her shoes and shucked her pants, trading them for the flowery skirt, which actually looked cute on her. Quinn gave her a pair of green Doc Marten's. I took the Zara culottes and pulled them on. They were grey, wide legged and cropped, which made my extra height irrelevant. I tied the big sash at the waist and held up my arms, turning.

"Put the Fluevogs on," Deanna ordered, and I obliged, lacing up the chunky multi-coloured brogues.

Deanna stood back, squinting at me. "Quinn, you have a red shirt?"

Quinn went to her closet and rummaged.

"The only red thing I have is this plaid flannel shirt." Quinn's style was more earth-mother crossed with logger, but after looking at the other options, we settled on a simple ribbed white sleeveless mock turtleneck shirt. I added Deanna's navy jacket, aware that I was running out of minutes.

"Perfect!" Deanna declared, pulling her necklace over her tangled blonde locks and looping it over my neck. Rainy and Quinn nodded in agreement.

"Wow, Ruby. Deanna did her magic again." Rainy exclaimed.

"Mirror?" I asked, and Quinn led me to her bathroom. I took a moment to ponder what impression I gave off, and wonder what Marzieh Farahdi would think when she saw me. "Not bad at all." What would it be like to wear normal clothes, clean and different ones every day, and meet people in offices and cafés instead of refugee camps and bombed-out buildings?

We all dashed back downstairs, and the rest of the gang reacted with oohs and aahs.

"You look really hot Ruby," Tate said.

Not too hot, I hoped. "But professional, right? Grown up?"

"Totally," Zach added.

Quinn went back to work, while Rainy ran over to a chair and dumped the contents of her satchel on the sofa seat. "Here," she said, shoving it at me.

I realized she was right. Her bag was soft black cowhide. Mine was brown and green and extremely well worn. I moved the contents of my bag into hers and offered her mine apologetically, my eyes filling with tears. "Thank you, Rainy."

"No problem," she said, passing me a pack of gum.

"No crying! No time to touch up your makeup."

"Ooh," Deanna rummaged in her bag and handed me a lipstick tube. "This is my lucky shade of red. Just the thing."

"Thanks, Deanna. Thank you, all of you, so much."

"Need a ride to the help-jet terminal?" Jae Soo asked. They'd all been filled in, apparently, while we were upstairs.

"I have my car outside, JJ, but thanks."

Phoenix had hung back, but stepped forward now. "Got one more minute, Ruby? I have something for you."

I smiled at the others and followed him towards the door, conscious that I literally had fifteen minutes to get to the harbour terminal.

Phoenix looked nervous, glancing at the floor. He shoved a hand into his pocket. "I met up with some guys I work with sometimes. And one of them just flew in from… Central America. He gave me this for you."

He held out his hand, and I looked down, confused. Until he opened his fingers and I saw, lying in the centre of his palm…

"My ring?" My heart did a flip, settling into a quick drumming.

He grunted in the affirmative. "There was some stuff confiscated when you were pulled out. It was being processed. But they concluded it must be yours. I actually... remember seeing it."

Any attempts at holding back tears at the enthusiastic support and help of my friends gave way utterly then. With trembling hands, I took the ring from his palm and slid it back into place on the ring finger of my left hand. Where it had always lived, when it wasn't too dangerous to wear it in plain sight. The rest of the time, it lived in a little pocket of my bag. My kidnappers must have rummaged through my things, though I hadn't known for sure that I hadn't lost it before then. All I knew was that, after carrying it with me all over the world for the last ten years, it had vanished.

As a sob tore from my throat, Phoenix gently wrapped his arms around me, patting me gently on the back. "Thought you'd appreciate having it back," he murmured quietly.

I nodded against his muscled chest, kind of stunned by how hard and solid he was, and pulled away, swiping under my eyes with my fingertips and blubbering, "I have to go."

He gave me a friendly shove, one side of his firm mouth quirking in an almost smile. "Fair winds."

I dashed out to my car, tore down Wharf Street, and screeched into a vacant parking spot outside the waterfront terminal. I jumped out and ran as fast as I could down the sloping dock towards the seaplane in Rainy's fancy Fluevog footwear, hoping I didn't sweat too much in the borrowed clothes my wonderful, amazing circle of friends had given me—literally, off their backs.

On the way to the harbour terminal, I again thought about Julian. I should have let him know I was heading out of town. My departure was so abrupt. And asking one of her friends to pass a message seemed presumptuous. I didn't want to burden them, as I had no idea what Julian and I were to each other.

Yet, leaving town without a word felt just as bad. I hoped he wouldn't read anything into it. But I had to do this. I had to figure out my path first. Without that, I had nothing to say to Julian. Nothing to offer him, nothing to ask of him.

I thought about the eager, supportive faces of my gathered circle of friends. They'd tell him where I went, anyway. Of course they would. And no matter what happened, I'd be back by tomorrow. To start a new life, perhaps. Or, at least, if the memoir deal fell through, to say a proper goodbye.

Once buckled up and in the air, I had less than half an hour alone with my thoughts. The last hour had zoomed by in such a blur of activity, I'd had not one moment to worry about my upcoming conversation with Marzieh. Now, the fear seeped in big time. Would I have the courage to confide my genuine concerns to her? Could I afford not to?

But over those worries and fears, draped like a warm blanket, was the feeling of being accepted, loved, and supported by my friends who, despite their protective feelings about Julian, were no less loyal and loving than they had ever been.

The cherry on top?

I held out my hand, gazing at the antique ruby and diamond ring on my finger, turning it so the bright light bouncing off the surface of the clouds sparkled on its facets. I had my engagement ring back.

***

Julian

The garden got the worst of it. Fortunately, there was never a shortage of hard physical labour to be found on a farm. And therefore, plenty of ways for me to take out my frustrations and my hurt.

Of course, I tried to call her right away, but my efforts went to voice mail.

You've reached Ruby Zimmer. I'm either on a call or away from my phone. Please leave a message and I'll get back to you at my earliest opportunity.

Then I called Tate, Deanna, and Quinn. The only one I reached was Tate, who hadn't talked to Ruby and knew nothing. He was also too preoccupied to understand how desperate I was to find her.

I tried Ruby once more, leaving a tight, brief message, afraid to show her how much I needed her and wanted her back. There were so many things we should have discussed while she was here. But I thought we'd have more time.

After sulking and storming around the house for a while, Finnegan trailing with a worried expression on his doggy face and pawing at me in concern, I finally came to terms with the fact that this was exactly what I'd expected from Ruby. I was a fool to have hoped for anything more. She'd never given me any reason to think she was staying; That I, or her relationship with me, had any bearing on her life decisions.

I assumed she'd got called away for a new assignment, or was off thinking about her book contract. Or maybe she just didn't want to hang around here with me anymore. Either way, I hadn't had the chance to make my intentions clear, if in fact I was clear about them myself. Maybe she misunderstood how I felt. I thought I'd been clear, so maybe she didn't have the heart to reject me again. At least to my face. That seemed to be her signature thing. The irony was that all my deliberations on the drive to the resort and back about how willing I was to accommodate her wanderlust and ambition were for nothing. She simply didn't want me.

And so I threw myself into chores, taking care of the routine animal care, shoveling mountains of manure out of the barn, hiking out to check on them all in the meadow and then reviewing the various repairs and projects that were ever on my rotating list. Breaking for water and a snack mid-afternoon, I called Matt finally to fill him in on my meeting with Ethan and see about calling a meeting of the Farm-to-Table Faire planning committee to move forward with our arrangements. He said he'd see about setting something up for the evening.

Then I spent another couple of hours harvesting and weeding the large vegetable garden, yanking out spent and overgrown plants—which was satisfyingly violent—and deciding to dig up one of the long beds to prepare it for planting winter crops.

When I finally staggered into the farmhouse, exhausted, sweat-soaked, and coated in garden dirt, I checked my messages and I discovered Matt had been successful and I was about to receive guests.

An hour and a half later, showered and dressed, I'd quickly tidied and thrown together some snacks, stocking the fridge with a few beers and wine, though I knew my foodie friends would invariably arrive with bounty of their own to share.

The meeting itself went well. The committee was so quick to agree with my recommendation that we accept significant sponsorship money from Ragged Mountain Resort I could no longer deny it had been my personal hang-ups that held us back thus far. Still, despite my changed feelings about Ethan's underlying motives and values, I wanted the committee to lay down clear boundaries around the scope and roles for what that sponsorship bought him. He could be a major sponsor, and that would buy him some limelight and a prime spot for his booth and his literature, but he couldn't be allowed to take over the event. We, collectively, had our own agenda and that must remain front and centre. They agreed.

But serious topics aside, this was a group of colleagues and friends; there was Hanns and Elinor the vintners, and Matt, Noah, and Arnie, who I liked a lot and whose company I enjoyed. I felt at ease in their company, and the evening devolved into relaxed social time and food talk before they all headed home for the night. And an early night since we were all farmers or ran businesses that required an early start. Food, after all, had to be prepared before our customers could eat it.

On that theme, early the next morning, I assembled a batch of sourdough bread, and while it was rising, resumed my chores. I'd awakened to a single voice mail message from Ruby. It must have come in last light while I was in my meeting and I hadn't noticed. It was curt and not very helpful, unless, like me, you were scrambling to read between the lines.

Jules. I'm so sorry. I had to leave, and I don't have a lot of time to explain. I —

Fuck. She'd been cut off. I could spend hours trying to figure out what she had meant to say but I was too tired and my heart hurt.

After feeding the animals, I finished fixing the section of paddock fence I'd abandoned last week, and set to digging in the garden bed again. The harder I worked, the less opportunity I had to wallow in my thoughts, or sink into self pity. That was something I knew how to do. This was the life I'd chosen and I was committed to it. I'd get through this, like I'd got through challenges and disappointments before.

Breaking to bake my loaves of bread mid-day, I ate lunch while researching alpacas online. Gradually, I'd made my peace with Nutmeg, and I didn't think I'd be able to get rid of him now. He'd always be associated with Ruby and her brief visit. His contact with her had seemed to settle him a bit too, so he wasn't inclined to aggression anymore, and seemed to be shyly waiting for some affection from me. The goats and he were getting used to each other, and I saw he spent more time racing back and forth and interacting with them. From my research, I learned they were sociable pack animals, and I thought in time I might have to get him some company.

The colourful knit hat Ruby had given me lay on the table, next to her cryptic note, untouched. I wasn't sure I'd ever be able to wear it, though I could imagine the field day Deanna would have curating a few posts and a video starring Nutmeg and my hat. There was value there, and perhaps in time I would have the strength to appreciate it.

I set up my lighting and shot a few photos of my bread, posting them and a delightful picture of a broody brown chicken with some quick updates about seasonal jobs around the farm, and then went back outside to dig.

"Hey, stranger," a teasing female voice interrupted my labours an hour later. "What have you got against that dirt, anyway?"

I stopped and looked up at my sister, leaning on the garden fence rail, grinning at me. "Hi, Molls." I swiped my hanky across my sweaty, dirty face, kicked my shovel into the ground, and strode over to her.

"Haven't seen or heard much from you these last few days," she said, giving me an opening.

I clicked my tongue against my teeth and raked a hand through my dirty hair, feeling it stand on end, sweat evaporating in a cool wave. "Baked some bread this morning."

"Are you inviting me in for tea and bread and butter?"

"Sure am."

We walked in silent companionship into the house, and I kicked off my dirt clumped boots at the door before washing up a little. By then, Molly had boiled the kettle and made a pot of tea, setting small plates, mugs, butter, and quince jam out on the table.

I chose a rustic round loaf, tapped its base to listen for that sweet drumming echo, raised it to my nose to inhale its heady sour scent, then brought it, a bread knife and a small wooden cutting board to the table. We'd want more than a slice or two.

Carving through the thick crust released a burst of steam and delicious scent into the kitchen from its fluffy, chewy centre. I cut a few thick tranches while Molly poured the tea into comfortable, old, chipped family mugs that we'd grown up with, and I pretended not to notice her curious gaze sliding sideways to the bright hat on the other end of the table with its scrawled note still tucked underneath. Of course, she'd read it while I was in the bathroom. But like me, she probably couldn't draw any conclusions from its spare words.

She asked about the Faire first, and I filled her in on my meeting with Ethan, the changes he'd implemented at the resort, and the committee meeting that had occurred last night.

"I'm glad. I admit knowing little about Ethan or his family's past, but I do vaguely recall how furious Dad was about that deal old Mr. Garwood screwed him over on. I never really understood what it was about."

I grunted. "Yeah. Dad didn't share the details of the arrangement with me, either. For all I know, Dad bullishly signed something he shouldn't have. He could be a bit naïve when it came to contracts." I paused for a big bite of bread and butter, closing my eyes to savour it before continuing. Gesturing with the bread, I continued, "The bit that I remembered was Dad telling me the money he'd set aside for my university education, small as it was, was gone to pay off the losses."

"I didn't know that," Molly said, frowning into her tea.

I shrugged. "Water under the bridge." Though I had no particular plans, that money would have given me some options.

"And now? Ethan's cool?"

"Seems so. Not that I'll be turning my back on him until he proves himself. But there's something else."

Molly tilted her head to the side, waiting, and I told her about the restaurant and Ethan's offer to me.

Her face opened in surprise and delight. "That's amazing, Jules. It's… it's what you've wanted! Isn't it?"

I shrugged, sticking out my bottom lip. "It's not how I thought I'd get it, though. I imagined it would take a few years before I had the resources to put together my own restaurant."

"And you can do whatever you want. With the food."

"Apparently." I took a big gulp of tea. "We'll see. First the Faire."

Finally, full and sated from our feast of bread and tea, I sat back, resting a hand on my belly, wondering if I had the energy to go back out to the garden for another shift. I'd already done double what I normally would in the time and could rest. Or maybe do up some preserves.

Glancing up, I caught my sister's patient gaze and sighed, relenting.

"What do you want to hear about first?"

She smiled. "I want to hear every detail about the reunion, of course, and how everyone reacted to your menu. But I'm picking up major vibes from you, and I'm assuming there's something else going on that's more important."

I rolled my eyes at the ceiling.

"Did Ruby go to the reunion?"

"I assume you heard she did."

"I might have picked up some gossip at the market."

I chuckled. "I'll just bet you did."

"Aaaaand?"

I sighed. "We avoided each other for most of the evening. But of course, we have all the same friends, so the pressure was intense."

Molly waited.

"Well, it might have ended like that." I recalled the horrible moments on stage when April had done her best to make us painfully uncomfortable, and largely succeeded. "Honestly, I guess it was inevitable that we would end up talking."

"I expect so."

"Well, we left together. Spent the night at Dee's condo."

"Oh. Did she go home with Zach again?"

I grunted.

"And you spent the night together."

I nodded.

"And it was wonderful."

I hiked one shoulder. "Wonderful and awful, both." Did I tell Molly about the miscarriage? We'd kept the pregnancy to ourselves, Ruby and I. Maybe it was best to keep it that way, even though that knowledge burned a hole in my gut, and with

Ruby gone, there was no one to share it with. But it was more Ruby's tale to tell than mine.

"And then?"

I swung my gaze away, thinking. "She came here. A couple of days later. We had dinner. A kind of... intense night. And then she left."

Molly said nothing, just studied me, her gaze thoughtful and assessing, and I stared back.

"So you think she's done it again?"

Narrowing my eyes, I grunted. "I think... she went back to her life. Her work."

"But she didn't say." Molly jerked her head at the hat and the note. "Is that all you got?"

I sucked in my cheek, nodding. "And a cut-off voicemail saying she had to leave in a hurry and she's sorry."

"I suppose you think that's the end of it."

I lifted my brows, way up, as a challenge. "You suggesting otherwise?"

Molly set down her mug and sat forward, pulling back her shoulders and jutting her chin, which told me I was about to get the 'big sister talk.' I really didn't need that right now. I rubbed my thumb and fingers into my eyes, sighing. "Molly—" I attempted to block.

"Just listen for a minute. Then I'll leave you alone in your misery."

I groaned.

"If you'd gone after her ten years ago. If you'd chosen to, you could have found her. You could have changed the outcome, or gotten closure, at least."

I glared at her. How had she made this my fault?

"You two obviously haven't finished with each other or nothing would have happened this week. Am I right?"

Swallowing, I conceded the truth in that with a slow blink. Ruby had even said she felt she owed me something. That we had unfinished business. But what did she mean by that? That she needed to apologize, or explain about the baby? How could she have felt we resolved anything enough to leave a note and disappear?

"That," Molly jabbed a forefinger onto the hard wooden tabletop, indicating the note, as if it were a smoking gun, "is not the end, Jules. That is not enough."

She'd pushed my last button, and my patience snapped. "What am I supposed to do about it, Molly? She left!"

"Tell me this. Honestly." She reached forward and pulled my hand between hers, jiggling it a little as if I was still a boy. "Can you ever be happy without her?"

That caused my stomach to fall like a stone to the bottom of a well. It wasn't a question I'd asked myself. I didn't feel I had a choice. So what was the point of asking? I swallowed thickly, my throat suddenly dry. Without my permission, my head shook slightly side to side, as if my subconscious knew the answer, though I refused to look at it.

"You could go after her. You could..." Molly dropped my hand and threw out her palms, leaving my options wide open. "Nothing is set in stone. If you want her, do something about it."

I felt the skin on my face tighten, my eyes heat. "If she doesn't want me, there's nothing there but more hurt."

"Wouldn't you rather know? And move on?"

"I don't know." Maybe not.

"What if you're wrong? What if she's waiting for you?"

I made a skeptical face. How likely was that? Ruby was a pretty straight shooter. She said what she meant. She didn't play coy. On the other hand, she was messed up, broken, vulnerable. Maybe she needed nurturing back to health. Again. Maybe I was letting her down again.

I chewed on my cheek, thinking.

"I have given this a lot of thought," I finally said to Molly. "Ruby isn't the only one with commitments, with goals and dreams. I have a lot going on here."

She nodded. "I know that."

"I can't leave now. Not with the Faire coming together. Too many people are depending on me. And…" I gestured at the door, indicating all that lay beyond that I had built. "I've invested so much."

"It's not like Ruby's hard to find. She's a public figure. All you have to do is watch the news."

I pushed my tongue against my teeth, pondering what that might mean. Maybe I had more time than I thought, but it didn't feel like it.

Molly sighed, leaning back in her chair. "You know, Julian. Dad would have been happy that you came back to the farm, and especially that you made it yours, made it meaningful to you. But you know he always understood your need to do your own thing. He was so incredibly proud of your work as a chef. You should have seen him, with his chest all puffed out like a rooster, showing photos and articles to his friends and his clients. 'That's my son!' he'd say, his face all red. Even if it means leaving the farm, leasing it out. Either way, it's okay. It'll be here if you want to come back. You have to do what makes you happy."

I filled my lungs and blew air out through my puffed cheeks, processing her words.

"Yesterday, I actually thought I could give it all up and follow her. Go back to the international restaurant scene, follow her around or something."

I studied the weathered grain on the top of the old farm table, chasing a crumb of crust around with the tip of my finger. "But I can't do that. I'm not a teenager with no obligations. I have an objective now, plans and opportunities. I can't leave."

"But you could ask her to stay. Or come back when she can."

I didn't reply, but the idea bounced around my nervous system like a jolt of electricity, causing me to twitch and jerk, my pulse kicking up. It was if my body had already agreed, and was on the verge of leaping up, jumping into my truck in pursuit.

"You'll never be happy without her. You might as well just do it; do whatever you need to do to convince her you want her to stay. If she says no, then at least you'll know. Don't spend the next ten or twenty years wondering, what if? Just fucking do it Julian. I won't be able to stand you if you don't. No one will."

I stood up, grabbed the toque, fingered it in both hands, thinking and staring at the note. Which, truly, told me nothing.

Fuck!

Yes. I had to find out. I had to take the risk and ask for what I wanted. Even if the answer was no.

I'd drive into town. Try to find Ruby. At least, I'd talk to Quinn. Maybe she knew something. Or maybe she'd talk some sense into me.

Chapter 28

Ruby

I RECOGNIZED MARZIEH AT ONCE, sitting alone in the lobby lounge of the Waterfront hotel, refined and matronly in an ivory skirt suit, her grey streaked dark hair pulled back into a soft knot. She was the picture of class. Colleagues had introduced us in passing at a couple of industry award events, and of course, knew her byline well.

Her head came up as I approached, and she stood. "Ruby Zimmer. Hello."

We shook hands.

"Marzieh Farahdi. I'm kind of in awe."

She laughed softly and gestured to take a seat opposite her. Closing the folder she'd been reading, she gave me an assessing look. "The admiration is mutual. How are you finding your time back home?" She had such a wonderful, accented voice; it was deep, liquid, and infused with wisdom that had always mesmerized me, even though she'd spent most of her career behind the scenes.

"I've had a lovely break, thank you. I happened upon my

tenth high school reunion last week, so I've caught up with a lot of old friends the past few days."

Her smile was warm and genuine. "Stuart and I are so glad you could fly over and meet me with no warning. We thought you might have questions about the project."

Down to business then. I sobered, chewing my cheek a little as I tried to figure out how to broach my concerns.

"Stuart may have mentioned that I'm a fan of your work, Ruby. I've followed your career with intense interest ever since you broke out with that story on the Crimea."

"I'm… gob-smacked, frankly, that someone like you even knows my name, Marzieh."

Marzieh laughed elegantly, lifting her pointed chin. "In fact, you are very well known, Ruby, among your peers. And we women must look out for each other. You are one of the special ones."

I stared at my laced hands, my knuckles white with the pressure of squeezing them together. "That's just it. I don't think I'm special. I've been very fortunate to have been given so many opportunities to contribute."

"On the contrary, you have accomplished a tremendous amount and earned the respect you've gained."

"I'm only twenty-eight. In some ways, I've just gotten started. I haven't even paid my dues yet. I feel, very much, as if I have so much more to do. So much I have to give back."

"Who is to say what is the right amount? This is a unique life we have chosen, Ruby. You are young, yes, but this career takes its toll on us simple human beings."

Her sympathetic words triggered something deep inside me. My body heated, and my throat and chest constricted with a sudden spasm. Knowing she knew what I'd been through, or something very like it, in her own career unlocked and unleashed a flood of emotion that I'd tamped down hard.

As if she understood I was on the edge of losing it, she turned her gaze out the tall windows beside us that overlooked some shrubbery in a long concrete planter, screening us from passersby on the sidewalk.

"I have been in this business much longer than you, and have known several outstanding reporters. Many women who've blazed the way. You were still in school in 2012. A terrible year for reporters. Frankly, I'm surprised that you carried on as you did. You have tremendous courage."

While I sniffled and stared at the floor, working to draw my tears back inside me where they belonged, she went on.

"When I got my start in Tehran and London, there were few women working as foreign correspondents. They considered it too dangerous, and it is. Those that were, were tough. We all looked up to Marie Colvin, but few have that kind of mad addiction to it. Nothing could have convinced her to live another way, and she kept at it until it took her life." I was listening intently now, fully focussed on the message she was sharing with me. "I don't think you are like that."

Without meaning to, I let out a feeble mewl of agreement.

"Janine G, who I know you admire—and rightly so—is a contemporary of mine. She threw herself into field work more than I could. But then, I had children earlier. That... changes your priorities."

By this time, I was staring at her, more composed, and she finally looked back at me and met my gaze. My stomach spasmed. I knew it then and knew it still. If our baby had survived, my life and career would have taken a very different path.

"Janine understood her limits and knew when to get out. Her work since then is no less valuable. Unless you are driven to do it; I'm not suggesting that you imagine what you have done so far is a sustainable career plan, Ruby. The experience you have gained, in some ways, is enough to fuel your work for decades to come."

My skin tingled, and the muscles on my face tightened into a frown. "Part of my dilemma with this offer is leaving the paper that launched my career, and abandoning this…" I shook my head, searching for the words. I lifted one hand, arcing it through the air. "This trajectory onto which I feel I've been catapulted."

"You do not have to be in the war zones to observe and to make a contribution. And you need not cut ties with the Times to work for Maclean's. You can take this one step at a time."

That came as a relief and lessened the pressure to get this right. "I don't know how to make this choice. I don't know how to stop doing what I'm doing."

Marzieh's lips pressed together, highlighting their outline and shape. "Every flying thing must eventually land, Ruby. Perhaps you are merely afraid of the impact."

I swayed as her words slammed into me. I nodded, feeling my chest tighten with emotion, mortified to feel my mouth twitch and chin quiver again.

Marzieh's steady gaze rested on my face, searched my eyes; it felt like a soothing balm. Like a cooling rain on a hot tropical day. Something about her calm acceptance of my words compelled me to go on.

"That's part of it, of course."

"I understand, my dear." Marzieh reached across the small table between us and covered my hand with hers. "We at the magazine are aware of recent events in Venezuela. People in this business are well connected, and they talk."

My voice, when it appeared, was a thin and reedy version of itself; it trembled with imminent tears. "I feel as though maybe I've already crash-landed, and can't remember how to fly anymore."

Marzieh hummed thoughtfully. "And, sorry to mix metaphors here, but you believe you have to climb back on the horse now or you never will."

I nodded. "That and… this idea that if I stop, I've failed."

She sighed, pursing her lips. "With all that you've accomplished, that will never be true, my dear. Even if you never wrote another piece."

I shook my head, disbelieving. How could I end my career before it had begun?

"I had to fight so hard, for permission, for access and for respect. Part of me believes that I'll lose that edge."

"I believe that now is a good time for you to pause and reflect before choosing your next path. Once you complete this memoir, we very much hope you agree to stay on as correspondent to the magazine. You could take that in many directions, once you have some perspective."

I took back my hand and buried my face in my palms, trying to pull myself together, trying to bolster the courage to say what I knew I had to say.

Lifting my warm face, aware that it was probably flushed and pink, I said, "That's part of the problem, Marzieh. In my heart, I would very much like to lie low, to hide out and rest. And I guess I know that I need a bit of normalcy and whatever comes afterwards, but…" I swallowed thickly, my throat suddenly dry with fear.

She dipped her chin, encouraging me to go on with her clear, steady gaze.

"I think you and Stuart," I circled my left hand to indicate the company as a whole, "have a particular understanding of who I am, and my experiences. And I think I know what you want from me. But I don't know whether I can give you that book. "

Marzieh leaned back slightly, narrowing her eyes. "Do you?"

I drew a long, slow breath, hesitating on what I had to say next, but she went on.

"Do you think we solicit memoirs from accomplished or interesting persons and then tell them what to write?"

I hesitated.

"What do you think we want?"

"I think you, like most people, want to hear about the risk and the courage, the high ideals. And the adventure. But in truth, it was more about misery and boredom, bad decisions, and fear."

"You think we don't know that? Despite those challenges, you produced award-winning, compassionate work that cut to the heart of the matter; making those stories accessible to the public."

"I feel that if I tell my whole truth, I'm being unfaithful to the people who gave me this chance, and maybe burning bridges."

She let out a low, gravelly laugh. "If you suffered from discrimination, unkindness or abuse from your employers or colleagues, don't you think those that inflicted it deserve to be called out? Reporters have a thick skin, Ruby. They'll survive. Maybe they'll respect you more for it. Perhaps that's part of the battle, hmm?"

Still uncertain but feeling the beginning of reassurance, I said, "So you're saying you want… my complete story, no matter what that entails? No matter how I tell it?"

"It's your story we want. And we have faith in you, Ruby Zimmer. Write your own truth. How those experiences affected you—the wars, the killing, the crime, the poverty and human rights violations. But we also want to hear about your own isolation, your doubts and struggles of the business. Being a woman alone. That, too, requires strength and determination. Don't underestimate what that cost you. That's a story worth telling."

Julian

Molly took Finnegan home with her to visit the kids and I left shortly afterwards, taking just enough time to shower and change into clean clothes.

On the familiar drive into town, I had time to think.

It frankly surprised me that Molly seemed to be urging me to chase Ruby. She was usually the pragmatic one, the one that argued for family, community, responsibility, stability. Though truthfully, we'd both been raised to value those things. Not that I needed her permission to do anything, but it almost seemed like she'd been trying to talk me into going away.

Maybe she had more faith in my career as an international chef than she did in my current venture, which, granted, wasn't exactly a ticket to fame and fortune. Maybe fame judging by my recent Instagram popularity, but hardly fortune. And it was entirely possible that my fifteen minutes of fame would come to an abrupt end next week and I'd have to face the fact that I had nothing. Fame was fickle like that.

Though, apparently I had a restaurant to run, if I wanted it. That was encouraging. It was also here, in Port Cam. We'd see about that, but it felt good to be wanted and to have a fall-back plan.

I ground my teeth, gripping the steering wheel harder. What were my options here?

A. Just let Ruby go? My chest squeezed with anticipatory grief at the idea of severing ties and never seeing her again.

B. Abandon my half-baked mission to save the world and commit to following her around so we could be together? Making the best of whatever that presented? I had serious skills, but you couldn't get anywhere in the food industry as casual labour. You needed stakes.

Or, C. Ask her to stay here with me. Ask her to compromise and sacrifice so that we could be together. My stomach almost heaved at that thought. It so went against my very character to make demands. I'd always seen what Ruby did as taking precedence. Being more important than anything I could do.

Maybe that wasn't true anymore.

Yes, it felt selfish to make demands. But it was high time I championed my own cause.

It might be selfish to ask Ruby to stay, but leaving everything that I cared about, that I'd invested in, was the wrong choice for me. For once, I had to choose my own path instead of reacting to what she did. The right thing, if it came to that, was to let her go, no matter how hard. But that didn't mean I couldn't, or shouldn't, ask for what I wanted.

I'd made my choice. Now it was time for her to make hers.

If she neither needed nor wanted me, I had to accept it. It was time to grow up. I might not be perfectly happy, but I would, I could, sacrifice perfect happiness for the greater good.

My foot pressed harder on the pedal, hurrying now to get there. To see her and tell her how I felt. What I wanted.

I briefly considered driving to Ruby's parents' house to look for her. But if I found her there, I was pretty certain I didn't want to have this conversation on their turf.

Best to head to the café and figure out my next steps from there. Hopefully someone there, likely Quinn, would know where Ruby was.

I burst through the café door. As usual, several of my friends were there. Quinn worked behind the counter. A quick scan of the café showed me that Ruby, however, was not present.

"Hey, Julian!" Deanna called out, waving.

Everyone else looked up, their faces curious, questioning, smiling.

"Hey, bro," Parker said.

"Dude," murmured Zach, jogging towards me, grabbing the door as I released it. "I gotta head out to the gym. S'up?"

Shaking my head, I came to a stop in the gap between the two big chairs. Deanna's long yoga pant clad legs stuck out over the overstuffed arm, crossing my path.

"Later." I turned to wave off Zach, who slipped out the door, a gym bag slung over his shoulder.

"We haven't seen you since Saturday night," Tate said, a sly teasing note to his voice. "A lot going on, I hear."

I grunted. "You could say that."

"Are you looking for Ruby?" Aislin asked, point blank.

I paused before answering. She clearly wasn't here now, but maybe I'd just missed her. "Was she here today?"

A few heads shook, and Deanna piped in. "She came in yesterday, but got a call and suddenly had to fly over to Vancouver to do an interview with some important person. She left yesterday afternoon in a big hurry."

My heart tumbled like a shrivelled October apple, falling to the frozen ground with a thud.

I was too late.

Chapter 29

Ruby

WHEN I ARRIVED BACK in Port Cam the next day, after signing a contract and enjoying a celebratory dinner with Marzieh, I headed home to regroup. I needed to sit alone in my room to absorb all that had happened. And I needed to tell my employer and my family what I had decided.

I took my time composing a long email to Richard at the paper. I'd much rather talk to him on the phone once he had all the facts than deal with his reaction live. He'd be angry, and disappointed, but I hoped, in time, he'd understand and forgive me for this choice.

Dad would be thrilled, but I had concerns about Mom's reaction to my news. She'd always been my biggest supporter in pursuing every angle to advance my career. Whether she'd agree that this tangent to write my memoir was an acceptable elevation of my status remained to be seen.

In the end, she was teaching on campus and I could get away with a quick conversation with Dad, whose relief was so palpable it brought tears to my eyes. When I talked over the idea that I'd move back to Port Camosun while I worked on the book, regardless of what I did afterwards, he was even happier.

"You can't know how much it means to me, to have you close again, sweetheart," he said, his eyes glassy. "And you're always welcome to live here, as long as you need to."

"Thanks Dad." We embraced, and his familiar scent comforted like it had when I was a little girl; his hugs were all I needed to feel safe and happy. I had to hold back the sudden rush of tears stinging my nose. I knew I'd made the right decision. "You'll help me deal with Mom, right?" I added, laughing.

"Don't worry about Mom. She's very proud of you no matter what." He paused, scratching his chin, his big hand sliding around the back of his neck as his gaze slid sideways. "I can't help wondering how Julian factors into this."

My heart stuttered. How did Julian fit into the next chapter of my life? Well, I'd see about that. In my more pleasant dreams, he was happy I was staying in town. In a perfect world, he'd have fully forgiven me for my past betrayal. And he'd be excited about the possibility of building a new future together. None of this was, to my knowledge, true. Despite the icy feeling of fear and dread that trickled through my veins, I had to go on. This was what I had to do, with or without Julian.

Pressing my lips together, I met Dad's gaze steadily. "I just don't know yet, Dad. But I have to do what's right for me."

I could finally see myself from his perspective now. Selfish, unstable, unreliable. I could hardly blame him for protecting his heart from me after what I'd done to him. Sure, we were obviously still wildly attracted to each other. And there would always be love between us. We'd shared so much, both good and bad.

But commitment. Sacrifice. That was another thing.

I knew I'd made the right decision to live in Port Cam to write my book—even if Julian didn't want me, and couldn't support me while I did it. It was okay. I'd get my own place.

I accepted that I needed my family, my friends, and my

familiar hometown turf to help me heal from my PTSD. Probably even pursue the counselling that Phoenix had recommended, to work through it all. I'd face down my demons and write my story, no matter what it took. I knew writing my memoir the way I wanted to would take its toll on me emotionally. It would require me to dig deep and be vulnerable; to do that, I needed to feel safe and secure, and supported while I did so.

Even though I'd behaved selfishly, I hadn't been thinking about myself. About my identity and my values. What drove me was human connection, empathy, and it was time I had empathy for myself.

It would be a different flavour of adventure.

My struggle would be personal and internal.

I hoped Julian would come around when he saw I was staying and, given time, would give me another chance.

I had to embrace my vulnerability, and what better place to start than with my heart's desire. I would tell him my truth and ask Julian to hold me.

But first, I would return to the café to thank my friends for their help getting me to my meeting and to share with them my plans to stay in town.

Julian

I'd stormed through the café and stomped straight upstairs to Quinn's apartment in a crazed huff, calling her name like a wounded dog, and she'd faithfully followed me up.

Before we we'd even sat down to talk, Deanna tumbled in too.

"Ugh. Dee. I need to talk to Quinn."

"Never mind," Deanna said. "I'm here too. Whatever you're dealing with, I want to hear it." She plopped down beside me on

Quinn's sofa and squeezed my arm. Well, that was a different kind of comfort than I'd get from Quinn.

I shook my head and dropped it into both hands, propped on my knees, groaning. What was I doing here? I sounded as desperate and hopeless as I felt.

"What happened? Ruby told us nothing much before she left." Quinn asked softly.

I groaned again. "It's not what happened before. It's the fact that she left at all, without a word."

"Did you argue?"

I rocked my head back and forth like another one of those late season apples, ready to fall. My chest felt cold and hard, my heart behind my ribs inert, like the dying fruit, spent, ready to melt back into the bitter rime.

"You guys had it out?" Deanna said.

I sat back. "Well, yes, but no… not like—"

"She seemed cheerful enough when we saw her yesterday," Deanna said. "She had nothing but sweet things to say about you."

A tiny droplet of hope stirred in my frozen heart, like a snowflake melting in a ray of sunshine. The dormant seed at the heart of the apple twitched and stirred to life.

"Really?"

"Yeah. But then she got some kind of urgent work call and had to fly over the Strait fast."

"So it was work," I mumbled. I'd thought as much. But what had made her leave the farm so abruptly when she hadn't got that call yet? "Was she leaving the country? Did she say?"

Quinn scowled, thinking. "Someone was flying out early this morning, but I don't think it was Ruby."

"No. Right. It was for some kind of interview," Deanna added.

I threw my hands up, exasperated. "That's literally what she does for work, Dee. She interviews people."

"I don't know," she whined. "She was worried about her clothes. You're so salty."

I shook my head, frustration building. I wasn't getting any useful information. "I'm sorry. I'm at my wit's end. So you don't know if she's coming back, or gone for good?"

Deanna blinked at me, at a loss. "Um…"

"For the love of coffee," Quinn cut in. "Let Jules tell us what happened."

My gaze scanned their faces, looking expectantly at me. "I just… I don't… nothing!" I barked, then let out an exasperated huff. "I mean, it was good. We had a great time together, actually." I felt my face soften into a half smile at the memory of our dinner. The evening had been very fine indeed, and nothing to scare her away. At least, until her nightmare and confession. I didn't think being vulnerable made her happy.

That elicited expressions of curiousity and encouragement; I scowled, shaking my head, and carried on. "We had it out, as you put it, but we didn't argue. Ruby and I never argue. It's only that, yesterday I raced out to my meeting in the morning, expecting Ruby to be there when I got home and she wasn't."

"So?"

"She just took off?"

I waggled my head. "She left a note and I couldn't reach her."

Quinn flicked her fingers at me, and I dutifully withdrew the wrinkled note from my pocket and handed it to her.

Reading it, she screwed up her face. Deanna leaned over her to read it. "She signed it with an 'x'" she said, her voice climbing to a mouse squeak. "That's good, right?"

"It doesn't tell us anything, really. What's 'this'?" asked Quinn, using air quotes.

"A hat. She left me a toque she'd knit."

She hummed. "Weird. Why did she imagine you in it?"

"Exactly! Doesn't that sound like she's won't be here to see me in it?"

We were all quiet for a moment, pondering.

"Why don't you just ask her?" Quinn said. "I suppose you didn't talk about the future. It didn't sound like she was leaving the country, to me. Not yet, anyway."

"No. We didn't talk about us, at all. It's always work with Ruby. But is she gone? That's the question. Is she going back to London? Or the Middle East or somewhere?"

They both shrugged.

"It's what she does. What if she doesn't want to be here?" My voice sounded hollow and small.

"What if she doesn't?" Quinn echoed. "What will you do?"

"I thought about giving everything up and following her. But I decided I can't."

Quinn leaned back. "No way, Jules. We just got you back."

"I just said I wasn't."

"That doesn't sound like what you want, Jules," Deanna set her hand on my shoulder, rubbing. "You've put so much work into your farm and your branding, and the Faire!"

"I know!" I knew all of this. Of course, they were right. I had family and friends here. I had land, animals, a business, even a job, which I had told no one about. I knew all of this. I was no further ahead than I was before. "Look, this is… I appreciate your support, Dee, but I just can't think straight. Can I please have a private word with Quinn?"

"Oh!" Deanna's face fell. I didn't want to offend her, of all people. She'd done so much for me, but Dee was my business advisor. We didn't talk about relationships. She and Tate had been supportive when Ruby left me, working hard to stay in touch and welcome me home last year. But only Quinn would give me the thoughtful, balanced advice I sought, without judgement.

"No problem, hun." Deanna wrapped her arms around my shoulders. She dipped her chin and met my gaze steadily. "Of course I want you to stay here, Jules. Just know, whatever you decide to do, I only want what's best for you. You deserve better."

I returned her squeeze with a wry smile. "Thanks, Dee."

And she left, the apartment falling into hushed stillness, not even a murmur of voices evident from downstairs. Quinn sat quietly beside me. "I don't know what happened between you and Ruby this week, and I don't need to know." She pursed her lips, narrowing her eyes at me. "But Deanna's right. I love Ruby. We all do. But you, of all people Jules, deserve to be with someone who loves you wholeheartedly."

I felt my throat tighten as my nose burned, and I drew in a breath to dispel the crushing feeling of despair that pressed in on me. "I've had a long time to get over Ruby, Quinn." I paused.

Ruby might not have proven her love with her choices, with her actions, but when we were together, I felt her love in every cell of my body with absolute certainty. The connection between us was unparalleled. It was all-encompassing.

When we were together, I couldn't imagine life being any better or brighter. Without her, colour faded from my eyes, music muted in my ears, my pulse dulled to a murmur. In some ways, my grief and loneliness had driven me to cooking and experimenting with food by a desire to feel more alive and to lose myself in something sensory that I could share.

"I've had ample opportunities to meet and even fall in love with someone else. But I didn't. I don't believe I ever will. I love only Ruby. And I don't think I'll ever stop. Even if she leaves me again."

"What do you want to do?"

I heaved a deep sigh and shrugged. "I raced into town because… I was going to ask her to stay." I raised a hand in a gesture of hopelessness. "Beg her, even. And she's not even here. She didn't pay me the courtesy of saying a proper good-bye." My voice garbled on the last words, and I lost any hope I had of holding back the hot tears that escaped. At least it was only in front of Quinn. She'd seen plenty of my tears over the years.

I shot to my feet, striding to the windows overlooking the Upper Harbour; raking my hands through my hair, I was desperate to rid myself of this overwhelming flood of frustration and loss.

"Aw, Jules. It kills me to see you hurting." She stood up and took my hand in hers. "I know you're trying to figure this out. But honestly, I think you're reading too much into this stupid note. Who knows why Ruby left the farm? Maybe she had shit to do. And I don't think she expected that call she got yesterday. She was in a flap." She picked up the note again and screwed up her nose, her freckles bunching together. "But this doesn't seem like a cavalier goodbye to me. I think you'll get another chance to talk to her. What you're agonizing over, it's a decision that you can't make alone, anyway."

Was I over-reacting? Assuming the worst? It's true this crushing desperation I felt in my gut, in my heart, was a too familiar feeling. The grooves of those scars were deep enough to distort what I experienced now. The tiny seed swelled, split, sprouted. Even the possibility that I still had a chance soothed the roil of fear in my belly, filled my chest with lightness. I turned back to face her. "You think I'll—"

The door opened, and Deanna popped her head back in. "Can you two come down to the café, please? There's someone here that wants to see you."

Ruby

I held my breath, my stomach a bag of angry bees as I entered the café. Parker leaned behind the counter alone, his head bent over his phone, thumb flicking intently over its surface. This late in the afternoon, the weekday customers had thinned to a stalwart two or three loners staring vacantly at their laptops. In our comfy seating corner, a few of my friends still hung out. The mood was more subdued, with sombre Aislin and Jae Soo flanking another brunette woman with glasses I didn't recognize, showing them her phone, tilting it back and forth while they leaned in, intent. No Julian.

Strung as tightly as a rubber band, on the edge of snapping, I had been given an inch of slack. Barely enough to take a full breath.

Stepping to the counter first, I stood a moment, waiting for Parker to notice me. "What would the boss say about you surfing on your phone while you're at work?"

He jerked and his head shot up as he slipped his phone into his back pocket in one smooth move. "Uh, sorry. What can I get you?"

I laughed silently at him, and a beat later, he blinked and his mouth tilted up at one corner, the tips of his ears going pink. "Damn. Hi, Ruby. You're back, eh?"

"Yup. You swiping for a hook up?"

Jae Soo's laughter amplified my teasing question. "Yaas. He's a thirsty boy."

He scoffed, a flush sweeping up his fair neck and cheeks like a red tide. "Maybe."

"You look like you could use some cheering up. Is Quinn out?"

"Red Oni's always in a mood. Aren't you, P!" Jae hollered from the sofa.

Parker scoffed quietly, ignoring the dig with a headshake, his mouth quirking into a half smile with a flash of white teeth, despite himself. "Nah. Mom's upstairs with... ah... she'll be back down soon. You want a bev?"

"Sure, yeah. I'll just have a cuppa regular joe, thanks. The Sumatra's good. Thanks."

I carried my coffee over to the sofa, feeling a little shy, since my main girls were AWOL. "Hey, Ash. Hi, Jae."

They all glanced up. Jae Soo, as dapper as ever in an expensive-looking pullover and flashy plaid pants, his long hair flopping over his dark eyes, flashed a welcoming smile up at me. "Ruby! Join us. Jeannie's showing pics of her son. Can you believe it?"

I stilled, peering intently at the unfamiliar woman in the middle of the sofa. "Jeannie? Jeannie van Bellen? Is that really you?" My missing friend. The last of our clique.

Her smile was as shy as a feral cat. "Hi, Ruby. It's nice to see you."

I flopped down into the cushy armchair opposite. "Likewise, girl. Welcome back to Port Cam." I gave myself a shake. Yet another disorienting connection with my past. Jeannie and I used to be really close. And then, abruptly, we weren't. "You look amazing. I don't think I would have recognized you if I walked past you on the street."

She dipped her head. "Yeah. I… heh, finished growing up, I guess you'd say."

I smiled. She was taller than I remembered, and curvier, with a more mature, defined face, and she wore so little makeup, I knew it wasn't artful contouring. "I mean, you're still you, of course. It's such a shock to see you."

"We've both been away a long time, but I haven't been on tv like you," she said, her cheeks pinking.

"True." It was strange to think of my old friends watching me on the news, aging month by month, year after year. "I'm sorry you missed the reunion."

"Oh, me too. I tried, but our flight just didn't work out."

"Yaas, Jeannie. We missed you," said Jae, leaning forward, elbows on knees. "It was so lit. Awesome seeing the squad again. And Julian slayed the food. I'm still dreaming about it."

"Aw, Julian. I haven't seen him yet," Jeannie mused. "Unfortunately, I had a lot of things to organize before leaving Kingston, since we moved back permanently."

"You and… your family?" I probed.

"Just me and my son, Will." She flipped the phone around to flash a picture at me of a cute, dark-haired boy with big owlish brown eyes peeping through glasses. Somehow like Jeannie, and yet not. "We're living with my parents while I do my MBA."

"Oh, wow. A son! How old is he?" Ugh. I sounded so lame. My mind flooded with questions I couldn't ask her while my heart jolted in my chest. She had a son! But no partner. Who was his father? What happened to him? How our life paths had diverged.

"He's nine," Aislin blurted, her dark eyes wide with meaning.

Jeannie's face flushed again, and her gaze darted away. "Yes. Will's, um, nine." She tucked her phone between her hands on her lap.

The same age our daughter would have been. Meaning, Jeannie was pregnant at the same time that I was, right after grad. Was it Zach's child? I didn't think so. I felt my face heat, and my heart rate speed up, flicking my gaze from Jeannie to Jae Soo to Aislin, whose gaze darted back and forth, struggling as usual to understand the social nuances.

Jae, at least, had the good sense not to grill her within a few seconds of saying hello after a decade long estrangement. An enormous lump formed low in my belly, a heavy wad of wet cotton, like the physical manifestation of a memory, a missing organ. An ache for something that would never be.

"So, you stayed with math. Did you major in business or commerce or stay with theory?"

Jeannie's tongue darted across her lips, her cheeks turning an even rosier shade. Then, as if making a decision, she jutted her chin. "No. I had to drop out of university, so I studied on my own while supporting us with freelance bookkeeping and accounting." She wiggled her phone again, as explanation. "I got my CGA first, then worked my way up to a CMA. This MBA is the final step."

I hesitated, unable to think of a diplomatic response. I'd put my foot in it again. An MBA was what she'd set out to do after grad. My mind whirled with facts and calculations. Jeannie, our class prodigy and math wiz, voted "Most Likely to Win a Nobel Prize" dropped out of university? Clearly because she got pregnant with her now nine-year-old son... who has no father in the picture. Like I probably would have had to do. Changing the entire course of my life and career.

She should have been an assistant university economics professor by now or something wildly ambitious. "That's... so admirable." I cleared my throat, embarrassed at my lack of sensitivity. "Sorry. Can't help interviewing people..." I laughed awkwardly, hiding my awkwardness in a sip of coffee.

"Are you and Julian—"

I caught her glancing at my ring, and I tucked my hand between my knees as I smoothly redirected. "What's happening with you, Jae? Are you staying in town long? Quinn said you got engaged?"

His bright smile faded. "Ah, she told you. Yeah. Yeah." He shifted his shoulders in his sweater and stretched his neck, grimacing as if his clothes felt suddenly too tight. "It's a family connection. Someone I knew as a kid."

"So you reconnected over this last visit, then?" Didn't exactly sound like he'd fallen head over heels.

He made a sound somewhere between a hum and a grunt. "You could say that, yes. I've had to get more involved in the family business these past couple of years." He bobbed his head, as if he were listening to voices that were trying to persuade him of something.

"So when's the wedding?" Jeannie asked, clearly missing something subtle in Jae's response.

Jae Soo's complexion turned a little green. "Erm, not for a while yet." He didn't come across as excited about it, and I know Quinn was having a hard time with him leaving, too.

"That'll be a big change. You'll be the first of us to do it. Do you have to return to Korea soon?" I asked softly.

"Not til after Julian's Faire thing. I can stay until, maybe, end of September. Thanksgiving if I can manage it."

"I'm glad, Jae Soo," Jeannie said, touching his arm, and I remembered how kind she was, and why we'd been close friends. "We'll have time to catch up more. What's this thing of Julian's?" She'd turned to direct her question at me, as if I'd be the most likely to know anything about Julian. My mouth opened obligingly, but I hesitated, feeling like a gasping fish.

Aislin jumped in. "A Farm-to-Table Faire. He's very passionate about it. It's on the Labour Day weekend."

There followed a lull in the conversation, and I wished for one of my bubblier, more outgoing friends to appear magically.

Into the awkward void, I finally thrust, "Well, I have news, too —"

Luckily for me, Deanna arrived then from the apartment upstairs. "Hi guys! Oh, Ruby, you're back." She strode over and flopped into the chair that mirrored mine, then tilted her head at the trio on the sofa, her voice dropping to a near whisper. "Can I believe my eyes? Jeannie?"

Jeannie grinned, her shoulders hitching up shyly. "It's me."

"OMG!" Deanna bounced back out of her chair and flung herself at Jeannie with a big gangly hug. "You're here at last. Wow. Let me look at you." Holding Jeannie by the upper arms, she leaned back and let her eyes roam over our friend, readjusting to her unfamiliar look.

Jae smiled at Jeannie and said, kindly, "She looks great, huh? Wait til Quinn finds out she's here."

"She doesn't know you're here?" Deanna turned to look at me, her voice turning strange, slowing, her expression narrowing. "And she doesn't know you're back either, Ruby. I'd better go get her right now. "I'll... just... be right back..." She made an excited squee noise and shuffled back to Quinn's apartment door on her high-heeled wedge sandals.

Just then, a woman came through the front door.

A tall, slender, very attractive dark-skinned stranger. We turned away, thinking she was just a customer, but then Tate came in right on her heels and cupped her elbow.

"What do you want to drink?" he asked.

"Just water, thanks, babe." She hesitated and Tate gestured to us. "Have a seat with my friends there. I'll bring it."

We hesitated, staring at her. She did not look like one of his usual fan girls. With my back to the woman, I widened my eyes at Aislin. Aislin, who, given the choice, would not be the first one to speak to a stranger. She gave a tiny shrug, flicking her eyes up in a half roll.

With a sigh, she said, "Hi?"

I turned to see the woman tilt her head. "Hello. I'm Nomi. Tate's date." She flashed a polite pretty Hollywood smile and perched on the other armchair, crossing an incredibly long, sexy leg over the other and bouncing her designer high-heeled shoe.

"How did you meet Tate?" Aislin asked, wary.

"Oh, work." The woman said. "From the show?" She angled her head in query, as if she doubted our veracity as Tate's friends.

Jae perked up. "Oh! Right! You played Lieutenant Shammura. I saw that episode." Apparently, Jae was the only one of the three of us who watched Tate's series, causing a twinge of guilt. Aislin and I pulled subtle faces at each other.

Nomi's face shone at his recognition. "That's right."

"Cool, cool, cool," Jae added as the exchange petered out, all of us no doubt speculating whether Tate was sleeping with his co-star. Likely, I decided.

Tate returned, rocking his own brand of handsome, handing Nomi a bottle of spring water and perching on the arm of her chair with his coffee, one arm leaning on the back, not touching her. I didn't get the impression they knew each other very well. Yet. Perhaps they'd just met on set.

While Tate introduced each of us to Nomi, secretly I

wondered if anyone could 'know' Tate. To me, it felt like he'd been in character since he discovered theatre in the eleventh grade. The geeky book-loving boy I knew in English class before that wasn't so confident, gregarious or vain, and I wondered whether even he knew who he was anymore.

It's funny, but we all seemed to be dealing with something, some secret or sensitive underbelly. It made the last ten years seem like a lifetime away from high school. We'd all got hit hard with adulting. Except possibly Deanna living in her pink social media bubble, and child-like Zach, who I now glimpsed through the front windows, standing with Phoenix.

"I'll have to make a point of catching up with the show, now that I'm going to be staying in one place for a while," I said, trying again to broach the subject of my plans.

Aislin caught my meaning, shooting a sharp glance my way, a question in her dark eyes.

"Are you—" she began, just as Zach and Phoenix stomped into the café hauling gym bags, laughing and talking animatedly, all rough and tumble in damp workout gear, their exposed skin shining with perspiration, muscles pumped up and bulging. Their wide smiles made them even more appealing, their usual grumpy moods chased away by the endorphins of their workout. Together, they were quite a sight, the professional athlete and the naval officer. A double pull-out centrefold of awesome masculinity.

No one else could tear their gaze away, including Nomi, whose eyes went wide as she took them in. Even I thought they were beautiful specimens of manhood, and it made me wonder if my friends were really that gorgeous, or if they only seemed that way to me because I loved them all so much.

"I have a new—" I tried again, stopping mid-sentence as Deanna reappeared from upstairs.

I sighed. With one thing and another, there never seemed to be the right moment to announce my big plans. I felt deflated, and didn't know how to bring it up without making it all about myself.

"Hey, guys," she said. "Great timing."

"Huh?" Zack blinked at her. "Why?"

Phoenix glanced up, catching my eye, and his mouth crooked up on one side. I dipped my chin in greeting just as his shrewd gaze caught on Jeannie.

"Parker, my man!" Zack said, turning to the counter. "Is this place licensed yet? I could really use a cold brewski."

Parker guffawed. "I wish, dude." Dropping his voice, he added, "If the last proper customer left, I could lock the door and pull out the personal stuff. But not until Quinn says it's—"

Speaking of the devil, Quinn popped out of the back door on Deanna's heels. I wasn't used to keeping tabs on so many people; my interactions with others usually focused on two or three colleagues, guides, or interview subjects. I felt a little dizzy, and there seemed little hope I'd get a chance to share my news this afternoon unless I wanted to grab a megaphone and jump up on my chair like Tom Cruise to get everyone's attention. I'd have to try again tomorrow.

Then Julian followed her through the door, his face the most handsome of all, frowning and scanning everyone in the room. When his gaze fell on me, he froze, looking me up and down, his jaw dropping. The scowl lifted from his sweet face, his brilliant white smile cracking wide open.

"Ruby," he said, stopping a few feet away, his gaze locked on mine. "You came back."

Chapter 30

Ruby

HE APPEARED as if he'd climbed a mountain and just crested the rise, winded, his cheeks rosy, his eyes glassy from cold and glare. My heart swelled in my chest at the sight of him, and I knew in that moment that we were special. That we belonged to each other, and we belonged together. This was a fact that could not be denied.

I don't know how many heartbeats passed while Julian and I just stood there, staring at each other like awkward teenagers. My beautiful friends disappeared into the background, my ears deaf to their murmured conversations. Or perhaps the hubbub petered out around us, but I barely noticed. Every cell in my body was standing up and reaching for Julian.

I'd both desperately longed for and feared seeing him again. This meeting felt auspicious.

I stepped closer to him. "I'm so happy you're here," I whispered. "I have something I need to tell you."

"Me too. I was looking for you. But go ahead." Julian's eyes shone bright, and my pulse hammered at the sight of him, my throat thickening with a swelling joy.

"No." I smiled, my voice choked by tears that had suddenly burned my throat, making speech difficult. I'd waited this long to share my plans. Now it seemed more important to hear what Julian had to say. "You first."

"I've been... I thought..." he stammered. He cupped my elbow and drew me gently away from the seating area, though I felt the many eyes of our friends follow us. Parker, alone behind the counter, made himself busy polishing the espresso machine. Julian drew a deep breath, as if searching for words.

He reached up, rubbing a hand behind his neck, his bicep flexing, his Henley stretching over his chiseled chest and I pictured the image he'd inscribed on his skin, so tragic and permanent. I ached to pull the fabric back and set my lips against his wound, to take back that betraying knife, to kiss him until his heart healed. But it would always be there, a reminder of my faithlessness, my cowardice. That was the scar I had to wear forever.

"You left the farm so suddenly, I worried. No, I was terrified." His throat choked off the word, drowning it, and he swallowed. "Scared that being with me... somehow felt wrong for you. Even though, I can't believe that's true. I feel your love, even if you don't want to feel it, or it's inconvenient for you. And when you left, it devastated me. I thought you'd gone for good."

With a sob, I lifted my hands and covered my face, feeling the tears that wet my hot cheeks.

Julian

When she lifted her hands, burying her face in them, I saw something that caused my heart to trip, skip a beat and throb, exploding like a supernova. My grandmother's ring.

It stole the words from my throat.

There it sat, on her third finger, as it had the summer after graduation, when I'd asked her to marry me. When we believed we were making a family together. When the future seemed simple and bright. But it hadn't been there at the reunion, and she didn't wear it to the farm. Its absence ate at me like a cancer. I thought she might have lost it, sold it, thrown it away in some fit of temper and that felt ominous.

But here it was. Back again.

That tiny apple sprout dared to shoot from the ground, trembling in the welcoming air of a fresh spring.

The ring had reappeared, and the fact that she wore it sent a message I couldn't ignore. It gave me courage to say the words I'd been so afraid to say, to express the feelings and desires that had built up inside me like torrential floodwater behind a dam.

The ground flooded, and the sprout drank deeply and stretched, its first leaves unfurling cautiously but bravely.

I stepped closer, pulling her hands from her face, tracing the oval shape of the old ruby with my calloused thumb, my heart trying to burst out of my chest with every passing second like a battering ram.

Dropping my voice to a murmur, for her ears only, I soldiered on. "You and me, Ruby. We belong together. We are together. Even when thousands of miles and tens of years separate us, we are still connected. I feel my heart searching for you, reaching out for you, always. I'll never be happy or complete unless you're near me. So..."

I drew a deep breath, from the very bottom of my well of courage, because what did it matter, what did any of it matter, without Ruby. "So, I'm asking you, will you, please, this time, finally... stay with me. I w-want you to stay with me, here, in Port Cam, and make a life with me. I don't know what that means, for you. Maybe compromise, maybe sacrifice. But this is my place and I'm committed to staying here now. Maybe not forever. And it would make me so, so happy, if you would stay here with me."

You could hear the birds chirping in the street trees outside in the profound silence that followed my declaration. My blood rushed in my ears like a wild mountain river as I waited for her response. My mouth had forgotten how to produce saliva, and my chest hurt.

Ruby lifted her gaze to mine, her eyes as wet, her expression as raw and honest as my own.

"I love you, Julian, so much." She pulled one hand from my grasp, lifting it to cup my cheek, and I couldn't stop myself from tilting my head and leaning into her touch. "I have always loved you. I never stopped loving you, not for one moment, no matter where I was, how far away, no matter what I was doing. You were always on my mind."

I turned my face slightly to kiss her palm.

My little apple tree shot up, its trunk firm and straight, reaching for the sky.

"For all I thought my purpose and my ideals were so much more important than what we were so lucky to find when we were children, I've discovered that I was wrong. What I had to go out into the world to discover was that… you had it right all along. I will never forgive myself for betraying you, and hurting you, but it would mean the world to me if you would give me the chance to try to make it up to you. To earn your trust, and your love, again."

"You never lost my love, Ruby." My heart crashing in my chest like a locomotive, I pulled her to me, pressing our hearts closer, and bent my forehead to touch hers as she went on.

"You are the pin on my map, the post in the heart of my homeland, the anchor in my harbour. I'm so sorry that I left you, but I was always destined to return home to you. You are my home Julian."

The apple tree's branches flexed and stretched wide in a broad embrace, leaves and blossoms sprouting, promising a bright future.

Trust Ruby, the wordsmith, to express herself so unequivocally and eloquently. Her meaning was clear, and it filled me with unparalleled joy, my eyes flooding with the tears that had pooled in my throat. My arms wrapped around her, crushing her to me tightly as I dropped my face to her neck, breathing her in like life itself. I held on so tightly, my arms trembled. I thought our ribs would crack, and the breath whooshed from both our lungs.

For all the joy I felt at her declaration, I still didn't have my answer. Yes, she'd returned to me. Yes, we were, at least spiritually, emotionally, joined. But would she, could she, stay?

I pulled away from her, meeting her swimming emerald gaze. She sensed my hesitation and looked up at me warily.

"Does this mean you're staying? Can you really make that happen?"

Her beautiful face split open in a wide smile. "That's what I wanted to tell you. What I've been trying to share with everyone for the past half hour." She spun one hand out toward our friends, who unabashedly stared at us like a gripping drama on Netflix. "Maclean's asked me to meet with the editor that I'd be working with if I agreed to do the memoir. That's why I went to Vancouver yesterday."

There were murmurs of understanding from our audience, and my comprehension crystalized. "I thought you were called away for another assignment. Somewhere... far."

She shook her head vigorously. "No! No. You know how I told you I had doubts and insecurities about the book project. Well, I could air them, and Marzieh, the editor, was so wonderful, so understanding and inspiring. She put my fears to rest. She helped me see that I'm free to work out what my story is on my terms. So, I..." She shrugged, her smile widening, clasping her hands together in front of her heart. "I signed the contract. And I spoke to my editor at the Times about taking a long leave of absence. It was Marzieh who helped me see I needn't burn any bridges. That I can determine the course of my career on my own terms now. That I'd more than paid my dues."

My breath left my lungs in a whoosh. Pushing words past the void in my chest, hope fizzing like sparklers on my skin, I whispered, "You're staying here. To write the book?"

She nodded. "I'm staying here. This is my home, as long as you're here. Who knows what the future holds? But I so need to put down roots again and have a home."

Speechless, unable to hold back the thunder that roared through my veins, despite the lack of privacy, I took her face between my hands and took possession of her mouth, passionately and earnestly, trying to pour my relief, my joy, and my love into the kiss. And she met me halfway, her lips seeking mine, holding nothing back. I couldn't wait to take her home again and show her, in every way possible, how happy she'd made me.

Parker let out a whoop and flung his rag into the air.

A cheer rose around us, and we broke apart, blushing and a little stunned, to smiles and congratulations and questions. Everyone gathered around us then, treating us to hugs and back-slapping in turns.

"This calls for a celebration!" Tate announced.

Chapter 31

Julian

"Well, I guess we're stuck with each other now," Ruby quipped, and I laughed and squeezed her, lifting her feet from the floor.

"Not a problem for me."

At Quinn's command, Parker locked the front door with a whoop, and dashed upstairs for his private stash of beer. It turned out Quinn had some wine in the cooler behind the bar, and in a flash the coffee shop was transformed into a private party.

Parker handed me a cold beer, and my head whirled in a blur of contentment, slouched into a corner of the big sofa with Ruby next to me, tucked under my arm.

Jeannie sat beside Ruby, Dee beside her, answering all her questions to bring her up to speed. Because she'd kept in touch with Quinn, she'd known that Ruby had left town, but she seemed unaware that Ruby and I hadn't seen each other for ten years, until this week. Somehow, our story belonged to the entire group, and in some ways it did. Certainly, the friends that had got stuck with my miserable ass after Ruby left had carried their share of the weight.

I scanned the room, my heart overflowing. Quinn, Parker, and JJ huddled, teasing and bantering as they always did. Though JJ had come and gone, Parker and especially Quinn had always, always been there for me. My rocks. Parker hopped from group to group, offering drinks, playing host. He seemed torn between his besties, and the boys, though whenever I took a moment to watch JJ and Quinn, some rapid fire fast-paced debate absorbed them, their faces bright and animated.

Zach, though his personal life was kind of a mess, was in his own way ever constant in three things, his devotion to his family, soccer, and his friends. He stood laughing with Phoenix, the two of them still in their sweaty workout gear, probably starting to get ripe. No one, least of all me, expected this day to end as it did. As they talked, they kept looking our way, so I imagined we were the subject of their conversation, though Phoenix kept stealing glances at Jeannie, obviously intrigued with her new look, between studying Zach in that quiet, strategic way of his. Zach, true to form, managed to pretend that she wasn't here.

Tate still perched on the arm of Nomi's chair, though from the looks of it, she was feeling out of her depth with our tight group, and was urging Tate to leave to whatever event they'd been heading to, and he was reluctantly agreeing to go.

"Will you be staying with Julian at the farm, Ruby?" asked Jeannie.

She sputtered. "Oh, er, this is all happening so fast." Her gaze darted to me with an embarrassed grimace. "I think… that… uh, would be maybe premature. I mean, I've barely got back to town. I really haven't had a moment to think about living arrangements. He has his life figured out at last, and I want to make sure he has the space to do what he needs to do. Right, Dee?"

"What do you want, Jules?" Dee said, grinning at me.

Pretending nonchalance, I said, "Oh, yeah, well, whatever Ruby wants to do. I agree, we've got time to figure it out."

"See?" Ruby started.

I kept talking, curling her towards me, bringing my nose close to hers. "As long as I can go to bed with her every night, wake up with her in my arms, and am allowed to feed her three meals a day, I'm flexible," I joked. "Whatever works best for Ruby."

That brought a flutter of laughter, and then they backed off asking questions we didn't have answers to.

"Oh, my god, I'm swooning," said Tate in a high falsetto. "Wait 'til Rainy hears the news."

"Oh, she knows," said Deanna. "I texted her already. She'll stop by after work."

People moved on to grill Ruby about her memoir contract.

In a moment of honesty, Ruby looked around at our newly reunited circle of friends and said, "I really don't have any idea how this writing project will go. It will be hard, and I have to do what I need to do, but it will be here. At home. With as much support as you all can give me. It will be challenging, and I can't do it alone."

"You, my love, will never be alone again." I planted a possessive kiss on her mouth, counting my blessings. I lifted her hand and ran my thumb over her ring, thinking.

Jeannie leaned closer, lowering her voice. "Who is that tall guy with Zach? He keeps staring at me, but I don't remember him. Was he in school with us?"

We glanced across the room. "You mean Phoenix?" Ruby answered. "Yeah, he changed a lot, hey? And surprised the hell out of us all when he showed up at the reunion last week."

"I don't remember anyone named Phoenix," Jeannie said, her brow pulled down in confusion.

"Oh, that's just a nickname he picked up in the forces. You knew him. I'm pretty sure you took honours math together,"

Ruby said. "You used to talk about him sometimes. Had a really rough family situation. His real name's Peter. Peter Corbin."

Jeannie flinched, gasping, her jaw going slack, her eyes wide, as though she'd seen a ghost, literally. I guess we'd all adjusted to the new reality, and she hadn't known. "But… but he… he died! He died in that fire. Didn't he?"

"That's what everyone thought," I said. "Apparently he didn't bother correcting the impression and went and joined the navy. He's been away for ten years, too."

"That can't be," Jeannie said, her voice a choked whisper. "He's dead. He can't be alive."

"Nope. Definitely alive." I narrowed my eyes at her sudden pallor.

"You okay, Jeannie? You don't look well," Ruby said, tucking an arm around Jeannie's suddenly trembling shoulders. Her face had gone from ashen to hot pink, her head shaking back and forth.

"I think I might be sick. I feel sick." She clenched her hands over her stomach, mewling.

"Oh, honey," Deanna jumped in, helping her up off the sofa. She stumbled, and it seemed something really suddenly swamped her with some affliction. "Come to the washroom. I'll get you cold water. Quinn?"

Quinn handed Deanna a bottle of water, and she led Jeannie to the washrooms, following them.

"That was weird. And sudden." I glanced across the room at Phoenix, puzzled. "I wonder what's wrong with her?"

Ruby shrugged, frowning over her shoulder, then inclining her chin towards Phoenix, who watched Jeannie's retreat with concern. "You know it's Phoenix who got this back for me." She held up her hand, the soft pink ruby glowing. "He gave it to me yesterday, just before I left for Vancouver."

"Back?"

"Mhm. I lost it in Venezuela, during the hostage-taking. I

wasn't wearing it. But I always kept it in my bag. I assume they rummaged through, looking for valuables. "

"Oh, babe. That on top of everything else you went through." I leaned in and pressed my lips to her temple through her hair. "I wondered what happened to it. I secretly thought you didn't wear it because you'd got rid of it or hadn't taken our commitment as seriously as I did. I confess it hurt."

"No. It's my most prized possession, and I kept it with me always." Ruby met my gaze with moist eyes full of sympathy and love. "I was heartbroken when it disappeared, after all these years." She was silent for a long moment, gazing at the ring. "I took it as an omen that it was over for me—that something had irrevocably been broken. For a while, I'd almost wished I'd died in the jungle because the one thing I wished for while captured seemed to have been ripped away. I had no hope I'd ever see you again."

"I can't believe you got it back."

"I can't believe I got you back." She cupped my cheek and pressed her soft lips to mine, sending swirling sensations through me, body and soul. Pulling away, she said, "Phoenix's military colleagues found it somehow. I guess he'd made enquiries about the event. I was so shocked. It seemed like a miracle, a sign that there was still hope for us."

"I for one am filled with hope today."

Epilogue

Julian

"GRAB THE DOOR, ZACH, THANKS," I said, my arms groaning with aluminum catering trays stacked with party food. He did, and I manoeuvred my load sideways into the café as Phoenix stood back, his own enormous arms laden with cases of beer, letting me pass. I looked them up and down, both of them, for once, in regular clothes instead of shorts and tanks or sweaty t-shirts. "Looking good, guys. You just arriving?"

"Yeah," Zach said, laughing. "The big P had to buy a fancy new shirt, and it took for-fuckin'-ever to find the perfect one."

"Fugoff, Chapman," Phoenix mumbled. I glanced at Phoenix, who Zach had taken to calling 'the big P' since they'd been at the gym together almost every day. A not very subtle reference to his unflattering high school nickname of The Penis. Stoic as ever, he narrowed his eyes, almost cracking a smile at Zach's teasing.

Leaving them to join the party, which was well underway, I carried my trays to replenish the long buffet table Quinn and Parker had set up against the brick wall of the café. The party was planned to be super casual, but of course Deanna got involved and made sure there were fresh flowers, funky boho candles and a banner on the wall that read, "The Prodigal Daughter Returns!"

Not sure what Jeannie thought of that, given her history.

Parker stood behind the counter filling a tub of ice with drinks, hailing the guys over to add theirs to the mix. Jae lounged against the bar, a glass in hand, laughing and joking with Parker, as always.

Quinn stood with her back to Jae, talking with Rainy and Jeannie. Still, she and Jae elbowed and pinched each other periodically like kids in middle school, and it appeared they were having a side conversation at the same time. More than likely an argument about something unresolvable, such as Jae's fashion choices, or Quinn's opinions about organic food.

Zach and Phoenix dropped their loads and stepped back outside, everyone twitching towards the door with flicked gazes and lifted chins, curious.

Ruby had spent a grand total of five days officially "living" at home with her parents before stuffing what little she owned into her duffle and fully moving in with me at the farm. Of those five, she'd actually slept there only twice, having spent most days and nights with me.

Or one-and-a-half, if you counted the time she'd called me in the middle of the night after she'd woken up from another nightmare and I'd hopped in my truck and driven into town to get her and bring her home. She said she slept much better in my arms, and I wasn't about to complain. I'd been waiting ten years to call her mine again. Waking to find her in my bed was becoming my new normal, though it would never, ever get old.

It seemed both so meteoric that it made my head spin, and inevitable and right. It's where she belonged, after all.

Now, she'd taken over a small upstairs bedroom, my old one, as her office, and we'd dragged an assortment of old family furniture around, making it comfortable for her. Next week, we'd head out to buy her a new laptop; something state-of-the-art to replace her heavy-duty field machine. Her excitement buzzed and mine for her. The knowledge that she'd be there with me every day, gazing out her window as I do my farm chores, spending time every day on long walks, slow meals and steamy nights, remained a waking dream.

On the day Ruby and I had overcome our fears and ask each other for what we truly desired, there'd been an impromptu party at Quinn's café. Jeannie had taken ill almost immediately, and rushed off home that night, missing the fun.

It had been a really fun evening, so relaxed and different from the actual reunion event, which had been fraught with anticipation and anxiety. Though I'd wanted to take Ruby home so we could be alone, we ended up staying very late that night. It seemed appropriate to mark the occasion with our circle of friends.

So much had changed in such a short time.

It was Quinn's idea to throw another party this weekend, a little better planned, with a few additional friends added to the group, as an official welcome home for Jeannie. Jeannie's protestations had been blithely ignored.

Jae, Quinn, and Tate had insisted I recreate some of the same food I'd made for the reunion, so Jeannie could experience it. I'd happily obliged.

"Julian! Julian!"

There they were, right on cue. Already warmed up with a few drinks, Deanna, Quinn, and Rainy flocked around me, making noises about all the food, fawning in that exaggerated way they'd taken to teasing me. My girl followed them, sidling up to my side with a smirk.

"I'm available if you need an extra dairy maid, Gorgeous," said Quinn.

"Am I crushing? Yes, I'm crushing," crooned Rainy, batting her dark eyes at me.

"Julian, can I have your babies?" squealed Deanna, then let out a telltale snort.

"Enough!" I couldn't stop myself from laughing.

Though I always half expected it, that they actually read the over-the-top comments my Insta feed got and threw them back at me still drew heat to my cheeks. I tried not to overthink it, but there were many that were clearly not about my food or my goats.

"Ooh, that smile! I'm pinning you to my bedroom wall," Quinn added.

"All right, ladies. Back the hell away from my guy. He's taken," Ruby joked, shooing them away.

"See. I told you, Jules. She's gonna kill your brand vibe," Deanna said, bending over the table to pick up an amuse-bouche, wrinkling her nose. "Is this one vegan?"

I picked up one of my new creations, holding it to Ruby's lips. "You've all got to try this new one." Ruby obligingly opened her mouth to receive my offering, and I tucked it in, delaying my retreat just long enough to make sure her sexy lips caught my thumb and fingertip. She darted her tongue out to lick my finger as it retreated, and I met her naughty gaze with a wink and a steamy smile.

Everything these days reminded me of some detail of our constant lovemaking, making my blood rush to my groin and my skin shiver with anticipation.

Closing her eyes, she squirmed, shimmied, and made orgasmic, moaning sounds as she chewed and swallowed; I caught her dramatic fake swoon right on cue with a laugh, as if I weren't in Billy Crystal-like shock. We'd made up for lost time sharing a lot of amazing food and cooking and sex. I guess it was going to be our new thing, but I didn't know what to make of her public display.

Ruby righted herself with a smile. "That is so delicious."

I leaned in for a kiss, slick with oil and garlic, which immediately slowed, turned sensual and drew a chorus of oohs and aahhs from the girls. Which naturally cut our enjoyment short as we pulled apart, blushing.

"Jeannie, you've got to try that one," Ruby said, redirecting. "It's to-die-for."

Jeannie obliged by taking a sample, quietly gloating at the ridiculous fan-girling I was subjected to constantly.

"Is it veggie?" mewled Deanna.

"Anchovies," I replied, accustomed to vetting my ingredients for her diet. She made a face, as if contemplating whether anchovies counted as real animals. "God, just eat one, Dee, it won't change the world."

"Here's your drink, babe," said Ruby, handing me my half-finished beer.

"Thanks." I hooked my arm around her shoulders and bent to kiss her temple. "Who's that with Tate?"

"Oh, some new girl," replied Quinn, glancing over her shoulder. "Uh, Daisy? Dusty?"

"Destin," Rainy said. "She came with me. We graduated from Psych Counselling together."

"What happened to Nomi?" Deanna asked, braving the anchovy thing with her nose curled up, poking her tongue at it.

"Didn't you warn her about Tate?" Ruby slid her arm around my waist, slipping her fingers into my pocket like she used to do when we were in high school; a rush of contentment swamped me in a warm wave, my heart kicking.

Everyone laughed again. Putting on a cross face, I said, "I don't know why you all give me such a hard time when it's Tate who's earned his reputation as a ladies' man."

"Yeah, he really is in full movie star mode, isn't he?" Ruby murmured. "I feel like I hardly know him."

Quinn hummed, chewing one of the new olive oil flatbread rounds with aioli, anchovy crumb and fresh garlic buds, her head nodding in appreciation. "He's still good ol' Tate underneath all the gloss and glam."

"I sure hope so," Ruby said.

Quinn licked her lips. "You've got to serve that new one at your open-air pop-up restaurant at the Faire, Jules."

"I plan to."

"He's been testing recipes on me. I'm not complaining."

"I thought all you ate was canned tuna and beans," Jeannie teased.

"Not anymore," Ruby sing-songed, sliding her appreciative gaze to me with a sly smile.

Deanna said, "See, I knew Ruby would be bad for your brand, Julian. We have to keep her off camera."

"If you look at the camera like you look at Ruby, you'll triple your following by Christmas," Rainy said.

That inspired a round of laughter from the entire group, and I imagined it was true. I couldn't look at Ruby without feeling a little faint myself, my heart rate speeding up just having her near me, being able to touch her whenever I wanted to. Which was always.

"As long as it brings more people to the Farm-to-Table Faire, and customers to my new restaurant at the Ragged Mountain Resort."

"So you're actually doing it?" Rainy asked.

"Hmm. Ethan and I have been negotiating terms."

"Jules wants to buy in as a part owner. He wants to maintain control."

"Have a stake," I corrected. "He's selling the idea to his old man."

"Do you have a name yet?" Beth asked.

"Getting there. It's between Forage & Feast or Wild Feast."

"Ooh, I like that. Wild Feast." Deanna said. "That'll bring in people even if they don't know what you're doing."

"Maybe. Or maybe the wrong people who will grumble when I serve them weed salad instead of roast boar."

Ruby bobbed her head back and forth, teasing. "Weed salad's not that bad, with the right vinaigrette, she said, making a face.

Zach and Phoenix returned, carrying more cases of beer and boxes of wine and tequila. Jeannie faltered, froze mid-expression, staring at them. Exchanging sly glances over her head, I think we all assumed she was staring at her ex, Zach. But he was oblivious, and it was Phoenix who stared back, smiling.

Jeannie blushed, dipped her chin, and looked away.

Deanna noticed the exchange and approached stiffly, stopping to face Jeannie.

"Hey Jeannie. Can I talk to you a sec?"

Her eyes narrowing slightly, Jeannie said, "Sure, Dee."

"I don't want to raise any ghosts, but I feel like I need to apologize for grad night." Despite trying not to eavesdrop, we all perked up at that.

Deanna continued. "I didn't mean to be such a bitch and hurt you. Me and Zach were just friends, and Zach was upset. We were both so fucked up that night, and one thing led to another. I've never forgiven myself for breaking you guys up.

"Oh, I don't... um..."

"Have you spoken with Zach since you got back? I know he felt bad about it."

"No." Jeannie paused, her gaze sliding over to Zach, her lips pursing, a thin line forming between her brows. "I haven't and I really don't need to. It's been ages, you know?"

"I'm sorry if I made coming home harder for you."

"No. You didn't. Promise. Old news. Okay?"

"Sure." Deanna gave her a grateful smile.

Jeannie, having gathered her thoughts, went on. "I have no regrets. In retrospect, I would have left him anyway when I went to school out east. And he was always going to stay close to his mom, wasn't he?"

This brought nods and hums of confirmation from the rest of us. Zach's family was pretty tight, because his mom had been sick for pretty much forever, and needed a ton of help. That's why he always played for the local team, passing up drafts to better ones.

"Besides, we were a terrible match and never meant to be together. It was just that nerd-jock high school thing."

I chuckled at the truth of that. I guess he wasn't her son's father, after all. They were not like Ruby and me.

"Zach was always a stupid jerk anyway, in retrospect. I mean… a loveable one," she amended. "I hold no grudge against you, Deanna."

Deanna sighed and hugged her. "I'm so relieved. Now that you're back in town, and Ruby and Beth are back, too, I'd so love for us all to be close friends again like we were." Deanna met Ruby's eye over Jeannie's shoulder, her gaze wistful.

"Me too," Jeannie said softly as they pulled apart. "It's going to ease our transition home so much."

Ruby reached out to give Jeannie a squeeze on the arm, and I was glad she was returning to a whole community of support, and not just me.

"Are you and Zach… together, Deanna?" Jeannie asked.

Deanna scoffed. "Oh, fuck, no. We're still just friends."

"Still with benefits," Rainy quipped with a disapproving smile.

Deanna shot her a pissy glare, waving off the implied criticism, her bracelets jangling. "Ignore her. It's not a thing now any more than it was then."

Jae arriving at the buffet with a quip drew a round of laughter that broke the group up into smaller conversations, when Quinn and Rainy turned toward him. Jeannie stood close to Ruby and me. Aside from Quinn, I knew Jeannie had been closest to Ruby, and the two of them were gently feeling their way back towards friendship, both of them still shy within the larger group.

Jeannie continued to stare at Zach and Phoenix, and I caught Phoenix noticing.

"How are you settling in at home with your parents, Jeannie?" I asked her.

Still distracted, she said, "Fine. I'm all registered and ready to start my new program at the university in September. Will and I are adjusting to living with my mom and dad, but it's challenging. We're used to our privacy, and I'm used to running my own home and… life. It's a change, for sure."

Ruby and I exchanged a glance and small smile, remembering her brief stay with her parents and how eager she was to move in with me, despite their good intentions.

"I forgot how… hard it is to deal with my bossy, controlling, passive-aggressive mother who still hasn't forgiven me for everything."

"Having their only grandchild live with them has got to soften them up, I'll bet," Ruby said.

Jeannie nodded, then shook her head from side to side, rolling her eyes. "Will is sulky about the move, leaving his friends in Kingston. My parents are working hard to connect with him. I'm afraid they'll spoil him rotten. But I can't go to grad school without their support, so we have to make it work." She shrugged.

"Is Will starting school too?" I asked.

"Yes. We have an appointment with the principal at Will's new school next week, to talk about his transition into grade four. Will's a January baby, so at least he won't be the smallest runt in the class. He's bright, but he struggles with anxiety, so I want the teachers to understand that going in. He'll need some help."

January baby? I mentally did math, catching Ruby's gaze. Wow. She got knocked up shortly after Ruby did. "Is he a math whiz like you?"

"Um, strangely no, that's the subject he has the most trouble with, and I'm the worst tutor. My efforts seem to trigger his anxiety more than anything."

"I might know someone, if you're looking for a counsellor," Rainy offered over her shoulder.

"So what's the deal with Peter Corbin?" Jeannie asked, when it seemed she'd finally forgotten them. "Has he moved back permanently too?"

"He's not a big one to share, but I get the impression he's undecided," Ruby said, leaning into me.

I curled my arm around her waist, tugging her closer and taking a pull on my beer. I nodded. "He told Zach he's got a couple of months to choose a new posting since his old platoon split up. Apparently it's between Ottawa, Halifax, and here."

"No contest, hey." Jae scoffed as the others rejoined us, holding napkins with several hors d'oeuvres on each hand.

"He gets to choose? That's pretty rare, isn't it?" Rainy said, stealing one from his pile.

"He seems to have a lot of autonomy," Ruby said. "I have the sense he might be in a pretty special unit."

We all shrugged, not knowing enough about how the Navy assigned jobs and distributed their people. I assumed wherever they were needed, but maybe that was just for the rank and file.

"His friends are there. One of his buddies is in Halifax, the other in Ottawa now. And apparently his mom and baby sister are in Vancouver, so he's feeling it out."

"He has a baby sister? Was she born after?" Quinn asked.

"No." Jeannie jumped in. "She's about nine or ten years younger, though. I remember his mom taking her away when we were just starting high school."

"And he stayed? In that awful trailer park?" Ruby asked.

Jeannie nodded.

"But…"

She pulled her lips tight. "He told me he didn't want to leave his dad alone."

"That surprises me," Quinn said. "He was kind of a grumpy jerkface."

"That's why everyone called him The Penis," Deanna said, snort-laughing in that way of hers.

"Hey, I resemble that remark." I laughed. It's true a lot of people called him The Penis, his enemies as an insult, his friends jokingly. He always claimed it was an improvement on what his dad's friends called him, which was apparently 'Little Prick.'

"Shush, that's rude," Jeannie said, smacking Dee's arm lightly. Her voice dropped, soft and wistful. "He wasn't really like that. He was super smart and thoughtful. It was tough at home alone with his dad. He was prickly, but nice if you gave him a chance."

"So you really knew him, then?" Quinn asked. "He only hung with the guys."

Jeannie shrugged, backpedaling, her face going a suspicious shade of rosy pink, her golden freckles jumping out as her gaze dropped to the floor. "Um. Very little. We talked a bit. In honours math mostly."

"Huh. Well, he's apparently a communications engineer now."

Jeannie looked up, her gaze intent, "I don't understand, though, about the fire. How is it that everyone thought he died in it, but he didn't?"

Ruby answered for the group. "I don't know the details, but apparently he got home on grad night at about four in the morning to find the trailer already engulfed by flames. He ran away, I guess, maybe when the fire trucks showed up? Maybe to his mom's?"

Jeannie hissed, her voice dropping, "But they found two bodies! It was in the paper that summer. Everyone was so shocked."

Ruby nodded. "I remember. They said a drug deal gone bad. Or burglary, maybe. Someone started the fire deliberately."

"Yeah, it was hot. Fuel-fed," Quinn said. "I guess they were so charred there was no way to identify them, so they assumed it was Peter with his dad since it was their trailer."

"God," Ruby whispered, her gaze unfocused and distant.

"Poor kid," I said, remembering how tough he had it, with his disabled, drug-addled dad, his mom gone. "His life was already miserable enough, hey?"

As if sensing us talking about him, Phoenix peeled away from Zach and Parker and made his way towards us in a straight line, his gaze steady, his solid gait intimidating. He stopped in front of Jeannie, dipping his chin to meet her eyes, which widened in panic.

"Hey Jeannie. Welcome back. It's really great to see you again."

Jeannie fumbled, the strap of her bag slipping from her shoulder, and she jerked, catching it and slinging it back on. She hesitated before replying, staring up at his face like she'd forgotten how to speak. "Uh-um. Yes. Peter. You too." A storm of colour had overtaken her cheeks.

Phoenix's lips pulled to the side and tucked in ever so slightly, a mere hint of a smile, and his warm eyes crinkled at the corners. "Nobody but my mother calls me Peter anymore. Everyone calls me Phoenix now."

"Right. Of course. Sorry." Could she blush any harder?

"No problem. I hear you're going back to school."

She swallowed, nodding, her gaze flicking up and down his impressive body, but skipping across his face. "Uh-huh. Yes. MBA."

"I hope we can reconnect this summer. Spend some time together before you get too busy." He stepped back, grinning at her, but kept one hand lightly touching her arm, almost possessively.

She let out a yip of nervous laughter, her translucent cheeks flaring with flags of bright pink. "Sure. Yup. Maybe. Um. I'll have to see."

He leaned in and dropped a kiss on her cheek, winked and went back to the guys, accepting a fresh beer from Parker while we all stared after him with slack jawed expressions.

"OMG!" Quinn hissed with suppressed thrill, pulling her shoulders to her ears and stretching her smile wide.

"What was that? He was practically effusive. He's been so cool towards everyone else!" Ruby added, drawing a curious glance from me.

"He was flirting with you," Rainy said. "Definitely."

"Oh, dear," Jeannie whimpered, her head shaking. "Oh, God. Why did I say yes? I can't... Oh, my God. No. This can't... I don't..."

Everyone chuckled at her shyness. Despite it, her reciprocal attraction was more than obvious.

I laughed, teasing, "Looks like you're going to be really busy this summer, Jeannie."

Laughing, Quinn and Rainy dragged Jeannie away. "Come on, you've got to try every single one of Julian's treats before Jae eats them all."

Alone at last, I turned to Ruby, planting a light, grateful kiss on her mouth, my heart full to bursting with contentment. I murmured for Ruby's ears only, "That was... weird, huh?"

"Yes. Yes it was." Ruby's eyes narrowed, staring after Jeannie, slanting a glance to Phoenix.

"Are your investigative senses tingling, Ms. Reporter?"

Ruby twisted her lips to one side. "Yes, Chef, they are."

DID you enjoy The Reporter's Unlikely Reunion? You can read Book 2 in the Most UNLIKELY To series now. Find The Phoenix's UNLIKELY Prodigy here: https://www.amazon.com/dp/B09DWJM1QY

WANT TO READ THE FIRST BOOK IN THE HAVING IT ALL SERIES?
BUY EBOOK ON AMAZON : BeMineThisTime

WANT TO CONNECT WITH ME?
www.maryannclarkescott.com
maryann@maryannclarkescott.com

If you enjoy reading this book, please rate it and leave a review on Amazon HERE. Your opinion can make or break an author's success, and it means the world to me.
Go here to leave a review: https://amzn.to/3qquxcU

The Phoenix's UNLIKELY
Prodigy - Chapter 1

Jeannie

My moment of hesitation before joining my welcome back party at Millhouse Coffee was just long enough to notice that my hand on the old brass door handle trembled uncontrollably. I pulled my hand away, clenching it into a fist. My feet stayed cemented to the sidewalk while I gathered my thoughts and my courage. Filling my lungs, I braced myself for what lay ahead.

Not just the next few minutes, but the next few days, weeks, and months.

Until last week, I hadn't been home for ten years. I hadn't seen my group of closest friends from high school in a decade. Even I could hardly believe it, and I'm the only one, except for my best friend Quinn, who knew what I'd been through since graduation. My road had been long and strewn with obstacles.

I was nervous enough returning to my hometown. Nervous enough that I'd conveniently-oh-so-strategically missed the ten-year Port Camosun High School reunion last weekend. That felt like more than I could handle all at once. A soft re-entry was what I needed, and the casual after-the-party gathering at my best friend's new café had seemed like the perfect speed. Or so I'd assumed.

Despite avoiding the reunion, I'd ended up reconnecting with pretty much everyone in our group a few days later instead of individually the way I wanted. It transpired that the biggest event at the reunion was Julian and Ruby getting together again. I thought my own history was fraught. But those two, it seemed, had it… Well, at least as bad.

Everyone assumed that from the moment Julian and Ruby set eyes on each other the summer before tenth grade, they'd be together forever. They were that rare couple who seemed like soulmates. But something happened the summer after grad that tore them apart, and broke Julian's heart, according to Quinn.

I realized that what I found inside Quinn's café might be hard to recognize. Everyone else would have changed, too. For better, or, like me, for worse. The girl voted 'Most Likely to Succeed' had become the 'Prodigal Daughter' returning from exile with her tail firmly tucked between her legs. I dreaded being the focus of everyone's attention. Fortunately, that day, I was able to reconnect with just a few friends at a time as people wandered in and gathered around the battered old wooden coffee table. For a while, I'd thought maybe it'd all be okay.

Until he walked in.

Initially, I felt most nervous seeing Zach Chapman, my high school boyfriend, after all this time, especially after the catastrophic way our relationship imploded on grad night.

But the incredibly hot, intense guy Zach came in with stole my attention instantly, casting a large shadow over my old beau. Taller, wider, with an imposing presence, his sweat-dampened t-shirt clung to impressive bulging muscles covered in ink like a *Men's Health* cover model. He was pure man-candy and sucked the breath from my lungs.

I honestly didn't know who he was. Just the most perfectly exquisite man to melt my inhibitions and distract me from my restorative mission—exactly the type of man who haunted my pathetic, lonely single-mom dreams.

My belly had swirled with heat and a shiver of excitement at the idea that maybe my future, now that I was home, might include something beyond motherhood, endless study, and hard work. Something decadent and delicious just for me. Now that I'd have my family's support while I was going to school, maybe there'd be time for a little dating, at last.

When his warm, steady gaze made its way across the room to me time and again, setting my face on fire, I finally leaned over to whisper in Ruby's ear.

"Who *is* that tall guy with Zach? He keeps staring at me."

"Who? Phoenix?" She laughed. "Yeah, he changed a lot, hey? And surprised the hell out of us all when he showed up at the reunion last week."

"I don't remember anyone named Phoenix," I said, mentally scrolling our grad class list.

Her reply turned that thrill of attraction and hope into a solid wall of fiery dread. "Oh, that's just a nickname he picked up in The Navy. You knew him. I'm pretty sure you took honours math together," Ruby said. "You used to talk about him sometimes. Had a really rough family situation? His real name's Peter. Peter Corbin."

In a nanosecond, everything I knew—about my past, my present, and most certainly my hopeful future—irrevocably changed.

<hr>

Phoenix

Jeannie hadn't yet shown up to her own party. Her late arrival had me rethinking my approach. She was obviously gun-shy about being with our group of old friends. I could relate, sort of, but it didn't scare or inhibit me. She was different, and I needed to find out more about her before approaching her. I didn't want to overwhelm her by coming on too strong, too soon.

Within about fifteen minutes of arriving, Quinn asked Zach and me to get a load of liquor from Parker's truck, parked just down the block. We lifted the cases of beer, and boxes of wine and tequila bottles, into two piles. I could see Zach fighting the urge to compete with me, and failing.

"Don't overdo it, Chapman. You don't want to overwork your muscles so soon after an intense workout."

We'd already spent hours at the gym today, Zach watching my routine and quizzing me on how to improve. Considering he'd been training and playing professional ball for a long time, I was frankly surprised at his desire to get stronger now.

"I'm good," he insisted. "I'm recovering nicely."

Having watched him lift weights, I knew this was patently untrue. He nursed his lumbar and was obviously in pain.

"I can take another one," I said.

"What about you?"

I shook my head. "I'm not nursing a sore back. And this is well within my normal load." I routinely ran twelve kilometres with a thirty-five-kilo pack plus gear, so I could easily carry a few more pounds a half a block.

Zach tentatively added another case onto the stack in my arms.

I hardly felt it. "One more."

Scowling, he piled it on, and I shifted it and reconsidered. "Nah. Take it off. I don't want to get my shirt sweaty."

Scoffing, he removed it, setting it down inside the truck. "Show off."

"We can get more later if we run low."

"So what's with the new shirt? I swear you've never bought new clothes. You tried on maybe twenty options this afternoon and fussed like a girl going to prom."

He wasn't wrong. After our morning workout, I'd talked Zach into showing me a couple of local places to shop for clothes, and made him sit and rate me. Because I seriously didn't have a clue.

"I haven't bought civvies, except to work out or hang out. Other than that, I'm on duty, so I have uniforms for…stuff." So many uniforms.

"Huh."

I hesitated. Technically, I didn't have to say anything to Zach, but we were rebuilding some kind of friendship here. "Have you talked to Jeannie yet?"

He straightened his stack of cases, not looking up at me. "No. Why should I?"

I continued staring at him until he looked up, and I held his gaze. "Because you owe it to her? Because it's the right thing to do."

His gaze narrowed, then darted away. "It's been for-fuckin-ever. I dunno. S'pose." He jerked his chin at me. "Why do you care?"

I tongued a tooth, twisting my mouth to the side. "Jeannie and I were good friends in school." I waited for a beat. "I, uh, might be interested."

Zach's face brightened as he processed what I meant. "No shit. Huh." He coughed. "So…the new shirt." He tilted his head towards the café where we headed, and I quirked a small smile. His next shrug conveyed permission, of sorts. "Not my business, man."

"Still. You ought to talk to her. Once. Clear up old hurts."

We carried our loads towards the café entrance. I could practically hear the gears working in Zach's brain.

"Hey, Big P."

"Yep?"

"I was wondering. If maybe you can walk me through your routine. Take me through it step by step."

He'd obviously finished thinking about Jeannie. "You planning on enlisting? It'll just make you hurt."

His mouth flattened, and his brow quirked. "I just want to try it."

I scoffed. Guys were always curious about what it took to train for special forces. Wondering if they had what it took. They usually didn't.

"Yeah, sure. I'll watch you sweat and beg to stop and then kiss my ass."

We laughed, and as we neared the door, Julian arrived at the same time with a stack of food trays from his van.

"Guys."

"Hey, man."

Zach set down his load to grab the door, and I followed Julian inside, where the party crowd had thickened.

***

Jeannie

I ripped off the Band-Aid and finally hauled the café door open, a wall of music and voices enveloping me. On the other side, I waded into a miasma of rich scents—coffee, spicy food, and beer—that pushed my queasy stomach further to the edge. The chill café that now served as our gang's daily hangout, which I'd avoided since that encounter last week, had been transformed into a sparkling bar scene with a standing crowd of people all talking at once.

It had been a struggle to stay away until now, but I was getting good at excuses. My first task, scanning for Peter Corbin, turned up nothing, and I breathed a sigh of relief. I was safe for now. I squinted into the dimly lit space, eager to find and attach myself to Quinn.

Seeing Quinn again had been—continued to be—amazing. She was the only one of our rag-tag and unlikely group of friends who I stayed in touch with all this time, keeping me from desperation, though a long-distance friendship just wasn't the same. Even during those first few years when I barely called my parents because I was so devastatingly ashamed. She was the only one who knew my secret.

And even Quinn didn't know *all* my secrets.

Quinn and I were honour roll geeks, math whizzes, and popular but nerdy good girls. Unlike many in our group, she took a different path. She didn't go to uni either, though everyone expected her to as well. But she knew what she wanted, and she went out and grabbed it by the throat.

Quinn's twin brother, goofy Parker, was not the brilliant student his sister was, but clever enough, combined with athletic ability, to get a scholarship to the uni here in town. I laughed, recalling he'd been voted 'Most Likely to be a Justin Bieber Impersonator in Vegas' because of his glib tongue and boyish good looks. That family never had the patience for desk jobs, more hands-on and pragmatic in their skills and passions than bookish, like me. Instead, Quinn took business classes at the local college, worked a long but strategic series of grunt jobs at shops, restaurants, and cafés and saved her money.

Two years ago, she bought this historic brick building in Old Town before anyone else fully realized how valuable and popular this blue-collar warehouse waterfront district next to the downtown would become.

But Quinn the entrepreneur knew. She had her finger on the pulse of the city. At least a third of the old warehouses were already converted to trendy lofts, and new construction was happening everywhere. So now the girl voted 'Most Likely to Own a Café' was finally the proprietor of the trendiest café in the trendiest neighbourhood, at only twenty-eight years of age.

She told me her dream was to make a place where people could hang out and feel at home. Where people could have a superior cuppa ethically sourced joe and a delicious healthy snack and chill with their friends. Where have you heard that before? *Starbunckles ain't got nothin' on this place*, she told me in her emails.

And in spite of my deep desire to run and hide from the inevitable, Quinn, along with Deanna, had insisted on throwing a proper welcome back party at the café just for me. How could I say no when I was the guest of honour? Not something I could get out of.

And I knew that, along with everyone else, Peter would be here.

And so, here I was. Now my girl squad was all together again. Even the famous war correspondent, ambitious and elusive Ruby Zimmer, had returned to our hometown, apparently to stay.

I spotted Ruby, Rainy, and Quinn near the bar, where Jae Soo leaned at the front, and Parker served as bartender behind. I cut a beeline through the crowd before anyone else noticed me arrive.

"Here she is!" JJ called, spotting me first as I neared.

Quinn's face opened in a rare but broad and welcoming smile. She stepped towards me and enveloped me in her arms, murmuring in my ear, "I'm so glad you came."

As if I wouldn't, but she had excellent people senses and, being my bestie, obviously noticed my reluctance to be with people.

Rainy kissed my cheek, and Parker offered me a glass of wine, which I accepted only too happily. I needed that and something stronger to calm my nerves.

"Thought we'd see more of you before now," JJ said, sipping his beer. "I have so many questions."

I sighed, smiling at him. Jay-Soo the Suit, voted 'Most Likely to be on the Cover of Forbes,' proud owner of the MBA I should have had. That I still wanted. He used to have a floppy mop of beautiful silky black hair. Now, severe chiselled cheeks and trendy hair dyed all shades of burgundy and pink, with sculpted sides, slicked on top.

Seriously though, everyone thought he'd have been whisked home to Korea long ago, swallowed up by the mega family business that supplied him with money to burn. And according to Quinn, he did disappear for years at a time. Some kind of apprenticeship, we supposed. Yet he was here again.

He still wore expensive fashionable clothes, but now he seemed harder, like a buttoned-up, no-nonsense businessman. Until he opened his mouth and laughed that ridiculous donkey bray, flashing those million-dollar white teeth and you realized that inside he was still the same old crazy rebel he'd always been. Yet tempered somehow, with a quiet determination.

My smile tightened, and panic swelled in my chest. This was the part I dreaded. The questions.

I replied, "Of course, sure, JJ. I can't wait to hear everything that you've done during the last ten years. I'm so excited to be here. I'll make the rounds first, say hello to a few people, and catch up with you, okay?" I was babbling. I always babbled when I was nervous.

He nodded, grinning, and turned to say something to Parker.

I'm sure by now word had got around, and everyone knew I had a nine-year-old son. I just hoped they were too polite to ask too many questions about him, though I doubted that very much.

As if to underscore my concern, as I turned the door opened and Julian entered carrying covered trays, presumably of his yummy food, while Zach held the door open for him. On Julian's heels, entered Peter—or Phoenix, I guess I had to get used to calling him that—his short dark hair gelled, his muscles straining against a dark-coloured short-sleeved shirt, sending my pulse hammering in my chest, like a prisoner demanding escape. I could relate. But there was no escape.

I spun towards Quinn. I needed time to sort out this crisis— and get my story straight. Yet first, somehow, I had to get through this night.

I didn't know how I would, but I'd survived worse, and I

had to trust myself. I filled my lungs, setting my teeth. *I will get through it. I will find a way.*

Phoenix

I didn't recognize half the people here and assumed our friends had brought friends, and probably dates or partners.

We hauled the cases of liquor behind the counter and set them down. Parker dumped a bucket of ice cubes into a half-full tub on the counter.

"Rip a couple of cases open and toss some bottles in here," he said. "We need to cool them down."

Jae Soo, glass in hand, leaned on the counter. "Fried chicken once a week isn't going to kill me," he drawled.

"But think of the poor chickens!" Quinn prodded his arm, grinning.

Once Parker was satisfied, Zach and I each grabbed a fresh cold one and circled the counter to hover near Jae Soo, watching the crowd. It was curious, observing how certain pairs of people related to each other, especially old friends or siblings like Parker and Quinn. The subtext. The habits. The emotional shifts were visible to me now, after running missions and leading units of soldiers for years. The dynamic between Jae Soo, Parker, and Quinn was complex and fascinating.

Ruby, as usual, caught my eye. She had an air of exhaustion about her that I'd noted before. But now, standing next to Julian, one or the other of them always touching the other, with a glow of elation and…relief, like a marathon runner who'd finally reached the finish line, like she'd been pushing through with her last ounce of energy.

I could wish my love life sorted itself out as quickly as theirs did, but I knew it couldn't have been easy with what Ruby had gone through. I could never let on all that I knew. But she'd suffered a lot. I'd seen people do much worse, really, after experiences like that.

She'd made the tough call, stepping away from her war correspondent work to stay here with Julian, near her family and friends. It was the right one. Going out on assignment, again and again, was no life. She'd used herself up that way. Even though she was smiling now, I knew from experience her battle with PTSD wouldn't be over any time soon. I had Dad to thank for that knowledge.

She was here now—Jeannie. A shrinking violet next to Quinn and Rainy, trying not to take up too much space. I wondered where the self-assured girl that I knew was hiding. Ten years ago, I'd found her pretty and poised, but also envied the shit out of her. She had her family, and lived in that big old heritage house at the crest of the rise a few blocks beyond the house I'd grown up in before we had to move to the trailer park. Everyone knew her mom who had taught at the elementary school nearby.

It was only after we'd been in the same classes for a couple of years, and become friendlier, that she confided in me about her little sister drowning when she was twelve. My baby sister Bess was only six at the time, and the thought of losing her killed me. But even then, Jeannie rose above it and was so strong and determined to succeed, and she believed she would.

She'd been an inspiration to me. I never got the chance to tell her, but I could start now.

Even though there was a brittle edge to her that hadn't been there before, there was also a ripe softness that had come with maturity. I found I liked it very much, my body responding with a rush of blood, and twitching fingers whenever my gaze traced her curves, or the soft blush of her freckled cheeks whenever I caught her looking at me.

I'd be a fool to think she was unchanged, unaffected by the past decade. I was hardly the angry scrawny teenager I was then. I'd heard she had a child, and that meant a complicated story. I needed to know more. To understand what had happened to her. No better time to start than now.

More than just Jeannie was glancing my way, so I figured this was my moment. I pushed away from the counter and strode towards her. Her eyes widened when I stopped in front of her, leaving no ambiguity that I was there to speak with her.

"Hey, Jeannie. Welcome back. It's really great to see you again."

"Uh-um. Yes! Peter. I heard you were home too. Nice to — You too," she stuttered, her blush ramping up to a cotton candy pink as she fumbled with her purse. The bright colour on her cheeks made her golden freckles pop. "I mean, it's nice to see you, too."

Her embarrassment was too sweet. She was eyeing me like I was a bag of licky-chewies. *She likes you, sailor.*

I couldn't stop my face from twisting into a smile. "Nobody but my mom calls me Peter anymore. Everyone calls me Phoenix now."

"Right. Of course. Sorry."

I hadn't meant to embarrass her further, but it was damned weird hearing my old name on her lips. Like I'd time-travelled back to high school.

"No problem. It takes getting used to. I hear you're going to school."

It wasn't a hard question. I was trying to put her at ease. But she was completely flustered. Her lake-blue eyes darkened to navy as her pupils grew large, and I pretended not to notice her gaze dart over my chest and arms and down my body, avoiding my face.

"Uh-huh. Yes. I'm finally going to get my MBA," she choked out.

"I hope we can reconnect this summer. Spend some time catching up before you get too busy." I took a small step away to give her a bit of breathing room, my smile growing at how flustered she was. I wanted to wrap her in my arms and give her a bear hug. Reaching forwards, I satisfied the impulse by setting my fingertips against her arm.

She squeaked and recoiled as if I'd set a torch to her smooth pale skin. *Sensitive.*

I took a deep breath and let it out slowly, picturing her response if I touched her all over the way I wanted to, my chest filling as if I'd come upon a secret buried treasure. It felt like I'd breached a fortress she'd built around herself, catching her off-guard. Her fine smooth cheeks flared an even brighter shade of pink like summer rose petals.

With a sputter of nervous laughter, she replied, "Sure. Yup. Maybe. Um. I'll have to see. Busy schedule. Busy."

Okay. *Back away, dude.* She was really delicate. Even more than I thought. Or maybe it was just me that rattled her. This thought both thrilled and concerned me. I hoped her memories of grad night were not unpleasant.

Shit. Is it possible she didn't even remember our stolen night of intimacy? That night, she'd been upset, and did have a lot to drink, and hadn't appeared used to it. But I hoped her memories were as pleasant as mine. Despite everything that happened before, and afterwards, I still held that secret memory close to my heart, treasuring it like a precious jewel. I'd had dreams of Jeannie.

Well, I didn't want to pressure her. This wasn't the time. I'd catch up with her later, when she wasn't on the spot, and give her my number. I'd make sure she felt in control.

Smiling, I bent forwards to kiss her cheek lightly, straightened, winked, and returned to my post at the bar. I took the beer Parker handed to me and ignored the knowing stare Zach angled my way.

"Obvious, much?" he muttered under his breath, nudging me with his elbow.

I chuckled. "What's wrong with that? I know what I want, and I'm going for it."

Jeannie

My pulse skittered wildly as I watched Phoenix walk over to his friends at the bar. I tried so hard to stay in the moment, to follow the conversations all around me, enjoy the party and pay attention to my lovely friends. But my mind had withdrawn, turned inward, drilled down on my own situation in a buzz of panic and worry.

What was I going to do? How had the universe turned against me once more? Would nothing ever be easy?

My body felt numb and tingly, and spots danced in front of my eyes. I couldn't let it get the better of me. I had to stay calm. At least this time, I knew what I was getting into.

Last Sunday, the day Ruby returned to say she was staying in town, and she and Julian got together, was my first time at the café, and everything had been going so well. I thought.

I was happy for them. Ruby was going to write a book or something. And I guess she was going to live with Julian on his farm. Unlike me, who would be stuck for the foreseeable future living with my parents. But then that gathering had turned into an impromptu party to celebrate them. That's when everything went sideways.

That's when Peter walked in, and the floor fell out from under me.

I wasn't faking to get away when I excused myself early, feeling sick. I truly was sick to my stomach, sweating, with a splitting headache. Stress and anxiety will do that. And shock.

Now the dizziness and nausea were returning, despite my being prepared. This stress sickness was new. I'd already been through so much, and managed everything just fine. I was strong. I was in control. I could do anything. But lately, I seemed to be losing my composure.

Maybe I was exhausted and overwhelmed by all I had to do

to make the move west. There'd been so many affairs to wrap up in Kingston. Everything to sell, give away, or pack up. And Will. Managing his expectations, stress, and resentment at having to leave his home, his school, and his friends. But I'd done it. And I'd dealt with far worse in my life. Why was I so frazzled now?

I couldn't stop myself from stealing glances at Phoenix, compulsively searching for the boy Peter that I knew in his unrecognizable masculine face, with its hard jaw, chiselled cheekbones, and thick neck. And that body, a huge wall of solid muscle, bore no resemblance to the gangly teen I'd known. From time to time I caught a twinge of something familiar—his straight nose was the same shape maybe, and why wouldn't it be? The whorls of his ears seemed familiar, though why I even knew that, I'm not sure. A tiny mole on his cheek. And most importantly, his eyes. The intense, serious, intelligence of his eyes, and their colour—a deep fathomless bottle green like the sea. Somehow, I remembered that.

An image flashed through my mind. A visceral memory, old and buried. The intense focus and wonder in those green eyes as they looked into mine. That wasn't a memory from math class. Shivering, I blinked the picture away.

Now he reminded me of a big cat—watching everyone with those feline eyes. You just knew he saw things others missed. Watching and waiting. Waiting for the right moment, but for what?

When he looked at me, which I couldn't help but notice was often, I felt naked. Whether it was because he was mentally peeling off my clothes, or because he could see right through me, right into me, I didn't know. One thing I knew in my bones was that he was dangerous.

It wasn't just his massive size or his solid muscles, or the intriguing ink that decorated his skin and drew my gaze over each bulging curve and hard plane, making me want more, though they were as intimidating as they were appealing. There was also his dark hair, cut short, and the intimate fit of his clothes, close but roomy enough for instant, powerful movement.

My body seemed to react to his presence with an agenda all its own. My skin tingled, my pulse raced, and my brain turned to mush. Just that, alone, set alarm bells ringing in my head.

It was him. Who he was. Who he was to me, and to my son, made him a ticking bomb.

I knew virtually nothing about him. And what I did know didn't put my mind at rest. He'd changed so much, it felt like the past meant nothing. I was starting from scratch.

What could I know, based on the past? His rough life as a teen had made me feel so sorry for him. Under the brittle toughness that he showed everyone else, once I'd got to know him a little better, I saw his kindness, his vulnerability, his will to survive, and his drive to succeed. His love and loyalty for his broken father that kept him close when a better life became available. It was those things that had made me the most sad when I'd learned he'd died with his father in the trailer fire. What a waste. It was one of those moments in life when something happens that felt both tragic and inevitable. I was hardly surprised, and maybe wouldn't have given it much thought, if it hadn't been for that one night we'd spent together.

Beyond that, I hadn't mourned him. I hadn't the luxury of time or attention to dwell on him later. If he hadn't died, I'm not sure how I would have handled the pregnancy differently. Would I have reached out and told him? What could I have expected from him in the way of help? The fact that he was gone was, in a small way, a blessing. I had enough problems on my own without getting tangled up in his.

Of course, I'd wondered who he might have become if he'd lived. His blood flowed in my son's veins, so I was curious. Now, I'd find out.

My God, so many of the facts had changed in a flash. I could hardly trust the ground I stood on. I felt dizzy with the need to rearrange my whole view of the world. Before long, I'd have to come to terms with these changes and face up to my moral duty. But I wasn't ready for that yet.

What I didn't understand was why he'd singled me out. Why was he staring at me? Why would he come over just to talk to me when he was so cool to everyone else? And how could I resist my attraction to the sexy wall of hunky man he'd become? How long could I hold out?

Continue reading The Phoenix's Unlikely Prodigy now. Find The Phoenix's UNLIKELY Prodigy here: https://www.books2read.com/phoenixsprodigy

Acknowledgments

Thank you's must go first to my HEA Marketing squad, Donna, Erryn, Jeanine, Natasha, Reshma & Stacy for being part of my process every day, and for helping me to really look at what you, the reader, are looking for in a romance book. Just like me, you love the tropes that help define our genre and this book, and this series, are my response to that. I hope it delivers, and more than that, meets all your expectations.

As well, special thanks go to my first, close and final readers of the manuscript: Natasha, John & my insightful editor Tracy. Thank you for finding and helping to repair those places where the story tripped on my verbosity and bad writing habits. I hope I managed to fix them all, and take full responsibility for those places where my stubbornness or blindness won out.

I hope you, my final reader are happy, and share the love in reviews. That's really the only way I'll ever know what you thought of my story, so I hope you share your views with me as well as other readers who might be searching for just this story.

Thank you also to subscribers of my newsletter who were part of the creative journey as I shared this manuscript, albeit in a slightly rougher form, chapter by chapter before final edits and publication. I hope you found the experiment fun and 'novel' and enjoyed the story as well.

And finally, thanks to my new crew of characters who've kept me company this past couple of years as I built, piece by piece, my imaginary world of Port Camosun. I hope you, reader, have fallen in love with this crew of friends as much as I

have, and stick around as I tell you their individual stories, one
by one. It's going to be bumpy ride, and it's good to have your
friends along.

    xo,

    MA

About the Author

MaryAnn Clarke ~ USA Today Bestselling author MaryAnn Clarke is a Chatelaine Grand Prize winner and Next Generation Indie Book Award finalist for The Art of Enchantment, first in the Life is a Journey series about young women on journeys abroad who discover themselves and fall in love while getting embroiled in someone else's problems. Her Having it All series is about professional women struggling to balance the challenge and fulfillment of their careers with their search for identity, love, family and home.

Always eager to fill blank pages and empty canvases with ideas swirling in her head, MaryAnn set out to write emotionally engaging stories that walk a tightrope between intelligent Women's Fiction and heart-warming Romance.

A socially awkward polymath with ASD who studied Fine Arts, Urbanism, Architecture and Gerontology at university on both coasts of Canada, she turned to her first love, writing stories, when she realized she could have more fun with fewer rules to follow. When not writing, she meditates while hiking wooded mountain trails, does yoga and Pilates to fend off decrepitude, reads eclectically, contemplates wormholes, experiments with painting abstract expressionism, kills plants and tries not to burn dinner while solving her next plot problem. Now that her chick has flown the coop, Clarke lives on beautiful Vancouver Island, Canada with her husband and cats. Although she knows she lives in Paradise, she still loves travelling the world in search of romance, art, good food and new story ideas.

Get MaryAnn's newsletter and never miss a new release!

Want to receive a FREE book? Join MaryAnn's mailing list to get all new and exclusive Single Dad in Studio 7D. Stay in touch to hear book news, special deals and updates about her new series release schedule.

You can read more about MaryAnn, her books and ideas that strike her fancy at www.maryannclarkescott.com.

FIND ALL OF HER BOOKS ON AMAZON AT
https://www.amazon.com/MaryAnn-Clarke/e/B01KPSGXNO

WANT TO CONNECT WITH ME?
www.maryannclarkescott.com
maryann@maryannclarkescott.com

Subscribe & Follow MACS!
www.maryannclarkescott.com
Question? Fan mail? Sure, you can reach me here.

Be Mine This Time

Making Room For You

Before You Knew Me

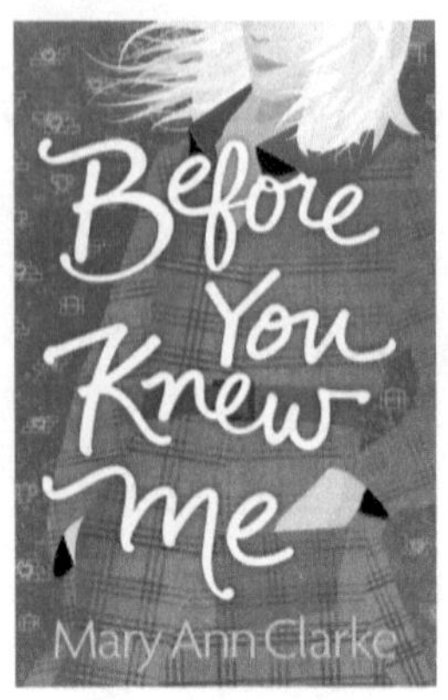

The Art of Enchantment

A Forged Affair

Hiding From Christmas

www.ingramcontent.com/pod-product-compliance
Lightning Source LLC
Chambersburg PA
CBHW021755190726
48290CB00005B/1279